I0693013

B'taav lifted his leg. The figure remained still for a fraction of a second as B'taav's foot left the ground.

And then the figure's fusion gun came up.

For the Independent, time slowed to a crawl. He lurched forward even as the ear splitting blast roared throughout the corridor. A wave of searing heat passed just over his head, a fraction of a second before his body hit the cold metal floor. He hoped none of the passengers behind him were in the path of this deadly blast.

B'taav rolled away just as another blast slammed into the ground, splintering and melting sections of the walkway.

Other Titles by E. R. Torre

Books

Shadows at Dawn
Haze
Cold Hemispheres
Mechanic
Chameleon
Nox
Ghost of the Argus
Foundry of the Gods

Graphic Novels

The Dark Fringe (with John Kissee)

THE LAST FLIGHT OF THE
ARGUS

E. R. Torre

The novel contained within this volume is a work of fiction. Names, characters, places, and incidents are the product of the author's imagination. Any resemblance to actual persons, living or dead, businesses, events, or locals is entirely coincidental.

B'taav, Inquisitor Cer, and all characters within this novel were created and are Copyright © 2010 E. R. Torre

The Last Flight of the Argus is Copyright © 2010 E. R. Torre

All Rights Reserved

Cover and Interior Artwork by E. R. Torre

Please visit my website:

www.ertorre.com

Comments or questions? Email me at:

atrocket@aol.com

ISBN: 0-9729115-5-3
ISBN-13: 978-0-9729115-5-9

Publisher:
CreateSpace Publishing
North Charleston, South Carolina

PROLOGUE

THE EREBUS WAR

MERCHANT SHIP "VIRTUOUS", on the edge of the Erebus System

Doctor Mark Stephenson wiped the sweat from his face. He shook as he rose from his cot and the room spun.

"Damn," he whispered while steadying himself.

He approached the medicine cabinet and knocked over several of the plastic vials and small containers inside it before finding the bottle he needed.

Stephenson popped the bottle's cap and poured several blue and green pills onto the palm of his hand.

Twenty of your fellow crewmembers in the lower decks are dead now. The air circulating through their rooms and compartments was replaced with a toxic substance. You made sure there were no alarms.

The thought made Stephenson sweat even more. He swallowed the pills and put the bottle back.

They're dead because of you.

It took a while for the pills to act. In the meantime, Stephenson found it hard to walk without shaking. He returned to his cot and stared out the ship's window and at the distant sun of Erebus. Somewhere between it and their ship, in the neighborhood of the fourth planet of this system, the backbone of the Epsillon Empire's fleet was massing either to fortify their defenses or initiate an attack. The forces of the Phaecian Empire lay a few million miles past them, probably doing the very same.

And here you are, in the middle of it all.

Doctor Stephenson closed his eyes and felt another chill. Visions of dead crewmates only a couple of floors below flashed through his mind.

Damn them for making what's to come necessary...

For millennia the Erebus system served as the uneasy border between the Phaecian and Epsillon Empires. Through treaties and negotiation, it was designated a no man's land, off limits to either side. Once established, the Empires tested those limits on a day to day, even hour to hour basis. Countless space crafts, both officially and unofficially, were intercepted "straying" into the Erebus system. Things eventually heated up and a new treaty was ratified. The system was split in half. The two empires were allowed to have their flotillas patrol their "side" of the system.

The politicians thought this a good compromise. In reality, they put the rival militaries that much closer to each other.

Traders established routes and merchandise was exchanged. Some, the more naïve among the politicians, thought this exchange would eventually lead to peace. But, a little over a year ago, an Epsillon passenger and cargo vessel was destroyed near Erebus' third planet. Six hundred people were lost, including close relatives of one of Epsillon's top ambassadors.

Early word hinted at a catastrophic accident, but rumors of a Phaecian military ambush took hold. Making matters worse, the Phaecian Empire was slow to deny these rumors. Some of the more outspoken Territorial Cardinals claimed the destroyed ship conducted espionage missions into their territory. The implication was obvious: The doomed craft deserved what she got.

It was hardly surprising tensions escalated to a boiling point.

And then one side fired upon the other.

Who fired first is, and would remain, a source of dispute. What could not be argued was the slaughter that followed. Skirmishes grew and fighter crafts were deployed. Diplomacy was attempted one final time, to no avail. The flotillas were massing at Erebus and it was only a matter of time before the first battle of an all-out war was fought.

Whoever emerged victorious from this lonely place would earn a base of operations from which they could launch an attack on their rivals.

Dr. Stephenson let out a low grunt. The medication was kicking in.

He again rose from the cot and headed to the door leading out of his room.

The crew of this ship was loyal to Epsillon. Half of them had family out there, fighting against the Phaecian Empire. That included Helen O'Hara, the ship's engineer.

Stephenson recalled how she smiled at him whenever they passed. They talked a few times and he even invited her to dinner. There was, he was certain, the possibility their friendship could grow, blossom, and become something more. Something he yearned for all his life...

Stephenson stopped. He reached for the corridor wall and used it to keep upright.

She's down there, in the lower levels, with the rest of them.

Bile rose from his stomach. He could barely hold it down.

"It had to be done," Stephenson mumbled. He wasn't sure he meant it.

Every member of this crew was willing to take up arms for Epsillon. Everyone but Dr. Stephenson. His comrades, in their own fighter craft, shadowed the *Virtuous'* movements for several weeks, until they were certain the ship's course took them through this particular zone. By then, his men were ready to act. On the *Titus* Space Station, floating just outside the Erebus solar system, his men originally waited for the crew of the *Virtuous* to disembark. The crew of the ship welcomed their shore leave and wound up in the Jackal, the station's bar. That's where Stephenson's agents identified each and every one of them.

Dr. Ely Corrigan, the *Virtuous'* resident doctor, was their target. Luckily for them, he was a loner. It proved a simple job to lace his drinks with Naranja. It was an even simpler job to call the local police and report the doctor's use of the illegal narcotic.

When he was arrested, Dr. Corrigan claimed he was innocent. It proved impossible to argue the blood tests. So, on the eve of its latest voyage, the *Virtuous* found itself in need of a new resident doctor. Lucky for them, Doctor Mark Stephenson happened to be available. As they say in the Phaecian Military OPs, it's a simple thing to infiltrate a group: Make yourself necessary to them and let *them* take you in.

Stephenson shook off the memories and glanced at his wristwatch.

13:42.

If all went well, the final act of betrayal would soon be done.

Captain Posner studied the computer monitor and frowned. His features were stern, hardened by ten years of military service and close to twenty years of running transport crafts. During this time, he lost two wives and outlived most of his friends. He bankrupted twice, yet always clawed his way back.

It took him a while, but he saved enough money to buy this ship. He had ten more years of payments to go. Thanks to the coming war and the incredible profits from transporting cargo, that schedule was cut in half.

Captain Posner's frown faded. In all these years he never thought about retiring. Now, that thought was a pleasant dream not so far off into the future. But first, the Phaecian Empire needed to be crushed.

Captain Posner's thoughts were interrupted when the small blip reappeared on his sensor monitor.

"There she is," he told his Senior Officer. "045 by 30."

"Yes sir," the Senior Officer replied. "I've completed the database check. There was no other traffic scheduled in these parts and at this time."

"Yet there she is."

"It might be an echo, sir. A ghost trace."

"It's possible," the Captain admitted. "But it's more likely someone is shadowing us, trying to hide in our blind spot and slipping out now and again."

"It could be an Epsillon Corporate ship. Smuggling operations are surging. They might be checking up on us, making sure we're sticking to our transit log and aren't running contraband."

"A Corporation ship wouldn't play around for that long. If they think we're doing something untoward, they'd hail us, make us stop, and come on board to inspect our cargo."

The Senior Officer offered no reply to this.

"On the other hand," the Captain continued. "If it is a hostile ship, where did she come from? She couldn't have arrived through the *Titus* Displacer, not with the lock over transportion the Empire has on it."

The senior officer nodded. The discovery of the Displacer revolutionized interstellar exploration. Essentially an artificial fold in space, the Displacer was a man made portal that vessels both large and small used to travel to their desired location in a matter of minutes, provided their destination had its own Displacer unit.

The Displacers were built in either triangular or rectangular shapes. Their center was hollow. When charged with high-density proto-matter, an energy field occupied this hollow center. Sophisticated computers controlled these energy bursts, refining the power signature until it took on the form of an artificial wormhole. Any vessel entering the wormhole was transported to a target Displacer in operation anywhere throughout known space. The trips range could be as close as three or as far as thousands of light years away.

To date, two hundred fifty six solar systems on the Epsillon side carried Displacer units while robotic probes carried another hundred at maximum thruster speeds toward distant and unexplored solar systems. Some of these probes were generations away from their destinations. But once they arrived and activated their Displacers, exploratory vessels would immediately follow.

Provided, of course, the war was resolved and the thirst for discovery was not quenched.

"If it is a hostile craft, what should we do?" the Senior Officer asked.

"They're far enough away that we can dodge them for quite some time. Follow our route and don't deviate. On the slim chance they are fellow Epsillon, they won't take too kindly if we lose them."

The Senior Officer smiled. His smile vanished almost as quickly as it appeared. A red light flicked in the upper right of his sensor monitor.

"I've got a signal. Strong and true."

Captain Posner hit a series of buttons on his computer panel and swore. The monitor displayed several lines of information.

"It's an Antigon class ship!" the Senior Officer swallowed hard. "They're speeding up, heading right at us!"

The Senior Officer leaned in his chair.

"Initiate evasive maneuvering?"

"Yes," Captain Posner said. "And send out a distress signal."

The Senior Officer typed in a series of commands on another keypad.

"Sir, our distress signal is being blocked."

Captain Posner focused on his personal computer. He pressed a series of keys and plotted a route back to the *Titus* Space Station. It would take them a full three weeks to return, provided they didn't hit any bumps along the way.

"The maximum speed of an Antigon class craft, assuming her crew didn't make any modifications, is roughly equal to our own," the Senior Officer said. "If we maintain maximum speed, they won't catch us before we return to *Titus*."

"Agreed," Posner said. He pressed the intercom button. "Engineering, we need to alter course and apply maximum thrust."

Captain Posner allowed a few seconds for a reply. None came.

"Engineering, are you reading me?"

"Sir?" the Senior Officer interrupted.

"Not now," Captain Posner spat. "Engineering, do you read me?"

"They have their hands full."

The voice came from the other side of the bridge. Doctor Stephenson stood at the door. He held a fusion gun.

"What is the meaning of this?"

"Your engines are about to seize up," Stephenson continued. "Unfortunately, your crew will not be able to do anything about this."

"You son of a bitch," Captain Posner yelled. Without thinking, he leaped from his chair and rushed Stephenson.

In Captain Posner's mind he already held the scrawny Doctor's neck in his hands.

In his mind, he squeezed the life out of this traitor. Stephenson would surely beg for mercy, but none would be given. The Doctor's lean face would turn blue in Posner's hands and he'd rattle off one last gasp before falling to the floor. Afterwards, Captain Posner would run down to the engine of his beloved ship and figure out exactly what Stephenson did. He'd fix his ship. He'd get her running again. He'd been in worse trouble than this. The *Virtuous* would survive. Captain Posner knew it would.

In Captain Posner's mind, all would work out in the end. Everything.

But Doctor Stephenson anticipated the Captain's moves and, without hesitation, pulled the gun's trigger. A concentrated blast of fusion energy hit Captain Posner's midsection. His body ruptured, bursting open in a kaleidoscope of blood and seared guts. The torn body hung in the air for a fraction of a second before landing with a wet thud on the bridge's metal floor.

"By the Gods!" the Senior Officer exclaimed. The smell of burnt flesh filled the tiny bridge and he felt he was going to throw up.

Doctor Stephenson made sure he didn't.

ERF SUPER-JUGGERNAUT "ARGUS," in the Deadelous Constellation

"The war goes badly."

The words echoed through Captain Nathaniel Torin's office like metal striking bone.

They came from Admiral Lester Cambridge. His haggard face was displayed on the view screen. It was plump and weathered and very unhealthy looking. The man appeared years beyond his actual age. Hushed whispers from those in the fleet questioned how much longer he could take the strain of command. Some wondered when the Royal Council would replace him.

Captain Torin, the man receiving the Admiral's transmission, knew doing so would be a grave mistake.

"Understood," Torin replied.

Admiral Cambridge nodded. He, like most members of royalty in the Epsillon Empire, was a distant relative –in this case a second cousin– of Torin's. When they were kids, they spent many weeks together at the Royal Palace in Winterhaven. They were good friends despite the blood rivalries that littered the history books.

It was when they entered the Space Corps as young adolescents that their paths diverged. Cambridge was fascinated with the intrigue of politics while Torin longed to escape the terrestrial bureaucracies and experience the freedom of space exploration. Even though his family tried to convince him not to, Torin eventually achieved his goal of becoming a Captain within the Royal Fleet.

He was offered no easy path to this rank, despite his royal blood. His immediate superiors felt he was nothing more than a pampered blue-blood. But after passing their rigorous training, they reluctantly assigned him a small ship and ordered he circle backwater solar systems hunting small time smugglers or quelling petty tribal disputes. In time, Torin's skills at both diplomacy and policing proved undisputable. His superiors had to acknowledge that beneath his royal surface lay a hungry, and highly competent, officer. Torin was eventually rewarded with a series of well-deserved promotions. His final promotion, his crowning achievement, was that of Captain of the super juggernaut *Argus*.

Admiral Cambridge, his childhood friend and second cousin, became his supervisor.

The past melted and Torin faced his old friend.

"What are your orders, sir?"

Admiral Cambridge stared deep into Torin's eyes, as if he were in the same room instead of fifty light years away. He took a deep, noisy breath and said, "We must speak of Erebus, and the way to end this war."

"Has intelligence determined—?" Torin inquired. He was surprised by the anxiety in his own voice. "Sir, is Project Phoenix..?"

"Yes," Cambridge replied. "As of the last two days, consensus has been reached."

"How close are we to action?"

"We received the green light this very morning. That's why I called."

Torin fell back into his stiff chair. He turned away from the view screen and stared out the cabin's window and at the stars beyond.

"Are we...are we to go?" he said. His voice was a whisper.

"Yes," Cambridge replied. "I have read your briefings, and commend you on your anticipation. Your actions have already saved many lives."

"Thank you sir," Torin said. His voice remained weak. "What exactly am I to do?"

"Proceed to the Erebus System. Your Navigator has the course. Take the Displacer in the Monnel system to *Erebus Military Prime*. Once there, you are to get in touch with the *Basilica* and Commander Desjardins. He will give you further orders."

"Understood."

"I was..." Admiral Cambridge began but stopped. He shook his head. "I was hoping it would never come to this."

"But it is our only chance."

"I wish there were other alternatives, Captain. But to save two empires...we must go through with this."

"Yes sir," Torin said. He managed a smile. "Sir..."

"Yes?"

"How...how are your kids?"

"Well, Nathaniel. They miss you."

"I miss them. Tell Judy...give her my greetings."

"I will."

An awkward silence followed. Captain Torin's familiar cabin felt darker, colder.

"I wish I could say more," Cambridge began. "Good luck, Captain Torin. And the Gods' speed."

The view screen went black and the darkness within Captain Torin's quarters was overwhelming. Torin again looked out his window and at the stars. His eyes scanned the constellations and locked in on a tiny star on the upper right side of the window.

Erebus. Such a tiny, insignificant thing. So impossibly far away.

Captain Torin rose. He walked to the window and laid his hand on the tinsel glass. It felt cool to his touch. He focused on Erebus, as if the few feet walk from his desk to the glass somehow afforded him a closer look.

A chill ran down his spine. What happened in the next day at that distant, dull light would not only impact billions of citizens of both Empires, but it would have an even more immediate impact on the *Argus* and the crew that remained on board.

For Project Phoenix meant the death of everyone left on board the ship.

Captain Torin slammed his fists against the glass. He returned to his desk and pressed the intercom button. The youthful face of Ryan Mills, Captain Torin's First Officer, appeared on the central monitor.

"Yes sir?" Mills inquired.

"We need to talk."

Captain Torin and First Officer Ryan Mills walked down the empty hallway of Corridor 31. In the past few months, few had ventured to this area. The accumulation of dust testified to this fact.

Visible at the end of Corridor 31 was a door. It led to a large, sealed room. The room housed Project Geist, one of the more than three thousand experiments conducted on board the super juggernaut. This experiment, unlike those others, was shut down due to ethical questions. The scientists involved in the project and on board the *Argus* were transferred, but their equipment remained behind.

"Are you sure about this?" Mills inquired when they reached the door. "There remain great risks."

Captain Torin pressed his hand against a thermal pad beside the door's frame. A soft red light bathed his hand.

"I'm well aware of them all," Torin said. "I need to do this. If anything goes wrong..."

"I have your orders, sir."

"Please identify yourself," a computerized voice asked after the palm print was analyzed.

"Captain Nathaniel Torin of the juggernaut *Argus*, identification prefixes 1000334a."

The jarring sound of unassailable locks disengaging filled the empty hallway. The immense door leading into Project Geist opened.

Captain Torin and First Officer Ryan Mills stepped past the door and into the room. As soon as they did, the mighty door closed behind them.

An hour later, Captain Torin was back in his quarters, reading the day's intelligence reports and making certain everything was proceeding as it should. When he was satisfied all was ready, he exited his room and walked to the elevator at the far end of the ship's principal corridor.

After entering the lift, he marveled at the number of levels within the ship. *His* ship.

Large as some of the destroyers in the RES Corps were, the *Argus* was the only super juggernaut class ship in the entire fleet. As such, it possessed the most conveniences. Despite her military classification, she had several large entertainment centers, food stations, and a unique, and very large, Hydroponics Level. The gardens were used to supplement the tasteless, and universally despised, nutrition rations and refresh the at times stagnant, artificially purified air within the ship.

It was to this level that Captain Torin headed.

He did so because his wife, Angela Torin, would be there among the plants. She spent most of the morning hours in that heavy humidity. It was her personal escape from the more stressful work in the Bio-Labs. There were many times she asked her husband to accompany her down there. But each time she did, Captain Torin found something more important to do.

After a while, Angela Torin gave up asking.

My loss, Captain Torin thought. Lost time was another burden to carry with him into Erebus.

Captain Torin stepped out of the elevator and was immediately hit with a wave of humidity. Extending for several miles in front of him were rows upon rows of lush plants. He could not identify even one species of plant from the rest, yet marveled at what he saw nonetheless.

It is beautiful, he thought.

Captain Torin's eyes followed a coiled vine that rose several floors up and beyond the evenly spaced lights hanging above the Hydroponics Level. Beyond the lights were hundreds of panels of tinsel glass. Beyond the glass and creeping through the artificial lights was the darkness of outer space. Without meaning to, Captain Torin spotted the faint light of Erebus...

No, he thought. *Not here. Not now.*

He took a breath and, despite his souring mood, forced a smile.

Captain Torin walked on. He was soon surrounded by the plants. After rounding a couple of corners, Captain Torin spotted his wife leaning over a beautiful red flower. She held it gently in her hand but did not pull it off its stem.

Captain Torin silently watched his wife. Her loose fitting clothes could no longer hide her pregnancy. In another few months, Captain Torin would be a first time father.

"Well, well, look who's here," Angela Torin said and released the flower. Her eyes were icy blue and her hair light brown. She was several inches shorter than her mate and, when she was by his side, had to stand on her toes to kiss him. Afterwards, Angela pointed to the lush green bush and flower. "What do you think of her?"

"Her?"

"She's far too pretty to be a 'he'."

"It –she– looks beautiful," Torin agreed. "What is she?"

"That, my dear, is a rose. You've never seen one before?"

"Maybe, at some point," Torin replied. He reached for the flower.

"Careful, she's delicate."

Torin drew his hand back. "She also has thorns."

"Beautiful but dangerous. Not unlike many things in nature."

"I'll have to take your word for it. Of all the plants we have, why your interest in this particular one?"

"The rose plant doesn't bear any fruit nor provide nutrients, so the Hydro Techs didn't bother with her when she arrived with the rest of the crops. They alternately starved or drowned or cooked her, yet she somehow survived. When I finally found her, she was near death. It was a pity to see something that could be so beautiful ignored. All she needed was a human touch."

"Are we still talking about the rose?"

Angela turned away from the bush. On a metal platform overlooking the Hydroponics level, she saw the elevator doors open. Two security guards exited and came to a stop.

"Looks like you're wanted," Angela said.

Captain Torin offered the guards a wave. They acknowledged him with a salute but remained in place.

"Must not be terribly important," Angela said. "Otherwise they'd be dragging you away."

"I sent for them."

"You did? Has someone been stealing the carrots?" She giggled. "I've had some strange cravings of late, but I swear it wasn't me."

"We've been ordered into Erebus."

Angela Torin's hand came to her mouth.

"By the Gods," she whispered. "Project Phoenix?"

"We'll reach the *Monnel* Displacer within the hour."

"But the Queen said we were making progress. She said the war would be over."

"The Queen tells her subjects what they want to hear. In this case, and unknown to her, she does not lie. The war will be over very soon. It's why you are going to evacuate the ship."

"You can't be serious. I would sooner leave than—"

"Hush. There's no need for you...for our child, to go into Erebus."

"The hell there isn't," Angela yelled. "I will not leave you!"

"You will," Torin growled. He grabbed his wife by her shoulders and held her still. "Please don't make me order the guards to escort you out. I...I don't want my last memory of you to be like that."

"You're hurting me," Angela whispered.

Torin released his wife.

"Angela...I'm sorry."

They faced each other for several seconds, neither saying anything. Angela finally broke the silence.

"I can't leave you. Even if you are going to Erebus."

"You've put up with so much from me...from my family. The Queen mother, my brothers...they never accepted you as they should have. But you're everything I've lived for, Angela, and that's why I can't let you stay. If not for you, then for our child."

"What about the others?"

"If it were in my power, I'd evacuate everyone. Everyone but me. Unfortunately, the *Argus* requires a crew. Even if it is the bare minimum."

"Please...please let me join you. Things might yet turn out well."

"I wish there was a chance," he said. "But we both know there isn't."

Captain Torin pulled a shiny crystal cube from his shirt pocket. When Angela saw it, her face went white.

"You didn't—"

"It's all there," he said before placing the cube into Angela's hands. "I want this ship's sacrifice to mean something. I want the Empire to live, even as so many will certainly die."

When she held the cube, a torrent of emotions flooded from Angela. Tears ran down her cheeks. Captain Torin tried to hold back but couldn't.

"I love you," he said. He wrapped his arms around his beloved wife and gave her a deep, passionate kiss. "Promise me our child will have a good life. Promise me my last wish will come true."

Angela shook her head. Her next words were barely audible. "I promise."

Torin wiped the tears from his wife's face and motioned to the security guards.

"They will take you to bay fifteen. An escape shuttlecraft is waiting for you there. It's...it's our last one. Controls and course are set. Other than my most trusted guards, no one will know you've left. You will be listed as one of those aboard the *Argus* when she departed for Erebus. Within the shuttle you'll find new identification and enough money to live a quiet, comfortable life. After our child is born and is strong enough for space travel, you should take him to Onia. I was raised there. It is my understanding the world has changed considerably, but I still have trusted friends living there. They will care for you. Say nothing to them about me or the fate of the *Argus*. Take advantage of your new life and make sure our son lives in a world free of wars."

"I love you," Angela said. "Even though making me leave your side is wrong."

Torin held her hands in his. "There is no wrong or right. There are choices that are made in the hopes they help more people than they hurt. I love you, Angela. I will always love you, as I will always love the Empire. Remember that my actions today were because of this."

The security guards approached but kept a courteous distance from Captain Torin and Angela. The two embraced one final time.

"I love you too," Angela said. "I will wait for you in Onia. I will wait for your return."

They separated and Angela walked past the guards. Captain Torin motioned to them and they followed his wife to the elevator. Tear soaked eyes stared at her husband until the elevator doors closed.

With a sharp burst of exhaust Shuttle 15 lifted off the floor and gently floated up into the cold vacuum that filled the *Argus'* primary landing bay. It spun around and let out another short burst of propellant. In seconds the shuttle cleared the bay doors and moved past the *Argus* and into outer space.

Angela Torin watched as the mighty super juggernaut grew smaller and smaller. It wasn't long before this fearsome war machine resembled a child's toy. Soon after, it was nothing more than a large white dot in a field filled with smaller white dots. One of them, Angela knew, was the *Monnel* Displacer. The *Argus* gained speed as it headed directly to toward its destination.

A sudden, steady burst of light indicated the Displacer's massive transportation machinery was powering up. A final burst of tears rolled down her cheeks and her hands settled on her stomach. She felt their child moving within her.

"You'll have to be brave," she told the child and herself. "You will get a chance to grow up."

Yes, Angela thought. Nathaniel Torin's child would grow up. The Torin name would live on.

Captain Torin walked the deck of the *Argus* with purpose. His eyes never straying far from the large view screen at the front of the bridge. In its center was the *Monnel* Displacer. The skeleton crew that remained on the *Argus* performed their functions with mechanical precision. There was little conversation or levity. The camaraderie that was usually shared on their journeys was replaced with a sober formality.

This was fine with Captain Torin.

When the particulars of their mission to Erebus were explained, Captain Torin feared his crew might panic. He was pleased to find them responding to their mission like the seasoned professionals they were.

The Argus neared the Displacer.

"*Monnel* Displacer, this is the *Argus*." The voice was that of First Officer Ryan Mills. "We are on course 0031, distance five point three thousand kilometers. On final approach."

"Acknowledged, *Argus*. We have jump coordinates. Displacer is powered up and awaiting your arrival."

On the bridge's view screen the *Monnel* Displacer's hollow core pulse with manic energy. Lights flickered and a mighty vortex of white light filled what was black, empty space.

"ETA is three, I repeat, three minutes."

"Acknowledged. All systems are green. Displacer is at full power and wormhole singularity is stable. Good luck."

"Thank you, *Monnel*," Mills concluded. He eyed his Captain.

Torin nodded. All twenty of the men and women seated in their posts on the bridge stared forward, resolute. Though Torin's face was hard, it displayed tremendous pride in those who stood at his side within the ship. Everyone knew what was coming and they were willing to follow their Captain to wherever he may lead them.

Captain Torin walked to the front of the bridge and turned to face his crew.

"When I was a younger man, I devoured every news article I could find," Torin began. "Back then, they proclaimed the inevitability of war between our two Empires. I was eager for the call of battle. But as I grew, I realized the ugly reality. There came a night, not so very long ago, that I had a dream. A dream of peace. I imagined our people reaching out to our rivals and finally, *finally*, putting away all these centuries of hatred. In these times, I've seen us move away from my dream and closer to a day of reckoning. Ladies and gentlemen, that day has arrived."

When Captain Torin paused, the bridge was deathly silent.

"We go now into a battle that will determine the fate of billions of innocents. There will be loss. There will be bloodshed. But despite the darkness of this hour, I see a shining light. I know that I will never live my dream, but I also know that what we do today, what we do from this very second forward, will ensure this dream becomes a reality. If not for us, then for everyone else. For despite the disappointments, despite the destruction, after today I *know* we will rise above our differences. Our sacrifice is the first step in the journey from darkness to light. We must all hold to that belief, for it is the truth."

Captain Torin pointed to the view screen.

"What lies beyond the Displacer is both our fate and that of *everyone* else. Let's make our next actions something we can be proud of. Forever."

Many of the crewmembers nodded. Others, their faces stony and resolute, turned from the Captain and focused on their stations. The flickering energy of the Displacer, as reflected on the view screen, was almost blinding.

Captain Torin walked to his chair.

"Navigator," he said. "Take her in."

MERCHANT SHIP "VIRTUOUS", on the edge of the Erebus Solar System

Doctor Stephenson sipped the synthetic orange juice and put the thin foil container on the side of his workbench. He straightened his glasses and watched as line after line of information appeared on the monitor before him. It was a maddening display. He rubbed his bearded chin and let out a deep sigh.

When will it end?

A week passed since his men took over the *Virtuous*, and today was looking very much like another day of mind numbing intelligence gathering. Here he was, deep in Epsillon territory at the birth of war, and the most exciting thing he'd done in the past two days was get a couple of extra hours of sleep.

Can't stay on stims forever.

Then again, Stephenson thought, too little excitement was preferable to too much. Taking over the *Virtuous* was a near perfect operation. After removing the bodies of the Captain and his First Officer, Stephenson's men, on board the light cargo cruiser *Xendos*, docked and, before any of the few remaining living staff of the *Virtuous* could react, spread out and took them down. Afterwards, all corpses were crated up. They would eventually be ejected into space and likely never found again.

All this was accomplished with only two injuries to his men. Both were serious enough for Stephenson to lock the men in stasis and send them back on the *Xendos* to the hidden Phaecian base. The stasis equipment on that ship would keep them alive and stable for at least a week. Stephenson knew that was not enough time. When he and the rest of his crew finally returned to Phaecian territory, the two men he sent ahead would be in body bags.

Stephenson frowned. His instructors back in the Corps would call this an acceptable loss considering the overall success of the mission, but what the hell did they know about loss?

It was one thing to talk about it in the comfortable confines of a classroom, and quite another to experience it first hand.

The Doctor tried to keep those grim thoughts from his mind and put his focus back on the mission. He was to continue the *Virtuous'* flight path along the periphery of Erebus and collect information on the constantly moving *Erebus Military Prime* Displacer, deep within the Erebus solar system. He was to do this for as long as possible.

"The *Monnel* Displacer has activated, sir," said Elliot Parker. He was Stephenson's chief intelligence officer. His equipment was wired throughout the *Virtuous'* computer room and was tasked solely to pick up and decipher stray signals emanating from the *Titus* Displacer, now over six weeks away. Though they could not link up to the *Erebus Military Prime* Displacer, they were able to intercept signals from *Titus* and these often provided sufficient information about all the Displacer activities in this solar system.

"So?" Doctor Stephenson said. His voice was so low Parker barely heard him.

"The incoming ship's status is classified."

Doctor Stephenson's dull expression perked up.

"Secret military vessel?"

"Most likely."

Stephenson rubbed his chin. "If it were a civilian or hospital craft they would give some kind of advanced word, just in case."

"It's the fifteenth such craft sent into Erebus in the past two days. Maybe the war isn't going too well for them?"

Stephenson shrugged.

"Wishful thinking. More likely it means the war is bogging down." From where the *Virtuous* sailed, it took days, sometimes weeks, to receive accurate data from the other side, his side, of Erebus. "I'm sure our boys are loading the solar system with as many ships as the Epsillon are."

"If we are to assume that's the case, the backbone of both Empires' fleets is parked out there. It's like a kid's game of Grover. Line up all the big boys and dash forward. Whoever breaks through will have their enemy's home worlds ripe for the picking."

"It begins and ends here," Stephenson said. "Keep a close eye on what's coming out of the *Erebus Military Prime* Displacer. The boys upstream love it when we give them hard data that isn't more than a half hour old."

Stephenson flipped a button before him and his monitor displayed the information on Parker's computer.

"Arrival at *Erebus Military Prime* is imminent."

"Prepare a coded transmission to Phaecian command."

"Yes sir. Power levels are rising. Twenty percent. Thirty percent. Arrival of craft in two minutes, maximum."

"Are the lines open?"

"Yes sir. I'm sending data to home base as we receive it." Parker pressed another series of buttons and smiled. "We'll have the exact information on this space craft in a moment."

"Eighty percent"

"Starting to get a trace on the craft," Parker said. "Mass is... by the Gods!"

Parker double-checked his readings.

"It's a juggernaut–no, even *larger* class craft!"

"Ninety percent."

"She's coming through. Gods, can this reading be accurate? What the—"

"Ninety five."

"I'm getting a—"

Parker rose. "I've lost the signal!"

"So have I. What?"

All the monitors before them went dead.

"Energy readings are at zero."

"That's not possible."

"Unless...unless the Displacer was somehow destroyed," Dr. Stephenson said. "Could we have gotten that lucky?"

"No. All transmissions in the vicinity of the *Erebus Military Prime* Displacer are gone. I'm going wider."

Doctor Stephenson grabbed his juice and took a deep sip. He turned away from Parker and looked out the window and at the Erebus sun. For a moment he thought he saw a flicker of light in its lower corner. Whatever he was seeing happened at least two hours ago, the time it took for light to travel this far. The flicker disappeared but soon returned. With a start, Dr. Stephenson realized it was growing. It originated from behind the sun. From the Phaecian side.

His side.

Parker slammed his fist on the counter.

"I'm not getting anything! No communication signals, no emergency traffic, *nothing*." His voice quivered with fear. "How is that possible?

Doctor Stephenson didn't answer. His eyes remained on the distant Erebus sun. The flicker grew even more pronounced. The sun appeared to first bend, then wobble and turn, eventually becoming a flattened sphere. The light shining from her dimmed and Doctor Stephenson felt an involuntary shiver. What the *hell* had happened on the Phaecian side of Erebus?

Incredibly, the sun rippled even more. This time, her light increased. Her shape became even more compressed, smaller and smaller, until, as if it were a candle, it simply went out.

"What happened?" Parker asked.

"By the Gods," Doctor Stephenson whispered. His voice was filled with awe and intense fear.

Even as the words left his mouth, he spotted a burst of unimaginable energy approaching their ship like a nightmarishly large tidal wave. In the fraction of a second it took to see it, the *Virtuous* and its crew were torn to pieces.

PHAECIAN INTELLIGENCE CENTER, PLANET HELIOS - *Four days later.*

The conference room was in turmoil. High level researchers and decorated Generals shouted at each other. A pair of Territorial Cardinals, the third highest ranking members of the Holy Empire, sat in a corner, watching the near anarchy before them. They kept their calm despite the harsh words. Twenty Security Guards spread at the fringes of the room and watched them and wondered what, if anything, they should do. They felt more like bouncers at a low class bar than security for the Phaecian Empire's top military and scientific minds.

So loud were the shouts that no one heard the outer door slide open. The man who entered the room wore a plain white robe. Over his chest lay the crescent of the Holy Empire. He was known as Dante, although this was his chosen, and not actual, name. His real name, if indeed he even had one, was unknown. He was one of the twelve Overlords that, along with the Grand Overlord, ruled the Phaecian Empire.

The researcher closest to the door noted the Overlord's presence and approached. The heightened emotions of the moment took control of him, and he approached dangerously close to the Overlord. Instead of offering a bow, the man tapped at a line of data among the documents he carried with such ferocity that it was a wonder his finger didn't snap.

"What do you make of this?" the researcher yelled. "The whole of Erebus is gone! And with it our entire fleet!"

For the first time since being approached by the researcher, Overlord Dante eyed the scientist. His look froze the man. The scientist stumbled back several steps.

"My apologies, Overlord," he said and bowed.

The Overlord motioned to the Security Guards closest to him and said:

"I want this room cleared out. Everyone is to leave. All but Cardinals Lazarus and Beck."

The room instantly grew quiet. Within that silence, the Security Guards performed their job.

"Where would you like them escorted to, sir?" one asked the Overlord.

"Far away from here. Otherwise, I don't care."

"By your command."

In a matter of seconds the room was cleared and the exit doors closed. Overlord Dante was alone with Cardinals Lazarus and Beck.

"It's good to communicate without shouting," the Overlord said. "Please, Cardinals, have a seat."

Both Cardinal Beck and Lazarus waited for the Overlord to sit before they did the same. The strain of the past few days was evident on their faces.

"Care to offer a briefing?"

The Cardinals eyed each other. Cardinal Beck was the first to talk.

"It's true what they say. Erebus is gone. We lost contact with our Displacer four days ago. At that same time, Erebus' sun evaporated. High range telescopes and sensors show her five planets were reduced to a large and highly radioactive asteroid field."

"And our fleet?"

"With all due respect, most holy, the Solar System was destroyed. What chance do you think our ships had?" Cardinal Lazarus replied. Realizing his response bordered on insulting, he bowed his head. "I'm sorry sir, I'm—"

"Don't apologize. How many ships were there?"

"Just about all of them."

"How many?"

"Sixty-three, including the *Founder*, the *Pastor*, the *Light*, and the *Miraglo*. The *Luxor*, too. I could go on..."

Overlord Dante shook his head.

"No need, for now. How many vessels did the Epsillon fleet lose?"

"According to intelligence they had no less than sixty-five battle class ships stationed there. They matched our fleet tit-for-tat."

"Bottom line?"

"The bottom line is we both lost our armadas."

Overlord Dante took a few moments to digest that information. He pointed to Cardinal Beck and said, "What about outgoing messages? What did the people caught in the blast say, before...before they were taken?"

"The source of Erebus' destruction traveled at speeds approaching light. The energy wave was massive. For the most part, we were getting standard communications and then nothing at all."

"What do our researchers feel happened?"

"Would you like me to bring them back in?"

Despite the seriousness of the moment, Overlord Dante let out a soft chuckle.

"Given their current state, I'd rather hear your summaries."

"There are two camps of opinions. The first is that Erebus was destroyed by some kind of unknown natural phenomena. Some think the system was swallowed by a black hole. Others think the sun somehow went supernova. Still others think we witnessed a release of antimatter."

"And the second camp's opinion?"

"They're open to the natural phenomena theory, but are hesitant to fully accept it. They wonder..."

"Yes?"

"They wonder if the explosion was man made."

"Really?"

"Yes sir. They are in a minority. Even those willing to consider that possibility can't fully accept it. If the Epsillon fleet had a weapon capable of destroying an entire solar system, why set if off while their fleet was standing in the way?"

"Given that fact, do you think they will eventually accept the idea that the explosion was the result of natural phenomenon?"

"Perhaps. In time."

Overlord Dante nodded. He flipped through one of the many folders the researchers left behind on the conference room table. A mass of numbers and symbols filled the folder's pages, as other numbers and symbols surely filled the others. Off to the side were stacks of disks and several small personal computers.

"Then everything proceeds as we planned."

"What about the confirmation?" Cardinal Lazarus inquired.

"Yes, your holiness," Cardinal Beck said. "Did you get the proof?"

Overlord Dante turned to the monitor on the wall behind him.

"Computer, security code alpha alpha three one three. Identification: Overlord Dante."

The computer's monitor came on.

"Acknowledged," a computerized voice replied. "Please proceed."

"Play message code 455-233."

The monitor replayed the last minutes of the space merchant craft *Virtuous*. The Cardinals and Overlord watched as Dr. Mark Stephenson and his intelligence officer worked on discovering the identity of the ship exiting the *Erebus Military Prime* Displacer. They watched in mounting horror as the two Phaecian agents puzzled over the Displacer's loss of signal. The image went black a split second after Dr. Stephenson looked out the window of his craft.

"The ship coming out of the Displacer...was it the *Argus*?"

"Yes. It arrived roughly at the same moment as the energy wave passed."

"Do we know if they set off their device?"

Overlord Dante shrugged.

"She was there when the explosion occurred. At this point, it doesn't make much of a difference, does it?"

"I suppose not," Cardinal Beck acknowledged.

The Overlord walked to the window at the opposite end of the conference room. It was dark outside, and stars littered the sky. Overlord Dante took a few seconds to find the Erebus star. From Helios' vantage point two thousand light years away, it was still full of life. In two thousand years, the people of Helios would see that light die.

"What do we do now?" Cardinal Lazarus inquired.

"The Epsillon Empire is in exactly the same position as we are, toothless and clawless. Just as we planned."

"Do you think...?" Cardinal Beck said.

"They've lost their big sticks," Overlord Dante said. "As have we."

The Overlord let out a sigh. It was going to be a very long series of days and weeks, what with sorting through the intelligence documents and debriefing all the government officials over and over again about the theories as to what happened at Erebus. Studies would proceed but if all went as planned, results would be very slow in coming.

If they come at all.

Overlord Dante noticed the bewildered and scared look on Cardinals Lazarus and Beck's faces. He smiled.

"The Gods be praised, gentlemen," he said. "The war is over."

1

AZUL NEBULA – 233 years later

The *Red Pelican*, a decrepit freighter running the route between Salvation and Orion, spotted the aberrant sensor blip purely by accident on the fifth week of its long trip.

The Captain of the freighter, who normally killed time inspecting his cargo or drinking himself into one long sleep after another, happened to be at the controls of his craft the day the blip appeared on his proximity sensors. He was familiar with this particularly desolate sector of space, and there was nothing in the outskirts of the Azul Nebula that should have triggered any alert.

The Captain, neither curious nor particularly interested in examining the source of this alert, nonetheless reported his findings as a warning to incoming merchant traffic and moved on. He eventually delivered his cargo to the planet Salvation.

Word of his find made its way to Merrick Enterprise's corporate headquarters. They sent a scout ship to investigate the unidentified mass and the crew were shocked to discover a dark, lifeless luxury cruise ship drifting in the Nebula. The ship was identified as the *DeCarlo*, the crown jewel of Merrick Enterprise's Cruise Lines. She was lost with all hands nearly a full year before and over ten light years away. It was presumed her engines malfunctioned and the craft burned up in the Persepolis' red sun, one of the five stops on her usual voyage.

A salvage and rescue operation was quietly initiated.

What the Merrick officers found inside the cruise ship would give them nightmares for the rest of their lives.

CRUISE SHIP "MERRICK", on the fringes of the Orion System – Two months later

Anyone fortunate enough to see her could not help but be mesmerized by her opulence. The *Merrick's* yellow surface looked like gold. The arches along her sides resembled flowing water. Her engines were among the most modern, and efficient, in the Epsillon Empire.

Like her owner and namesake, the *Merrick* was born to cruise the heavens.

The small cargo craft approaching her port side, on the other hand, was quite the opposite. Her bow bore the scars of considerable travel. Her lights flickered like weak candles against the darkness of space. She slowed to a crawl as she came alongside the mighty cruise ship, then eased her way into the first of the larger ship's twenty docking births.

Jonah Merrick sat behind an enormous oak desk and stared at a handful of financial reports. He was an elderly man with very thin and very gray hair. His face was stern; his eyes the color of charcoal. Now in his eighties, he was a small, frail man. The ravages of age masked the young and sturdy explorer he once was. The one whose fearlessness in exploring distant worlds bordered on reckless...and heroic.

With the passage of time, Merrick's wanderlust faded. But he used the prestige of his name to gain valuable loans which he parlayed into a cruise line empire. His clients represented the Empire's very rich; his ships' destinations were exotic. Thanks to the runaway success of his cruise line, his personal wealth was incalculable.

Jonah Merrick put aside the last of the financial reports and stared out his cabin's window. Like everything else on his personal cruise ship, the window was made to Merrick's specifications and, thus, was enormous. Staring at the quiet star field offered Merrick an escape from the drudgery of the business world.

At this moment, however, the Epsillon magnate found the view distracting. His guest was due and Merrick needed to stay sharp. He pressed a button on the right side of his desk and the enormous window turned opaque. He then activated his intercom system.

"Is he on his way yet?" Merrick inquired. Impatience hung heavy in his voice.

"I'm here."

The voice came from the far side of the room. The man who uttered the words stood at the office door. He was tall and muscular and had short, platinum blonde hair. His eyes were sunken deep within their sockets. To the casual observer, it appeared he had no eyes at all. Standing beside the man was Merrick's personal secretary. She had escorted the man to this point.

"You may leave," Merrick told her.

She did so without saying a word. The office door slid closed behind her.

"Please, have a seat," Merrick told the man with the sunken eyes.

He sat in the chair opposite Merrick's desk.

"How may I help you, Mr. Merrick?" the man asked. His voice was low and controlled and cold as ice.

Merrick laid a black diskette on the table.

"That's a report on the recent... troubles...we've had with our cruise ships," Merrick said. He pushed the disk forward, toward the platinum haired man. "I don't like to waste time, so I'll leave it to you to acquaint yourself with the details."

The man did not reach for the diskette. He kept his hands folded.

"I've spent considerable resources getting in touch with you, Mr. B'taav."

"I've noticed," the man replied.

"When I'm looking for certain...help...I demand the best. A few inquiries revealed those with even a passing acquaintance with you were impressed by your efficiency and successes. Several more inquiries revealed you were under contract with Octi Corporation. A curious choice, as they're not the most reliable corporation to do business with."

"They pay."

"They also work for both Empires and have a habit of stabbing their employees in the back."

B'taav offered no retort to this accusation. There was none worth giving.

"Anyway, I contacted Octi and they were willing, after some negotiation, to let me take on your contract, at least for three months."

B'taav's eyebrow lifted.

"As you no doubt have guessed, the cost to me was not inconsiderable," Merrick continued. "But as of now, you're my employee."

"I'm touched by your confidence. What makes you think I want to work with you?"

Merrick's cold features softened. He let out a low chuckle.

"What makes you think you won't?"

"Go on."

"The job I have requires you to travel to the Tauric System. More specifically, you are to go to the planet Salvation. One of the main ports of calls for my cruise ship fleet is located there and I suspect that office has been infiltrated by hostiles. Given that I am to make a major presentation there in the coming weeks, I want you to check the office out before I arrive. All your expenses will be paid for, and I will extend a healthy bonus for any positive resolution."

B'taav stared deep into Merrick's eyes.

"I'll need more incentive."

"Like?"

"Can you get me out of the Octi contract? Permanently?"

"It's certainly possible. Can we do business together?"

B'taav picked up the diskette.

"We can do business."

SALVATION, third planet in the Tauric System

Salvation was so named three millennia before by a group of weary explorers whose journey veered perilously close to catastrophe. During those early years of space exploration, if you found yourself in trouble, there was no armada of ships to turn to for help. An uncomfortably high percentage of exploration crafts were never heard from again.

One such ship, the *Maria*, suffered major structural damage after colliding with space debris. Most of the ship's major instruments were damaged while many of the crucial instruments, including the food distributor, were completely destroyed. Hurt and very hungry, the crew was forced to take a detour through the Tauric system. They were in desperate need of a safe harbor to conduct much needed repairs. They were also hoping, though this seemed a very long shot, to find a world that offered any sort of nutrients.

They feared the worst.

Cursory exploration of the Tauric system a few years before indicated the explorers would find neither food nor shelter. But luck was on their side. The early exploration data proved invalid and the third planet in the system not only had a breathable atmosphere, but also luscious fields of green and thousands of clear, fresh water lakes and a diverse resident fauna.

The crew of the *Maria* took their time repairing and re-supplying their ship. An exploration that appeared headed for disaster was thus saved.

And that's how Salvation got its name.

Three thousand years later, the fauna and lush green fields were long gone, replaced by rusted walls and decaying concretal buildings. The lakes were contaminated with spill off from the ports. Rocket fuel, oils, and some three hundred man made substances labeled as "unknown" flowed through the once pristine waters. The planet's soil turned into a chemical wasteland, her clear skies grew hazy and gray. In less than a thousand years' time, Salvation become just like the other space port worlds in the Epsillon Empire.

The old cargo craft's sides were still smoking from orbital entry as she glided into one of Salvation's landing bay ports. The pilot watched with diminished interest as the automated systems did their work. His left hand lay at his side; his right hand held a thermos. It took an hour to travel from Salvation's Displacer to the planet's atmosphere and then another half-hour to approach the landing strip.

The pilot took a sip of his warm tea. At this point it was the only thing keeping him awake.

"Here she comes," the man in the dark trench coat said. He pointed beyond the smudged glass in the waiting room and at the skies over the Ferro City Star port. The four men with him looked up but didn't move from their chairs.

"Now we just gotta wait an hour or so for him to get through customs."

One of the seated men shook his balding head.

"He'll be out as soon as the ship lands. Mayor's orders."

"No kidding? This guy has that much clout?"

"Enough," the balding man said. He rose from his chair and said: "Come with me."

The group followed him through the waiting room's exit doors. A customs officer watched the group as they approached his post. He was ready to tell them to leave, that this was a restricted area.

When they showed him their Police badges, he let them through.

B'taav stepped off the rear exit of the weathered cargo craft and onto the greasy landing strip. While he stretched, he took a cautious breath of the air and found it, despite the strong scent of gasoline, adequate. He gripped his black duffel bag tight and, using a remote control, shut the doors to his craft. When he was certain the ship's security lock was engaged, he followed the markings on the ground to the south side of the landing strip.

Another cargo ship screamed overhead as it lifted off. The burst of its after burners sent a stiff, warm breeze in B'taav's direction. He increased his pace and reached a rail beside the doors leading into the Customs Building. He looked up at the doors, and a scowl appeared on his face.

A group of five men exited the building, waved at him, and approached. B'taav's free hand reached into the black duffel bag he carried and gripped the handle of his fusion gun. They smiled and appeared friendly enough, but experience told him he could never be too careful. Especially when outnumbered five to one.

"Hey!" the balding man at the front of the group called out. "I'm Len Herbert."

Whether the balding man noted B'taav's right hand was in the duffle bag or not, he nonetheless slowly, *very* slowly, reached into his coat and pulled out his ID badge. "We were contacted by your company. Merrick Enterprises wanted us to give you a hand while you were here."

B'taav eyed the badge. He recognized the standard shield of the Epsillon Law Enforcement Agency.

"I'm the chief of police in Ferro City," Herbert continued. "What can we do for you?"

B'taav released the fusion gun and slung the bag over his shoulder.

"Get me a phone," he said.

Deep within the fiftieth floor of the Ferro Police Center building was a large, well-kept room whose walls were lined with dozens of yellowed citations and worn photographs. Normally, B'taav would take his time examining the items on the wall and get a feel for the man whose office he currently occupied. In his line of work, it was helpful to understand potential allies or enemies. But at this time, the platinum haired man was more interested in making his call. After an hour of trying, he finally was connected via video link with Constable Bill Goodwin, the local representative of the Merrick Cruise Lines. The man looked and sounded like a depressingly typical middle management number cruncher.

"How can I help you?" Goodwin asked. His thin, angular face filled the monitor.

"Who told the police I was arriving at Salvation today?"

Goodwin straightened his thin black tie and said, "Why, we did."

It was impossible for B'taav to keep the exasperation from his face, something Goodwin noted.

"We...we figured you could use some help once you got here," Goodwin quickly added. "The local authorities and Merrick Industries are working together and we thought you'd want to join us and, you know, hit the ground running. We want to put an end to all these shenanigans as soon as possible. Pooling our resources should expedite this task."

B'taav's darkened eyes drew level with the image on the monitor. He stared at Goodwin for several long, uncomfortable seconds before turning his attention to Police Commissioner Herbert. The bald man stood very silently by the door to his office.

"Other than the commissioner and his four men, how many other people know I'm here?" B'taav inquired.

"We just called Commissioner Herbert. He's been very thorough on our behalf in the past and is above reproach. We thought—"

"*We?*" B'taav interrupted.

"Me," Goodwin admitted. "I made the decision."

B'taav shook his head.

"I was hired to investigate acts of piracy committed against your company's cruise ships. In case you weren't aware, I'm an Independent, a free agent. The reason people like your boss hire people like me is because the work I'm tasked to do is often...sensitive. It may involve skirting certain established boundaries..."

B'taav paused. He offered the Commissioner a cold stare.

"Constable Goodwin, Mister Merrick hired me *because* he expects me to work as a true Independent, without having to answer to, or stumble around with, anyone else. I've done considerable research regarding your problems here, and it is clear Merrick Enterprises is dealing with a group of people who don't follow *any* rules and don't think twice about killing innocents. This makes them, and my job, very dangerous. That being the case, I require full control over every aspect of it."

"I don't do this because I'm a person who savors his solitude, nor do I do this because it irritates me to deal with bureaucratic clowns. I do this because these bad people tend to bear grudges.

If I'm working alone and I screw up, bad things could happen to me. If I screw up while others are supposedly helping me, I endanger *their* lives as well as my own. Thanks to your actions, Constable, I am responsible not only for my welfare, but also yours, Mr. Herbert's, and that of the four men that accompanied him to the spaceport. So please, forgive me if I sound harsh, but it upsets me when the people employing me decide to call others behind my back and tell them where the fuck I am and what the fuck I'm doing."

"Sir, I—"

"Shut up and listen," B'taav growled. "You tell Mr. Merrick my fee went up. And while you're at it, tell him my next call comes when I'm done. I'm sure he'll understand. Oh, and Mr. Goodwin?"

"Yes?" the Constable stammered.

"Don't tell anyone else I'm here, ok?"

Goodwin opened his mouth to say something but B'taav switched the monitor off before he did.

"Son, who the hell do you think you—" Herbert started.

Before he could say another word, B'taav was directly in front of him, pressing the Commissioner against the door to his office.

"I'm nobody," B'taav said. "As far as this department is concerned I'm not here now nor was I ever. You're going to make sure the four men who accompanied you to the air strip say the same thing."

"You're not my boss."

"No. I'm just a working man, like you. Thing is, if I can't resolve old man Merrick's problems here in Ferro City, there's a strong possibility he will find himself another space port for his operations. I'd hate to think what happens to your local economy when Merrick Enterprises packs up and leaves."

Herbert opened his mouth but said nothing. The Independent eased back.

"I see we finally understand each other."

"My...my men will do what I ask," Herbert said. He stepped around B'taav and to his coffee machine. The Commissioner poured himself a drink but didn't offer any to the Independent.

"That was quite a speech you gave Goodwin," Herbert said. He sipped his coffee and, despite some lingering anger, a smile formed on his face. "I've butted heads with him before. Can't say I never wanted to tell him a thing or two."

B'taav returned to his chair. His black duffel bag lay on the floor. He grabbed it.

"Constable Goodwin may not be right about many things, but he did right by telling me you were coming," Herbert continued. "Whether you like it or not, it's my job to keep the citizens of Ferro City safe. If there are Independents circulating around here chasing pirates or fairies or pussy, it's my business."

"I suppose. I read your file."

"Then you know I'm clean."

"Clean enough. It's the only reason I didn't turn around at the star port and leave."

"You also know I've been busting my ass trying to solve Merrick's piracy problem."

"What exactly do you know?"

"Most of it has reached the news. The pirates are more of a nuisance than anything else. They've sabotaged some of Merrick's equipment, rifled through his warehouses, even stolen cargo. Nothing big. Nothing worth sending an Independent to check out."

"Your information is outdated," B'taav said. "Did you hear about a Merrick cruise ship by the name of *DeCarlo*?"

"Sure," Herbert said. "Lost with all hands when she fell into a sun, right? An accident?"

"No. The *DeCarlo* took on two thousand passengers at the port world of Bathurst. The passengers expected a real treat: Visiting five systems in two weeks with an eventual return to Bathurst to disembark. The official story was what you said, that her engines malfunctioned and she dropped into a gravity well and was crushed. But that's not what happened."

"No?"

"Somewhere in the Persepolis system our group of pirates raided the ship. They had inside help, because all communications between the *DeCarlo* and Merrick's home base were jammed. She was unable to send out even one distress signal. The pirates boarded her and quickly took control. It wasn't too hard. She was a luxury ship filled with unarmed, and well pampered, civilians. The pirates held the crew and passengers at bay and stripped them of their valuables. Afterwards, they parked the *DeCarlo* off the Azul Nebula and tore up every piece of hardware that wasn't disabled in the initial attack. They then gathered up their loot and left the passengers and crew adrift and helpless. What followed was a nightmare."

B'taav paused.

"Imagine you're trapped in a cave without food or water and with very little or maybe no light. You're alive and well but you're stuck. Escape might be as little as a few feet away but you're blocked behind a wall of unmovable rocks you could never push aside. Now imagine the hours passing very slowly, one after the other. Imagine realizing that this is the way you're going to die."

"You scream, even though you know no one can hear you. You claw at your cage until your fingers are bloody pulps. But you can't escape that hunger, that thirst. The terror. There's no hope."

"Now imagine you're not alone in that dark cave," B'taav continued. "Imagine you're trapped with hundreds, maybe even a thousand, other people. They all know there's no escape and that it is only a matter of time before they die. *What would they do to each other?*"

"By the Gods," Herbert muttered.

"The *DeCarlo* was found a few weeks ago. She was a lifeless derelict. Based on the ship's logs and personal notes found onboard, Merrick's officials pieced together what the passengers did after the pirates left. They found strength in groups. These groups attacked each other. The first to go were the weak. The elderly, the frail, then women and children. All were killed, all for two reasons. The first was because the pirates disabled the air-purification systems. The survivors knew they needed to save as much air as possible..."

"A-and the second reason?"

"The pirates also disabled their food dispensers. They needed to eat."

Herbert's hand shook, spilling droplets of coffee on the floor.

"Merrick Enterprises paid out a large amount of money to the relatives of the lost. They'll pay out even more when the truth of what happened to the *DeCarlo* comes out, as it eventually will."

"Why are you telling me this?" Herbert asked.

"I want you to understand why I was brought in and why this job is so important."

"I can help."

"How?"

"I have someone who can escort you around Ferro City. Someone I trust. He has very good contacts, and he can keep his mouth shut."

B'taav thought about that for a few seconds.

"You trust him?"

"With my life."

B'taav nodded.

"Let's get started."

B'taav followed Herbert through concrete corridors and down humid stairs before arriving at the station's firing range. Only one man occupied the cavernous room. He was a short, graying man who sported a tight crew cut. He was reloading his weapon.

"This is Officer Ken Shepherd," Herbert said. "Shepherd, this gentleman is B'taav. He's an Independent, hired by Merrick Cruise Lines."

"Independent?" Shepherd said. There was suspicion in his voice. "Since when do you fellows consult with the police?"

Herbert frowned. Shepherd caught his superior's look and extended his hand. B'taav shook it.

"Pleased to meet you, Mr. B'taav," Shepherd said. "What can I do for you?"

"You'll be Mr. B'taav's escort while he's here," Herbert said. "If he has any questions about Ferro City and its citizens, you will provide him with whatever insight or knowledge you can. If he has any really tough questions, you can always direct him back to me."

"You've been moonlighting outside the office, sir?"

Herbert's frown deepened.

"I'm heading back there right now. Someone has to keep Ferro City running." Herbert turned from Shepherd and addressed B'taav.

"Good luck," he said before exiting the firing range.

When he was gone, Shepherd took another long look at the Independent.

"I guess I'm at your disposal, Mr. B'taav," Shepherd drawled. "I can't help but think company is the very last thing you wanted."

B'taav stared at the Shepherd's target. The officer's aim was quite good.

"We make do with what we have," B'taav said. "I need to go over Salvation's customs records for the past year."

"Past year?" Shepherd said. "I'm not a member of the tourist board, but I'm guessing we're talking about over a half million entries."

"More like seven hundred and fifty thousand. Give or take."

"What are we looking for?"

"Long term visitors. Where do you keep these records?"

"Seventy second floor."

"Let's go."

After a few hours of work in the record room, they come up with a preliminary list of over five hundred thousand visas for people who came into Salvation in the last six months. They discarded half of these visas outright because the individuals remained planet side less than a month before moving off world.

"Now what?" Shepherd asked. His body was almost entirely hidden behind a noisy old computer.

B'taav sat behind an equally noisy terminal on the opposite side of the room.

"Let's see how many of these people have felony histories."

"What kind?"

"Any."

"Even shoplifting when they were teens?"

"We'll sort them out afterwards."

Shepherd shook his head. It would be a very long day.

They took their first break at lunchtime. Shepherd wandered out of the record room and headed to the cafeteria on the third floor while B'taav remained behind his terminal.

They worked through thirty thousand records and still had two hundred and fifty thousand to go. B'taav estimated they wouldn't hit the streets for at least a couple of days.

The slow pace didn't sit well with the Independent. If only, he wished, he had these records in his possession on the way to Salvation.

Shepherd approached B'taav's side. In his hands were two cups of coffee. He offered one to B'taav.

"No thanks," B'taav said.

Shepherd shrugged. "More for me."

Shepherd got back to work at his terminal.

At five in the afternoon of their second day they got their first break.

"Take a look at this," Shepherd said.

B'taav approached Shepherd. On the officer's monitor was a picture of a twenty-six year old woman. Her hair was straight and fair, her face lean and long.

"Her name is Gail Griffen," Shepherd said. "She doesn't have any serious felony records, but I found this—"

Shepherd pointed to a line of information on the monitor. It read: "Joined the Salvation Liberation movement, 20009."

"That movement came into their own about twenty years ago," Shepherd explained. "They're against pretty much *all* the businesses interests within Salvation."

"They were linked to the Black Friday group."

"Never heard of them."

B'taav's eyes narrowed. "They've done the same sort of things as the Salvation Liberation movement, except their actions are more militant and—"

B'taav stopped in mid-sentence. He bit his lower lip.

"When did she arrive in Salvation?"

"Two months ago. She was born here but left Salvation at twenty. This is the first time she's been back in six years. She's unemployed and has no family or means of support yet has traveled around a bit."

"Where was she in the interim?"

Shepherd punched several buttons and the information on the monitor changed.

"She's bounced from planet to planet but stayed mostly in the Azul Nebula sectors."

"Azul Nebula? When?"

"Last time was, let's see...It was two and a half years ago. Is that important?"

"Yeah. It might just be."

2

Gail Griffen lived in apartment 6345 of the Tropic Hotel. Depending on your point of view, the building was either a treasure of the Industrial Art Movement or another of the many dilapidated structures that littered the south side of Ferro City. When asked, the hotel's manager couldn't recall much about this tenant, other than what was on her registration records. She checked in the week before and paid her rent on time and, so far, didn't have any strange visitors coming in late at night.

"That makes her a saint as far as I'm concerned," he concluded. The manager returned to chewing on his cigar. "If you guys tell me otherwise, I'll throw her out."

Shepherd shook his head. "That isn't necessary. We're running checks on some recent arrivals and she happens to be one of many."

The manager gave Shepherd a *whatever-you-say* smile. Then, realizing he there was a golden opportunity before him said, "The room next to hers is available. Would you like to rent it? You know, to check up on her real close? I mean, if you needed to."

B'taav laid a bill on the counter. The manager raised a partition in the unbreakable glass that separated his station from the hotel's lobby and grabbed the money. In return he handed the duo a plastic key card.

"Room 6344," he said. "Enjoy."

Room 6344 had a small living room, an even smaller bedroom, a tiny bathroom, and a microscopic closet. According to the manager, it was a mirror image of Gail Griffen's apartment next door.

B'taav stuck a small black button against the wall that separated the apartments and placed a larger black tab in his ear.

"Partner, we locals aren't allowed to do that without a warrant," Shepherd said.

"Good thing I'm not local," B'taav responded. He activated the device.

"Someone's in there," he said after listening for a few seconds. "They're watching television."

"One person?"

"Possibly.   They're getting up and...going to the kitchen. Subject turned on the faucet. Now they're activating the food system."

Shepherd eyed their apartment's food system.

"Can that thing tell you what she's eating, and if it's any good?"

B'taav ignored the officer's comment and sat on one of the chairs in the living room. He closed his eyes and listened for a long while. The food system churned before shutting down. Gail Griffen or whoever was in the adjacent apartment stepped out of the kitchen and returned to the living room. There were groans coming from the sofa springs as the person sat down.

While B'taav listened, Shepherd walked to the apartment window and stared out at Ferro City. He lit a cigarette, smoked it down, and lit another. When the second cigarette was finished, he eyed B'taav and said, "You figure we'll be here all night?"

B'taav raised his hand to silence his partner.

"A call is coming in," the Independent said.   "Subject answered. She's a female. She's talking."

It was their first real indication Gail Griffen was the person in the apartment. Her conversation proved brief.

"She's done," B'taav said. "She's turning the television off and...She's leaving the apartment."

"Where is she going?"

"I didn't get an address, but she's meeting someone. She said she'd see them in an hour. We should follow."

"Yes. Is she the only one in the apartment?"

"As far as I can tell."

"It might be a good time to get electronic eyes in there."

"Vid Bugs? If listening into her apartment is illegal without a warrant..."

"Whoa," Shepherd said while extending his hands. "I'm going to follow Gail Griffen to wherever she's going. When she gets there, I'll give you a call. In the meantime, I'll contact a judge I know and get the proper warrants for our listening devices. Until then, we haven't used them, right?"

"Right," B'taav said. "You better get going."

Shepherd casually stepped into the hallway, just another tenant on his way out, and closed the door behind him.

B'taav listened for several more minutes to make sure there was no one left in Gail Griffen's apartment. When he was sure, he exited his apartment and broke into hers.

An hour and a half later Shepherd contacted B'taav.   The officer was at the Longshore Club, a steak house on the west end of Ferro City. B'taav took the elevator to the lobby of the Tropic Hotel and, from there, grabbed a cab. It took a half hour to get to the Club.

B'taav paid the driver and took a quick look up the street. He spotted Shepherd in his car on the corner of the block. From where he parked, the officer had a clear view of the Longshore Club and the large window that made up its front façade. B'taav entered Shepherd's vehicle.

"Here's our warrant," Shepherd said. It was a hard copy, freshly printed and bearing a Ferro judge's signature.

"What about Gail?"

"At the front of the restaurant and to our right."

B'taav spotted Gail Griffen sitting alone. She cradled a glass of some clear liquid and looked younger than her already youthful age.   Her hair was darker than that on her file photograph. She was very skinny, almost frail.

"What did she do after leaving the hotel?"

"Not much," Shepherd said. "She took a cab and a long –a *really* long– route here. She switched rides several times."

"She was looking for a tail?"

"Absolutely.   Funny business for someone off to a dinner date."

"Did she spot you?"

"I don't think so."

"Are you sure?"

"There are only three things in life I'm sure of: That we pay too damn much in taxes, that we have an unfortunate habit of electing crooks to office, and that we're all going to die. Other than that, I'm *reasonably* sure she didn't spot me."

"Has she tried to communicate with anyone?"

"No. After getting the warrant, I had central lock in on any signals emanating from her assorted rides. She didn't make any calls."

"Good. Let's wait and see who she's meeting."

During the next hour, Gail Griffen finished her meal and nibbled on a light dessert. She also took down two more shots of the clear liquid that looked a lot like Seco. She remained alone but didn't seem particularly lonely.

B'taav, on the other hand, grew worried. The fact that Gail Griffen was looking for tails en route to the restaurant was proof she was up to something. The fact that nothing else happened since she arrived here suggested she had indeed spotted Shepherd's tail and cancelled whatever meeting was originally scheduled.

"That lady can put down some serious food," Shepherd said. "Reminds me of my wife. Only she ain't so thin."

"Gail Griffen arrived from a higher gravity world. Her body burns more calories."

"That's exactly what my wife says."

"Ms. Griffen might be on to us."

"No way."

"Yeah."

"How can you be sure?"

"Only three things I'm sure about..."

Shepherd let out a laugh. It died abruptly.

"Look!"

B'taav followed Shepherd's gaze. A compact green vehicle pulled up in front of the restaurant. It held two occupants, both young men in their mid to upper twenties.

"I know them."

"Who are they?"

"They're," Shepherd began and stopped. He pulled out his Police Comp Pad and activated it. "I don't remember their names. But I've seen their photographs on our actives list. Hang on."

The man in the passenger seat of the compact green car exited the vehicle and walked to the entrance of the restaurant. He waved aside a waiter and pointed to Gail Griffen. The waiter retreated while the young man sat opposite the young lady and scanned the restaurant, as if making sure no one looked in their direction. Once certain, he whispered a few words into Griffen's ear. He then stood up, stepped out of the restaurant, and headed back to his car.

The meeting lasted less than a minute.

"Short and sweet," Shepherd said.

"What did you find?"

Shepherd pointed to an image of the two young men followed by a short description displayed on his Comp Pad.

"Orlando Echo is the tall guy," Shepherd said. "The driver's name is Carlo Giny. A couple of months back we ran a security check for Merrick Cruise Lines. The high tourist season was about to begin and they were subletting jobs. Anyway, these two guys were among many that worked for the Lewitt Catering Company. Their background information raised a few flags."

"But not enough to refuse them the job?"

"Like Gail Griffen, they were involved in some juvie stuff. Small time arson, some shoplifting. Like you said, nothing big enough to refuse them the job. Still, who better to provide inside information on the comings and goings of Merrick Cruise Enterprises than a catering company?" Shepherd turned the Comp Pad off. "We made progress, no?"

B'taav's gaze returned to Gail Griffen. She was done eating and exited the restaurant.

"Some," B'taav admitted.

Two days later Officer Ken Shepherd stood at the corner of the street in front of the Tropic Hotel. He looked away from the hazy early evening sky and at the rusty blue car parked across and at the end of the street. The fingers of his right hand tapped a small plastic tab that filled the cavity within his right ear.

"You hear me?" he whispered.

"Loud and clear."

"Good."

Shepherd rocked back and forth in place while trying to keep warm. Two day's worth of stubble covered his oval jaw and he chewed on a cigar that looked like it was badly in need of last rites.

"Tell me something," B'taav's voice came through the tab in Shepherd's ear. "Is this Ferro City's tourist spot?"

"If you're looking for tourist spots, I recommend the local jail. With all those guards surrounding it, she's the safest place we've got."

Shepherd rubbed his nose and marveled at the rapid drop in temperature. As if things weren't uncomfortable enough, the wind kicked up.

"Any more of this and you'll need to chip me off the corner," Shepherd whispered. "What time were they meeting?"

"Now," came his response. He heard the sound of B'taav shifting in his seat in the car. "There they come."

Shepherd spotted the same green compact from the Longshore Club a few days before approach the Tropic Hotel. The officer shuffled away from his lookout post and approached a trash bin. He rummaged through the refuse, sorting through the rotted food and acting as if he was looking for buried treasure.

"They're coming right at you," B'taav said.

"Ok," Shepherd said. He spotted a worn porno mag and flipped through it.

"Not bad," he muttered.

"Say again?"

"Never mind."

The green compact came to a stop only a few feet away from Shepherd. Orlando Echo, the tall, young man who met Gail Griffen in the Longshore Club, stepped out. In his left hand was a black briefcase.

The driver of the car, Carlo Giny, shut the car down. He too exited the vehicle. His black hair flickered in the stiff breeze. He closed his door and nodded to Orlando before locking the vehicle up. Together, the two walked past Shepherd and into the Tropic Hotel.

"Get ready to move," B'taav whispered.

Shepherd held the porno mag and took a slow walk to the entrance of the Tropic Hotel. Through the broad windows at the front of the building he saw the young men walk through the lobby and approach the elevator.

"They're heading up," Shepherd whispered as the elevator doors closed. A LCD panel over the elevator doors flickered with ascending numbers. The duo came to a stop on the 63rd floor.

"They're on her floor," Shepherd said. "We are set."

Shepherd took one last look at the magazine before throwing it back in the trashcan. He then ran across the street and into the rusty blue car. He was pleased to find it warm inside.

"How exactly did you convince me to wait out there?"

"You flipped the coin."

B'taav put away the camera he used to photograph the two men entering the Tropic Hotel.

"So I did. Have they made it to her apartment?"

"No," B'taav said. He reached for a small display screen between the car's front seats. Four images took up equal sections of the monitor's display. Gail Griffen sat in the chair before her television, waiting. Her eyes were on the apartment door.

Setting up the Vid Bugs in Gail Griffen's room proved useful. In the days since doing so, B'taav and Shepherd discovered she offered the two men from Lewitt Catering ten thousand credits for information regarding any and all Merrick cruise ship maintenance schedules. It was the sort of inside information anyone could use to plot a raid.

The sound of a light knock was heard over their headphones.

"There they are," B'taav muttered.

On the monitor, Gail Griffen rose from her chair.

"Who's there?" she asked.

"Us," came the muted reply.

Gail opened her door and allowed the two visitors entry. After they were in, she quickly closed the door.

"Sit down," she ordered.

"She sounds tense," B'taav said.

"She's probably new to this."

"Yeah," B'taav said. "It might be time to call the police in."

"And here I thought you were a loner."

"Normally, I am. But there's little sense—"

"Look, we can get backup in a matter of minutes. But so far, the only thing we've got on Gail Griffen and those two boys is conspiracy and minor industrial espionage. The worse they get is six months to a year in a minimum security jail. I doubt Merrick sent you all this way for that. How about we give her a little more time and see if she talks the boys into admitting something more substantial?"

On the monitor, Gail Griffen's two visitors sat down. Gail did not. She paced just behind them, saying nothing. The visitors watched her movements and, after a second or two, Orlando said:

"So are we doing this?"

Gail Griffen stopped pacing.

"The information is worth every penny," Carlo, the driver, said. "We went through a lot of shit to get you this. If anyone finds out we're out of a job."

"I don't much care for your troubles," Gail Griffen replied. "You should have thought about that before you set your price."

"Funny you should mention that," Orlando said. "We figure what you want is worth a little more. But we're not greedy. We just want another thousand."

Shepherd grinned.

"If you want to buy something in Salvation, you gotta bargain for it. We pride ourselves on our strong belief in capitalism."

"I'll give you five hundred extra," Gail countered.

Shepherd whistled. "She's been out of Salvation too long. Now they'll ask for seven fifty. She should have lowballed them."

"How about seven fifty?" Carlo said.

Shepherd let out a laugh. On the monitor, the image flickered.

"I can't do that. You'll have to settle for five," Gail Griffen said. Her voice was high strung, impatient. She rocked in place, tense and full of energy.

There was a long pause. Too long. The monitor flickered again.

"Something isn't right," B'taav said.

Indeed, Gail Griffen seemed to not care about what the duo brought her, nor terribly interested in finalizing their deal. On the monitor, the image steadily grew worse.

"What's wrong with the camera?" Shepherd asked.

"Interference," B'taav replied.

"Fuck this," Orlando muttered. He got to his feet and reached for something in his jacket pocket. A gun. "You don't want our stuff? Fine. We'll keep it. Give us our money and we'll leave."

The images on the monitor dissolved to black.

"Call the squad cars in!" B'taav yelled. As if by magic, a fusion gun appeared in the Independent's hands. He was out of the car and running to the entrance of the Hotel.

Shepherd fumbled for his phone while he too exited the vehicle.

By the time he stepped onto the street, B'taav was already at the Hotel's entrance. The sound of gunfire exploded in Shepherd's ear. He cursed and reached for the ear tab. He heard a dull electric whine and, thinking better of it, left the tab in place.

He too headed for the entrance of the Hotel.

3

B'taav was at the Tropic Hotel's elevators when the sound of gunfire roared in his ear piece. Someone was shooting at Gail Griffen's apartment. He pressed hard on the elevator's "up" button. The nearest of the three elevators was on the 4th floor and heading down.

"Call the police," B'taav yelled to the Hotel's Manager. The man crouched low behind his glass case.

He grabbed the phone and did as told.

By the time the police answered his call, the platinum haired man was in the elevator and gone. Shepherd stepped into the Hotel's lobby. The officer drew his weapon and walked to the manager's glass booth.

"Where did my partner go?" Shepherd asked.

The manager put the phone down.

"Into the elevator. What's going on? Is this about Gail Griffen?"

"I'm afraid so. Did my partner tell you anything?"

"Yeah, he said to call the police."

"Did you?"

"Of course."

Shepherd nodded. He looked back at the Hotel's entrance and within seconds spotted the distant lights of several squad cars converging on the Hotel.

They're running quick tonight, Shepherd thought.

"The police will cordon off this place. Any guests show up down here, tell them to go outside. Don't get in our way."

"I won't."

Shepherd smiled.

"Take it easy, we won't mess up the room you rented us."

"What about Gail Griffen's room?"

"Can't promise anything there," Shepherd said. He remained in the lobby as long as he could. When the police cars screeched to a stop before the Hotel's entrance, he headed for the elevator.

Just as the elevator reached the halfway point of its journey the Independent heard a second gunshot through his earpiece.

B'taav winced. The sound slammed through his already numb ear. Afterwards, all B'taav heard was garbled electronic feedback.

B'taav considered the distortion and his pale face grew pale.

She jammed the Vid feed and now she's jamming the audio signal, B'taav thought. *She knew we were watching and listening.*

The elevator passed the fifty-fourth floor. B'taav removed his ear tab and put it away. He then checked his gun to make sure it was loaded and ready.

The elevator doors opened on the 63rd floor.

B'taav took a quick glance at the south hallway and leaned back inside the elevator. He did the same for the north hallway. Both sides were clear.

B'taav stepped out of the elevator and slowly walked to Gail Griffen's apartment door. He was thankful for the hallway carpeting. It muffled his footsteps.

Shepherd swore. The elevators were descending too slowly. He looked at the hotel manager. The man shrugged.

"They're old," he said.

Shepherd shook his head. Several officers emerged from their vehicles and headed to the Hotel's front entrance. More squad cars were coming from down the street.

And Shepherd needed to be in the goddamn elevator.

B'taav leaned against the hallway wall. In front and to his right was the door to apartment 6345. There was a small hole in the upper half of the door and a similar hole on the wall opposite the door. Smoke rose from each. The two holes were the result of fusion blasts.

B'taav's body tensed as he reached for the doorknob. Abruptly, he stopped. Another door, the one to apartment 6348 across the hall, opened. An elderly lady stuck her head out of her apartment to see what was going on.

B'taav put his index finger in front of his mouth and then pointed at his gun.

"Fucking Independents," the old lady muttered. "If it isn't the heavy metal music it's the fucking shooting."

She disappeared into her room and sealing the apartment door.

The elevator doors closed just as the first of a group of officers entered the Hotel's lobby.

Sorry I couldn't wait, Shepherd thought.

"B'taav, do you read me?"

His ear tab emitted a low electric whine.

"If you can hear me, don't bother answering. My earphone is dead. I'm in the elevator passing the... uh...20th floor. Squad cars have surrounded the building. I'll be up in a moment."

Shepherd swore. If his tab went dead after the second gunshot, there was every reason to assume that B'taav's tab was also gone.

B'taav pressed the side of his head against the door to apartment 6345. He listened for any sounds coming from within. Someone inside the apartment groaned. The voice belonged to a man. The groan was followed by the sound of something large hitting the floor.

"Your suitcase is empty," said an angry female voice.

B'taav recognized the voice as Gail Griffen's, but her tone was far deeper, more guttural than ever before. Regardless, she was alive and seemingly uninjured while at least one of the men who came to see her was in pain.

B'taav was surprised by this. Was it possible someone as petite and frail as Gail Griffen could disarm and incapacitate two men, at least one of whom was carrying a weapon? If so, she was far more dangerous than she outwardly appeared.

"For the last time, where are those documents?" Gail said. Incredibly, her voice was even deeper than the moment before. There came the sounds of movement and someone walking away.

B'taav held his gun tight. He took a step back and kicked the door open. What he saw inside Gail Griffen's room made his blood run cold.

Shepherd checked his gun for what felt like the hundredth time while in the tight confines of the elevator. He muttered meaningless words to himself.

The elevator approached the fiftieth floor.

Shepherd was ready for what was coming.

Blood splatters covered the walls of Gail Griffen's room.

Lying just a few feet from the apartment door was the shattered body of Orlando Echo. His face was a bloody pulp. His crushed left eyeball dangled from the mass of flesh that was once his face. He still held the fusion gun in his right hand.

A few feet away from him and also lying on the floor was Carlo Giny. The face of this man was also mangled, though not quite as badly. He breathed, but barely. He wouldn't last without immediate medical attention. On the floor next to his ravaged body was an open and empty black briefcase. It was the briefcase the two men brought to Gail Griffen's apartment.

B'taav aimed his gun at the center of the apartment as he entered. He knew the dwelling's layout well. To his right was a small bathroom. To his left was the bedroom. The doors leading to both rooms were closed.

Gail Griffen was hiding in either of the two closed rooms or had escaped out the window. B'taav stepped over the first of the two men and knelt down. He felt for a pulse on Orlando Echo. It was no surprise when he found none. He picked up and put away the man's gun.

B'taav stole a quick look at the body and considered what had caused the man his brutal injuries. Orlando was hit with a blunt object, B'taav guessed. Perhaps a wood plank or stone or...

B'taav shook his head. Could Gail Griffen do this kind of damage to an armed man with her bare *fists*?

No, B'taav thought. *Some person –persons– were hidden in the room. They jumped the men and held them down and beat them...*

No.

If there were more people hidden in the apartment, B'taav and Shepherd would have seen or heard them through the various Vid Bugs. Apart from the two men lying in the living room, Gail Griffen was always alone. Always.

Maybe, he thought, she had partners who kept another apartment somewhere else on this floor.

B'taav approached Carlo Giny. The wounds on him were also the result of a severe beating. Fresh blood seeped from a jagged cut on his forehead.

"Can you hear me?" B'taav whispered. He didn't look directly at the man, but keep his eyes on the closed doors on either side of the room.

"Yes," came a barely audible reply. The man spit up a mouthful of blood.

"How many people does she have here?"

"She's alone," Carlo muttered. From his throat came a rattling sound that might have been moan. "All alone."

Carlo Giny took one final breath and was gone.

4

After what seemed too long a delay, the elevator doors opened. Shepherd stepped into the hallway and pointed his gun in the direction of Gail Griffen's room. The corridor before him was empty.

"Ok," Shepherd said.

He walked to apartment 6345.

B'taav moved away from the second corpse and edged closer to the apartment window. Outside, there was no ledge. With a sixty-three floor drop, there was no way Gail Griffen could escape that way. It meant she was still in the apartment.

B'taav stared at the doors to either side of him. The bedroom or the bathroom. Gail Griffen was behind one of them. Gail Griffen, the petite, frail looking twenty six year old woman who had somehow beaten two men –one of them armed with a fusion gun– to death.

Gail Griffen. There was more to her. Much more.

You're either in the bathroom or the bedroom, B'taav thought. *Door number one or door number two.*

The bathroom was small, confined. To the Independent, it was more likely she'd be in the bedroom.

B'taav stepped to the bedroom door and, with his free hand, grasped the doorknob. He slowly, gently, turned it. The door wasn't locked. With great care, He pushed it open.

The door let out a soft creak but otherwise gave. B'taav stepped back, unsure what to expect. He pressed his body against the wall beside the door and waited. Nothing happened. After a few seconds, he eased off the wall and stared into the room. He found inky darkness.

B'taav's eyes took only a few seconds to adjust. While they did, the Independent's stomach churning with thoughts of what lay within, waiting for him to step inside.

Soon, B'taav identified the freshly made bed. Beside it was a night table. On the night table was an antique paperback novel. Beside the night table was a covered window. Beyond that the double door to the closet. One of those doors was open. B'taav spotted no clothing on the hanger and a black suitcase against the inner wall. Gail Griffen was packed up and ready to go.

B'taav aimed his gun at the closet door. He could only see half of the closet's contents. For all he knew, Gail Griffen was hidden behind the second, closed door.

He had little choice but to check.

Shepherd reached the door to apartment 6345 and found it open. Like B'taav had done moments before, he listened for any sounds coming from within.

He heard nothing. He thought about calling out for B'taav, but he needed to assess the situation before letting anyone know about his presence.

It was the prudent thing to do.

He also thought about waiting for backup to arrive. By now, Police Officers were on their way up. An overwhelming force would ensure control over the situation.

But what if B'taav lay injured in the apartment?

Gail Griffen's buy of Merrick Enterprises information had gone sour. A gun was drawn and shots fired. B'taav was in there.

He might be injured.

Officer Shepherd had no choice in the matter. He stepped forward, past the door, stopping at the threshold.

"By the Gods," he whispered.

In fifteen years of duty, Officer Shepherd saw plenty of horrors. As the old adage went, you never got used to such sights. But he had never seen anything like *this* before.

Shepherd walked to the first body and shuddered as he checked for a pulse. When he found none he approached the other victim.

B'taav rested his hand on the closet door. He slid the closet door open and pointed his gun at the darkness within.

There was no one there.

B'taav found the light switch and clicked the closet lights on. A single change of clothes were on a hanger. It was what Gail Griffen wore a few days back, to the restaurant. B'taav reached for the light switch and was about to turn it off when he noticed something lying beside her suitcase.

It was a plastic vial and syringe. B'taav picked the items up. The vial was labeled Ac2. B'taav gasped. The massacre in the apartment suddenly made sense.

"B'taav?" came a voice from the living room.

B'taav dropped the vial and syringe and rushed to the door leading back to the living room.

"She's in the bathroom!" the Independent yelled.

For the first time since knowing him, Shepherd heard terror in the Independent's voice.

B'taav sprung out of the bedroom as Gail Griffen smashed the bathroom door from its hinges. Her petite body was transformed into a hulking, muscular monster. Her face was bloated and distorted. Engorged veins ran across her forehead and the blood within them beat wildly against her hideously stretched skin. Her eyes were likewise swollen and wild. Her body, with the exception of her left hand, which hung limp at her side, appeared supercharged. Blood from a fusion gun blast dripped down the length of the limp arm.

The monster that was once Gail Griffen tore into the living room with lightning speed. Her good hand reached out and, before Shepherd could react, locked around the police officer's neck. Gail Griffen let out a guttural roar and twisted Shepherd's head to the right and left. His body flailed about as if it were a child's doll.

There followed a grotesque crack and Shepherd's body went limp. His service revolver tumbled to the ground. Though he was dead, the being that was once Gail Griffen continued shaking the officer. The flesh that held the dead man's head to his body ripped away. Shepherd's headless body tumbled to the ground while his head remained in Gail's monstrous right hand.

B'taav fired his gun over and over and over again. The blasts tore into the woman, producing five gaping holes in her chest. From each spewed a fountain of blood.

The creature roared once again. She slammed Shepherd's head to the ground and moved toward B'taav. But her movements were sluggish. The blood flowing out of her body was too much, even for this monster.

B'taav ran back to the bedroom and slammed the door shut. It was the only barrier he had between himself and that creature.

If it holds.

The creature pounded against the door, splintering panels just inches from B'taav's face. B'taav held the door tight while the creature continued pounding. Her blows grew weaker, until they finally stopped.

B'taav waited a few more moments before inching the shattered remains of door open. Gail Griffen lay on the floor, her body no longer bloated and muscular. In death her features were serene. All traces of the monster that killed Orlando Echo, Carlo Giny, and Officer Shepherd were gone. All around her and sprayed against the wall and floor was a thick layer of her blood.

In the end, it was the blood loss that killed her.

5

The sixty-third floor of the Tropic Hotel was tightly cordoned off and filled with police and crime scene technicians.

B'taav was led to the room next door to Gail Griffen's. It was the same room Shepherd and he rented several nights before. The Independent was told to sit there with three fresh-faced Ferro City Police Officers. He was asked no questions during that initial wait. Through the door leading out into the hallway B'taav spotted a small army of technicians pacing back and forth. Photograph flashes went off at a steady clip. Another technician walked very slowly past his room. In his hand was a three-dimensional holograph quality Vid Camera. He talked into it as he panned the instrument back and forth. The three-dimensional imaging would offer anyone interested a virtual walkthrough of the crime scene.

After a half-hour, B'taav got to his feet. The police officers said nothing, though one of them momentarily tensed. B'taav slowed down. There was no need to alarm his babysitters. He walked to the room's window. A mob had formed outside the hotel. They were held back by at least twenty police cars and a plethora of officers.

"It's crazy down there."

The voice came from the entrance to the room. Though calm in tone, there was a discernable edge to it.

Len Herbert, the Commissioner of the Ferro City Police, stood at the doorway. He wore a dull gray trench coat and smoked a thin white cigar. The lines on his face were pronounced. There was a genuine sadness in his eyes.

"I've taken a look around next door," he said. "Care to tell me what the hell happened?"

B'taav pulled out the vial labeled Ac2 and the syringe. He handed them to Herbert

"What is this?"

"Amidoadrenalin. Some call it an adrenalizer. Others call it Accelerant."

"Accelerant? I don't believe I've heard—"

"It's a stimulant. It works on the user's body, speeding up their system. If you're a miner and work on commission you take a small dose and it gives you the energy to work three or four days in a row without needing sleep."

"I suppose it also increases your strength?"

"Yes, though if used in the regular doses this increase is minimal. Gail Griffen overdosed. On purpose. Even if I, or Officer Shepherd, hadn't shown up, she would have been dead within the hour."

"Are you saying Officer Shepherd's death wasn't necessary?"

"She could have left the apartment, crashed into a number of other rooms and killed many more before the drug eventually killed her."

"She didn't want to be taken alive?"

"That's my guess."

"Why? According to your own reports, you had her on relatively small charges. Why go nuclear?"

"She was a member of the Black Bird organization. The pirates I was tasked with rooting out used their members as potential recruits."

"You have proof she was a recruit?"

B'taav didn't answer.

"Figures," Herbert said.

There was movement in the outside hallway. Bill Goodwin, the Merrick representative of Salvation, entered the room. He wore a heavy gray coat and was in the process of removing an expensive pair of black leather gloves. He wasted no time greeting Herbert or acknowledging B'taav's presence.

"What a fucking mess," Goodwin began. He poked his finger in Herbert's chest. "You'll tell the media this was a case of domestic violence or a lover's quarrel or whatever story you come up with that sounds good. You will not even whisper any mention of Merrick Cruise Lines in your report."

"A lover's quarrel? One of our officers is dead and you want us to pretend nothing happened?"

Goodwin stared down the chief of police.

"As far as Merrick Cruise Lines is concerned, nothing *has* happened."

Herbert nodded. There was no use arguing the point. He stepped back and said:

"You two should get going. It seems we've got a domestic violence case that needs to be cleaned up."

B'taav and Goodwin followed two police officers to the elevator. They were taken down to the second floor and escorted to the Hotel's rear exit. There were no news crews there. When the officer was satisfied no one might see the Independent or the Merrick official, he whistled and waved. A sleek white limousine pulled up. Its rear passenger door opened.

"This way," the officer said.

Goodwin and B'taav hurried out the Hotel's exit and into the limousine.

When they were inside, the vehicle hurried down the darkened back alley streets. Goodwin nervously looked out the rear window until he was certain no one spotted their departure or was following. He then sat back and pulled out a long brown cigarette. He searched in vain for a lighter in his coat pocket before giving up.

"Must've left it at home," Goodwin sighed. "You got a match?"

"Don't smoke," B'taav replied.

"Just as well," Goodwin said. He returned the cigarette to its packet. "That was some business."

B'taav nodded. Outside, neon signs flashed. A light rain fell and the splash of water broke the silence.

"Mr. Merrick called yesterday," Goodwin said. "His ship should be in orbit around Salvation by now. He wanted to know how we were doing. He's arriving at Ferro City tomorrow morning."

Goodwin paused and shook his head.

"I gave him a rundown of what little I knew about your investigation. Couldn't offer him more than the date of your arrival and details of our one phone conversation."

"And?"

"He said I shouldn't have told Commissioner Herbert about you."

"I see."

"Mr. Merrick was angry. He said you knew what you were doing and that if you needed any help, you'd ask." A ghost of a smile appeared on his face. "He told me my job was in jeopardy."

The smile slipped away into nothingness.

"He didn't exactly come out and say I was fired. His type never does. I took on the job of running a cruise ship port of call. If I knew the position required dealing with pirates, industrial spies, Independents, and the police, I wouldn't have taken it."

In the distance, a mega-mall shone in blue neon. The lights reflected off the side of Goodwin's face.

"For what it's worth, I'm sorry. I'm sorry for this whole mess."

"Did Shepherd have any family?"

"A wife and two kids. His wife's name is Susan. His boys are Elias and Thomas. Eight and ten years of age."

"You knew him?"

"Well enough. When my family first arrived in Ferro City and began the transition with the previous Port Director, I was told it would be in my best interests to contact the local police and procure a bodyguard. Back in those days –hell, it was only ten years ago– the big corporations weren't at all welcome. The locals figured all they did was use up Salvation's resources and, once exhausted, split. In many respects, the people here were right."

"Anyway, we put off getting a bodyguard. We figured the stories about violence against corporate types were an exaggeration. That is, until we started getting threatening calls. The usual stuff. Environmentalists, nationalists. Freaks, protestors. I got in touch with Commissioner Herbert and he pointed me to Shepherd. He was our bodyguard for nearly a year. During that time, we smoothed over most of the bad feelings the locals had about Merrick Cruise Lines and painted a positive picture of our interests in Salvation. Now, the locals welcome the work and money we bring in."

The rain fell harder as the limousine entered a rundown neighborhood. Goodwin pointed out the window.

"That's Salvation," Goodwin said. "The real Salvation. When we're done here, she'll rot. Maybe in another million years the plants and animals that inhabited this place will take over. By that time they'll be another business conglomerate just like ours ready to chew the planet up again."

Goodwin sighed.

"Talking about Merrick Enterprises doesn't bother me anymore, Mr. B'taav, seeing as how I'll be an ex-employee very soon."

B'taav was familiar with people like Goodwin. They were honorable to their bosses and sung their corporation's praises as long as they held their job. Once it was threatened, they were quick to bite the hand that fed them.

"At least you took care of your business," Goodwin said. "I suppose you're done here. Where to next?"

B'taav thought about the question and ultimately shrugged. Goodwin laughed.

"Before I leave Ferro City, I should talk to Shepherd's family and tell them what he did. What he *really* did," Goodwin said. "It may not be worth much to them, but maybe they'll feel his death wasn't completely in vain." Goodwin straightened in his chair and added, "They'll get a pension from the force. I doubt Merrick will offer them anything for their loss."

Goodwin's face twisted in on itself while the outside neon colored him in a rainbow of artificial lights.

6

MINING CRAFT "SANDSTONE", on the outer edges of Erebus

Kelly Lang entered his ship's decompression chamber and removed his helmet. Bright red dust fell off his suit and danced around the room before being sucked into the ship's purification system.

The old man ignored the rush of air and hurriedly walked to the door leading into the body of his craft. He pressed a series of buttons in a panel beside the door and, when the all clear light flashed, he re-entered his ship.

The old man removed the remainder of his space suit, revealing a sweaty blue thermal suit underneath. He hung the space suit on its rack and walked the narrow corridor leading to ship Ops. He sat behind the ship's navigational controls and worked the central computer.

Images recorded during his latest spacewalk appeared on the monitor and were cross referenced with known landmarks in the navigational computer's memory. The old man focused on one spot, a distant light he saw during his many hours outside. It was a reflection. He saw it only once before it faded away.

To anyone else, the light was a blip and nothing more. To Kelly Lang, the aberrant flash meant there might be something out there worth scavenging. This was his vocation, after all, and over the years he developed a sense of the importance of spotting anything out of the ordinary.

Kelly Lang replayed the flash of light several more times on the monitor before a broad smile appeared on his face.

"Metal," he mumbled with delight.

There was no doubt the light was indeed a reflection off something metallic. But was the object man made? Could it be a remnant of the Erebus War? The larger the remnant, the bigger the reward.

Kelly Lang could not contain his growing elation. Though the Epsillon government ordered most of the Erebus system off limits following the war, there were plenty of people like Lang skirting the security perimeters in the hopes of finding any of the war's debris. There were collectors from the Homeworlds willing to pay top credit to buy the stuff.

Kelly Lang steered the nose of his ship in the general direction of the reflection and worked some more on locating the reflection's source. While he was pleased with the possibility of finding vintage Erebus War era material, the thought that there might be an Epsillon security ship or, even worse, claim jumpers also occupied his mind.

If he were found by either in this section of Erebus, his ship could be impounded or stolen. Since the *Sandstorm* was his only means of income, he'd be forced to do whatever he could to stop anyone from taking her.

"Where are you?" he muttered. He held the ship steady and initiated a gentle acceleration. Huge asteroids, the remains of Erebus Planet E, drifted past him.

The planet, along with the rest of the planets in the Erebus system, was reduced to rubble at the abrupt end of the war. Thoughts of the massive wave of destruction haunted those who flew these parts, but Kelly Lang was not one to dwell on the Great Unanswered Question of what exactly happened here so many years before.

He knew government officials ruled the cause of this destruction "unknown natural phenomena", but he also knew there were plenty of alternate theories, from government conspiracies to the idea that some dark, unknown alien force that would not tolerate interstellar war ended it, once and for all. The later theory, he always felt, made the most sense.

Kelly Lang's eyes opened wide.

"There you are!" he yelled.

The object he briefly saw while on his spacewalk was revealed in his ship's sensor equipment. Kelly Lang steered the *Sandstorm* in even closer. As he did, he found it harder and harder to contain his excitement. The object was the largest intact piece of machinery he had ever come upon. It measured at least five feet by seven and looked like a rectangular box. Several bent antennae and crumpled wires protruding from its body. Despite considerable charring and a few scars left behind from small asteroid impacts, the object was essentially intact.

Lang licked his lips and parked the *Sandstorm* mere feet from his prize. He ran back down the corridor and picked up his space suit before returning to the decompression chamber. By the time he was locked inside, his suit was on. After checking the suit's status, he opened the outer hatch doors.

Lang guided the suit's thruster and floated away from the

Sandstorm and toward the object. He clicked on the short-range scanner and prayed no one was close enough to detect them. Floating in space unarmed and a good distance from his craft was, after all, a scavenger's greatest moment of vulnerability.

The scanner gave minimal radioactive readings on the device, so Kelly Lang shut it off and applied more power to the thrusters. The closer he got to his prize, the more he found it looked like nothing more than a very dirty gray box. Kelly Lang spotted several dark marks and cuts along the length of its body and faint red lettering half buried under a layer of dust.

Lang applied a counter thrust and stopped a couple of feet away from his prize. Cautiously, he reached out and touched it. Dust crumbled off the object's surface and floated off. Lang swept more dust off, until he could read the letters hidden below.

ISP. Information and Scientific Probe.

The smile on Kelly Lang's face grew larger. He hit the jackpot after all. There were more markings on the lower half of the probe, but for the moment Lang ignored them. He removed a tinsel wire from his belt and connected it to the probe. Afterwards, he again activated his suit's thrusters. The burst of energy sent both Lang and his tethered cargo back toward the *Sandstorm*.

Once inside the ship's decompression chamber, Kelly Lang locked the probe down and closed the *Sandstorm's* outer doors. He then made a more detailed examination of his find.

To get top credits for this prize, Kelly Lang had to verify the probe was part of the armada that met its end in Erebus two hundred years before and not some more recently discarded equipment.

After a few minutes of detailed examination and clean up, Kelly Lang found a protruding metal plate on the lower half of the probe. He brushed the dust from it and found a set of serial numbers.

"11345-23400," Kelly read.

The scavenger let out a laugh. The numbers could be easily cross-checked and the space craft that held this probe would then be found.

Once it was, Kelly Lang stood to make a whole lot of cash.

In minutes Lang was back at the *Sandstorm's* Ops center.

"Computer, access Epsillon common database," he said. "Locate all information pertaining to scientific probe, serial number 11345-23400."

The computer worked on the information for a few seconds before saying, "Identification number belongs to a class 4 scientific probe."

"Which ship carried this probe?"

The computer worked on that for a second.

"The *Argus*, military designation PE-332. Juggernaut class."

"Status of ship?"

"Ship was lost with all hands, May 21st, 50789, in the Vega system."

Lang's eyebrow lifted. The timing was right: The ship was operational until the end of the Erebus War. But its final listed location had to be a mistake.

"Vega system? Please verify."

The computer was silent for a few more seconds.

"All hands lost in the Vega system. Craft lost communication with Epsillon Command on May 21st, 50789. Last reports indicate engine failure while approaching a class three gas giant. Craft was believed to be pulled into planet and crushed."

"And no way to check for wreckage," Lang muttered.

Though the records indicated the *Argus* met her end in the Vega system, finding the scientific probe here in Erebus proved otherwise. In the days leading up to the Erebus War, there was a great deal of misinformation floating around about the location of various warships. It hardly mattered that the *Argus* was one of many Epsillon ships whose existence in Erebus was, until this moment, kept secret.

Kelly Lang strapped himself into the navigator's chair. He activated the *Sandstorm's* thrusters and began the slow trip back to the *Titus* Space Station.

7

FERRO CITY, the planet Salvation

Goodwin's limousine dropped B'taav off at the James Hotel.

B'taav exited the car and stepped quickly under the faded awning at the Hotel's entrance and out of the rain. Goodwin's limousine pulled off to the edge of the street. It paused a moment to allow traffic to pass before turning to the right and heading off toward the city's high class residential zone.

B'taav stood under the awning for a few seconds and thought about the events that transpired over the course of this, and the past couple, of days. Being an Independent was a messy business, no more so than when things went so very wrong.

B'taav ran his hand through his damp hair and walked into the lobby of the hotel. He slipped past the receptionist and made a brief call on one of the public phones before stepping into an elevator. He reached out to press his floor button, but paused as the memory of Gail Griffen and Ken Shepherd and their gruesome ends intruded upon his thoughts. He let the memories go and pressed the 32nd floor button.

Beyond the elevator's glass paneling B'taav was treated to a view of downtown Ferro City. Heavy rain soaked the buildings and sent bystanders running for shelter.

A loud ring brought B'taav around. The elevator doors opened, revealing the 32nd floor hallway. B'taav again ran his hands through his wet hair once more and, with a heavy sigh, reached for the fusion gun in his holster.

B'taav walked silently to the stairwell door. His movements were controlled and precise. He turned the doorknob and carefully opened the door, slid past it, and examined his surroundings.

The stairwell was encased in concrete and smelled of mildew. The stairs were concretal metal and their lower base was corroded. B'taav peeked over the edge of the stairs and down. There was no one below. B'taav turned his attention to the stairs leading up. Again he saw no one.

The Independent walked up the stairs, past three flights, before stopping in front of the door to the 35th floor hallway. The door was solid metal. There was no way B'taav could see what lay beyond without opening it.

B'taav crouched down to his knees and, while keeping his gun steady in his right hand, gripped the doorknob with his left and turned. B'taav opened the door just a crack, enough to see the 35th floor hallway. Despite the gloomy illumination, he could see no one was there.

B'taav opened the door fully and slid into the hallway. He pressed his body against the wall and gently closed the stairway door. He silently moved forward, until he stood before the door to apartment 3514.

His apartment.

With his free hand, B'taav's reached into his pant pocket. He pulled out a slim metal keypad and inserted it into the slot over the door's handle. The keypad mechanism issued a faint click and the green light over the handle came on.

B'taav put the keypad away and pushed the door's handle down. The lock made another faint click. B'taav released the handle. His left hand came down and joined his right in grasping the fusion gun.

B'taav's left foot slid to the base of the door. He used it to push the door open and pressed his back against the wall, as if expecting something from within his room to burst out. When the door was fully open and nothing happened, B'taav exhaled. He leaned past the doorway and gazed into his room.

In his apartment was darkness and formless shadows. B'taav returned to his previous position against the wall. He made a mental picture of what the room looked like when he left earlier in the day. He could account for most of the shadowy forms.

Most, not all.

A chair and table were moved slightly to the left. The chair that was by the window was turned over and lay near the door. A video entertainment unit was lying close beside it. Worse, B'taav detected a pungent smell: oil and sulfur.

B'taav remained in place. After a few seconds, he heard a faint metallic click coming from within. The sound increased, as did the smells. B'taav lowered the gun and aimed it at the base of his apartment door. The clicking increased some more. Whatever was making the sound approached the open door.

It stopped, turned, and moved away.

B'taav kept his gun trained at the door's base and entered the room. He looked to his left and spotted a body. Crouched on top of it were four metal spiders. They walked the length of the swollen corpse and, every few seconds, stung the dead man with a thin spike that protruded from their belly. The tension B'taav felt eased. Each of the spiders, the Independent knew, was harmless now. The venom in their bodies was spent.

The spider that approached the door remained close to B'taav. The Independent put his fusion gun back into its holster and grabbed it.

"Black Widow," B'taav muttered. He searched the still moving beast's body for any identification marks. He was not surprised to find there were none.

These metallic devices were used for any number of tasks, some of them even legitimate. In B'taav's field, Black Widows were primarily used for either industrial espionage or remote control murder. The would-be assassin leaves the activated device within his victim's room. When the victim arrives, the spider senses their target's movement or body heat and attacks.

The machines were very efficient, but like any mechanical device, this efficiency was tied in to the sophistication of their programming. If you weren't careful, once activated your remote control assassin would not distinguish between victims and perpetrators.

B'taav wondered if this was the case here.

The Independent stared at the swollen features of the corpse. He didn't recognize the man, although he was certain he was the one that brought the mechanical assassins to this room.

The mechanical spider in B'taav's hands stopped moving and its body heated up. It wouldn't be long before the spider melted into a puddle of unidentifiable metal.

B'taav dropped the device on the ground and grabbed the plastic card hanging on the other side of the entry door. He then stepped out of the room, closed the door to his apartment, and placed the plastic card on the doorknob.

The card read: "Do Not Disturb."

B'taav exited through the rear of the building and was careful not to be seen leaving. He walked three blocks to the north and two to the west in the pouring rain before hailing a cab.

He asked the driver to take him to Mr. Goodwin's residence on the outskirts of Ferro City. The driver grunted an acknowledgement and headed to the highway entrance. When they got there, they found a long line of cars and, in the far distance, a police barricade.

"That's quite a jam," the Cabby said. He reached for the monitor on his dashboard and turned it to the traffic news network. "Let's see what's going on."

After a few minutes of commercials, an announcer appeared on the screen.

"For those hoping to catch the North 631, we recommend seeking alternate routes. There has been an accident just outside exit 54."

The image on the monitor changed to flaming wreckage on the highway. B'taav recognized the charred vehicle as the one that brought him to his hotel.

Goodwin's.

"Early word is that the driver somehow lost control and, before the anti-crash software was activated, his vehicle crashed into the steelcrete barrier," the announcer continued. "It is our understanding there were two passengers. Both were killed instantly. The highway will be closed until further notice."

"How about that?" the cabbie said. "I can get you where you want to go, but it'll take a while."

"Never mind," B'taav said. "Turn around. Take me to the star port."

The *Merrick* floated over Salvation and a large docking crew floated around her like bees swarming their hive. They serviced and inspected the ship. All at once, several of their heads turned.

A weathered cargo ship approached and slowed. A radio signal, a request to dock, was sent from the cargo ship.

The request was granted.

8

EPSILLON MILITARY COMPLEX - HOMEWORLD

General Anton Jurgens was in a very bad mood.

The angry little lines on his weathered face threatened to rip his skin into pieces. It was always like this at the end of the fiscal year. The business interests that owned the biggest share of the Epsillon Government and made up most of the Council were always looking at every single credit the military spent rather than focusing on the potential dangers the Empire might face in the future.

General Jurgens worried the constant interest in the bottom line would come back to bite the councilmen in their collective asses. One day, perhaps. And then they would all come screaming to him to save them.

Of course Jurgens would put up a fight for more funds, just like he did every year. He would argue that more money was needed *–required–* for any number of contingencies. He would plead his case until he was practically on his knees.

To that, the council majority would inevitably scan their spreadsheets, give their calculators a good workout, and eventually say something to the effect that whenever future problems presented themselves, they would be resolved at that point. When they occurred. There was little use in spending money on things that "might" happen. *Besides*, at least one of the councilmen would inevitably add, *the Phaecian Empire hasn't tried anything in over two hundred years. Why would they do something now?*

Jurgens felt his blood pressure soar. As if the Phaecian Empire was the only threat.

At least he had four of the Council member's ears. They were far from a majority but enough to keep the military budget from shrinking. Then again, these particular councilmen were sympathetic to increasing military spending because the planets they represented provided the fleet with most of its weaponry and maintenance docks.

Jurgens smirked. The Council members were a collection of liars and thieves, each and every one of them in this for their own profit.

The elevator stopped on the fiftieth floor of the Complex.

General Jurgens stepped out of the elevator and into the waiting area of his office. He found the regular group of advisers and military officials sitting in chairs waiting for him. They rose and saluted, each looking on in hopeful anticipation. Before they spoke even a single word, General Jurgens knew what they would ask: Was the budget a go? If not, can our department get its full funding? If not, can we at least get...

General Jurgens stepped past the group without acknowledging their presence and entered his secretary's office. As was his habit, his next stop was the coffee machine at the back of that room.

"Tough meeting?" his secretary asked.

"I have yet to be in one that wasn't."

The General reached for a cup and poured some coffee. He pointed to the outside waiting room. "If they had their way, they'd surgically attach themselves to my ass."

"And if you had your way?"

"I could think of a few worse places."

The Secretary let out a gentle laugh and said, "I can't promise you anything, but I just might be able to fit in a bathroom break at two, then six, then perhaps one more by midnight."

"That would be nice. So how would you like me to see them? In the order they arrived or alphabetically or...?"

"I think you should see Corporal Ewing first."

Whatever levity General Jurgens displayed abruptly vanished.

"Ewing is out there?" he said. "Why didn't you say so?"

"I'm sorry, sir. I thought you noticed him when you came in. I'll escort him in right away."

Jurgens put the coffee down and entered his office. He was sitting behind his desk when Corporal Theodore Ewing was shown in. The Corporal was very young, almost too young to be one of the heads of Epsillon Intelligence. Yet his service to the Empire was exemplary and he had a reputation for being all business. When he came to see you, it was for a reason.

Ewing gave General Jurgens a crisp salute. Jurgens motioned for the Intelligence Officer to sit down.

"What have you got?" he asked.

Ewing laid a small computer pad on Jurgens' desk. Information flashed on the pad's screen.

"We picked up someone making inquiries regarding flagged information."

Jurgens nodded.   Any search for information on the government's main database was routed through another search engine installed by the military many years before.   Flagged material related to undesirables, state secrets, or anything that might fall into the purview of military command was brought to the attention of those higher up on the information food chain.

"Go on," Jurgens said.

"This inquiry came from the *Sandstorm*, a salvage ship operating outside the Erebus system.   She is, according to our most recent information, docked in space station *Titus*."

"What was the inquiry?"

"The ship's pilot, a man named Kelly Lang, asked for information on a Class 4 Scientific Probe with the serial number 11345-23400."

"And?"

"When the captain of the *Sandstorm* made that inquiry, it triggered a warning message on our system.   The message reads: Code Omega-Omega 3321."

Jurgens' face froze.   He mumbled his thanks and motioned Ewing out of the room.

"If you need anything else, please call me," the Corporal said.

"Thank you," Jurgens replied.

When Ewing was gone Jurgens returned to his desk and read the information on the computer pad.   He felt strong chills run down his back.   The Omega-Omega codes hadn't been used in a very, very long time.   Certainly not since the Erebus war.   Almost all references to them were deleted over the years.   So why had the *Sandstorm's* inquiry set off such a code?

"Computer," General Jurgens said, addressing the larger machine on his desk. "Open file code named Theta Omega 3321."

"Please enter security code."

Jurgens did so.

For the next hour he read the information provided about the lost super juggernaut *Argus*.   When he finished, he paged his secretary and told her to send all those kind, patient officers waiting to see him back to their respective offices.   He would have no time for them today.

General Jurgens then called up the four members of the Council who were sympathetic to the military.   He told them they had to call an emergency session right away.

He told them it involved the fate of the Epsillon Empire.

9

TITUS SPACE STATION, on the outer border of Erebus

The *Titus* space station served the Empire well as a listening post and a center for transportation of cargo in the years leading up to the Erebus War. She was the only remaining structure on the Epsillon side to survive the explosion that decimated that system. At the height of her golden age and just before that tragedy, she housed over one million citizens.

Today, after various upgrades, she was as large as a medium sized city. Yet in spite of her upgrades, she was a living anachronism. Shortly after the war, she was abandoned. Soon after that, and following years of negotiation with private interest groups, *Titus* was purchased by investors catering to historians, preservationists, and vacationers.

When it was clear the Erebus system was stable, the area became a point of interest to hundreds of thousands of tourists curious to see where what should have been the greatest galactic war started and, very abruptly, ended. The luxury crafts that brought tourists into this area needed a place to dock and *Titus* was the only station around.

Unknown to the tourists was the fact that deep within *Titus* operated a vast illegal salvage trade. Scavengers skirted the law and flew out into the remains of the system seeking any memorabilia that survived the war. They brought their finds to *Titus* to sell.

Far away from the main docking section and occupying a place by the common quarters was the refurbished Jackal Bar. Over time, it became the watering hole for those scavengers. They met and tried sniffing out where the latest hot spots for prospecting lay. Because of the illegal nature of their activities, talk was usually hushed and information well-guarded. Despite this, rumors had a tendency to spread like butter on hot toast.

When Kelly Lang walked into the bar, few paid attention to him. He was one of several dozen scavengers who filtered in and out of the place. He headed for his usual seat at the foot of the bar. It took great effort to contain a growing smile.

"What do you want?" Dave Maddox, the Jackal Bar's head bartender, asked. He was a short man in his late thirties that carried a slight build. His hair was jet black and his face a sturdy mask of neutrality.

"The usual," Lang replied.

"You look kind of funny today," Maddox said as he poured Lang a beer.

"I'm fine," Lang said, even as his voice told another story.

If Maddox noticed, he didn't say. He acted as if their conversation was about nothing more than the too-steady artificial weather within the station. Maddox pulled a tin plate from the Food Dispenser and laid it before Lang. Lang removed the lid and dug into the brown mush.

"Steak and potatoes," Maddox said. "Just like momma used to make."

"Provided your momma was a five hundred pound grease machine."

"Who says she wasn't?"

"Something tells me you've had a good day."

"Maybe I did," Lang replied cryptically.

Maddox leaned in close to the scavenger and said: "I hear the Pritchett boys found some shielding in quadrant 5423. Might be from one of the destroyers."

"Good for them."

"They say it's in good shape. Hardly any dings or warps," Maddox continued. He knew if he gave out information, even information that may not interest the person he was speaking with, it increased the odds of reciprocation.

"I'm happy for them. Really I am," Lang said. He drank some more beer, took another spoonful of the brown slop, and winced. "Momma should be shot."

"She's seen better days."

"Haven't we all."

Lang took a long look around the bar before his eyes returned to Maddox.

"Tell the man in white I've got something he might find interesting," Lang whispered. "I'll give him a first look, but only if he's willing to come to my ship in the next hour."

"Come on, Lang. You go to him. He doesn't go to—"

"This is gold, Maddox. One hundred percent. If he doesn't come see me, I'm heading elsewhere."

Maddox laid down another cup of beer.

"There isn't a day that passes where someone tells me they've got the goods."

"I'm not bullshitting," Lang retorted. "What I've got he'll want. I guarantee it."

Maddox sighed. "You know he's a busy man. If you want him to jump, you have to show him a reason to do so. You know he won't do it just for me."

"Yeah. I suppose so."

Lang reached into his shirt and pulled out a small photograph. He handed it to Maddox and said, "If this doesn't convince him, nothing will."

The photograph displayed a side view of the probe Lang found on the outskirts of Erebus.

"What is it?" Maddox asked.

"It's from the war and it's just about intact. Anything else, the man in white can figure out on his own. Tell him I've got it."

Lang laid down some change. With a nod and a wink, he headed out the bar.

Kelly Lang whistled a cheerful tune while returning to his ship's docking berth. At some point in the distant past, the corridor before him was immaculately clean. It was now filled with reddish dust and a stampede of footprints both old and new.

It took Lang a few minutes to pass this corridor and reach the entrance to his craft. At the foot of the door, he punched in his security code and waited. His ship's outer doors opened and he entered an even narrower and grimier corridor.

Home sweet home.

He took only a couple of steps before hearing a ring.

Lang returned to the ship's outer doors and pressed a button beside a monitor on the wall. It lit up with a view of the *Titus* station's docking berth doors. Walking into the area was a man dressed in immaculate white.

"That was quick," Lang said.

The scavenger pressed a button and the outer doors opened. The man in white stepped through them and out of the camera's sight. Lang shut the monitor off and opened his ship's outer doors once again.

Lang met up with the man in white just as he reached the pressurized doors leading into the *Sandstorm*. The man's white suit was immaculate. His face was chiseled and very thin. Icy blue eyes gave Lang an impatient stare.

"Maddox showed me your photograph," the man in white said. "What you're selling better be real, Mr. Lang. I don't take kindly to people wasting my time."

"Wouldn't think of it."

"It would be an even bigger shame if I discovered you were trying to pass off a forgery."

The smile on Lang's face evaporated. The man in white, otherwise known as Ned Frasier, was one of the chief engineers of the *Titus* space station. Though he worked for the Epsillon government, those in the salvage business knew he was also one of the elite middlemen that dealt with Erebus War material. His clients paid very well and no one crossed him. That was because it was rumored he had very deep ties to the underworld.

"I wouldn't call you out if what I was selling wasn't big, and real," Lang said.

The scavenger escorted Frasier to the rear section of his ship. The two paused before the double doors leading into *Sandstorm's* decompression chamber. Lang punched in the appropriate access code and when the doors opened he motioned for Frasier inside.

Frasier did so and stopped a few feet short of the probe.

"She's a beauty, isn't she?" Lang said.

Frasier did not reply. Instead, he scanned the machine as if he were a starving man admiring an elaborate banquet. After a few seconds, he walked to the probe's side and leaned down to get a better look at her faded red lettering.

"I did some research," Lang said. "The probe's from the *Argus*. She was a juggernaut class ship that –get this– wasn't even supposed to be here during the war."

"*Argus*," Frasier repeated. His voice was a whisper. He touched the probe gently, as if feeling for a pulse. "Where did you find her?"

"Among the asteroids."

"*Where?*"

"You're kidding, right?"

Frasier's cold eyes stared hard at the scavenger. Lang wasn't sure what to make of the intense expression on the man in white's face.

"No offense, Mr. Frasier," Lang sputtered. "But I tell anyone where I found this and whatever claims I've got for any future discoveries are gone."

"I will pay you well for this item," Frasier countered. "Well enough that you won't have to worry about making any further forays into Erebus. But I will not pay you one credit until I know where exactly you found this probe."

"Why?" Lang asked. "You think there's more treasure out there?"

Frasier drew an impatient breath. He rubbed his eyes before letting out the breath.

"As a historian, an *amateur* historian anyway, I make it my hobby to know as much as possible about the Erebus War. As you said, the *Argus* was not one of the Epsillon warships listed as perishing within this system when it erupted. Unfortunately, I've had more than a few scavengers offer me items they claim were from ships stationed here at the time of this explosion. They demand top dollar for what amounts to planted items. I need to know where you found this probe, Mr. Lang, because that's the only way I can verify the *Argus* was indeed in system when it exploded."

Kelly Lang scratched the back of his neck.

"I see," he finally said.

"Is this all you found?"

"Yes sir," Lang said. "I guess...I can understand your concern, Mr. Frasier. If you're willing to pay extra, I'll throw in the location of this find along with the probe itself."

"I didn't mean to question your honesty," Frasier said. "The fact is, your discovery has taken me by surprise. How many others have you told?"

"You're the first," Lang said. He didn't consider Maddox. After all, talking to Maddox was the same as talking to the man in white.

"I'll give you fifteen thousand credits for the probe, and the information on where you found her."

Lang had to keep from gasping. The sum was more than he'd make in five years of scraping and struggle. Tempting as it was to agree right away to this exchange, Lang knew he could get more, provided there was more to be salvaged from the *Argus*.

"Your offer is very generous," Lang said. "I'll need a while to think about it."

Frasier shook his head. "This offer remains as long as I'm standing on your ship. I will not be drawn into a bidding war."

Lang considered arguing, but ultimately relented.

"My momma always told me I didn't have much business sense. How about, just for my peace of mind, we make it an even twenty thousand credits?"

Frasier considered this for no longer than two seconds

before agreeing. The coldness in his outer expression melted. "Your mother was a bit harsh in her judgment. Twenty thousand credits for one day's work isn't bad at all. Now tell me, where did you find this magnificent item?"

Frasier waited within the decompression chamber of the *Sandstorm* for his crew of five men to box and remove the probe.

Lang ate a late afternoon snack as the men worked.

The scavenger no longer cared about the probe and was at peace with the fact that he disclosed the location of his find. His mind was on the money Frasier transferred to his account and, even more specifically, how he would use it. The first thing he'd do was get the *Sandstorm* updated. He had taken her in for full service a couple of months before, but he always wanted a speedier craft.

After the *Sandstorm* was upgraded, he'd travel to all those places he dreamed of when he was a child. Maybe somewhere out there he'd find another woman like Elizabeth, his recently departed wife. It was too bad she couldn't share in this good fortune.

Frasier's men hauled the boxed probe past Lang. Ned Frasier followed close behind them but stopped when they reached the ship's exit doors. Maddox was there, waiting for the men to pass.

"We're done," Frasier said.   He offered Lang his hand. "Thanks for coming to me first."

"Absolutely," Lang replied.   He shook hands with Frasier before the man left his ship.

Frasier walked into the narrow corridor outside the berthing dock and approached Maddox. The two walked several steps behind the men carrying Frasier's crate and spoke in a low voice.

"We examined Lang's flight recordings," Maddox said. "They're genuine."

"And the location of the probe?"

"Exactly where he said he found it. I hired another scavenger to take Rasp to the area. So far, they haven't seen any other material."

"It is irrelevant," Frasier said. "I'm afraid our greatest fears are a reality. The *Argus* was not destroyed in the Erebus explosion."

"After all this time," Maddox said. "But are you sure? All we have is the one probe. Maybe the ship was destroyed and the probe somehow survived."

"No. The probe is nothing more than a small box. A reinforced small box, yes, but compared to the hull of the *Argus*...No. That ship was designed to withstand the harshest conditions. The ship survived, but was rendered inoperative. The crew, those still alive, released that probe after the explosion. It was a message in a bottle, so to speak. It's the only reasonable explanation for its present condition."

"What should we do?"

"Gather our people. All of them."

10

STARSHIP MERRICK, orbiting the planet Salvation

B'taav's footsteps echoed against the metal mesh when he stepped out of his ship and onto the landing bay of the *Merrick*. Jonah Merrick's personal secretary silently joined him. The two exited the landing bay and eventually reached the plush carpeting that filled the ship's inner corridors. Their footsteps went silent.

During their brief walk to Merrick's office, the Secretary said nothing. It was just as well. B'taav didn't feel much like talking anyway.

The doors to Merrick's office were made of a metallic alloy that reflected cold blue light off the fluorescent cells on either side of the corridor. They were security grade reinforced, befitting the head of industry of such a prestigious corporation. Merrick's secretary pressed her hand against a sensor. There came a faint hiss as the blue metal doors parted, revealing Jonah Merrick's enormous office. The Epsillon industrialist sat behind his enormous oak desk.

For the moment Jonah Merrick ignored his visitors and instead stared out the window that filled the rear of his office. Beyond it laid the planet Salvation. Farther in the distance, rising above the equator, was its third moon.

B'taav walked to the center of the room and froze. A lean, brown haired woman sat on a chair at the far side of the room. Unlike Merrick, her pale green eyes were on B'taav from the moment he first entered. She was sizing him up, calculating the means with which she could best him, either in physical combat or through other, more subtle efforts. B'taav returned her gaze in kind, despite his weariness of these Independents' games.

"Mr. B'taav," Jonah Merrick said. "Please have a seat."

Merrick's secretary remained by the door while B'taav stepped into the room. He sat in a chair opposite the Epsillon Industrialist's desk. Merrick's attention remained on the breathtaking view of outer space.

"So pretty," he said. "In all my years of exploration, I have yet to see an ugly planet. From orbit, anyway."

"Things look better from far away."

Merrick nodded. The window turned completely black and

the Epsillon Industrialist's focus was on B'taav. "Please give me your report."

B'taav explained in detail what happened on Salvation, from the moment he landed on Ferro City to the events of the past hour, including finding the mechanical spiders in his room and Goodwin's death.

"Those are the dry details," Merrick said when B'taav was done. "Now give me the rest of it."

"When I was met at the Salvation star port by the police and assigned an escort, it was clear someone within your organization leaked my arrival and status for the purpose of neutralizing my effectiveness. When Bill Goodwin acknowledged he was the one to leak the information, it momentarily threw me off. The leaking of the information, I thought, was deliberate sabotage, yet here he was, admitting to doing this as if it were some colossal, unintentional mistake. Either he was very dumb…"

"Not likely, given his position," Merrick said.

"…Or he was very, very clever. That's why I put up an act of being furious with his supposed bungling. It's why I told him to tell *you* I wanted more money."

"I got your message loud and clear," Merrick said. He pointed to the female Independent at the back of the room. "It's the reason I sent Latitia in after you."

"That wasn't necessary."

"She comes from a long, prestigious line of Independents."

B'taav felt a dull anger grow within. He drew a breath and calmed himself down.

"After some give and take, I agreed to allow an escort be assigned to me," the Independent continued. "He was an officer named Ken Shepherd. I figured he, like Goodwin, might try to slow me down. Only the exact opposite happened. He turned out to be very smart. Too smart."

"How do you mean?"

"Even on the best of days I couldn't sift through literally thousands of documents and hit on a good, solid bit of information as quickly as he did. He discovered Gail Griffen. He was the one that made me stay behind to bug her apartment while he followed her. He then called me when she was in the restaurant and he was able to identify, just like that, the two men she met from the Lewitt Catering Company."

"In the business world we appreciate efficiency," Merrick

said. "But are suspicious when there's a little too much of it."

"When we discovered the details of the meeting between Gail Griffen and the Lewitt Catering boys, Ken Shepherd was the one that insisted we stay outside of the hotel, ostensibly to make sure everyone entered the place and, thus, were trapped within. He was also the one that didn't want the police coming in too fast. He said we had too little on them. He said we should wait for them to reveal more serious crimes."

"Not a recommend procedure."

"Officer Shepherd portrayed himself as someone who worked by the book. He had issues with me using surveillance devices without the proper authorization, yet in a situation like this, where we had the suspects in a confined place and with officers potentially feet away in case of any trouble, Shepherd had us on the road, far away from them, and without any nearby backup. I went along with his plan, but by that point I no longer trusted him. I knew something bad was going to happen in Gail Griffen's room."

"And it did, of course."

"She overdosed on Accelerant, but remained lucid enough to keep hidden and draw me into her room. The only way she could beef up while retaining her intellect was to take incremental doses of the drug for at least two hours before the meeting with the Levitt Catering boys."

"Is it not possible she took it after they arrived and pulled their weapons?"

"No. If she had, her brain would have fried and her heart burst. She knew she was trapped, even before they arrived."

"Premeditated suicide?"

"Someone tipped her off. Someone deeply involved in this case."

"Officer Shepherd."

"That's my guess. It explains why he kept the police and I away, at least until it served his purposes. It also explains how Gail Griffen knew about our video and audio bugs and disabled them before I showed up in her room."

"But Shepherd went in after you?"

"He had to. When I left him, I told him to call in the police. When I entered the Tropic Hotel, I also told the manager to make that call. Only one call was made."

"It wasn't Shepherd's?"

"Exactly. I got in touch with the Police after being driven

back to my hotel. They told me the only call they received about the commotion at the Tropic Hotel was from the Hotel's manager. I made a second call, to that same manager, and asked him what Officer Shepherd did after I left the lobby. He said Shepherd took his time moving from the Hotel's entrance to the elevator. A curious thing to do, especially after several gunshots were fired and I flew into the place with gun in hand. The manager said Shepherd started moving only when the cops were on their way into the Hotel's lobby."

"Shepherd gave you time to confront Gail Griffen, then had to go up before the police did, to make sure you, and she, were dead."

"If everything worked according to his plan and the police hadn't been called in prematurely, Shepherd would have waited several more minutes in the lobby, no doubt checking his watch and grumbling about the police's late arrival. Upstairs, I'd become Gail Griffen's last victim, and her Accelerant poisoned heart finally explodes. When the appropriate time passed and the police still didn't arrive, I have no doubt Officer Shepherd would have finally called them in. He would have chewed out the operator and wondered out loud, so the manager could hear, what happened to his backup. Afterwards, when all the bodies were discovered, Officer Shepherd would cry some genuine tears when he told the story of how he waited for the police but they arrived just a little too late. His final report on this whole mess would complement me for taking care of the pirate presence on Salvation while, simultaneously, falling victim to it."

"Bloody, but neat," Merrick said. "Shepherd was recommended to you by Police Commissioner Herbert."

"Which meant he was in on it as well," B'taav said. "But Herbert was put onto me by Constable Goodwin. On the ride back to my hotel, I asked Constable Goodwin if he knew Shepherd. He admitted to knowing him. Very well."

"All three were in league."

"Yeah. Because I was still alive, I was in danger. I figured either Goodwin or Herbert sent an assassin to my hotel room to finish me off. He was dead when I found him, a victim of his own Black Widow devices."

"Latitia did an admirable job countering the spiders' original computer programming, didn't she?"

B'taav didn't reply.

"I don't expect gratitude from you, B'taav," Latitia said. "We

Independents usually try eliminating, rather than aiding, each other."

"Did you take out Goodwin?" B'taav asked her.

"I thought he died in a traffic accident," she replied.

"What about Police Commissioner Herbert?"

"Tomorrow's another day."

"Thank you for your work," Merrick told Latitia. "You're excused."

Latitia approached B'taav.

"You shouldn't take things so hard," she said to him. "This business is just a game, after all."

With that she walked to the door leading out of the office. Merrick's secretary, who remained silently in the back of the room, opened the large doors to let her out. When she was gone, Merrick motioned for the secretary to leave as well. Without saying a word, she too departed. The large door closed, leaving Merrick and B'taav alone.

"You shouldn't have brought her in," B'taav said. "This could have been resolved without further bloodshed."

"Sometimes the solution to your problems is the most drastic one," Merrick replied. "As it was, I did hold back. I only sent the *one* Independent in after you."

"She's untrustworthy."

"This new generation of Independents isn't to your liking?"

B'taav did not reply. Merrick let out a chuckle.

"You've been an Independent far longer than everyone else in the business. Most of them, like Latitia, are lucky if they make it five years before either stopping a bullet or venturing out to greener pastures. Not you."

Merrick smoothed the ruffles on the front of his suit.

"There's no way you can enjoy your work *that* much, B'taav. All these betrayals and death and blood...they'll rot your soul. After a while, you won't feel anything at all."

"Maybe I should take a vacation."

"Might do you some good."

"Goodwin said you were firing him. Why did you order Latitia to kill Goodwin if he was gone anyway?"

"A message needed to be sent. When I ordered Latitia to get rid of Goodwin, she told me to ask *you* if it was OK. Since you were the primary Independent on the job, she wanted to defer to your judgment in that matter. Never mind that I was the one paying for this whole fucking thing."

"She has some redemptive qualities after all."

"Perhaps. You did well, B'taav."

"All I figured out was that Goodwin, Herbert, and Shepherd were part of some larger organization and were intent on deceiving, and ultimately killing, me," B'taav said. "Gail Griffen and the Lewitt Catering boys were nothing more than a group of young fools that trio paraded before me. If I'm closer to the pirates, that distance can be measured in centimeters."

"Maybe. But if their plans worked out, those three clowns would still be in place, rotting my company from the inside out. The people behind Goodwin, Herbert, and Shepherd will be taking some hard looks over their shoulders for the next couple of years."

Merrick pressed a button on his desk and the blackened window behind him returned to its previous clarity. Salvation once again shone like a jewel below them.

"I'll give the boys down there a few more hours to run around and tidy things up before arriving. Once I'm there, I'll raise holy hell. When I'm done, the place will run like new."

"I assume you have replacements ready to take Goodwin and Herbert's jobs?"

"Of course. Latitia wasn't too far off, you know. It is a game, and that's the way the game goes."

"You're satisfied?"

"As much as I can be. My only worry is that the pirates have some backup plan, an alternative target somewhere else."

"You can count on that."

"And away we'll go again," Merrick said and smiled. "B'taav, our contract is at its end. Are you still interested in that extension?"

"That depends on what you're offering."

Merrick opened a drawer and pulled out a gold credit chip. He laid it before B'taav. B'taav picked the chip up and stared at its surface display.

"That's...that's most generous."

"Consider it not only a bonus for a job well done, but an advance for the job you're about to do."

"I'm listening."

"So am I. In my field you talk as little as possible and hear everything going on around you. You never know what you'll learn." Merrick again reached into his desk and produced a micro disk. He offered it to B'taav. "Give the disk a look. I'd like you to take on this job."

"Only on one condition."

"Yes?"

"No more babysitters."

Merrick thought about that and nodded.

"Fair enough."

11

SALVAGE CRAFT SANDSTORM – on the border of Erebus

Kelly Lang slept well for the first time in a very long time. When he awoke, he felt like a new man. When he double-checked the balance in his bank account, he knew yesterday wasn't simply a beautiful dream.

Today, on this bright brand new day, it was Lang's intention to make the most of his new life. He showered, made a quick breakfast, and dressed for travel.

After checking all the systems on his ship, he settled into the navigator's chair and activated the communicator. He directed a transmission to the *Titus* space station's flight control.

"This is the *Sandstorm*. Requesting clearance for departure. Destination is the Displacer."

There was a crackle of static followed by a lady's voice.

"Departure clearance granted. Please maintain a path along coordinates 523 by 099. Use minimal speed until advised otherwise."

"Yes ma'am."

In minutes Lang's ship uncoupled from the space station. After a very short burst of thrust, she drifted away from *Titus* and slowly turned until Lang had her pointed in the direction of the Erebus Displacer.

"Erebus Displacer, this is *Sandstorm*," he said. "Request transit passage."

"Acknowledged. Please provide destination point."

Lang was silent for several seconds. In his eagerness to leave this place, he hadn't fully considered where he wanted to go, and with all that money, he had the freedom to choose.

"*Sandstorm*?"

"The Castillo system," Lang blurted. It was where he first met his wife. It was where he spent his youth. It was where he longed to return.

"That will be fifty credits."

Lang pressed a series of buttons on his console. The fifty credits were transferred from his account and to that of the Erebus Displacer.

"Fee has been received," the Displacer Operator said. "Please allow thirty five minutes for incoming traffic."

"Will do," Lang said. He slowed his ship to a stop a few miles for the enormous entrance of the Displacer. Freedom from his lowly salvage job lay so tantalizingly close.

Lang checked his sensors to see if any other ships were approaching. Though it didn't happen often, once in a while a free rider would try to enter the Displacer alongside the legitimate traveler. Doing so was incredibly dangerous, as the only way this could be done and not be detected by the Displacer's Security was by traveling very close to the paying space craft. That type of proximity could lead to a collision, and no private pilot needed that kind of trouble.

His sensors detected no ships in the immediate vicinity.

Lang relaxed. He locked his ship down and exited his chair. He still had time to double-check his equipment and make some last minute preparations.

The scavenger stowed away all remaining loose gear and made sure his cargo containers were properly locked down. When he reached the decompression chamber he noted the reddish dust that still filled the area. It was all that remained of the *Argus* probe.

Lang looked at his watch. There were still ten minutes left before he could travel. Lang pressed a button on the wall and opened the compartment where he stored his cleaning gear. He grabbed a slender vacuum tube and ran it across the floor, sucking up most of the asteroid dust. Once done, Lang folded the tube back into the storage compartment.

As he did, he noticed a small black box sitting in the corner of the compartment and behind a pair of disinfectant containers.

"What the hell?" Lang muttered.

The scavenger bent down and picked up the strange box. It was light and measured no more than a square foot. Lang saw no seams or latches on its surface. When he turned it over, he found a single blinking white light at the box's center.

"What the hell?" he repeated.

The blinking became faster, and faster...

The *Sandstorm* noiselessly exploded into tiny jagged pieces.

Only a few people in the upper lounge area of the *Titus* space station noticed the explosion, but they thought they were witnessing a meteorite collision or the peculiar twinkling of a distant star.

An hour later a group of fellow scavengers within the station pressed their faces against the lounge area's tinsel glass walls and watched the police ships pick up fragments of the *Sandstorm* before they drifted away. When most of the pieces of the ship were collected and the police ships were gone, they lowered their heads and mourned for their fallen comrade.

12

The investigation into the *Sandstorm's* destruction started strong, with promises to the public that the cause of this terrible accident, as it was originally labeled, would be quickly found.

Less than a week later, public interest in the *Sandstorm* waned.

Lang's ship, like most used by local scavengers, was an older craft, and many assumed it experienced some kind of terminal malfunction. Those in charge of investigating the craft's destruction focused more and more on what damage, if any, the *Sandstorm's* debris might have caused the Erebus Displacer.

That device was, after all, the only means to get back into the Epsillon Empire.

In the control room of the Erebus Displacer, the day moved slowly. Interstellar traffic was low and the high tourist season was still a month away. Jeb Smitheen manned the communications station but his attention was on the latest transmissions from Segaru IV. His view screen displayed the forty-fifth World Cup Leatherball match, and Jeb couldn't think of a better way to spend this quiet afternoon than losing himself in this game.

Halfway into the match, the lights over his display flashed on. Jeb scowled.

"What now?" he muttered.

He shut his monitor off and activated the communicator.

"Erebus Displacer, this is Aloida One. Please respond."

"Aloida One, this is Erebus. How can I help you?"

"Craft incoming. Activate receptacles."

"Incoming? We didn't have anything schedu—"

"Code 53."

The corners of Jeb's mouth tightened.

"Code 53?"

"Yes, Erebus Displacer. Code 53."

Incoming military craft. A chill ran down Jeb's spine. *What did we do to deserve a military visit?*

Jeb Smitheen pressed a series of buttons. In seconds the screens before him flashed acknowledgement of all his requests.

"Aloida One, Erebus Displacer is active."

He received no reply.

The Erebus Displacer's hollow core came alive in a wall of shimmering energy. The gulf between millions of light years was negated as an artificial fold in space was activated. A large, sinister black mass appeared in the center of this gap. In moments it stepped from Aloida One, one hundred light years away, and into Erebus space.

Even those unfamiliar with Epsillon military attack crafts would recognize the *Wake* as one of the more modern ships of the fleet. Visible along the length of her body was an array of fearsome short and long range weaponry.

The craft moved out of the Erebus Displacer and into the ample space between the Displacer and the *Titus* space station. It turned starboard ever so slightly, until its nose was pointed at the station.

"Erebus Displacer, this is the *Wake*."

"This is the Erebus Displacer."

"By order of the Epsillon Council, we assume full control of Erebus space. Any requested use of the Displacer, both for incoming or outgoing traffic, must be forwarded to us for approval. Understood?"

"U...Understood," Jeb Smitheen stammered.

There was a brief pause.

"Well?"

"Yes?"

An audible sigh was heard over Jeb's communicator speaker.

"Would you be so kind as to forward us all incoming and outgoing craft requests? *Right now.*"

"Oh! Yes sir."

Jeb tapped at the computer and the requested material was sent to the military craft. Jeb considered the information on the files. There was one scheduled departure and arrival for later in the day and a few more for later in the week. Otherwise, traffic was light.

After several minutes passed without a reply, Jeb keyed the communicator.

"*Wake*, this is Erebus Displacer. Did you receive the information?"

"Affirmative, Erebus Displacer."

"Uh...what should I do with regard to today's schedule?"

"For now, no crafts may leave the area."

"Acknowledged. What about the inbound ship?"

There was a momentary pause.

"Next scheduled entry is the *Wanderer*. She's a Class C small cargo vessel."

"Yes sir."

"A supply ship."

"Supply or scavenger. We place all small vessels under the former classification."

"Scavenging in the Erebus system is prohibited."

"Sorry, that's just our local colloquial expression. I meant she might be on a scientific mission. You know, archeology."

"Why classify her as a supply vessel?"

"The powers that be prefer the more neutral term."

"So is this a supply craft or a...scavenger?"

"I wouldn't know."

"Why should we let her in?"

"Guys, that's up to you," Jeb said. "But it's a meager business, sir. I'm sure the pilot spent all his, or her, funds just getting here. If it makes you feel any better, I doubt they'll try anything illegal with you around."

There was another pause.

"Approval granted. We'll present our recommendations about the other crafts shortly."

"Yes sir," Jeb said.

Eddie Robinson, the senior forensic technician on board the *Titus* Space Station, received the e-mail summons while in his office.

To: Eddie Robinson, TFT
Please proceed to Deck 52 for a meeting with Lieutenant Lester Daniels, EMC. Do not delay.

Robinson scratched his nose. *Epsillon Military Command?*

"At least they said please," the elderly man chuckled. He shut his computers off and headed for the door.

Deck 52 of the *Titus* Space Station was an enormous, but mostly unused, docking space. Its purpose was to house ships that required repairs that could not be performed in zero gravity space.

Eddie Robinson found the *Wake* there, taking up almost the entire one mile of empty space. The sight was mindboggling.

The few times he came down here all he saw was one cubic mile of emptiness, littered with one or two joggers who used the space as a track.

Several military officers walked around the base of the ship. One of them noticed Robinson and approached.

"This is a restricted area," the officer said.

"I'm here to see Lieutenant Daniels. My name is Eddie Robinson."

The officer's stern tone softened.

"We were expecting you. Come with me."

The officer motioned Robinson toward the stairs leading up into the *Wake*.

"You've got quite a ship," Robinson said. He eyed the ships smooth surface as well as her modern, sophisticated thrusters. Try as he might, it was impossible not to also notice her fusion cannons and torpedo launchers.

"Step inside, please."

They walked the metal plank up and into the *Wake*, then proceeded down several spacious corridors until arriving at a large metal door. On it was a plaque that identified the space beyond as a conference room.

During the trip, Robinson kept his mouth shut while taking in everything around him. He realized, after a fashion, that the route the officer escorted him on was semi-circular. More than likely he kept Robinson away from instruments and equipment civilian eyes were not permitted to see.

Within the conference room, Robinson found a single rectangular metal table. Around it were an even dozen chairs.

"Have a seat," the officer said.

Robinson sat at the chair closest to him, which turned out to be the head of the table. The officer frowned at Robinson's choice but didn't suggest he find an alternate seat. He disappeared through a door on the opposite side of the room and left the elderly forensic technician alone. Robinson stared at the room's walls and noted that, despite appearing plain, there were many small groves and subtle indentations throughout its surface.

From his days in the Epsillon military, he knew the room was likely equipped with the latest monitors, computers, and video/radio hybrids. With the flick of a switch, panels would slide away and hidden equipment would appear like magic. Despite the plain outward appearance, this room was probably an intelligence nerve center.

After a few minutes the door on the opposite side again opened. Out stepped a man in his mid-thirties. Like most military officers, his face was lean, his posture rigid. His eyes were dark and penetrating.

"Mr. Robinson? I'm Lieutenant Lester Daniels. I was ordered to the *Titus* Space Station to look into the destruction of the *Sandstorm.*"

"*Sandstorm?*" Robinson replied. "I thought you were here to check for possible damage to the Erebus Displacer."

"Not at this moment."

"Why would the military care—?"

"I require an examination of all recovered wreckage."

"Certainly. When would you like to—"

"Right now."

Most of the wreck is in Cargo Bay 144," Robinson said as he tried to keep up with Daniels' brisk pace. The elderly man spent too much time writing reports and too little time exercising.

"Exactly how much of the *Sandstorm* have you recovered?"

"Thirty to forty percent," Robinson replied. "Why is the Epsillon military so interested in this?"

"One of our citizens is dead and we have an interest in finding the cause of this death. Funny how it seems not be a terribly big concern to those aboard this space station."

"I beg your pardon, Lieutenant, but it's not like that at all. I'll grant you, few knew the guy personally, but he was a scavenger."

"And?"

"They tend to fly second and third class ships, the type that make it a habit of breaking down. Just last week we had three ships we were forced to tow back into *Titus.*"

"I see. And exactly how many of these second and third class ships have exploded into tiny little pieces for no obvious reasons in the past five years?"

Robinson considered the question, but before he could say anything Daniels provided an answer:

"Not a single one. In fact, this is the first time in the last five *decades* that we've witnessed such an occurrence."

"That can't be right."

"I assure you it is," Daniels said. "Certainly there have been ship failures and accidental collisions. And there have been crew fatalities. But ships today, even those that are second or third class, have a wealth of safety features. They may suffer from breaches or system malfunctions or even fires. In worst case scenarios, they might even be crippled beyond any possibility of repair or break into several large pieces. But exploding?"

"You said it's been five decades since something like that's happened. Did they ever find the cause of that explosion?"

"Yes."

"What was it?"

"Sabotage."

Robinson let out a whistle.

"Are you suggesting that's what happened to the *Sandstorm*?"

"I'm here to collect evidence, Mr. Robinson, not make guesses."

"But that's what your superiors think, right? That's why you're here."

Lieutenant Daniels did not reply. Robinson shook his head and smiled.

"Come now, Lieutenant. I'm sure when the evidence is sorted, we'll find the *Sandstorm* had some kind of accident."

"Then consider my presence a way to move quickly toward this solution," Daniels replied.

He continued walking toward the entrance of Cargo Bay 144.

13

The *Wanderer*, a class C small cargo vessel, exited the Erebus Displacer and began its slow approach to the *Titus* space station. It requested clearance for docking and, when granted, pulled into berth number 23.

Once locked in place, her lone occupant shut down all major systems and rose from the navigator's chair. The pilot wore a full body space suit, something forced upon him when the heating system within his vessel malfunctioned. He walked to the storage deck but stopped before a series of cabinets. He opened one of them and pulled out a spent Accelerant cartridge.

The man took a hard look at the cartridge and returned it to its place. In the dark shadows of the storage deck he removed his space suit and headed for the docking clamp.

Lieutenant Daniels and Eddie Robinson entered Cargo Bay 144 through one of the side doors. The cargo bay was dark and very cool. Daniels could just make out the remains of the *Sandstorm* littered on the otherwise empty bay floor.

"How about some lights?"

"Lights," Robinson yelled. The lights in the bay came on in full force. Revealed before them was a very long rectangular cargo storage room. Twisted metal and charred plastic lay on the ground and took up nearly one third of the area.

"This is it?" Daniels inquired.

"Yes sir. As I said before, it amounts to thirty or forty percent of the *Sandstorm*."

Daniels approached the ship's remains but made sure not to touch anything. The pieces of the doomed craft were arranged like a burned out jigsaw puzzle. Daniels made out the vessel's general shape and could draw some obvious conclusions from the directions of the twists in her shattered metal frame.

"The explosion likely came from the rear of the craft, perhaps from the decompression chamber," Robinson said.

"Agreed," Daniels replied. "My understanding is the *Sandstorm* was a '64 Class E Habberlight."

"That's true."

"Then her fuel cells were located just below the decompression chamber. If one of them was leaking, even the smallest spark might cause an explosion."

"So it could have been an accident after all?"

Daniels pulled a small camera from his shirt pocket and took pictures and video images of the wreckage. He did so with great care and deliberation, making sure to get a complete record of all the material on the deck. After forty-five minutes he was done. He made a call to his ship and then faced Robinson.

"My boys will be here in a few minutes," Daniels said.

Several hours later, Eddie Robinson entered the Jackal Bar.

He wearily waved to his co-workers. A group of military officers, all members of the *Wake's* crew, were enjoying a quiet break at the other side of the bar. Their table was filled with empty and half-empty bottles of beer, but their conversation was low and, unlike the scavengers, they kept entirely to themselves.

Robinson approached the center of the bar and sat at a table. A female bartender made her way toward him, but he motioned her off. Dave Maddox noticed the elderly man's actions and approached.

"How are you doing?" Maddox asked. He handed Robinson a freshly poured glass of beer.

"I'm exhausted," Robinson said. "Busy today?"

"You bet."

"Yeah? Does it have anything to do with our military guests?"

"Oh, just about everything," Robinson said and chuckled. "They're looking into the destruction of the *Sandstorm*."

"They're specialists?"

"I suppose. They took over the operation."

"Really?"

"Yup. It's out of my hands."

"What's the matter? They don't trust you?"

"I don't think it's as simple as that."

"No?"

"They're looking into something else," Robinson said. His voice lowered until it was a soft whisper. "They think the ship was sabotaged."

"Really?"

"Would I lie about something like that?"

"No. I don't suppose you would."

"Anyway, the guy in charge is a Lieutenant, a Lester Daniels."

"What's he like?"

"He's young and seems smart enough."

"Why would the Epsillon military care about the destruction of a scavenger vessel way the hell out here?"

"You got me. Maybe his orders came from higher up."

"Industry?"

"Could be."

"What's he done so far?"

"Had me take him to the *Sandstorm's* wreckage. He took a shit load of pictures and then had his forensic teams go over the wreckage piece by piece. I was ordered to take a few of his people to my office, so they could go over my computer files."

"Why?"

"They're piecing together the *Sandstorm's* final journey. But they're also looking into everything Kelly Lang did since he first arrived at *Titus*."

"Why would anyone care? And what about the Displacer? There's no telling what damage it might have sustained in the explosion. Isn't he interested in that?"

"I offered to take him or his boys in for a closer examination of the hits she took, but he didn't care."

"That's really strange. Even if Lang was the victim of sabotage, why would the Epsillon military or industry care?"

Robinson shrugged. He took another sip of beer.

"You got me. But I'll tell you something even stranger than all that."

"Go on."

"Think about how quickly they got here. It takes a while to put together a crew and equipment to investigate something like what happened to the *Sandstorm*, even on the best of days. Yet here they are."

"Someone lit a fire under their asses."

"A thermonuclear fire," Robinson said.

They continued their conversation, oblivious to the tall, platinum-haired man that stepped into the bar.

14

EPSILLON MILITARY COMPLEX, HOMEWORLD

General Jurgens retreated into his office and turned his communicator on. After his security software verified the line was secure, he pressed one final button. Lieutenant Lester Daniels' face appeared on the monitor. His message was four hours old.

"General Jurgens, I've completed my preliminary investigation into the *Sandstorm*. Through examination of the ship's remains, I've determined that the explosion originated in the cargo hold, near the fuel cell storage. I've ordered the wreckage crated and sent to the Analysis Division on Homeworld. It should be there by the time you receive this message."

"There was no evidence of a Class 3 type probe aboard the *Sandstorm* at the time of the explosion. I would caution, however, that only a little over 30 percent of the wreckage was recovered. It is possible I won't be able to find the remains of the probe at all, even if it was originally there. Regardless, our focus is now on the last days of Kelly Lang. I will send another transmission before the end of the day."

DINAMIX WAREHOUSE, Titus space station

As usual, Ned Frasier was dressed in an elegant white suit. As he walked past the torn remains of assorted ships and ship parts that filled the Dinamix warehouse, he wondered why. He carefully avoided every protruding piece of scrap metal and dodged every bulky engine part. He didn't so much walk as limbo through the warehouse.

At the rear of the structure, he slinked past what looked like the remains of a greasy Turbo-jet and was pleased to see he made it unscathed to the door at the end of the junkyard. He pulled out a handkerchief and put it over the doorknob and turned it.

He spotted Janet Donaldson at the back of the room. She stood a little over five feet three inches and had a delightfully plump figure. Her nose was flat and her hair was too short and her manners weren't ladylike at all. Her clothes were covered with grease stains and rust and the Gods alone knew what else. The parts of her face that weren't covered in sweat had a thick layer of grit. Over her eyes was a pair of thick black glasses. Every few seconds the lenses would glow an eerie green, indicating the sensors embedded within were recording the insides of the Probe that lay before her and in the center of the room.

Ned Frasier allowed himself a full minute to take her in before letting out a sigh. She was the love of his life, and he wanted to do nothing more than reach out and hug her, here and now. But this wasn't the time and there was too much work to do. He cautiously approached her side.

Ned Frasier forced his eyes from his lover and onto the probe she was examining. The craft's central panel was open and lay on the floor. The wires within were exposed and lifeless.

"Anything?" Frasier said.

Donaldson pulled her sensor glasses off and gave Frasier a loving wink before shaking her head.

"These things were built to live a relatively short life," she said. "They're active up to ten years. I heard one of them managed to survive and transmit messages five years beyond that, but that was the exception rather than the rule."

"She survived until now."

"Yeah, but some one hundred and ninety or so years have passed since she lost power and began bouncing around the asteroids. It's a miracle she's whole, but to expect complete data is asking a bit much."

"Her computer files were corrupted?"

"To some degree. The internal computer is shot. I removed the memory chips and tried to activate them with conventional equipment. All I got was garbage. I'm guessing the probe passed through some heavy magnetic and radioactive fields."

"Can you reconstruct the data?"

"Give me time," she said. She gave Frasier a seductive smile. "Have I ever let you down before?"

Frasier folded his hands across his chest and suppressed a smile of his own.

"Not that I remember. Then again, it *has* been a while—"

Unable to resist her any longer, Frasier uncrossed his hands and placed them on Janet's broad shoulders. He pulled her near him and gave her a gentle kiss.

"You'll get dirty."

Frasier ignored her comment and kissed her again. All the while, he made a great effort to not soil his clothing.

"How did a grease monkey like me get involved with a cleanliness freak like you?" Janet said between kisses.

"Great luck."

Frasier released Janet and examined his suit. The front right side was badly stained.

"Looks like I'll have to change," Frasier groaned. "Again."

Janet laughed. She returned to the probe while Frasier used a handkerchief to wipe away what he could of that stain.

"When they sent it out, they must have anticipated the possibility –the probability– the batteries and hard drive could burn out before being found," Frasier said as he put the handkerchief away. "Might the crew have left behind marks on the probe itself? Either outside or in?"

"Now that you mention it," Donaldson said. She pulled the probe's outer plate from the ground and removed a greasy rag from her back pocket. She rubbed the rag across the plate and showed the results to Frasier.

"I found this. Someone scrapped it on the panel with a knife or a screwdriver."

Frasier leaned down. When he read the words scrawled across the plate, his face turned pale.

"Are you ok?" Janet Donaldson asked.

Frasier shook his head.

"No. Not at all. You should have told me about this before."

"I'm sorry," Donaldson said. "Is this important?"

"Very."

Without saying anything else, Frasier ran to the door leading out of the warehouse. He was in such a rush that he ignored the dirt around him and bumped into several pieces before exiting.

Janet Donaldson shrugged. It wasn't unusual for her lover to show such impulsiveness. He delivered merchandise, sometimes illicit merchandise, from sellers to buyers and she knew he had his secrets. There were times he went silent and disappeared for hours, even days, only to return abruptly, his passion for her intact. At first she demanded an accounting of his missing time, but eventually she realized there was little point in questioning his every move. He always returned to her, and that was the most, the only, important thing.

Still, there was a noticeable tension these last few days, and this coincided with the arrival of the *Argus* probe. Janet looked down at the scrawl and, without meaning to, felt a shiver run down her back.

The scrawl read: 133 of 400.

She wondered why Frasier was so scared about the possibility there were another three hundred and ninety nine probes from the *Argus* floating out there, in the remains of what was once the Erebus solar system.

15

THE JACKAL BAR – Titus space station

Lieutenant Lester Daniels and a group of five subordinates entered the Jackal Bar just after happy hour. To a man, the group had an intense look, as if any little thing might set them off. Their presence in the bar and at this time maximized awareness of them among the regulars. The place was filled to near capacity. That number would swell as the hours passed.

To Lieutenant Daniels, this visit was part of re-tracing Kelly Lang's final hours before his ship erupted. The Lieutenant and his group stepped up to the bar's counter. They forcibly made space for themselves between several scruffy pilots. Daniels motioned to the bartender. The man promptly approached Daniels' side.

"Beer," Daniels said.

The bartender shrugged and got to work. For the moment, Daniels ignored him and surveyed the area. The Jackal Bar was small, smaller than just about every bar he was familiar with on Homeworld. Its décor bordered on bland. You'd have to look long and hard to find even a hint of luxury.

"Here you are," the bartender said.

Daniels noted the single glass and gave the bartender a cold stare.

"What's your name?"

"Maddox."

"Mr. Maddox, would you be so kind as to serve my men as well?"

"I'm sorry," Maddox said. "When I was in the service, officers tended to drink alone."

Lieutenant Daniels offered the bartender a weary smile.

"Only when they want to get drunk."

Maddox nodded. He served Daniels' men.

"That'll be five credits each. Forty credits total."

Daniels laid an amber colored fifty-credit piece on the counter and realized there was at least one luxury item in this place: the price of liquor.

"Keep the change."

"Thanks," Maddox said. He grabbed the chip and slipped it into the cash register.

"Do you know who I am?" Daniels asked.

The bartender shook his head.

He knows, Daniels thought. *But he'll be damned if he admits to anything.*

"I'm here at the request of the Epsillon Government."

"They wanted you in this bar?"

"Your attempts at humor border on the insulting, Mr. Maddox."

"My apologies," Maddox said, his voice roaring with a mighty indifference. "We're honored to have you. Around these parts we see new faces just about every day, but rarely do we ever receive such distinguished guests."

Daniels let out a laugh.

"I'm...sorry. I didn't mean to be funny."

"I've never heard anyone say the word 'distinguished' in quite that way. If I didn't know better, it almost sounded like you were swearing."

"Heavens no."

"Skip it. I'm looking into the death of a prospector."

"Prospector?"

"Why condemn the recently deceased with the label of scavenger, when we both know such activity is strictly prohibited."

"Fair enough."

"The gentleman's name, as I'm sure you're aware, was Kelly Lang. His ship blew up on his way out of this system. My understanding is that it was good fortune he didn't take the Displacer with him."

"Isn't the first time something like that's happened."

"Someone else told me the very same thing. Like you, he too was wrong. But you know that also."

Daniels took a sip of his beer.

"In the past hour I discovered something else. Kelly Lang's ship had a full check-up not a month before it exploded. Luckily for us, the company doing the checking retained their data analysis of his ship's systems. It was running fine."

"Obviously not that fine," Maddox offered. He gazed at the ribbons on Daniels' suit. "I didn't get your name, Lieutenant."

"Lester Daniels, EMC."

"You think Lang was killed?"

"Twenty thousand credits were transferred to his bank account the day before he died."

"Someone killed Lang to steal his money?"

"If that was their goal, they didn't succeed. The money's still there."

"Why else kill him?"

"That's an excellent question."

"So, what? Was it an accident after all?"

"Maybe."

"I've never heard anyone say the word 'maybe' quite like that before, Lieutenant."

Daniels flashed Maddox a smile.

"You're one of the very last people Kelly Lang spoke to before his unfortunate...accident. Funny how, in all this chit chat, you didn't feel the need to point that out."

"What's there to tell? He came by, ordered a drink and food. He drank the drink and ate the food and after he was done he left."

"And that's all?"

"There's nothing more to tell."

"So many dead ends," Daniels told his men before addressing Maddox. "You know what I'm thinking of doing?"

"What?"

"I'm considering a section by section investigation of this station. Like we did at *Freedom Twenty*."

Maddox stiffened. The *Freedom Twenty* was a space station near the Marron System. It was a floating mega-city that housed over three million occupants. Powerful business interests within the Epsillon Empire unsuccessfully tried to gain control of the station's lucrative concessions. The attempts were rebuffed by the station's power brokers.

One day, a miner was found dead in his compartment within the station's lower decks. This proved the opening the rival business representatives needed. They used his death to get the Epsillon army into *Freedom Twenty* to investigate. When the miner's death was ruled a murder sixty-five individuals, including forty five concession stand owners, were imprisoned.

Now free to do what they wanted, the outside business interests literally walked into *Freedom Twenty* and took control of everything they were unable to get their hands on legitimately. It was no wonder small business interests feared any military presence in their area.

Maddox leaned close to Daniels.

"What exactly do you want to know?" he said. His eyes

glowed an unhealthy red.

"Simple," Daniels replied. "Tell me what Kelly Lang told you the day before he died."

"Look, we talked, all right? I don't remember details, but it was gossip, stuff about other scavengers."

"What did he find in Erebus?"

"Garbage."

"You know what they say. Your idea of garbage might be someone else's idea of treasure."

"Far as I'm concerned, all that's left out there is junk."

"Who buys this junk?"

"That depends on what you've got. There are at least one hundred buyers in this part of the station alone."

"Who did Lang deal with?"

"Come on, Lieutenant. He talked to *all* of them, just like the other scavengers did. When you're in that business you feel your way around, always looking for the best deal."

"He must have had his favorites."

"I'm sure he did. But I wouldn't know which of them actually bought things from him."

Daniels drank what remained of his beer. He laid the empty glass on the counter and exhaled loudly.

"You're going to have to do a lot better than that," he said. His voice rose above the others within the bar, silencing them. His icy gaze was on the bartender. "A lot better."

Several people quietly exited while others stole glances in the direction of the bar's counter. In the middle of this nervous silence, one man rose from his chair and stepped up to the bar. He stopped beside Daniels.

"It's my experience that threats are a poor way to gain information," the man said.

"Welcome to *Titus*, B'taav," Lieutenant Daniels said. His eyes stayed on Maddox. "When I heard your ship arrived, I wondered how long it would take before you showed your face. Four hours."

"Three and a half. But who's counting?"

"Have you been avoiding me?"

"What makes you think that?"

"Because it's been *my* experience that broken down Independents like you tend to hide in the Borderlands rather than stick their noses into Epsillon government business."

"I wouldn't know much about the Borderlands," B'taav said.

"Though 'broken down' might apply better to you than me."

Even as the words exited B'taav's mouth, a frigid wall of tension shot up between the two men. Daniels' face flushed and he fought back a volcanic rage. There was old blood, very bad old blood, between the platinum haired Independent and him.

"You're referring to my ship, not me," Daniels quietly said.

"The ship under one's command is an extension of its senior officer. That was quite a case we had back in Evalba, wasn't it Lieutenant?"

"Yes, quite a case," Daniels agreed. "Just as things were heating up and I had you in my sights, my ship malfunctions. Very fortuitous. For you anyway."

"I'm truly blessed."

"On the other hand, the boys and I came out of that looking like incompetents," Daniels continued. "I took the ship into dry dock to get her checked out. You know what the mechanics said?"

"I can't imagine."

"They told me her coolant coils were ruptured, that someone cut one of the main lines. I didn't think there was anyone – anyone– with the balls to infiltrate a Capital Guard ship and do something like that."

"It would take quite a bit of nerve."

"Especially when the penalty for this is a quick trip to the firing squad."

"Perhaps," Maddox interrupted, in the hopes of cooling things down. "We could all use another drink. On the house?"

"That's a good idea," Daniels said. "You boys enjoy your drink. B'taav and I have some catching up to do. Come with me, Independent."

"Is that an order?"

"A request."

"A friendly request?"

"Why not?"

B'taav followed Daniels to one of the now many empty tables in the rapidly emptying bar. Daniels motioned for B'taav to sit.

"What are you doing here?" Daniels asked.

"Taking in the sights of Erebus. It was time for a vacation."

"Good. In that case I'm sure you won't mind if we inspect your ship and cargo."

"I have no problem with that, as long as you do so accompanied by a neutral party. Say, the *Titus* police. I wouldn't want your boys finding something on my ship that wasn't there in the first place. Not that I don't trust your good intentions."

"I don't know why you're here and I don't care," Daniels said. "But I'll give you fair warning: Get back to your ship and stay far away from me and my men. Am I clear?"

"Very."

Daniels got to his feet.

"The only reason you're still alive is because you covered your tracks well back at Evalba. But I've seen your handiwork and I *don't* make the same mistakes twice."

Daniels returned to his men. He told them a few words and the group exited the bar. When they were all gone, a scowl appeared on B'taav's face. He could no longer hold back the disgust he felt for the Epsillon officer.

It took a while to compose himself. When he did, he noticed a lady sitting at a table on the opposite side of the bar.

She had long yellow hair wrapped tight in the back of her head. Her face was as smooth as porcelain and her eyes were hidden behind dark glasses. She wore a shiny black body suit and a heavy black jacket.

She was watching the Independent. Of that there was no doubt.

B'taav leaned back in his chair and looked her way, but by that point her interests had shifted. Or at least she made it look like that was the case. She didn't linger much longer in the bar. She paid her tab and departed only minutes after B'taav first noticed her.

The Independent made no move to approach or stop her, although his instincts told him he should. When she was gone, B'taav walked to the bar's counter. Maddox raised his hands.

"I don't need trouble," he said.

"Too late for that. Lieutenant Daniels wouldn't be here unless there was something that needed fixing."

"But there isn't anything—"

"Whatever it is, it's none of my business. I just need a little information and I'm gone. Can you help me out?"

"With what?"

"Accelerant. You know some suppliers?"

"I have no reason to talk to Daniels and even less reason to talk to you."

"At least I asked politely."

"So far."

"Look, I'm not a cop. I'm following a path of Accelerant sales, looking for a supplier who probably isn't even on this station anymore. I'm guessing he left to Salvation about four months ago."

"You're kidding," Maddox said. He sighed. "Look, friend, I'd be hard pressed to remember what happened yesterday, much less four months ago. Suppliers come and go just like everyone else in Erebus. If you want to find a specific supplier, your best bet is to get access to the Displacer's databanks and find the space craft traffic logs for the past four months. You check up on every flight coming in or heading out and maybe you'll find what you need."

"Daniels' boys aren't letting anyone access to the Displacer's computers."

"Then you wait patiently until they're gone. Either that or ask your buddy Daniels really nice if he can let bygones be bygones and maybe, possibly, give you access to the computer. Who knows, it might just work."

B'taav laid a two hundred credit piece on the counter.

"You know what I need," B'taav said. "If you hear anything, give me a call. I'm in dock 23."

Maddox's took the credit chip and whistled.

"You're easy with your money."

"Easy enough, as long as I get what I need."

When B'taav was in the outer corridors, he spotted three figures lurking nearby. They were dressed as civilians, but their posture gave them away as Daniels' men. The trio hung back and slipped in and out of the sparse crowds heading to their various destinations. B'taav knew the Lieutenant's game. The men would follow from a polite distance and bid their time until B'taav was alone.

Then, and only then, they'd attack.

B'taav considered his options as he walked through the corridors. There were few. The Independent sighed.

The show must go on.

After a few minutes of walking, the Independent abruptly stopped. His eyes settled on the closest of Daniels' shadows, a muscular man in his mid-twenties who looked like he could take a few punches. The man pretended scanning through a pile of used electronic games a corner merchant was selling.

B'taav approached quickly.

"Tell Daniels whatever he's looking into here doesn't involve me," B'taav said in voice loud enough to be heard by all those around.

"I don't think he cares," the young man replied. His lips cracked and he showed a perfect set of sharp white teeth.

The target proved too good to let pass.

B'taav slammed his fist into the young man's face. The man fell, hard. His mouth was a bloody mess. Several of his beautiful white teeth littered the floor. The game seller approached the downed man.

"What have you done?" he wailed.

The Independent helped the merchant pick the unconscious soldier up. He sat the man between piles of games and out of the way of pedestrians before offering the merchant a twenty credit piece.

"What's this?"

"For your troubles," B'taav said.

B'taav eyed Daniels' other men. They lingered some thirty feet away and did not approach. Instead, they glared at the Independent. One stood by a computer repair shop, the other by a synthetic food center. This man talked into his communicator.

B'taav knew who he was talking to. He figured now was a good time to walk away.

16

The two remaining military officers followed B'taav through a maze of floors on the upper deck of the station. At times they came very close to the Independent, but never close enough. Soon, B'taav grew worried.

It seemed Daniels' boys were content to hold back and give the Independent his space. As if—

B'taav felt a sudden urgency to get back to Docking Berth 23.

When the Independent arrived, he found a crowd of onlookers just outside the usually sparse area. Docking Berth 23, the berth leading to his spacecraft, was locked down. A flashing red light over the door indicated a catastrophic loss of pressure.

B'taav elbowed his way deeper into the crowd until he reached a side window. Floating just outside the station were two workers in environmental suits. They were doing heavy welding outside the docking door. B'taav looked past them, past the point where his ship should have been, and farther out into space itself.

Some five hundred meters away floated the Independent's ship. She had a large gash along her port side. Like blood from a mortal wound, her insides drifted into space.

"What happened?" B'taav asked no one in particular.

"I don't know," a woman standing beside him replied. "Emergency lights came on and the exit tunnel was sealed. Someone said a meteorite hit that ship."

"She's a goner," another person said. "The owner will be lucky to get scrap value."

Onlookers continued their conversations, offering speculation about the cause of the ship's destruction, but B'taav ignored them. The workers outside finished their welding job. One of them pressed a button on his arm pad and, after a few minutes, a rugged towing vessel drew in to pick them up. Gravimetric clamps drew out of the towing vessel's compartments and clamped onto the remains of B'taav's ship. It was towed away and out of view.

The show was over and people scattered. B'taav moved with them.

He didn't walk far before spotting Lieutenant Lester Daniels and the two men who were following him. They waited for him at the outer radius of the crowd.

"You know what I think?" Daniels said when B'taav was near enough to hear him. "It was sabotage."

Lieutenant Daniels leaned in close to the Independent, so close that his next words could only be heard by him.

"Nowhere to run. Now the show really begins."

With a laugh, the trio of Epsilon military officers walked away. After a while, so too did the Independent.

B'taav took a circuitous route through the main body of *Titus*. He had no specific destination in mind, but the trip allowed him to check for anyone following. No one was, of course. There was little reason for them to. B'taav was trapped.

The Independent spent the remains of the day finding and talking to transport pilots. He searched for anyone willing to fly him out of Erebus. But word spread quickly of the military's interest in him, and most pilots were unwilling to offer him passage. The few that were interested demanded a hefty fee.

B'taav told these pilots he would give them a call the next day, after he finished his business within *Titus*.

Afterwards, the Independent checked into the Titan Hotel on the main deck of the station. It was located only two hundred meters from the Jackal Bar and offered all the amenities of a lightly stocked broom closet.

B'taav's room, though it could be more accurately defined as a square cubicle, had enough space to fit six people standing next to each other. A stiff bed was folded up into the wall and, once pulled out, there was no longer space to stand.

B'taav grabbed the room's single towel and exited. He walked to the end of the hallway, where the other hundred and some odd guests within the hotel's floor shared a communal bathroom.

B'taav waited his turn outside. When he finally entered, he found showers capable of fitting thirty people at a time. His fellow inmates kept to themselves. Like B'taav, their eyes never lingered on any one person, yet a base survival instinct made them weary of any and everyone within their proximity.

B'taav removed his clothing and showered. The water was cold so the turns proved quick. When B'taav was done, he headed to the dressing area. He was on his way out when the rusty wall speakers came to life.

"Ladies and Gentlemen, this is *Titus* administration

speaking," the female voice began. "As many of you know, a small transport ship exploded near the Erebus Displacer a little over a week ago. At that time, our technicians examined the Displacer and felt she sustained no serious damage. However, out of an abundance of caution, we notified Epsillon authorities and were told EMC technicians would arrive to conduct a more thorough examination of our Displacer. A group of technicians arrived aboard the EMC craft *Wake*. They have concluded their more detailed examination of the Displacer and determined it is experiencing irregular energy fluctuations."

"These fluctuations are not, I repeat, not serious. However, they are a cause of concern. Lieutenant Lester Daniels, commander of the *Wake*, has for the time being cancelled all use of the Displacer. There will be one, and only one, exception: The battleship *Dakota* was called in to come to our aid in effecting repairs. Despite the risk, I'm pleased to say she arrived a few minutes ago. The *Dakota's* full complement of technicians is now looking over the Displacer's energy cells. If all goes well, they estimate she will be fully functional by the end of the week. We're sorry for this inconvenience. We will keep you informed and report the moment the Displacer is ready for use. That is all."

Only a few of the Hotel guests took the news in stride. Most could not hide their alarm. Like B'taav, they too were trapped on *Titus*. They, like B'taav, realized they were prisoners of Lieutenant Daniels, the *Wake*, and, now, the *Dakota*. One a cruiser, the other a full-fledged battleship.

Given this new reality, the Independent knew no one would dare make a run for the Displacer with him on board. Not even for all the credits in the Homeworlds.

B'taav's prison was fortified.

17

After sleeping a few hours in an uncomfortable fold up bed, B'taav exited his room and wandered *Titus*. The corridors were quiet this day, as the full realization of military control hit everyone. The citizens of *Titus* were willing to accept the *Wake's* arrival as part of the routine process of checking into the *Sandstorm's* destruction. They were even willing to accept when this interest turned to their Displacer. But with the arrival of the heavily armed battleship and the shutting down of their only means out of Erebus, a palpable sense of paranoia prevailed.

Something bad was happening, and no one was sure exactly what.

B'taav's wandering led him back to the Jackal Bar.

Clients within the place were sparse. The scavengers huddled in small pockets and their conversations consisted of barely audible whispers.

B'taav sat at a barstool. Dave Maddox served a few cups of beer and some rum to a group of patrons before slowly making his way to the Independent. When he was within earshot, he laid down a glass of water and whispered: "Go to the back room."

B'taav took the water and nodded ever so slightly. While Maddox focused on other clients, B'taav made sure the area was free of Daniels' men.

When he was satisfied this was the case, he walked to the door leading into the rear of the bar. It slid open automatically, revealing a small room furnished with a wooden table and a set of chairs. B'taav approached the table and sat down. The door he entered closed.

"Here I am," B'taav muttered. He took another sip of water and sat back.

And waited.

Fifteen minutes later, Maddox entered the room.

"What is Lieutenant Daniels doing?" Maddox said.

"Good morning to you, too."

"I'm not in the mood for jokes. What is Lieutenant Daniels doing?"

"I have no idea."

"Fine. Then what is he capable of?"

"What do you mean?"

"Maybe you didn't hear, but he's got a goddamned battle ship parked in front of our Displacer. It is our only way out. Every single one of its weapons is pointed directly at us. We may be in the middle of nowhere and many of us may not have much of a formal education, but we're not blind and we're not stupid. How far is he willing to go?"

"That depends on what he's after."

"He wants you."

"Certainly. But he isn't doing all this for me."

"I saw what he did to your ship. I saw the look on his face the other day. He wants you. Bad."

"If I were his primary target, he would have taken care of me a long time ago. Trust me, I don't merit all this fuss."

"Why haven't you tried to leave?"

"I have. I've talked to almost every pilot I could find on this station. There were a few willing to smuggle me on their ships, but they demanded more cash than I had, or could get. Not only did Daniels destroy my ship, he also froze all cash transfers from the Homelands. Anyway, I hoped to secure funds through some alternate means, but when the *Dakota's* arrived, that pretty much shut me down. There isn't a pilot willing to take me around the block, much less past her."

"Did you try the pilots on Deck—?"

"Come on, Maddox. You know there are very few pilots still willing to risk a run at the Displacer. The only ones that are are secessionists who hate the Epsillon military more than their ex-wives and in-laws combined and pilot some of the shittiest crafts this side of the Argon Nebula. To get past the *Dakota*, they'd have to run their ship's engines much hotter than they're capable of. So hot they might explode. Like Kelly Lang's ship did."

Maddox tensed.

"Easy, Maddox," the Independent said. "I've still got ears and our good Lieutenant's interest in Lang's death is a hot topic. When Daniels first arrived, his interest was Lang, *not* the Displacer. Now he's changing his tune completely and is focused entirely on the Displacer. People pick up on that."

"So they do."

"Look, when I got here I didn't care what the military was up to. I had work of my own and, in retrospect, probably should have kept a lower profile. Unfortunately, things didn't work out and now I'm trapped. So I figure it's time I learned exactly what's going on here. Tell me, Maddox: Why is Kelly Lang's death so damn important to the Epsillon military?"

Maddox's lips tightened until they became pale white slits. B'taav shook his head.

"If I can tell you know more about Lang than you're willing to admit, imagine what Lieutenant Daniels thinks. He may be an angry, vengeful little bastard, but he's also a member of the Epsillon Elite. The military doesn't give membership into that club to just anyone."

"What will he do?"

"If I was looking into Lang's death and had a battle ship backing me up, I'd do exactly what Daniels is doing. First I'd lock up the Displacer, so that no one gets past me. That way, all potential suspects can't skip town, so to speak."

"And then?"

"Then I'd announce some kind of temporary fix to the Displacer's energy cells. A minor miracle, but one with limits: Only a few people and ships will be allowed through it each day."

"What does that accomplish?"

"Use your head, Maddox. The Displacer's temporary fix is a great way for Daniels to get rid of everyone he knows isn't involved in Lang's death. Everyone here will be anxious as hell to get back to the Homeworlds and as far away from the *Dakota's* guns as possible. Daniels' men, of course, pick and choose who gets to leave while thoroughly searching each vessel that goes. In time, whoever or whatever he's looking for will be left behind on *Titus*."

"And then?"

"What do you think? Erebus is a dead end. If Daniels doesn't find who or what he wants, there's nothing to stop him from planting a bomb in the Displacer and setting it to blow the moment the *Wake* and *Dakota* head out. Whoever is left behind—"

B'taav let out a bitter laugh.

"Whoever's left behind with *me* will be trapped on this station with no ship and no way home. In the unlikely event that someone in the Homeworlds should miss us, it would take them seventy five years using the fastest cruisers available to make it back here without a Displacer. I doubt anyone would bother."

B'taav stepped past Maddox, pausing for a moment at the door leading back into the bar.

"*That's* how far I think Daniels is willing to go."

18

The following day moved slowly.

B'taav again ventured into the depths of the *Titus* station, alternately searching hard to reach areas and interviewing whatever pilots he might have missed the first time around. There were none.

Hours later, the Independent was back in his hotel room. He brooded on his situation. Military patrols, at first few and far between, were becoming a strong presence in *Titus*.

At a little after three in the afternoon, another announcement was sent through the station's intercom:

""Ladies and Gentlemen, this is *Titus* administration speaking," the female voice began. "The following is an update on the condition of the Erebus Displacer. The crew of the EMC *Wake* and *Dakota* has determined that damage to the Displacer is more severe than originally thought. Technicians have measured a significant surge within the energy containment units. While this surge threatens the integrity of the Erebus Displacer, technicians note it only occurs when the unit is activate for periods longer than one hour during each solar day."

"Because of these unique circumstances, Lieutenant Daniels, the acting commander of the *Wake*, has ordered the evacuation of the *Titus* station. A lottery will be set up to allow ships to return to the home worlds free of charge. All ships given clearance to depart must meet the absolute minimum specifications for space flight. Due to the nature of the energy containment surges, all cargo must be left behind and all ships and crew will be subjected to a search to insure this is the case. This is for your safety. Those scheduled to depart and were given military clearance will be instructed on their exact window of opportunity to leave. They are expected to be prepared and ready to go when their time comes. Those who are unable to make their schedule will be sent to the back of the line."

Outside in the hallway, just past the curtain door, B'taav heard people talking excitedly. They were ecstatic they could leave the now militarized Erebus space.

"All vessel Captains are now ordered to report to the main flight deck to begin the lottery and receive their printed evacuation procedures. Good luck."

A few hours later, the first lottery winners were announced

and their vessels were scheduled to depart that evening. B'taav knew a long line of ships would be hovering just outside the Displacer by that time, ready to go.

It wouldn't be long now.

The next day, B'taav returned to the Jackal Bar. Although only two rounds of evacuations were completed since the day before, the place was almost empty. Almost everyone with a ship was waiting in their crafts, ready to go.

B'taav proceeded to the bar's counter and motioned to Maddox. The bartender laid down a dark drink. It fit the mood.

"Daniels is doing what you said he would."

"I wish he didn't," B'taav replied. He held his drink up. "Here's to you, my friend. Get out while you can."

B'taav took down the drink in a single swallow. He laid the cup on the table and lowered his head. After a while B'taav turned from the bar's counter and examined the place. A couple of scavengers huddled here and there, their eyes turned inward. Another scavenger, this one alone, read the digital clock over the bar and headed out.

On the opposite side of the bar, B'taav saw a yellow haired woman sitting alone at one of the narrower tables pressed up against the back wall. It was the same woman he spotted the day he confronted Lieutenant Daniels. Today she sat in the thick shadows. Her eyes were covered with a pair of dark glasses and she gazed in his general direction.

B'taav returned her stare, but was unsure because of the glasses if she was indeed looking directly at him. After a while, he gave up. The Independent laid a credit note on the bar's counter and stumbled back to his room and its stiff bed.

B'taav returned to the Jackal Bar the following evening. The Independent's face reflected growing signs of helplessness. He motioned to Maddox and ordered Pesan. Maddox delivered a cup of the volatile liquid, but B'taav shook his head.

"The whole bottle," he said.

Maddox gave the Independent what he asked and watched with little surprise as the man took it down. He had nothing better to do as there were almost no other clients to take care of. In another couple of days, he figured, there wouldn't be anyone left on *Titus*.

No, Maddox thought as he watched the Independent drink

himself into oblivion. *That isn't entirely true.*

Maddox eventually left B'taav when a pair of new arrivals showed up. After serving them, he returned to his spot behind the counter. At times he looked B'taav's way, but his eyes never lingered. After their last conversation, Maddox did not appear interested in talking to the Independent anymore.

Still, the bartender did his job. After a while, he offered B'taav another bottle of the liquor. The Independent took down half that bottle in less than twenty minutes. Afterwards, his movements slowed and his already sour mood dampened.

At a little after seven, the yellow haired woman with the dark glasses entered the bar. She was dressed entirely in black, as she was the last two times. She walked past B'taav and sat in the same table she took the day before.

Her icy-cool looks and calm demeanor intrigued the Independent. He stole half-hidden glances at the woman and left the remainder of his liquor untouched. After a while Maddox approached her table and whispered a few words. As he did, he looked at the entrance of the bar, as if weary of being caught in her company.

At ten hundred hours, two of Daniels' men entered the Jackal Bar. By that time there were a little over a half dozen customers milling about. The flights out of Erebus were done for the day, and those few that remained in *Titus* decided to have one last drink before the next day's scheduled departures.

Daniels' men produced a computer pad. The younger of the two read off several names. Those listed were scheduled for the next evacuation. After their announcement was read, the men left.

Maddox nodded to the yellow haired woman. She was quickly on her feet and following Daniels' men.

B'taav considered the silent interaction between two. Having nothing better to do, he decided to follow her.

19

B'taav shadowed the yellow haired woman through three separate corridor levels before somehow losing her. Some fifty feet ahead of him were Daniels' men. They were oblivious to either tail.

B'taav stopped.

Slowly, carefully, he turned. The object of his pursuit stood behind him. Her right hand was hidden in her jacket pocket.

"There aren't many who can take down that much Pesan and still walk a straight line," the woman said. She pulled the hand out of the pocket just a little, enough to reveal the fusion gun in its grasp. "You don't look at all drunk. Not now, anyway."

B'taav kept still. His eyes looked her over, determining the woman's strengths and weaknesses, as surely as she did the same with him. After a few seconds of uneasy silence, she spoke.

"Move. Nice and easy."

B'taav did as told. The woman fell in place behind him. By then, Daniels' men were long gone and the corridor before them was empty. B'taav continued walking until he reached an intersection.

"To the right," the woman said.

B'taav walked down that corridor until the woman told him to stop. To B'taav's left was a bulky dock door. Visible through the window at its side was a small cargo craft attached to this docking berth. Worn black letters printed on her side identified her as the *Pilgrimage*. The woman tapped a series of buttons in the paneling beside the dock door. Air rushed into the vacuum beyond. In seconds a green light over the door flashed on and the security locks disengaged.

"After you," the woman said.

B'taav pulled the bulky door open and entered the dock corridor. The door leading into the *Pilgrimage* opened automatically as they approached. B'taav stepped into the spacecraft. He found a small, rectangular room with smooth metallic walls. An emergency kit was affixed to the far wall and beside it was a solid stormite door.

"Have a seat," the woman said. As she spoke, a gray slab slid out two feet from the far wall.

B'taav approached the slab and sat down. The cargo craft's outer door closed and sophisticated clamps locked into place.

The Independent heard a low hum and felt vibrations coming from deep within the ship. The *Pilgrimage's* engines were warming up.

The yellow haired woman stepped before B'taav and pulled the fusion gun out of her jacket pocket. She kept it pointed at B'taav while she removed her dark glasses. Revealed was a pair of stony brown eyes.

"Bad enough I'm threatened by the Epsillon Capital Guard," B'taav said. "At least they're on home turf. What brings a Phaecian Inquisitor across the border?"

The woman did not reply, although B'taav thought he saw the ghost of a smile flicker on the corner of her lips.

"You know me?" she asked.

"Not at first," the Independent admitted. "Although there was something familiar about you. Now that we're face to face, it's obvious. Pleased to see you again, Inquisitor Cer. We met ten years ago. At the Pan-Pacific Business Convention."

"I remember the event. I don't recall you."

"I was just another face in the crowd."

"That I doubt. What were you doing there?"

"Our Epsillon business personnel were... uncomfortable around Phaecian delegates."

"And even more uncomfortable around Inquisitors?"

"I was hired to watch you guys and make sure you didn't take any liberties with the hosts. Fortunately for everyone, you behaved well."

"Either that or we did what we wanted and you weren't the wiser. For all you know, you failed miserably at your job."

"Always a possibility," B'taav admitted. "I don't mean to pry, but if I remember correctly, your personnel file stated you were in good standing within the ranks of your fellow Inquisitors. Yet ten years later, here you are, in a rundown station at the edges of our mutual Empires' greatest trash heap. Are you still an Inquisitor, Cer? Or have you retired to pursue a lucrative scavenger job?"

"I read up on you, too, B'taav. Congratulations on keeping such a low profile. Most files referencing your...work...have you listed as a 'John Doe', yet you are an Independent of some note among the business elites. The best I could determine, your career began shortly after the Tamarin campaign, some thirty years ago. You were listed as a soldier in that campaign, though given the enormous amount of casualties and the poor record keeping at the time, it is possible you were never a part of any battle, but rather used the event to launch your –how can I put this?- most recent *identity*?"

"That's very old news, Inquisitor."

"You're also a proficient pilot. You're experienced with small arms and underground work and you've shown up in various solar systems and, despite your best attempts to hide it, have always left some kind of mark before leaving. High level corruption exposed, narcotic rings busted, even black markets shut down. Sterling stuff. What exactly did you do to Lieutenant Daniels in Evalba, or is that a secret too?"

"Depends on your level of clearance."

Inquisitor Cer raised her fusion gun.

"Let's assume my clearance is of the highest level."

"You, better than anyone else, should know."

"Ah," Inquisitor Cer said and smiled. "This involved Phaecian assets?"

"Lieutenant Daniels arrived three months after my arrival at Evalba. He was searching for a Phaecian mole."

"Same as you?"

"I caught the individual shortly after Lieutenant Daniels arrived. I was entitled to deliver him to the proper Industry and collect the bounty. Daniels didn't see things that way and tried to stop me. I had to smuggle your...asset out of the Gemini Council with Daniels on my ass. We were in a race to Evalba's Displacer. Just as he was about to overrun my ship, wouldn't you know it, his cruiser's engines seized up."

"Just like that?"

"Just like that."

"To touch an Inquisitor's ship is to court death. I imagine the same applies to anyone in Epsillon that dares sabotage a Capital Guard ship."

"Provided one can prove such malicious actions, yes. As far as anyone's concerned, that day Lieutenant Daniels had some very bad luck at a very bad time."

"Neither of us are friends of Lieutenant Daniels and his group so it's curious we find ourselves facing him in this particular place and at this particular time."

"You've had a run in with Daniels?"

"Yes, though the details are best left unsaid. What is more important is why General Jurgens sent Daniels here."

"You know about General Jurgens? Now I'm impressed. My

compliments to the Phaecian Empire's intelligence gathering."

"Ours is no better –or worse– than yours. We know what we know and make educated guesses about the rest. Now that you're before me, there is little reason to guess as to your purpose, when you can explain it in your own words. So B'taav, why are you here?"

"I could ask you the same question."

"You could, but I've got the gun."

"I'm checking into suppliers of Accelerant."

"Accelerant? The drug is barely illegal. Why would someone of your stature care about someone peddling such a petty item?"

"It's related to a bigger case involving piracy and mass murder."

"Very noble," Cer said. "For what it's worth, I'm glad we had this talk. Let me assure you I'm being very sincere when I say I'm sorry."

The gun in Cer's hand rose level with B'taav's head, but the Independent lunged forward and grabbed Cer's wrist before she could fire. He twisted her hand and pointing the barrel of the gun down and away. Cer elbowed the Independent in the jaw and, for a split second, all B'taav could see was darkness. He tasted blood in his mouth but continued twisting Inquisitor Cer's arm. Cer let out a grunt and the gun dropped to the floor and out of sight.

With the weapon gone, the two broke away. B'taav assumed a fighter's stance and squared his fists. Cer mirrored his moves with a similar posture. Though B'taav was bigger than Cer, her athleticism and fluid movements gave her advantages over the Independent's mass. B'taav knew it was no easy feat to best *any* Inquisitor in hand to hand combat.

The two circled each other in the cramped area, each waiting for the other to make the first move. They remained that way for several long moments, until Inquisitor Cer relaxed. She straightened up.

B'taav followed her lead. The two would be fighters stared at each other for several more seconds, until Inquisitor Cer folded her hands across her chest and leaned against the wall.

"Perhaps some other time," she said.

B'taav looked around the floor and spotted Cer's fusion gun. He picked it up.

"Not loaded," he said after checking the weapon.

"Surprised?"

"Somewhat," B'taav admitted. "When you struck me in the

jaw, it should have knocked me cold. You held back."

"I was curious to see what you were capable of."

"Did I measure up?"

"I'm afraid not."

"Sorry to disappoint you," B'taav said. He ran his hand over his jaw. "Then again, you had the advantage. You were carrying a gun and you were sober."

"You further disappoint me. There's nothing worse than a sore loser. Given your personnel files, I imagined you were a man of *some* honor."

"Independents can't trouble themselves with trivial things such as that. We've always been a practical group."

"Not unlike mercenaries."

"Why are you here, Inquisitor Cer?"

Inquisitor Cer's eyes narrowed. "Our empire's activities are our own, B'taav. Suffice to say that we are not interested in the pursuit of pirates and petty drug dealers. Nor do we worry about our next paycheck."

"What are you interested in?"

"That's for others to explain."

The door leading into the heart of the ship noisily came to life. Locks were disengaged and the solid mass slid to the side, revealing a dark corridor beyond. A shadowy figure walked the length of the corridor and came to a stop before Inquisitor Cer and B'taav. He said:

"The Inquisitor is correct."

It was Dave Maddox.

He carried a fusion gun and didn't look terribly happy about being alongside B'taav once again.

"Let me assure you my gun *is* loaded," the bartender said.

"Understood."

"Good," Maddox continued. "Time is scarce, so I'll tell you what you need to know. As you've no doubt surmised, Lieutenant Daniels' interest in *Titus* is directly related to us."

"What are you doing here?"

"In good time, Independent," Inquisitor Cer said.

"Or not at all," Maddox added. "We've come to believe, as do you, that Lt. Daniels is willing to go to great lengths to stop us from leaving this station. His boys pressed the pilots around here very hard. So hard that any potential flight crews we hired are on their way out. Permanently. No one, it seems, wants to take on a piloting job."

"You're telling me," B'taav said.

"This forces us to improvise. Among our group, Inquisitor Cer is the only one with military class flight skills. Given the fact that the moment we take off from *Titus* Daniels and his boys on the *Dakota* will be on our tail, it would be foolish to attempt our journey with only one experienced pilot."

"Which is where I come in," B'taav said.

"Our destination is within Erebus, but very far away," Maddox continued. "While Inquisitor Cer's stamina is great and she can fly the craft for many hours. But even with that great stamina, she will eventually need to be relieved, and we cannot afford to stop, even for a few minutes. We're aware that you too are a skilled pilot, as you arrived here with your own craft. We further assume that you know enough about starship maintenance to be able to fix things that might, in transit, break."

Maddox walked to the decompression chamber's outer door, the one that led to outer space. He activated it. The double doors slid open, revealing the small space where the ship's refuse is packed before being ejected.

"The way I see it, you have two options. You can help us get away from Lieutenant Daniels, or you can take a walk." He motioned beyond the door. "The choice is yours."

20

Lieutenant Lester Daniels swore.

The officer before him maintained a rigid pose and tried his best not to react to his superior officer's growing fury. When it peaked, and appeared to pass, the officer spoke. Meekly.

"The responsibility was mine," the young man said. "B'taav was there one moment and gone the next. I offer no excuses and accept whatever disciplinary actions you feel is appropriate."

"You're lucky I need every man I can muster," Daniels replied. "Get back out there and look around. Maybe we'll get lucky and spot B'taav when he returns to the hotel."

The young officer saluted before leaving the conference room. Daniels waited for the door to close before punching a sequence of buttons on the computer built into his desk. A door on the opposite side of the room slid open and revealed an opulent study. In the center of the study was a highly polished metal desk and sitting behind it was General Jurgens.

Daniels entered this room. The door closed behind him. Only a very select few on the *Dakota* knew of General Jurgens' presence in Erebus, but only General Jurgens and Lieutenant Daniels alone knew of their other, equally important guest held in the luxury suite beyond this chamber.

"I heard everything," Jurgens said. He switched off the monitor that transmitted the sounds and images from the conference room.

"I hope none of this proves a setback, General."

"For *all* our sakes."

"How's our guest doing?" Daniels asked and motioned toward the doors leading to the chamber beyond.

"About as expected, suffering from some mild cabin fever."

Daniels shivered. The last thing they needed was to make their guest uncomfortable.

"If he needs anything," Daniels said. A faint buzz interrupted his comments. It came from his communication badge.

"What is it?" General Jurgens asked.

"I'm wanted on the bridge," Daniels replied. He hurried out the room.

Lieutenant Daniels arrived at the bridge of the *Dakota* and quickly positioned himself before the central monitor. Sensors indicated an unauthorized craft departed from *Titus* only moments before and was heading straight for the Displacer. The ship showed no signs of slowing down and her pilot was oblivious to the Epsillon fighter crafts on an intercept course.

"The distance between the ship and the Displacer is four thousand kilometers and closing fast," the Sensor Op said.

"Must be some kind of maniac," Daniels muttered. "Have they responded to any transmissions?"

"No sir," replied the Comm Op. She sat to Daniels' left and shook her head in frustration. "They continue ignoring all warnings."

"What is the status of the *Tango* fighters?"

"Armed and ready," the Weapons Officer said. She sat in the corner of the bridge. Before her were three separate monitors. One plotted the course of the *Tango* fighters and the unidentified craft while the other two provided real time displays listing active weaponry and defensive shields. "They will intercept in forty seconds. What are your orders, sir?"

"Surround the unknown craft," Daniels said. "Has the ship taken any evasive actions?"

"No sir. Unknown's course remains consistent."

"Tell *Tango 13* to fire a missile across her bow. He is not to hit the ship, is that understood?"

"Yes sir."

Daniels' eyes returned to the sensor monitor. A second after the command was issued a blip, coming from the lead *Tango* fighter craft, appeared.

"Missile is away."

Daniels watched as a blip representing the missile streaked toward the approaching ship. The ship continued its course, just as oblivious to the missile as it was to the *Tango* fighters and the transmissions sent to her. The missile missed the ship by only a hundred meters.

"Any reaction?"

"None, sir. Distance is now two thousand five hundred kilometers."

"If they're trying to enter the Displacer, they should be slowing down," the Nav Op said. "Either their pilot is one of the bravest souls this side of Erebus or—"

Daniels gasped. He slammed a series of buttons to the side of the monitor. A larger sensor graphic of the *Titus* space station and its surrounding area filled the screen. Another small blip appeared on the screen. The ship this blip represented was heading in the exact opposite direction of the unauthorized craft, *into* the asteroid remains of Erebus.

Daniels' face went white. He turned to the Weapons Op and yelled:

"The ship approaching us is a decoy! Tell the fighters to take her down. Take her down *now!*"

Despite its distance from the Erebus Displacer, the explosion from the decoy ship lit up the area around the *Titus* space station like a fiery new sun.

B'taav shielded his eyes and looked away as the cockpit of the *Pilgrimage* burned with the white-hot light. Just as quickly as it flashed on, the light was gone. It took several seconds for the Independent's eyes to adjust to the dim lighting of the bridge. He double checked the ship's controls and verified their course into Erebus.

Maddox stood behind B'taav while Inquisitor Cer sat at the secondary ship controls next to the Independent. Both Maddox and Cer intently watched the navigational readout.

"It appears our diversion worked," Maddox said.

"You loaded the decoy with explosives?"

"How long did you think a decoy spacecraft would occupy a battleship and its complement of officers? A minute? Two? We needed much more time to make our getaway."

"There might be casualties," B'taav said.

"I doubt Lt. Daniels is stupid enough to let the decoy get that close," Maddox said. "Besides, whatever happens from now on does not matter, so long as our mission is accomplished."

"Easy for you to say," B'taav replied. He faced Inquisitor Cer. "What about you, Inquisitor? Our Empires have been at peace for two hundred years. What could possibly make you risk that peace?"

Inquisitor Cer did not reply. B'taav shook his head in frustration.

"Even if the *Dakota* and *Wake* are disabled, they'll lock onto us with their long range sensors and see where we're going," B'taav said. "When we're out of range of those sensors, all they have to do is sit back and wait for us to use our sensors to maneuver around the asteroid belt. They'll follow our progress as if we were carrying a flashlight into a dark room."

"We won't be using our sensors for quite some time."

"What do you mean? The asteroid field gets very thick. How will we know where we're going?"

"I see you're unaware of how scavengers explore the area before us."

"I didn't expect to trace their paths."

"For now, B'taav, we follow the navigational course plotted into the computer."

"And afterwards?"

"The scavengers don't use their sensors for the very reason you stated: They don't want to be followed. Should they give away their positions, there's the possibility claim jumpers will steal their hard earned discoveries. To avoid that particular problem, the scavengers laid out a series of small satellites over the years and arranged them into a grid. These satellites emit low level signals which the scavengers use to orient themselves and find their way."

"How deep into the asteroid field do the satellites go?"

"Deep enough, for now."

"You mean we're going in deeper than even the satellite grid?"

"Yes."

"What do we do when we're beyond those signals? More to the point, what if Daniels and his men log into the satellites' computer and scramble the signals around? They could have us fly in a circle and emerge right in front of them."

"They could try, but those satellites use very old tech," Maddox explained. "The only way to change their transmissions is manually. Quite literally, you have to fly out to them and press their control switches. We've kept a close watch on the *Dakota* and *Wake* since their arrival. They haven't sent even a single fighter craft outside the radius of the Displacer and *Titus*, and none anywhere near the start of the satellite grid."

Inquisitor Cer gazed at the view screen monitor. A mass of asteroids were already visible in the distance, the remnants of one of Erebus' original six planets.

"Even with those satellites, without the use of sensors there's a great danger of collision, especially if we follow this flight path."

"Relax, B'taav, this is the easy part," Maddox said. "We haven't even entered the first dense asteroid cluster."

Maddox tapped Inquisitor Cer on her shoulder.

"We'll let our new friend take the first shift," the bartender said. "Inquisitor Cer will relieve you in eight hours. I should warn you B'taav, the communication system is locked. Any attempt to tamper with it will result in a very loud alarm. This very loud alarm will also be activated should you deviate or slow from the prescribed course. Be a good boy. I'd really hate to have to send you outside."

Inquisitor Cer stepped past Maddox and exited the cockpit. Maddox took her seat and flashed B'taav a cold grin.

"Don't feel bad," Maddox said. "At least you're out of Lieutenant Daniels' hands."

"And into yours," B'taav replied. "Am I much better off?"

"Only time will tell," Maddox said. He closed his eyes and drifted off to sleep.

21

B'taav's first flight shift proved remarkably uneventful.

An hour into the trip Maddox awoke from his nap, stretched, and made a brief inter-ship communiqué. In seconds, a thin and morose looking man wandered into the cockpit. Maddox allowed the thin man to take his place.

"This is Rasp," Maddox said. "He will watch you from here on out. Make sure to stay on his good side."

Maddox said nothing more before leaving the ship's bridge. B'taav examined Rasp. He wasn't just thin: he was gaunt, with equally thin black hair and an avian look to his face. His eyes were clear blue and his mouth was locked tight.

Friendly sort, B'taav thought. He nonetheless extended his hand.

"Rasp? I'm B'taav."

The gaunt man's mouth, and arm, remained stubbornly unmoved.

"Pleased to meet you too," B'taav muttered before returning to controls.

The next hours found the *Pilgrimage* passing a series of impressively large asteroids. The craft entered the edges of Erebus' largest asteroid field. It wouldn't be long, B'taav knew, before he would have to reduce speed and maneuver carefully around these obstacles. By that time, the ever present star light would be choked off and an almost absolute darkness would surround them. It would feel like the ship entered a tight, mysterious cavern.

Good thing I'm not claustrophobic, the Independent thought.

On the sixth hour of flight, Maddox returned to the cockpit with a tray of food. He handed it to B'taav, gave the Independent a few minutes to eat, then took the tray, along with whatever the Independent didn't eat, and left.

At exactly the eighth hour of B'taav's shift, Inquisitor Cer and Maddox showed up. Rasp allowed Cer to take his seat. The Inquisitor activated her console and, simultaneously, deactivated B'taav's. Maddox checked the Navigator's controls and verified the *Pilgrimage's* course. He then put on a pair of sleek, metallic computer magnification glasses and stared through the ship's windows. From the cockpit, he had a clear view of everything but the underside of the ship.

"How ironic," B'taav said. He motioned to the deactivated instruments before him. "We've got all this sophisticated technology yet we're reduced to looking for Daniels' boys with our own two eyes."

"We've got some enhancements," Maddox said and removed the magnifying glasses.

"They can't be too far away."

"I expect so," Maddox said. "We'll keep following the course laid in. By the time we get to your next shift we'll switch to the satellite signals as guidance."

"Where do we go when we enter the heart of the asteroid field?"

"Keep the questions to yourself, Independent. You'll get no answers from me."

"I'm assuming your plan isn't just to go hide out among the rocks, because if it is, we will be caught."

Maddox motioned to Rasp.

"Take our guest to his quarters," Maddox said. "He should be well rested by the start of his next shift."

The remainder of the week passed largely without incident. B'taav and Inquisitor Cer exchanged piloting shifts every eight hours and, without fail, Rasp marched B'taav straight to his quarters at the end of the corridor outside the bridge.

It was obvious there were other passengers on board, but B'taav was kept away from them. Now and again, he heard bits of conversations emanating from the lower passages. He did not recognize any of the voices.

B'taav followed the prescribed course deeper and deeper into what had once been the orbit of Erebus E. Navigating through the planet's remains proved a challenge. The asteroid clusters were at times so thick the Independent was forced to slow the ship to a crawl. Maddox wasn't pleased with the delay, but he knew there was little choice.

When they made it through a particularly narrow stretch, B'taav was confronted by a field of asteroids the size of small moons. Several of them rotated at tremendous speeds, shattering anything they came in contact with. Even after two hundred years, the destruction of Erebus continued. In these circumstances, Daniels' men would have difficulties locating the *Pilgrimage*, even with the full use of their sensors. The very thick asteroid field provided an effective cover. Maddox must have known this, too, as he spent less time visually scanning for signs of Daniels' fighter crafts.

When Maddox wasn't on the bridge, Rasp guarded the Independent. The silent man offered no conversation and B'taav soon wondered if he was capable of speaking at all. So silent was Rasp that he said nothing when an alarm screeched throughout the cockpit. Instead, he gave B'taav a murderous glare.

"Don't look at me," B'taav said. "I didn't do anything."

Alarm lights flashed on one of the monitors. The port engine was reading highly elevated temperatures.

"What the hell is going on?"

Maddox and Inquisitor Cer ran into the room and, like Rasp, eyed the Independent with suspicion. Cer's hands hovered close to the fusion guns in her belt.

"Coolant systems on engine three are offline," B'taav said. "She's overheating."

Maddox looked over B'taav's shoulder and at the display monitor.

"How bad is it?"

"Bad enough."

"Can it be fixed?"

"With time, yes. But we should stop."

"Out of the question."

"We need to fully assess the damage. If we keep flying, there is a risk of burning the engines out completely. Do you have any ship techs on board who can look at this?"

Neither Maddox nor Inquisitor Cer replied. B'taav didn't expect any words from Rasp.

"Don't tell me: Daniels' boys scared any mechanics you were planning to hire on this trip as well."

Maddox nodded.

"I should have stayed on *Titus*. At least there I had a fighting chance."

"Inquisitor Cer knows quite a bit about ship mechanics, but she's more familiar with Phaecian models," Maddox said. "What about you, B'taav. Think you can fix our problem?"

"If it isn't too bad, I might be able to patch it up. But we need to find a hiding place to park."

"No. We keep moving."

"Listen, Maddox: At the very least we need to shut down engine three so we don't lose any more coolant. When we shut it down, we won't have full maneuverability." B'taav pointed out the window.   "Around these parts, we *need* all the maneuverability we can get."

"We're not stopping," Maddox said. "We've got the-Gods-alone-know how many fighter craft on our tail. We stop for any length of time and they will catch us."

"I'll fly her," Inquisitor Cer said. "You take care of the leak."

"Fine," B'taav said. "But if the damage is really bad, we will stop."

"How long before you know?"

"A half hour, give or take. Even with the air units at full blast, it's going to be hot as hell in the Engine room and the air within will be borderline toxic. A half hour is about all the time we'll have."

"Can't we suit up?"

"No. The place is cramped enough. Based on the speeds this ship is doing, I'm guessing you've made some improvements, the type that required a proportional elimination of the free space available within the engine compartments."

Maddox eyed Inquisitor Cer.

"Keep her moving," he said before escorting the Independent out of the cockpit.

B'taav and Maddox sprinted down to Engine Room 3.

For B'taav, it was the first time he saw other parts of this vessel. The view was hardly memorable. Empty corridors and shut doors gave B'taav precious little new information about the craft he was piloting or the passengers it carried.

"I'll need tools," B'taav said.

"We've got a room filled with them on the way down."

They stopped at the entrance of Engine 3. B'taav carried his bag of tools as well and replacement circuitry. The Independent felt the engine's door with the palm of his hand.

"She's running really hot," he said.

Maddox followed B'taav's lead and also laid his hand on the door. No sooner did he touch it that he let out a yelp and drew his hand back.

"Hot as blazes."

B'taav stepped up to an intercom unit on the wall beside the door.

"Inquisitor Cer," he called out.

"Yes, B'taav?" came his answer through the speaker.

"We're in the corridor outside engine room 3. I need you to set the air unit to maximum cooling for the engine room."

"The AC is already at a maximum."

"Then get the corridor cooled down as well."

"Acknowledged."

It took a few seconds for the air to filter in from the ceiling wall. The corridor's temperature dropped noticeably.

"OK," B'taav said. He grasped the engine room door's handle and gave it a sharp tug. He stepped back as a wave of steaming air flooded into the corridor.

"You can't go in there!" Maddox exclaimed. He held his hand to his mouth.

"Either I do, or we shut the engines down."

Maddox placed a cloth over his mouth and coughed.

"Let's go."

"No need for both of us inside," B'taav countered. "Just keep this door open. Whatever cool airs makes its way in there helps."

B'taav took a cautious sniff and sensed the bitter acid and oily discharges.

"On second thought, you should close the door and head back. The atmosphere is already turning poisonous."

"You're not leaving my sight, B'taav. Besides, I'm not losing one of the crew. Even if it is you."

"Fine, but if you feel lightheaded, don't stay." B'taav drew several sharp breaths. "Give me no more than twenty minutes…"

"I doubt this engine will last much longer than that," Maddox said before letting out another cough. "Well, what are you waiting for?"

22

As bad as the heat spilling into the outer corridor was, entering Engine Room 3 proved far worse.

B'taav covered his mouth with a strip of cloth, even though he knew it offered minimal protection. As expected, there was very little space to move within the engine room, and it was far too tight to bring in a fully functional breathing apparatus or environmental suit. Even without this bulky equipment, B'taav knew he would need to press his body through some very tight, and extremely hot, spaces.

This is going to hurt.

Before he moved deeper into the room, B'taav checked a computer panel before the engines. The panel's monitor displayed detailed information regarding the engine's status. It noted a loss of coolant pressure to subsection 3, at the farthest end of the room.

"Figures," B'taav sighed.

The Independent pushed forward. His path, a narrow walkway, was clear. The engine throbbed and hummed as it should, yet the Independent also noted the unmistakable sounds of heavy strain. At the end of the walkway he was forced to crouch past a red hot tube, and then climb over another rectangular piece of machinery. Deeper and deeper B'taav pushed and the air, throbbing sounds, and claustrophobic setting engulfed his senses.

Still he moved forward.

B'taav gingerly avoided brushing against any of the machinery, yet despite his best efforts he couldn't help but stray. Minor burns didn't affect him, but as he crawled forward, he accidentally pressed his left arm against one of the many tubes surrounding him. He let out a yell.

"How's it going?" Maddox called out.

"I'm having the time of my life," B'taav yelled back.

"You can't say it's been a dull date."

The Independent shook his head and squeezed between rectangular cases, searing his clothing as he moved, before finally sliding on his stomach through a particularly narrow aperture. He felt hot, oily liquids soak his shirt and pants.

Coolant fluid.

He knew he was very close to the problem. B'taav reached

into his bag and pulled out a flashlight. He ran it along the walls and spotted a ruptured feeding tube.

Let it be all that's wrong, the Independent prayed.

He crawled forward a couple of more feet, all the while fighting off a growing nausea, until he reached the leak. It was hard to tell the cause of the rupture, and B'taav decided not to try. From his bag B'taav removed a roll of Stern tape and wrapped a dense layer around the damaged tube.

At any other time, doing so would be an easy task, but B'taav found it difficult to concentrate on the job. His eyes were dry and a dull throbbing headache made it almost impossible to think clearly. Even worse, anytime the Independent leaned in too close, he felt a jolt of electricity.

"Come on," B'taav muttered.

He was taking too long, and the longer he remained...

Snap out of it. Get it done and get the hell out of here.

It took several agonizing minutes to cover the damage. By that point, the Stern tape had hardened until it became a solid mass. The only way to remove it would be to replace the feeding tube entirely. B'taav analyzed his work and was satisfied the leak was sealed.

He began the long trip back.

In the Independent's mind, this journey felt like it took hours. Meter after painful meter he moved, until, thankfully, he was free from the tight spaces. B'taav climbed to his feet and, for a second, blacked out.

He leaned against a hot wall and heard the sound of his clothing sizzle, yet the pain came from a million miles away. B'taav stumbled toward the exit door.

"I'm done," he said.

There was no reply.

Maddox sat beside the outer door, his head down. The fumes and heat had overwhelmed him.

B'taav ignored the bartender and examined the engine's computer monitor.

The sensors indicated the room's temperature was lower and the operating system was green. The danger that the engine would overheat was over. However, the air remained toxic. The air purifiers were offline.

B'taav coughed and stepped past Maddox and to the front corner of the room. The air system's controls were only a few feet away and did not require any contortion on B'taav's part to reach them. He leaned down and drew a screwdriver from his black tool bag and unscrewed the paneling.

As he did, the screwdriver slipped from his fingers and hit the floor. B'taav reached down to get it, and immediately felt his consciousness slip.

I have to do this, the Independent thought. He shook his head and momentarily cleared his mind.

The Independent grabbed the screwdriver and loosened the remaining bolts. With sluggish effort he pried the paneling off. It dropped to the ground with a bang and the Independent stared at the computer system. What he saw was a blur of darkness and blinking red lights.

He closed and rubbed his eyes several times and tried to get a better look at what lay in front of him. His vision worsened. Suddenly, all the sounds around him stopped.

B'taav felt his stomach churn. His body felt heavy, so very, very heavy. He needed to sit down. He needed to...

The Independent tried one last, desperate attempt to make out the controls before him. He couldn't. Everything was dark.

He saw nothing at all.

23

When he awoke, B'taav was lying flat on his back and staring up at the engine room's ceiling. His vision remained foggy, but at least he could see. Even better, the toxic air was all but gone. The air purification system was running.

B'taav closed his eyes and allowed a few seconds to pass. Whatever lingering nausea still bubbled within him was settling down. When he reopened his eyes, a young boy was standing over him.

The boy couldn't have been more than eight years old. He stood only five feet tall and had dark black hair and bright blue eyes. He held a small red ball. The child ignored the Independent lying just below him. His eyes were on the air purification paneling B'taav opened before blacking out.

"What are you doing here?" someone said.

The boy didn't turn or react to whoever spoke. B'taav sat up. The speaker was Maddox. His voice was weak.

"You shouldn't be here," he said.

Maddox was on his knees by the door leading into the engine room. His face was pale and his eyes were red. He tried to keep his voice soft and his words soothing. It took a great effort to do so but it was in vain. The boy did not answer. Instead, he bounced his ball and caught it, then bounced it again.

Maddox got to his feet and made his way to the boy's side. He gently grabbed his left hand.

"You need to get back to your mother," Maddox said.

B'taav sat up and rubbed his head. He followed the boy's gaze. The child was staring at the green lights flashing across the air purification system's controls. The burnt out microchips were replaced.

"You did a good job," Maddox told B'taav as he escorted the boy out of the engine room. "What say we get the hell out of here?"

"You'll get no argument from me."

B'taav rose. He couldn't recall finding, much less replacing, the inoperative coolant system microchips.

Don't know what you did, or how you did it, but it's fixed.

B'taav was in no condition to further analyze anything and decided it was best to simply follow Maddox and the boy out of the engine room.

B'taav tossed and turned and awoke feeling more exhausted than when he went to sleep. He washed his face and brushed his teeth before heading to the door leading out of his room. The Independent knocked twice and in seconds Rasp unlocked and opened it.

The silent man accompanied B'taav down the corridor and straight to the ship's cockpit. Along the way, B'taav heard the distant sound of a ball bouncing against the metal floor. It was a sound he had heard before, now and again, but only now realized its origin.

"Hello again," B'taav said.

The boy stood at the end of the corridor. He was dressed in a gray jumpsuit and had the same dull stare. He offered the Independent neither greeting nor reply.

Rasp laid his hand on B'taav's shoulder and squeezed.

B'taav said nothing more. He resumed his walk to the cockpit but abruptly stopped when a door beside them slid open. A gray haired lady in her mid-fifties rushed into the corridor and almost ran into the duo.

"Sorry," she muttered before looking away. She spotted the boy and the worry in her face faded.

"There you are!" she said. She tried to sound cheerful despite her obvious concern. "Come on child, it's time for dinner. What would you like to eat?"

She didn't expect any answer.

"I've got mashed potatoes and gravy and chocolate cake," she continues as she escorted the boy away.

When she passed the Independent, her eyes momentarily settled on his. Her lips tightened and she offered a nod, a small acknowledgement and greeting wrapped in one, before turning her attention back to her child. The two returned to the room the lady emerged from.

When they were gone, Rasp tugged at B'taav shoulder.

"Lead the way," the Independent said.

As he approached the sixth hour of his latest shift, B'taav found it hard to keep his eyes open. His time in the engine room wiped out his energy and the taste of toxic air lingered in the back of his throat. Even more bothersome were the burns on his hands and throughout his body.

Could have been worse.

Even as that thought entered in his mind, it suddenly was.

B'taav straightened in his chair and stared out the starboard side window. Running a parallel course to their ship and far off in the distance was another vessel.

B'taav gripped the steering yoke and pushed down hard, sending the ship into a steep dive. She skimmed a very large asteroid and hid behind it and out of the other ship's line of sight.

B'taav swore.

He didn't get a good look at this vessel and, for all he knew, she was a scavenger craft and not part of Daniels' search team. Then again, they were so far away from *Titus*...

B'taav eyed the long range sensor control. How useful it would be to click it on, for only a second, and get some idea of what –and who– lay so close by.

But then they'll get a very good look at us, won't they?

Maddox, who usually watched over B'taav near the end of his shifts, wasn't there at this hour. Sitting beside the Independent was Rasp. He eyed the Independent's actions with great curiosity.

"Sorry for sudden turn," B'taav told his companion. "I spotted a ship. She might be a scavenger, but I wouldn't count on it."

Rasp pressed a button beside the navigator's chair. A low, angry alarm buzzed through the cockpit.

"Turn that damned thing off," B'taav said. "I can't concentrate."

Rasp allowed the alarm to sound for a few more seconds before shutting it off. By that time, Maddox and Inquisitor Cer entered the bridge. They looked out the windows and at the monitors that displayed a view of outer space from the underside of the ship.

"What did you see?" Maddox asked.

"A single ship, off to the starboard side," B'taav said. "She couldn't have been much more than two hundred kilometers away."

Rasp allowed Inquisitor Cer to take the co-pilot's chair. She activated her console and hit several buttons before the whine of the engines decreased.

"You're slowing us down?" Maddox asked her. "Why?"

"Phaecian ships use energy readings as well as long range sensors to pinpoint nearby crafts. The less energy we expend the less chance they pick us up. I imagine it's the same with your Epsilon crafts."

"It is," B'taav said. "As long as we remain hidden behind these asteroids and don't send out too many energy flares, it'll be hard for them to spot us. But we will need to alter our course."

"Why?"

"If she's one of Daniels' craft, there are bound to be others nearby. We need to fall back, perhaps circle around."

"How far?"

"I'd recommend a thousand kilometer arc, at the very least."

"At this speed, it might take us an extra day," Maddox said and shook his head. "We can't afford to waste that much time."

"We'll waste considerably more if we're caught."

"No," Maddox insisted. "We need to find an alternative."

B'taav sighed.

"It's very difficult for me to figure out alternatives without knowing where we're going."

"Listen, Independent," Maddox began. "The last thing I need is—"

Inquisitor Cer turned away from her monitor and looked squarely into Maddox's eyes. Maddox caught her icy stare.

"Look," B'taav said. "So far I've done everything you've asked. I haven't made any demands and I haven't asked many questions. But things have changed. Daniels' boys are close, and if we make any mistakes, it will mean the end of our little trip. I need to know where we're going. That's the only way I could even begin to plan our route."

"You're hardly in a position to demand anything."

"That's enough," Inquisitor Cer said. "B'taav knows how to fly and he's had experience avoiding Daniels. Might I suggest, Mister Maddox, that we spare any more wasted time in pointless arguments and either give our co-pilot the coordinates of our destination and use his skills to plan our trip there or take him back to his room."

Maddox's face reddened, but he offered the Inquisitor no counter argument. Instead, he motioned for Rasp to leave the cockpit. The silent man did so.

When he was gone, Maddox squeezed between the two pilot chairs and pushed a series of buttons under the central monitor.

"We have two days flight left before arriving at our destination," the bartender said. He pressed another series of buttons and the navigational monitor before B'taav's side lit up.

"This is where we're going," Maddox continued. The center of the monitor displayed a single asteroid within a group of many more.

"An asteroid?" B'taav asked. "That's our destination?"

"Yes."

"Why?"

"You asked where we're going and I've told you. The rest can wait."

B'taav considered the coordinates. He pressed several buttons and the monitor screen split in four, displaying the current position of the *Pilgrimage* in relation to their destination. He pressed another series of buttons and a single blip indicated where the Independent guessed the ship he spotted was located along with the direction she was taking.

"What are our odds of getting where we need to go before they overtake us?"

B'taav ran several flight path simulations on the computer before settling on three he felt offered the best chance of a safe arrival. Each involved considerable use of asteroid cover.

"What are our odds?" Maddox repeated.

"We won't know until we try."

24

The first hour after spotting the spacecraft was tension filled. There was a very real fear that Lieutenant Daniels and his forces could descend on the *Pilgrimage* at any second. After that first hour passed, however, those tensions eased. Inquisitor Cer lingered in the bridge for a little afterwards. She reluctantly returned to her quarters, leaving B'taav, Maddox, and Rasp behind.

The last thing the ship needed, especially now, were two exhausted pilots.

B'taav skirted the edges of several large asteroids, more than once actually scraping the ship's underside. There were no complaints from either of his crewmates. As long as they were headed in the right direction and avoided detection, they were fine if their space craft suffered a few bumps and bruises.

By the end of his shift, B'taav was spent. His hands shook from the strain of gripping the ship's yoke and his head throbbed.

Inquisitor Cer took over the controls and noted the progress made to their destination. Because of the proximity the ship kept to the asteroids, her speed was much reduced. Instead of two full days before their arrival, they were looking at closer to three.

"We need to go faster," Inquisitor Cer said after taking control of the ship.

"I don't disagree," B'taav said. "But it's easier said than done. We could change things up."

"You have an idea?"

"Yes. We cut the shifts to four hours each. It'll keep us fresher."

"I'll see you in four hours," Inquisitor Cer said. "Rest up."

"I will," B'taav replied. "Good night."

The four hour shifts proved more intense than the eight hour shifts, if only because each time B'taav came on, he pushed the *Pilgrimage's* speed well beyond what he considered safe limits. Based on the distances covered while he rested, it was clear Inquisitor Cer did the same.

Once in a while, a loose piece of rock, at times the size of a human head, slammed against parts of the ship. The speed of the debris around them, thankfully, was slow in relation to their craft, and there was little danger of rupturing the hull. Over time, the near constant sounds of rocks slamming into the ship proved unnerving.

"She'll need a new paint job," B'taav said after one such object skipped off the hull.

Rasp, the Independent's sole audience, offered no response.

More hours passed.

Toward the end of his latest shift, and with their destination no longer very far away, the Independent's thoughts turned to what would happen when they did arrive. Would the crew still need him? If they didn't, then what? Would he be escorted to the decompression chamber once more, and this time offered only one way to leave?

"How are we doing?" Maddox asked as he entered the cockpit.

"Not bad," B'taav said. He barely noticed Rasp leave.

"Keeping the pilot shifts short has proven a good idea, Independent. We've trimmed some time."

"More importantly we're down to five more hours before our arrival at the...asteroid," B'taav said. "Give or take."

Maddox sat on the vacated navigator's chair just behind B'taav. He closed his eyes and let his head settle back. The stress of the trip was evident in his face as well.

"You should get some rest, too."

"They'll be plenty of time afterwards," Maddox said.

Despite his words, the bartender's eyelids dropped. A little while later, his breathing grew heavy.

B'taav let the bartender sleep. His eyes wandered across the length of the front windows, searching hard for any sign of pursuing craft while keeping the ship as close to cover as possible. So focused was he on this task that he was startled to find someone standing beside him.

It was the black haired boy from days before, the one he found –or rather had found him– in the engine room. In the boy's hands was his ever-present red ball.

"This isn't the time, kid" B'taav said. He kept his voice low so as not to startle the child or awaken Maddox. "You should get back to your quarters and your mother."

Instead of doing so, the boy walked to the co-pilot's chair, to the left of B'taav, and sat down. Curiosity got the better of the Independent.

"What's your name?" he asked the child.

The boy did not reply.

"How old are you?"

Again, no reply.

"Can you speak at all? No?"

The boy stared out the window.

"You're right," B'taav said.   "That's where my attention should be."

B'taav's focus returned to his piloting. Now and again, however, he glanced at the boy. He watched in fascination as the child examined the de-activated controls before him. After a while he let his red ball slip from his fingers. It fell to the floor. The boy pressed several of the de-activated buttons. His dull, sleepy eyes suddenly came alive. It was as if he had some primitive recognition of the function of what lay before him.

"That's how we fly the ship," B'taav said. The boy grabbed the co-pilot's yoke and pushed it forward. His movements proved graceful.

"That's how we maneuver."

The boy released the yoke and allowed it to settle into a neutral position. He then grabbed and pulled at it once more. B'taav allowed the boy to continue playing. After a few minutes, it dawned on him the boy wasn't playing after all. He was mimicking the Independent's moves. When B'taav turned the ship to the left, the boy turned his de-activated yoke in the same direction. When he pressed any series of buttons, the boy did the same on his station.

"You're a natural," B'taav said. At this point, he didn't expect the child to reply. He was shocked when the boy did.

"...nat..." the boy muttered.

"What was that?"

The boy's eyes were focused forward, his hands steering the ship with the inactive control.

B'taav pressed a couple of buttons before him and activated the monitors on the boy's side.

"Take a look," he said.

The boy's eyes shifted down to the monitors. On them were readouts of the ship's status and flight path. The boy stared at the monitors for a few seconds before looking out the front window again.   All the while, he continued copying B'taav's moves.

B'taav slowed the ship down and performed a tight glide past three tumbling rocks. He banked the craft then steered her hard to the right. He turned the ship's power up and fractionally increased her velocity before slowing her down and banking once again. The procedure required many actions on his part. When the ship cleared the latest barrier, he glanced at the boy. To his surprise, he realized the child was no longer mimicking his actions.

He was *anticipating* them.

"How could you know?"

A familiar hiss came from the rear of the cockpit, indicating the door leading inside slid open. The gray haired lady entered the bridge.

"Nathaniel!" she said.

Maddox stirred but did not awaken.

The woman hurriedly approached the boy. She picked his red ball up from the floor and spun the co-pilot's chair around.

"I hope he didn't bother you," she said.

"He's been great company," B'taav replied. "I'm sorry I didn't call to tell you he was here. Then again, I don't think I'm allowed to use the intercom. And even if I did, I wouldn't know who to address."

The boy noted the ball in his mother's hand. His right hand reached for it, but before it did he noticed B'taav. The sullen expression on his face melted. A very small smile found its way onto his faded lips.

The gray haired lady noticed this.

"He's never done anything like that before," she said. When she spoke, the child's smile disappeared. He again stared at his red ball.

"I gave Nathaniel his medication a while ago," the gray haired lady continued. "He usually goes to sleep afterwards and, frankly, so do I. And I did. He was sleeping, but at some point he must have gotten up and decided to wander."

"Medication?"

"He's not entirely well, as you've probably noticed. I do the best I can for him, but fear he will never function as an independent adult."

"I don't mean to pry, but have you taken him to a specialist?" B'taav asked. "There must be some kind of procedure...?"

"None," the gray haired lady said. "There was a chance, years ago, when he was a newborn, to treat the infection that crippled his nervous system. Unfortunately, my late husband and I were living in a rather distant world at that time and didn't have the advantages of modern medicine or technology. It wasn't until he was four years old that we were able to get him proper care. By then, it was too late."

"Sorry."

"At least the medication helps. And who knows, maybe one day..."

She didn't finish her thought. She motioned to Maddox.

"He's been through a lot."

"He's not the only one."

"Perhaps, when this is over, we can sit down and formally introduce ourselves."

"That would be illuminating."

"How are we doing?"

"We're getting very close to our destination and we haven't been discovered by Daniels' boys. I'd say we're doing pretty well."

"Where are they?"

"I wish I knew."

"Why don't you use the ship sensors?"

"That wouldn't be a very good idea."

"Why not?"

"The sensor's resonant waves give us a view of the area and whatever ships are within range, but the signal's source can be back-tracked. Those hunting us will have a very clear look at our location. Use the sensors and we see them, but they will see us."

"Oh. Well, we're confident you'll get us safety to where we're going."

"We?"

"If I say any more, your sleeping friend will get upset."

The gray haired lady leaned closer to the Independent.

"Suffice to say, B'taav, *we* have confidence that you'll get us to safety." She leaned back and looked around the blank monitors before staring out at the asteroids floating around the ship. The frustration of not knowing what lay around the *Pilgrimage* was evident on her face. "I really do wish we could use those sensors," she muttered.

All was quiet for a few seconds. B'taav took the ship through its paces while the gray haired lady watched. All was serene. All was peaceful.

And then an ear shattering clatter filled the bridge and the cockpit was bathed in a dull red light. Screeching alarms blared and B'taav lurched forward. His eyes ran across the control panel. It took him a moment to realize the ship's long-range sensors were activated. On the sensor monitor B'taav spotted nearly a dozen blips off the starboard side of the *Pilgrimage*. He immediately shut the sensor off, but the damage was done.

"What happened?" the gray haired lady asked.

"Someone turned on the long-range sensors," B'taav said. "I...I got a peek at where Daniels' boys were."

"And they saw us...?"

B'taav's normally pale features turned even paler.

"Of course."

25

"What the hell is going on?"

The voice was Maddox's. His eyes were still half closed but he was waking fast. The door leading into the bridge opened and Cer ran into the room. She drew her fusion gun and trained it at B'taav.

"What the hell happened?" Maddox continued. "Why did you set off the sensors?"

B'taav slowly lifted his hands. He did not respond, instead allowing Inquisitor Cer a clear view of the cockpit controls. The frown on her forehead deepened when she noted the boy sitting in the co-pilot's chair and the displays on his monitor.

"He didn't turn on the sensors," Cer said. She put the gun away.

"What do you mean?" Maddox asked.

"The sensors were activated from the co-pilot's chair," Cer said. "Where the boy sits."

All eyes turned to Nathaniel.

"What?" the gray haired lady began. "There's no way—"

Maddox was having none of it.

"Lady, get that boy out of here!" he yelled.

"You are here to serve us, not the other way around," the gray haired lady snapped back. "I will not have you yelling at Nathaniel or me. Is that understood?"

"Perfectly," Maddox said. "When the time comes, I'll make sure Lieutenant Daniels' men talk to you and your boy in nice, friendly tones from the very moment they stick us in their brig."

The gray haired lady pulled Nathaniel out of the co-pilot's chair and left the bridge. Inquisitor Cer sat in the just vacated chair.

"Where are Daniels' ships?" Maddox asked.

"Most of them are on our starboard side," B'taav replied. He pulled up the sensor scan image on his monitor. "No doubt they've moved by now."

"Right at us," Inquisitor Cer said.

She activated her controls as B'taav slid the *Pilgrimage* past a large red asteroid. Beyond it lay another of equal size that twisted in a wild arc. B'taav kept the *Pilgrimage* well away from it. He noted Inquisitor Cer was re-running the commands issued from the co-pilot's chair.

"Did the boy really set off the sensors?" B'taav asked.

"So it would seem."

"How could he do that?" Maddox asked. "Every bit of sensitive equipment in the bridge is password protected."

"The boy entered the correct password," Cer said. "He somehow figured it out."

"That can't be. He'd have to be some kind of genius, and that kid is *not* a genius."

"He mirrored my actions while I was piloting the ship."

"Perhaps he overheard someone mention the code."

Maddox considered this but ultimately shook his head.

"I can't recall ever mentioning the codes before the boy."

"Maybe someone else did."

"There is another question," Inquisitor Cer said. "Of all the things he could have done after accessing the ship's commands, why did he set off those sensors?"

B'taav thought about that for a few seconds.

"Just before they came on, Nathaniel's mother and I were talking about them. I told her we didn't know where Daniels' ships were and she wondered why we didn't use the sensors to detect their position. I explained the dangers of doing so. She said something to the effect that she wished they could be used."

"You think the boy did this to please his mother?" Inquisitor Cer asked.

"It's as good a theory as any."

"That's all well and good, but we need to move on before Daniels' boys pump a battle ship's worth of missiles up our collective asses," Maddox said.

"That time is past," Cer muttered. "They know where we are. We're as good as caught."

"You're giving up?"

"They know where we are, they know our maximum velocity, and they have a far superior force," Cer said. "By my estimate, we only have a few hours before we're surrounded. Once surrounded, we don't stand a chance."

"None?"

A heavy silence filled the bridge for several seconds.

"We have one chance," B'taav finally said. He faced Maddox. "But for it to work, you're going to have to give me some more information. I need to know why our destination is in the middle of nowhere. I also need to know how many people we have on board and exactly what cargo, if any, we need to get to that destination. You will tell me all this along with detailed specs on this ship's defensive and offensive weaponry and escape pod status."

"Like hell I will."

"Inquisitor Cer is correct, Maddox. Lieutenant Daniels has surely ordered his ships to surround us. They have the superior forces and the luxury of time. If you're unwilling to give me the information I ask, then may I suggest you instruct the others on board to start rehearsing what they'll say to Daniels when he captures us."

Maddox looked at Cer and found her staring right back at him.

"I'm out of options," Inquisitor Cer told the bartender. "But I'm not as well versed on Epsillon fighter specs nor have I escaped Daniels' pursuit before. B'taav has an advantage over me in both areas."

Maddox shook his head.

"I have to talk to—"

"We're short on time as it is," Cer interrupted. "Either the Independent is in on this, or he's not. If we're extraordinarily lucky, we might make it a little farther. You have to make a decision."

Maddox exhaled. The tension in the room was thick. After several seconds, Maddox closed his eyes and drew a deep breath.

"Fine," he muttered. He typed in several commands on the ship's central computer. When he was done, he took a step back. On the lower monitor appeared a file.

"Read it," Maddox said. "It gives the details of our destination. As for this ship, there are twelve total passengers on board."

"Including us?"

"Yes."

"What about the ship's cargo and equipment?"

Maddox retrieved another file.

"There you go."

B'taav opened the first file. Upon reading it, his dark eyes widened and his mouth opened. When he faced Maddox, he found the bartender holding his fusion gun. He powered a charge and pressed the barrel of the weapon against the Independent's neck.

"It's not that I don't trust you, B'taav," Maddox said. "But if we're caught, even after I'm convinced you've done everything you could to keep us away from Daniels, I'll still make damn sure you're the first to suffer. You understand?"

B'taav nodded.

"Good. Let's get to work."

26

Oscar Theodor, the senior pilot of fighter craft *Tango 13*, drew even with the wobbling gray asteroid and flipped his vessel over its large, spinning mass. He examined the view screen and his monitor. The other twenty fighter crafts were nearly in position. Their flight coordinates were exact and difficult to maintain, but to snare their prey, they had to form, and maintain, their circle.

"Is it too much to ask that you turn on your sensors one more time?" he muttered to his unseen prey, knowing full well the craft they were pursuing would do no such thing.

Four hours had passed since the occupants of the pursued craft committed their mistake, and in the interval the *Tango* ships were ordered to adopt a standard surround tactic. It worked well in the vast emptiness of outer space but proved tricky to implement in this dense asteroid field. Still, the circle was closed and capture was a matter of time.

Theodor gazed through the glass bubble that surrounded him and turned the magnification of his goggles on. The lenses over his eyes buzzed with mechanical life. He carefully examined the area around him.

We'll spot them. By any means available.

"This is *Tango 16* calling *Tango 13*," a voice crackled over Theodor's speaker. "Approaching section 1001.45. I...I have a visual of our target. Guys, I think I see her! She's right in front of me!"

Theodor turned to his right. The magnification lenses again buzzed as he zoomed in on that location. Euphoria quickly turned to disappointment.

"*Tango 16*, this is *Tango 13*," he said. "I have the object in sight. Sorry, Phil, it's just a piece of twisted metal."

There was a long pause.

"Acknowledged, *Tango 13*," the voice over the radio finally replied. "Shit. After this is over, I'm going to get my eyes checked."

"Better luck next time. *Tango 13* out."

Theodor steered his ship over and between several more asteroids. Every few seconds, he eyed the sensor readout.

Turn your sensors on, he again hoped. *End this misery.*

Without meaning to, Theodor whistled an impatient tune.

The week and a half they spent out here, in the middle of nowhere, was getting to everyone. The sensor flare couldn't have come at a better, or worse, time. Better for morale because many of the search crew worried the craft might have doubled back or somehow slipped past them. Worse because Theodor's eight hour shift would end soon, and he might not be the pilot on deck when the capture was finally made.

Think positive thoughts. Who knows, maybe in the next hour you'll be the one to corner them. You'll be the hero.

Yeah, right.

Theodore continued whistling, louder. He was hungry and he was tired and more than a little angry that—

"Wait until you're asleep," a gravely male voice crackled over the ship's intercom. It was Steve, one of the two replacement pilots. "They tell me I've got a lovely singing voice."

Theodor laughed and, to the eternal gratitude of those below decks, stopped whistling.

The rocks floated by as if Theodor were at the base of a mountain staring up at an avalanche dropping, in slow motion, toward him. Slow and peaceful...

Theodor's eyes closed for a second.

"Another half-hour," he said. "That's all. Unless you guys would like to tell us where you—"

Theodor never finished his thought. His long-range sensor flashed with a newly acquired blip. It was near the center of the circle the *Tango* fighter crafts had formed.

The communicator came alive with multiple voices. Theodor, the senior most officer in the current formation, activated his speaker and the communications computer silenced the other voices.

"Target ship's sensors are active," he said, both to the other craft and the *Dakota*, trailing many thousands of kilometers behind.

Theodor turned from the monitor and stared out the port window and in the direction of the sensor ping. He increased the magnification in his lenses to their maximum. After a moment he again clicked on the communicator. There was considerable excitement in his voice when he said:

"This is *Tango 13* to all units: I have a visual of our target. I repeat: I have a visual of our target. Her location is 2332.44."

"Acknowledged, *Tango 13.*"

The voice sliced through the tension within the *Dakota's* bridge like a machete splitting brush. Lieutenant Daniels took three long strides and sat in his chair at the center of the bridge. He leaned forward, as if preparing to sprint.

"Velocity of target?" he asked.

"Seventy five kilometers per hour."

Slow, Daniels thought. *Why?*

"All *Tango* crafts, this is Lieutenant Daniels. You are to close in to fifty kilometers of the subject."

Daniels rubbed his chin as one after another *Tango* ship acknowledged his order. It was only then that he pulled his personal monitor closer. He examined the visual readout which included the course of each of the *Tango* ships. The *Dakota*, the largest craft on the monitor, hobbled far behind the last of the *Tango* flight group.

We should be closer, just in case.

It was a miracle they had flight capacity at all. The entire mechanical staff was still working feverishly on the damage caused by the decoy ship sent toward the Erebus Displacer the week before. It was good fortune the explosion caused only minor structural damage to the ship's fourth propulsion engine.

And a good thing there were no fatalities, he thought. *Or else all hell would* really *break loose. Then again, the damage proved useful, didn't it?*

Once this was done, Daniels estimated the *Dakota* would require a month at the Central Docks to regain her full thruster capabilities. However, what happened that far in the future held little interest to him today.

"This is *Tango 13*," Oscar Theodor's voice came over the radio. "Confirming pursuit craft is a class VII Oscarlot."

Data on the craft appeared on Lieutenant Daniels' monitor. The Oscarlot was primarily used for cargo runs and was a favorite of the more successful scavengers operating out of *Titus*. Given her speed when she first escaped, it was obvious her engines had been modified. Preliminary video images of the craft appeared on Daniels' monitor. The ship looked intact.

Why did you use your sensors? Daniels thought. *You've been successful for so long and you're clearly undamaged. Why give up now?*

"*Tango 13*, this is *Dakota*," Daniels said into the communicator. "Are the target's long range sensors still active?"

Because of the distance they lagged behind, the sensor

readings received from the pursued craft by the *Dakota* were at least five minutes old. Communication transmissions relayed from *Tango* craft to *Tango* craft, on the other hand, were only a few seconds old.

"Yes sir."

Daniels shook his head.

"*Tango* group, be advised to use extreme caution. I have a feeling our friends are up to more of their tricks."

The *Pilgrimage* flew through the asteroid field as if an arrow sprung from a bow. It kicked through a cloud of debris as if plowing past a swarm of bugs.

"That's gotta hurt," Theodor muttered as the rocks, some the size of an armored vehicle, bounced off it.

After a few minutes of careful piloting, *Tango 13* pulled within the ordered fifty kilometers behind the craft. Theodor examined his instruments. While he did, *Tango 5* appeared beside his ship. The pilot of that craft, Jennifer Gibbs, was near enough to wave.

"This is *Tango 5*," she said over the communicator. "Theodor, I don't get it."

"What's that, *Tango 5*?"

"They've avoided us pretty well so far, yet now they're making themselves a juicy target. I don't know about you, but I've got missiles locked on their engines. They try anything funny and they're gone."

"Don't get jittery," Theodor countered. "The higher ups want them alive."

"Too bad," Gibbs responded. "We could have finished this a while ago. Why do you think they've given up?"

"Maybe their engine's cracked up. Hell, maybe they're just tired."

"Do you really think so?"

"No," Theodor admitted. "And neither does Lieutenant Daniels. That's why we're hanging back and surrounding them."

Theodor eyed the computer monitor and the various blips drawing around the *Pilgrimage*.

"Won't be long now."

The *Pilgrimage*, for her part, continued moving in a straight line. She approached, and barely avoided, a rock roughly half her size.

"That was damn close," Gibbs said. "You think their controls are frozen?"

"They better hope not," Theodor said. "You see what's coming?"

Jennifer Gidds stared forward and magnified her flight goggles. Not very far away and approaching fast was a massive asteroid fragment.

"Maybe they don't want to be taken alive."

"The Oscarlots are well reinforced. If they run into that rock at the speed they're going, they won't crack up."

"The ship might not crack up, but what will happen to the passengers?"

"They better strap themselves in real tight," Theodor replied.

Lieutenant Daniels' mind processed the developments presented in real time on the main view screen. He tried to understand what was happening, but ultimately shook his head.

"What the hell are you up to B'taav?" he muttered.

The *Pilgrimage's* approach to the asteroid fragment continued without the slightest deviation.

"This is *Tango 13* to *Dakota*. Maybe they're asleep and need a wakeup call. Permission to fire a shot across ship's bow?"

"Permission granted," Daniels replied. "Oh, and Theodor?"

"Yes sir? "

"Try not to make it quite as close as last time."

Oscar Theodor primed a port missile and set her course. After he double checked all systems, he pressed a large red button at the top of his directional joystick. A single missile shot out of *Tango 13*'s rack and flew toward the cargo ship.   It skimmed past the *Pilgrimage's* port side.

No one on board that ship appeared to notice the streaking projectile.

Oscar Theodor clicked on his communicator.

"*Dakota*, this is *Tango 13*. ETA for *Pilgrimage* impact is three minutes."

The lines on Daniels' forehead deepened.

He rubbed his hands and sat down. The cargo ship was going to crash. There was no longer any doubt about it, just as there was no longer the possibility of stopping her from doing so. The fighter craft could try, of course.   They could fire on the *Pilgrimage's* engines and hope to disable them. But the forward momentum guaranteed some kind of collision.

The only possibility to avoid this was to have a *Tango* craft roll up alongside the *Pilgrimage* and have the men aboard it jump the breach, board the errant ship, and take control. They could then guide her to safety. But time was too tight, and there was a very real possibility the ship could be primed with explosives just as the decoy ship was back at *Titus*. And if the ship's controls were indeed compromised, then boarding the craft served no purpose.

Daniels considered various scenarios and explanations for what was unfolding before him. The most logical explanation was also the grimmest: The crew of the ship was already dead, perhaps a mass suicide to prevent capture. But he had a hard time picturing B'taav going away that quietly. Maybe he was taken by surprise, the first victim...maybe his *Tango* group was following a ghost ship.

No. After all this, they wouldn't give up. Not—

A tiny smile suddenly appeared on Daniels' face. The lines so evident on his forehead disappeared.

"Very clever," he said. Just as quickly as it appeared, the smile faded.

"Maintain your distance from the ship," Daniels barked. "If they want to crash, let them."

The *Pilgrimage* came to a jarring stop when it collided head on with the asteroid. The ship's front section crumpled while her rear remained largely intact.

"This is *Tango 13* calling *Dakota*," Oscar Theodor said. "Cargo ship *Pilgrimage* has collided with the asteroid. Repeat, *Pilgrimage* has collided with the asteroid. She is heavily damaged but structure remains stable. I do not see –I repeat– I do *not* see any evidence of a breach or loss of internal atmosphere. It is possible there are survivors aboard. Awaiting further instructions."

"This is *Dakota*," Lieutenant Daniels replied. "Maintain your distance. Wait for us to arrive."

"Sir? If someone survived that crash, they'll need medical—"

"I heard you the first time. Now listen to me: Maintain your distance and wait for us to arrive."

"Yes sir," Theodor said and shut the communicator off. "I heard *you* the first time, too, you cold blooded bastard."

The twenty four *Tango* ships did as ordered and kept their distance from the damaged cargo ship. The asteroid the *Pilgrimage* collided against slowly spun away.

Idle chatter filled the communicators as members of the flight crews calculated how long it would take before the *Dakota* arrived and they would be allowed to help those trapped or injured within the useless craft. Ten minutes later, they were glad they were ordered to keep their distance.

It was at that point that an onboard explosive ripped the *Pilgrimage* to pieces.

27

In the shadow of an asteroid far from the *Pilgrimage's* remains and just outside the *Tango* fighter's snare, there was movement. At first slow, then quicker. The object was tiny, less than one twentieth the size of the *Pilgrimage*. Its slender, cylindrical shape identified her as an escape sled, a bare bones vessel used by crews either in the event of catastrophic failure of the mother craft or as a device to transport personnel from one ship to another.

The escape sled was a skeletal metal frame propelled by a small engine and open to space. Its range was short. Efficiency, and not comfort, was the primary concern in her construction and use.

The pilot eased the craft around several asteroids. He ignored the momentary flash of light that lit up the area far before him.

He and the co-pilot, their features hidden beneath bulky silver environmental suits, worked the controls and increased the sled's speed. They were still many kilometers from their destination, and there was the very real fear the craft would not have the fuel to make it that far.

The pilot stole a glance behind, at the other passengers in the sled. Somehow, ten people fit into the remaining cramped space. The passengers' features were also hidden beneath their environmental suits, but the pilot knew at least one of them for he was much smaller than the rest.

The boy with the red ball.

It took nearly a full day of careful piloting before the sled pulled in very close to an enormous gray asteroid. Its two pilots were directed by one of the passengers to the lower section of this rock and told to maintain their position. The passenger giving the orders then activated a transmitter and a faint red light come to life in the asteroid's lower quarter.

A small, perfectly rectangular section of the asteroid moved forward and slid away, like some rocky window, revealing a dark, cavernous space within. A faint pattern of white lights that faded into the distance came on. It was a landing strip used to direct ships inside the asteroid.

"Go on," Maddox, the man with the transmitter, instructed

the pilots.

They activated the sled's thrusters and their craft floated inside the hidden base. Afterwards, the rectangular doors shut behind them.

The pilots flew the sled forward, following the landing lights. Soon, they arrived at a small landing strip.

The sled's pilot couldn't help but marvel at what he saw. There was enough space here for three class C cargo ships like the *Pilgrimage*. There was little doubt that at more than one time in the past, this landing site was fully occupied. At this moment, however, there was only one large, and very old, spacecraft parked within. The escape sled landed beside her.

"*Xendos*," one of the pilots muttered, reading the faded lettering that identified the ancient craft.

In seconds the escape sled's magnetic landing clamps were activated and the vehicle was locked down. The pilots shut their control panel and the lights of their environmental suits came on.

"We're here," B'taav said. "Now what?"

The *Tango* squad pilots weren't experts when it came to salvage protocol, yet did the best they could in recovering the fragmented remains of the *Pilgrimage*. Afterwards, they returned to the *Dakota* which, by that point, was parked just outside the search zone.

One hour after returning to their mother ship, the pieces of the *Pilgrimage* were spread out on landing strip 12 of the battleship. Lieutenant Daniels eyed those pieces and motioned to the salvage specialists combing through the debris.

"Any sign of human remains?"

The salvage specialist closest to Lieutenant Daniels shook her head.

"None whatsoever, sir."

Lieutenant Daniels nodded.

"Just as I thought," he said. "That's the second decoy they've thrown our way."

B'taav and Inquisitor Cer stepped out of the escape sled and climbed down her short metal ladder. In the airless zero gravity within the asteroid, they did not feel the drag of the suit's weight on them. They were thankful to stretch, and imagined the other passengers were just as eager to get out of their seats as well. Maddox, however, instructed them to wait.

B'taav and Inquisitor Cer stepped lightly onto the landing strip floor and kicked up a layer of dust. The lights within the landing bay were very dim, and the duo could barely see the roof or far walls.

Inquisitor Cer removed a small black case from the underside of the sled and turned her attention to the *Xendos*. She admired the ancient craft for a few seconds while B'taav increased the power to his suit's lights. He walked past Cer and to a double door sculpted into the asteroid wall. It led, B'taav presumed, into the asteroid base itself. Inquisitor Cer approached his side and examined the door's controls. Her mind remained on the *Xendos*.

"Class 34 Phaecian Cargo ship," Inquisitor Cer said. "You don't see many of them around anymore. She was discontinued—"

"There will be time to admire her afterwards," Maddox said.

"Yes sir," B'taav replied and waved to the seated passengers.

"Remember, we'll hear everything you say," Maddox continued.

B'taav and Cer understood. The environmental suits on board the *Pilgrimage* were simple, and cheap, civilian fare and contained equally simple communication devices. The devices transmitted on a standard frequency and, as long as they were within range, all others in the environmental suits or using communication equipment could hear what was said between them. There were no secondary channels, there was no encryption software. All conversations were public.

B'taav glanced at his co-pilot. "Let's not keep our audience waiting."

Inquisitor Cer opened the door's control panel and replaced the long drained energy cell with a fresh one taken from her black case. Remarkably, the door's controls showed signs of life.

"I never would have believed this," B'taav said.

"Why not?"

"Because the base is an antique. There must have been some degradation of equipment in all this time."

"The last tenants appear to have taken great care in shutting her down properly. Without atmosphere, there is little decay. We just have to give the control panel time to warm up."

They did just that. Soon, the control readings were green. Inquisitor Cer entered a code and the door slid open, revealing a long, tight corridor. Here and there were dust covered boxes waiting to be loaded up or put away, but ultimately cursed to remain exactly where they were.

Cer and B'taav followed the corridor to a large metal door. A wilted yellow plaque identified the area beyond the door as the control tower.

Inquisitor Cer removed another, larger energy cell from her black case and, after opening this door's control panel, replaced a similarly sized depleted cell. In seconds, the door locks were charged and ready for operation.

"Two for two," B'taav marveled. "Say what you will, they don't make 'em like they used to."

Inquisitor Cer nodded.

"Maddox, this is Cer. We have the control room door powered up."

"Understood," Maddox replied. His voice was marred by static. The base was constructed to dampen communication signals, for fear that outside ears might hear.

"We'll need the code now," B'taav said.

Maddox listed a series of numbers and repeated them.

Inquisitor Cer keyed the code into the panel. Both Cer and B'taav then stepped back as the ancient door slid open, revealing the cramped control tower and walls filled with ancient computer equipment.

"We're in," Inquisitor Cer said.

B'taav examined the equipment and zeroed in on the base's life support system.

"Over here."

"I haven't seen anything like this in quite a while," Inquisitor Cer said. She removed a pair of panel covers, eventually finding the life support system's energy cells. They were far larger than those that operated either of the doors they already passed.

"This will take a few minutes."

Inquisitor Cer removed the straps which kept the cell in place. She set the depleted batteries aside and, for the third time, reached into her black case and retrieved fresh cells. The modern power cell was a fraction of the old cell's size, but Inquisitor Cer had anticipated the discrepancy. She reached deeper into her black case and pulled out a cradle. She placed the fresh power cell into this cradle and then snapped the cradle into place.

When Inquisitor Cer was done, she gazed at the terminal monitors. They flickered on after a minute or two. Three of the six monitors sputtered and immediately went dark. Another displayed a faint, blurry image. The remaining two, however, were as good as new. The command options were displayed with crystal clarity.

Inquisitor Cer keyed in a few commands.

"How long has it been since anyone was here?"

"Curious?"

"If I wasn't, you'd need to check if I still had a pulse."

"Obviously, she's been here for well over two hundred years and rendered obsolete the second the Erebus War ended. That might be the last time anyone was on board."

"When did the base become operational?"

"That I don't know," Cer said. "Could have been a hundred, maybe even two hundred years before the war. Back then, both sides spent unholy amounts of money on intelligence gathering."

"Both sides?"

"To date, we've found twenty Epsillon bases similar to this one hidden on our side of Erebus. I doubt we've found them all."

"Even if you did, I'm not so sure any of our equipment would work after all these years."

"You'd be surprised."

"You think they expected someone to come back?"

"We're here, aren't we?"

"Enough with the chit chat," Maddox interrupted. "How long before the life support is up?"

"It will take at least a half hour for the computers to complete a system review. Afterwards, the repair robots will be sent out to take care of whatever problems are found in the various systems. They will do this in order of seriousness."

"Let's just hope the repair robots don't need repairs themselves," B'taav said.

"Anything else, we'll have to wait and see," Cer said.

"What if we can't activate the life support systems?" Maddox asked.

"The environmental controls within our suits provide no more than two full days' worth of air and heat," Inquisitor Cer said. "If we are to make it any further, our only hope lies in getting these systems working."

28

They waited a little over a half hour before Inquisitor Cer activated the central computers. Their processing time was slow compared to modern systems and both she and B'taav worried the computer's internal organs might be damaged. In time, however, all command screens came up.

"We're in," Inquisitor Cer said. She worked the controls and asked for and received information on the status of each and every one of the life support systems within the asteroid base.

"What do you have?" Maddox asked after a while.

"I see a few interruptions in the auxiliary circuitry. Minor stuff."

"And the energy grid?"

Inquisitor Cer's fingers clumsily worked the keyboard.

"It's damaged," she said.

"How bad?"

"We've got roughly sixty percent power flow."

"Are you sure?" Maddox asked. There was alarm in his voice.

"Yes. The diagnostic system is crude compared to what we have today, but I've isolated at least five major problems."

"Are they repairable?"

"Yes."

"Sixty percent is pretty good for a system that hasn't been used for two hundred years," B'taav said.

"Good. But not good enough."

"What about the repair robots?"

"If these readings are accurate, only a third of them are still active. They are—"

Inquisitor Cer pointed to the other side of the room. One of the repair robots, a small square box with a set of black wheels, scurried past them and entered an open panel.

"Anything you can do to hurry the process?" an impatient Maddox asked.

"There's always something to do," Inquisitor Cer replied.

B'taav and Cer moved past dark corridors and deeper into the body of the abandoned Phaecian base. The place was a model of Spartan functionality. Rooms and corridors were no larger than they absolutely needed to be. The furniture, all of it bolted to the floors, was boxy, firm, and uncomfortable.

B'taav and Cer spent an hour criss-crossing the station and repairing energy lines and computer systems. The maintenance storage room proved the only room within the base still carrying a full complement of supplies. The station's last occupants removed all foods and weapons before departing.

"Other than the obvious, what did they do here during the war?" B'taav asked.

Inquisitor Cer lowered her tools. The faceplate of her helmet, as was the case with B'taav's, was fogged because of her heavy breathing resulting from their strenuous work.

"You mean other than spy on the Epsillon war efforts? They left behind a cargo craft. Perhaps at one time or another they used it to raids merchant vessels and confiscate their supplies."

"Wouldn't that attract unwanted attention?"

"Of course. More likely the ship was used for exactly what it was designed: To ferry cargo to the base. For its time, it was quick and she is armed. She has a single fusion cannon mounted on its front."

"Hardly a fearsome offensive, or defensive, weapon."

"Yet a weapon nonetheless."

"Ok, so she moved supplies to this base. Where did she get those supplies from? It's not like a Phaecian vessel could slip undetected into an Epsillon Displacer and take a ride across the border. Not unless—"

B'taav didn't finish his thought. A knowing smile appear on his face.

"You guys had your own Displacer around here, didn't you?"

"At one time. It didn't survive the explosion."

"I believe you," B'taav said after a while.

"Oh? Why?"

"If it still existed, I doubt you would have admitted you had it in the first place."

B'taav and Cer returned to the control room a full three full hours after originally leaving it. They were hungry and tired but pleased with their progress. The damaged energy grid was mostly patched up. Energy readings indicated that the station's power was a little over the desired seventy-five percent.

"Maddox, do you read me?" Inquisitor Cer said.

"Go ahead."

"We're ready to activate life support and artificial gravity."

"Understood. We're going to stay strapped in the sled until

you initiate the artificial gravity."

"Agreed."

"Easy with the increments," B'taav said. "We wouldn't want anything to come crashing down too hard."

Inquisitor Cer pressed a series of buttons and both she and B'taav felt a slow increase in the pull of gravity. After so long without it, it was a welcome feeling. On the opposite side of the room, a pair of crates floating knee-high gently touched down on the floor. All around the station similar items also dropped.

"The station now has standard gravity," Cer said.

"Acknowledged," Maddox replied. "Now, get the life support systems online. We'd like to get out of these suits."

"You're not the only one."

Inquisitor Cer worked the controls some more. Reading indicated a rise in temperature, but because of their environmental suits, neither B'taav nor Inquisitor Cer felt the change. Soon, the displays indicated the station once again had breathable air.

"I'm seeing no leaks. Atmosphere is stable."

"And the temperature?"

"Best I can do is three degrees Celsius."

"Chilly, but livable," B'taav said. "Now comes the hard part: Taking off our suits. How much faith do we have in the readouts from these old computers?"

"Just like an Independent to question an Inquisitor's faith," Cer said. She reached into one of her suit's pockets and removed a small black environmental sensor. She activated it and, after reading the results, nodded.

"That old computer had it right," Inquisitor Cer said and offered the Independent a wink. "Faith can take you far, but verification completes your journey."

Inquisitor Cer removed a series of bolts that kept her helmet in place. She unscrewed it. A loud hiss was heard as the air from her suit rushed out. After removing her helmet, she stood still. Her yellow hair was flat and her stony brown eyes stared forward.

Finally, she took a deep breath of the station's air.

B'taav watched her with equal parts fascination and dread. After a few seconds, the Inquisitor eyed the Independent and said:

"What are you waiting for?"

"The station is functional."

B'taav and Cer stood beside the escape sled. They no longer wore their helmets but remained in their environmental suits. The heat emitted from them was welcome. The passengers of the sled remained in their suits. But not for long.

One by one, they rose and eagerly removed their gear. A couple, Maddox and Rasp, stepped onto the landing strip before doing so.

B'taav watched them all, for it was the first time the Independent saw the faces of all the passengers aboard the *Pilgrimage*. When the decision was made to use the escape sled, B'taav and Cer were the last to suit up before putting the ship on autopilot. When they stepped into the control section of the escape sled, everyone else was already suited up and in place.

B'taav knew and had already seen Rasp, Maddox, Inquisitor Cer, Nathaniel, and the gray haired lady. The remaining six passengers were all men. The largest of them were a trio seated together in the last section of the sled. They laid their helmets down and quickly unzipped their suits. Each was dressed in thin gray plastic body armor. B'taav recognized it as belonging to the Veils, a well-known for-hire mercenary outfit. They were likely here to protect one or all the passengers, and they each carried steel suitcases. No doubt their weapons were stored within.

The remaining three men were seated immediately in front of the Mercs. They showed their inexperience with the environmental suits by the amount of time it took to remove them.

The man closest to the escape sled's ladder was in his late forties. He was dressed head to toe in an elegant, high quality white suit. There was an incredible sadness on this man's face, as if he recently suffered a great loss.

The man next to him took even longer to remove his gear. When it was off, B'taav immediately recognized him, but not by name. The man wore a regal dark green robe that identified him as one of the Phaecian Empire's Territorial Cardinals. In the centuries of history of the Phaecian Empire, none of the fifty six Cardinals had *ever* ventured outside that Empire's borders. According to their religious dogma, to do so invited temptation and was therefore strictly prohibited. All diplomatic meetings between the Epsillon and Phaecians, at least on this side of the border, were conducted through intermediaries. Inquisitor Cer's presence among this group suddenly made perfect sense. She, like the three Veil Mercs at the back of the escape sled, was here to protect specific passengers.

B'taav also recognized the third, and last, of this trio of men. He stood slightly less than six feet tall and carried a delicate, prematurely aging frame. His hair was thin, his cheeks sunken in. In spite of this, he projected considerable power. Even here, in the middle of nowhere.

Stephen Gray.

He was a high ranking Epsillon Empire Industrialist and owner of both the Bandilion and Seriana companies. Each company had a long reach within the Epsillon Empire, from sophisticated weapon manufacturing to heavy cargo hauling to entertainment productions.

To say the least, it was an odd group.

A hand fell on B'taav's shoulder. Maddox stood beside him.

"Well done," Maddox said. For the first time since the trip began, his face carried something other than a scowl. "It isn't often you successfully evade the Epsillon Empire's finest headhunters."

"It's getting to be a habit," B'taav replied.

"And here I thought you were humble," Inquisitor Cer said.

A couple of the passengers chuckled at Inquisitor Cer's statement. The tension they felt was replaced by levity. The passengers of the escape sled broke up into smaller groups. Their conversations were informal, mostly complaints about the station's stale and very cold air. A couple admired the architecture of the place, while the three Mercs quietly checked their luggage. They did this away from any prying eyes.

The only ones not engaged in conversation were B'taav, Inquisitor Cer, and the boy with the red ball. The boy didn't seem aware of anything occurring around him.

B'taav noisily cleared his throat. The conversations around him died out.

"I don't mean to ruin your good cheer, but I'm worried," the Independent said.

"About?" Maddox asked.

"Daniels' ships. We escaped, but only for the time being. If they haven't done so already, they will realize no one was on board the *Pilgrimage* when it exploded. Lieutenant Daniels' considerable resources will be directed toward finding us once again."

"How will he do this?" Stephen Gray asked.

"The life support systems in this base are old and noisy, both sonically and electronically. In time, his ships will pick us up. At the very least, his ship's sensors will note the increase in temperature within this rock."

"This base has existed many years without detection," Cer countered.

"That was back when sensor equipment wasn't quite as sophisticated as it is now. If we give them time, they will find us."

"That's true," Maddox said. "But given the number of asteroids in this area, and unless we're colossally unlucky, we should be fine. At least for a few days. Certainly long enough to get the *Xendos* operational."

"The *Xendos*?" B'taav said. "Why?"

"This base was never intended to be our ultimate destination. We still have a ways to go. We only agreed to sacrifice the *Pilgrimage* because we knew about this ship." A deep frown formed on the bartender's face. "Had I known we might eventually need her, I would have spent more time making sure she was functional. As it is, it's up to us to get her moving before Daniels finds us."

29

With each breath they took of the stagnant and frigid air, the more they grew used to it.

B'taav, Inquisitor Cer, and Maddox took two hours examining the *Xendos*.

On the first, cursory look, they found several personal items including photographs, diaries, jewel boxes, discarded magazines, and books the ship's last crew left behind. In the corner of the main engine room, B'taav found a half-finished letter a crewman wrote to either his wife or lover. It was addressed to "Helen" and the author wished he could return to her side. Whether this happened would remain unknown.

Inquisitor Cer treated the material with respect and swore she would return the more personal material to their families, if it was at all possible.

The trio left the effects in a crew compartment and turned their attention to the ship's engines. They were a relic of ancient times, but were well preserved. The trick, obviously, was to treat them with great care while fixing them up.

"The engine design is simple enough," Inquisitor Cer told both B'taav and Maddox. Given her familiarity with Phaecian designed ships, she took the lead in the engine's refurbishing. "Our first step is to fix any leaks and replace batteries, liquids, and fuels."

"There were some spare parts on the lower decks," Maddox said. "There are also some fuel tanks."

"Let's hope none of that material has degraded, and that there's enough to take us where we need to go," B'taav said. "Where do we need to go?"

"We'll worry about that when we get the ship moving," Maddox replied.

"Does the base have a machine shop?" B'taav asked.

"I think so. It should be in the lower decks of the station, as well."

"Any parts we don't have, we may be able to make."

"That will take time."

"How long do you think we have before Daniels finds us?" Maddox asked B'taav.

"Four or five days at the very most. Sooner if we've angered him enough."

"And how long before the *Xendos* is up and running?"
"If I gave any estimate it would be little more than a guess."
"Then guess."
"It'll be very tight," B'taav said after a few seconds. "Very."

By the end of the first day, the process of charging the ship's fuel lines was initiated. Inquisitor Cer found several useful parts in a warehouse on the base's lower level. Those they couldn't find, Inquisitor Cer was able to replicate in the machine shop.

The following day, when the ship's batteries were charged, Inquisitor Cer accessed the ship's computers and ran several diagnostic tests. The ship needed some major work, but at least it was something she and the Independent could accomplish with time.

"Now how does it look?" Maddox asked them.

"We need at least five days," Inquisitor Cer said. "Maybe even a week."

B'taav rubbed his hands to keep warm. The previous day he, like Inquisitor Cer, wore a light gray work suit. Like the Inquisitor, that suit was smeared with a mix of oil and soot and almost completely black.

"We'll have to work non-stop," B'taav offered. "Too bad I never found the Accelerant pushers in *Titus*. We could use some of their product right about now."

While Inquisitor Cer spent time in the machine shop, the mute Rasp shadowed B'taav's movements in the *Xendos'* engine room and made sure the Independent didn't stray from his prescribed duties.

B'taav was either in the main engine room or shuffling down to the machine shop to pick up new parts. Each time he emerged from the *Xendos* and walked the corridors of the base, he saw either Inquisitor Cer or Maddox, but rarely anyone else. The remaining passengers were still being kept away from him.

In spite of this, later that day B'taav saw Stephen Gray and the Phaecian Cardinal walking together down one of the base's corridors. Their discussion was low but animated, befitting the fact that each man had such a different philosophical background.

At least they aren't fighting, B'taav thought. *Yet, anyway.*

Rasp noted B'taav's gaze and gave the Independent a strong push. It caused him to stumble, and he nearly dropped the fuel cell he cradled.

"I wouldn't try that again," the Independent said. "If this hits the ground hard enough, none of us will have to worry about Daniels anymore."

Rasp eyed the power cell.

"Old tech," B'taav explained. "It ruptures and the inside of this asteroid becomes considerably hotter."

Early in the third day of their work, B'taav spotted the gray haired lady and her mute boy walking just past the open door to the engine room of the *Xendos*. The boy looked directly through a small window in the rear of the ancient craft's engine room and at B'taav, who in turn waved at them.

The boy's expression was sullen and distant and he clutched his ever-present red ball in both hands.

The two walked around the deck and, after a few minutes, Maddox appeared from a side door and approached them. He said a few words to the gray haired lady and both she and the boy departed.

Rasp noticed B'taav attention was focused elsewhere and, after making sure he wasn't carrying anything that looked like it might explode, gave the Independent a strong push. B'taav fell to the floor.

"You really shouldn't do that," the Independent said.

Rasp's body tightened. His hands balled up into fists. A sadistic smile crept onto his face. He welcomed B'taav's reaction, whatever it would be.

The Independent took a deep breath and rose.

"If that's the way it has to be," he said.

B'taav turned away, and Rasp took advantage. He ran at the Independent, his right fist in full swing. But B'taav was quicker. He dodged Rasp's sucker punch and rammed his knee into the mute man's midsection. The air exploded out of the silent man's lungs and he fell to his knees.

For several seconds, he gasped for air and was at the mercy of the Independent. He looked up at B'taav with hateful red eyes.

B'taav swung his fist and connected with the man's jaw. The hit was solid, and Rasp fell to the ground, unconscious.

"Don't say you weren't warned."

The Independent dragged Rasp's body to the edge of the engine room and laid him down. B'taav took the man's fusion gun, cradled it in his hand, and then extended his arm fully away from his body. He held the gun that way for a second or two before sliding it into a tight space below the ship's main engine. He then returned to his station. After a few seconds, he spotted Maddox hurriedly approaching the ship. The bartender held his own gun.

The Independent sighed.

"So much for getting any work done."

Maddox cautiously stepped into the main engine room. He held his fusion gun before him and his eyes locked on the unconscious Rasp.

"He'll live," B'taav said. He wiped his greasy hands on a rag and continued his work.

Maddox approached the Independent and pushed the barrel of his gun against the man's back. The Independent slowly raised his hands.

"Who do you think you are?" Maddox said.

B'taav didn't answer. The pressure of the gun's barrel increased. The Independent's muscles tightened. He didn't want to act, but the bartender was giving him little choice.

"Put the gun down."

The voice came from behind Maddox. It was the gray haired lady. She stood at the door leading into the Engine room. At her side was Inquisitor Cer.

"He attacked Rasp," Maddox said. "We're done with him—"

"B'taav's been good so far," the gray haired lady countered. "Much better than we would –and *should*– have expected. He hasn't asked many questions or proven much of a bother."

"What do you call this?" Maddox yelled while pointing to Rasp's prone form.

"He's been our prisoner for a long time now. It was inevitable he'd need to burn off some steam. Rasp made it easy for him to do so."

The gray haired lady reached into the tight space under the engine and just below where Maddox stood. She retrieved Rasp's fusion gun from the hiding place B'taav had wedged it into. She gave the weapon to Maddox.

"Because you rushed out so quickly to confront our Independent, you didn't see him so very deliberately put this gun away," the gray haired lady continued. She lady turned to B'taav. "You knew we had you under surveillance, didn't you?"

"I suspected as much."

"But you couldn't be certain?"

"If you didn't have me under surveillance, and Rasp woke up before you arrived, I wanted to make sure our next confrontation wasn't...life-threatening."

"To Rasp?" the gray haired lady asked and laughed. "That's perfectly understandable." She laid her hand on Maddox's arm, and forced him to lower his fusion gun. "As you see, Maddox, our Independent could easily have shot Rasp while he was down. Afterwards, he could have laid in wait, and ambushed whoever showed up next."

"That wouldn't be necessary," B'taav said. "I could have sealed myself up in the *Xendos*. You never would have been able to breach her hull. Not with the equipment you have here."

"And then, you could have waited until Lieutenant Daniels found us."

"Or I could have done something to get his attention."

"Your freedom in exchange for our hides."

Maddox's face turned red with anger. The gray haired lady leaned against a wall of machinery.

"You're a curious fellow, Independent," she continued. "Why are you still with us? Do you fear Lieutenant Daniels that much, or do you have other reasons?"

"At first I wanted to get away from Daniels," B'taav admitted. "But things got out of hand so quickly, and you didn't leave me much choice. When I realized you had an Inquisitor of the Phaecian Empire in your group, the thought of turning you in to Daniels in exchange for clemency did cross my mind."

"But turning in an Inquisitor on the wrong side of the border wasn't enough, was it?"

"You were wise to keep the others away from me," B'taav said. "No offence, Inquisitor, but the madam is right. Turning you in wouldn't have been enough to get a break from Daniels."

"And now?"

"He would certainly give me a deal, should I turn in your group."

"Still, you chose not to."

"Making a deal with Lieutenant Daniels and having him honor it are two very different things. Last I checked, we're in the middle of nowhere. If I were to give you guys up to the Lieutenant, what incentive would he have to honor our deal?"

"Point taken."

"That, more than anything else, makes me inclined to follow

along. Whatever Daniels wants with you, it's big. I'd be lying if I said I wasn't curious."

"I've made a tidy living studying other cultures," the gray haired lady said. "Every one of them has a saying about the dangers of being *too* curious."

"I'm familiar with these sayings as well. It's why I haven't asked too many questions. My goal, as with any job, is to get back home alive rather than in a box. If, during the course of this particular journey, there's the possibility of getting a cut of your action, even if it's only a fraction of a percent, I would consider it a bonus."

The gray haired lady again laughed.

"That's what I like about Independents. Always looking out for the bottom line."

She motioned to the still unconscious Rasp.

"What if our friend doesn't like the idea of giving you a pass? What if he is even less pleased with the idea of making you a partner?"

"He knows where I am. He's welcome to file a complaint."

The gray haired lady nodded. She motioned to Maddox and said, "Get Rasp out of here."

Maddox didn't move. His eyes were volcanic fire and locked onto the Independent.

"I suspect B'taav knows you don't like him, so staring him down is rather pointless," the gray haired lady said. "Get Rasp out of here."

Maddox finally relented. He put away his fusion gun and dragged Rasp out of the engine room.

"I'm no fool, B'taav," the gray haired lady said when they were gone. "But neither am I unappreciative. We keep this crazy pace up and it won't be long before you and Inquisitor Cer are also at each other's throats. As reluctant as I am to do so, I'll allow you both some rest. Five hours."

She headed to the door leading out of the engine room.

"Keep your cool, Independent, and maybe -*maybe*- we'll cut you in on the action. But get out of hand and I'll let Rasp, and Maddox, take care of you."

30

The five hour rest flew by, and Inquisitor Cer and B'taav both rose wearily from their cots just outside the engine room of the *Xendos*. They went back to work and progressed without the added burden of significant fatigue.

The two replaced almost all the burnt circuits in the engine's core computer system as well as the last of the fuel lines. Finally, they cleaned the primary energy connections.

Rasp no longer hovered over B'taav, but the Independent knew at least one camera was still trained on him.

Later in the evening Inquisitor Cer left him alone, only to return with a tray of food. She ate with the Independent.

"They said we can have another five hour rest."

"When?"

"Tomorrow morning."

"We should unionize. Force them to give us vacation and sick leave."

"We're not going to make the deadline," Inquisitor Cer said. "We are at great risk."

"Agreed. Given the amount of work left to do, I estimate we need at least three more days."

"Two days past our deadline."

Inquisitor Cer put down her drink.

"You said it would be dangerous to remain beyond four days, B'taav. What is the risk of staying six?"

"Lieutenant Daniels is probably using a standard search procedure. He'll keep his fighters spread out and circling. Their sensors will shine on each asteroid and every crevice within. They know we used some kind of escape craft, and therefore know we can't be too far away. If they get the *Dakota* in close enough, they could release the ship's complement of probes and rewire them so they sense any heat or electronic signature. Even assuming the probes aren't close, they likely will equip them with a motion detector system. You get a few hundred motion detectors spread out in this zone and every movement will be detected, however minute."

"Even if he doesn't find this base, we might already be trapped."

"On the plus side, the asteroids are not stationary. When we launch the *Xendos* we could emulate their movements. Doing so might allow us to slip through."

"You don't sound very optimistic."

"One should always maintain a sense of optimism, so long as it isn't blind," the Independent said. "Our advantage is that Lieutenant Daniels doesn't know when we bailed out of the *Pilgrimage* and therefore has a lot of space to cover. We need to have faith he doesn't get lucky."

"There you go, talking about faith again."

B'taav smiled and pulled a piece of paper out of his pocket.

"Here's another list of material we need."

Cer wearily eyed the paper.

"Since you brought dinner, it's a shame I can't offer a movie in return," B'taav said. "On the other hand, there isn't anything quite as romantic as slaving over an antique engine."

"That's funny," Inquisitor Cer replied. "I thought Rasp was more your type."

Cer and B'taav exited the *Xendos* and walked past the escape sled and to the main door leading into the station. It had been a while since B'taav was there and he found the rooms closest to the entry door tidied up and converted into living quarters for the rest of the passengers of the *Pilgrimage*. None of the room's occupants, however, were present.

The two made their way through the narrow passageway and to the storage room. The rooms on either side of this corridor were used as offices during the Erebus War. Their interiors were visible through large glass panels. B'taav noted several small cots within. Some were neatly tended while others showed signs of use.

When B'taav and Cer were halfway to the storage room, B'taav detected movement in one of the dark, adjoining rooms. The person ran quickly out of a side door, as if in a panic.

"What is it?" Cer asked

B'taav's jet black eyes pierced through the room's darkness. Inquisitor Cer followed B'taav's gaze but was unable to detect anything.

"Call the others," B'taav said. "Tell them to come here, *now*."

"What is it?"

"There's a body in there. Someone's been killed."

A communicator appeared in the Inquisitor's hand.

"This is Inquisitor Cer. I'm in the corridor outside the main storage room. We have a body in one of the rooms."

She put the device away. It took a little while for her eyes to adjust to the darkness. When they did, she too saw the corpse.

It was a male. He lay face down on a cot. Sheets draped over him spilled onto the floor. The clothing he wore was white, but a large, dark stain covered his back. At the center of the stain protruded the handle of a knife.

Inquisitor Cer slid her fusion gun from its holster and cautiously stepped through the room's front door. B'taav followed close behind.

The two leaned against a metal desk bolted to the floor. Cer tapped B'taav on the shoulder and pointed to a light switch. B'taav reached for it and the room lit up.

Inquisitor Cer aimed her gun in an arc, covering all corners of the space before her. The Independent approached and examined the body.

"He's dead alright," B'taav said.

Fresh blood covered the man's back as well as the handle of the knife sticking out of it.

"It went right through his heart."

Inquisitor Cer's rigid pose relaxed. The Independent and she were the only living occupants in the room. She approached B'taav's side and, with the Independent's help, gently turned the man over. The victim's face was twisted into a mask of pain. He survived only seconds after sustaining this fatal injury.

"Rasp," Inquisitor Cer said.

B'taav's eyes moved from the corpse and to the half-open side door leading out of the room and into a parallel hallway.

"Whoever did this went that way," the Independent said.

B'taav and Cer stepped to that door. B'taav inched his head closer to the threshold and listened for any sounds coming from beyond. He heard the shuffling of feet.

"Someone's heading down the hallway."

Cer nodded. She grabbed the door's handle and pulled. The door didn't move. Its hinges were frozen. B'taav lent his strength to Cer's and together they pulled it wide enough for them to pass through.

"Only a small person could get through that crack," Cer whispered.

"You mean the boy? He couldn't do this."

"Maybe he saw who did."

The two stepped into darkness. Inquisitor Cer motioned for the Independent to remain behind her. He looked over the hallway and noted it extended forward and to the right. A third corridor, the one behind them, headed back to the landing bay.

"Do you see anything?"

"No," B'taav replied.

"Which way?"

"I can't be sure, and we've got three choices," B'taav said. "It's best we split up. You go to the right. I'll scout back to the landing strip and the other hallway. I'll work my way here and to you."

"You might run into the killer."

"If I do, I'll appeal to their better nature."

Cer reached into her jacket pocket and produced a small knife similar to the one lodged in Rasp's back. Upon seeing it, B'taav's eyebrows lifted.

"Standard issue for Inquisitors?"

"Standard enough," Cer replied. "Take it."

B'taav did as told, although he noted Cer's fusion gun was now aimed at his stomach.

"Don't make me regret giving you this," Cer said.

"Inquisitor, we haven't left each other's side for the past day and Rasp was murdered only minutes ago. It's clear neither of us had anything to do with his death."

"The same can't be said about the rest."

"We share that knowledge, at the least."

B'taav examined his knife. It would be adequate in a close fight, but very inadequate should the Independent face someone carrying a gun. "If I see anything I can't handle, I'll yell."

"If you see anything at all, yell," Cer replied.

The two split up.

31

B'taav pressed his body against the cold metal walls and moved along the corridor. He inched his way deeper and deeper into the heart of the base. The area around him showed considerable age and neglect. A heavy layer of dust covered the floor and walls but heavy foot traffic indicated recent movement.

The Independent continued down the hall and stopped every few feet to listen. At one point he thought he heard the sound of someone moving in the area before him. The sounds died as suddenly as they began.

B'taav inched forward even more cautiously. In time, he again heard footsteps. The person making them was very close.

B'taav crouched down and stepped forward. He held his right hand and the knife ahead. After a few more steps B'taav paused and listened. A grim look filled his face. In spite of the darkness, he had located his target.

B'taav straightened up and took several more steps. The corridor took a sharp right turn a few feet away, and the footsteps were coming from just beyond that turn. B'taav licked his lips and eyed his blade.

Here we go.

The Independent was off, sprinting around the corner. The muscles on his face were tight; his eyes became thin slits and blood throbbed heavily through his veins. The darkness in his eyes was a cold void.

And, just as suddenly, the void and the tension vanished. B'taav slid to a stop and drew back his knife. Standing before him was the boy. His hands were bare. His face had the look of someone who had lost his way.

"Nathaniel," B'taav said. "What are you doing here?"

The boy walked forward, toward B'taav, seemingly unaware of the Independent's presence. B'taav took a deep breath and allowed the last of the tension to leave his body.

"Come here, Nathaniel," the Independent said. He laid his free hand on the boy's shoulder.

"Your mother must be worried," he said. "Let's get back to the—"

B'taav stopped talking. He heard the sound of another set of footsteps coming from farther down the corridor. Whoever it was, they were coming fast.

B'taav pulled the boy to the wall and again drew his knife. The footsteps started as a hasty jog. They turned into a full run.

B'taav pushed the boy further back, toward the corridor's turn. The Independent held the knife against the darkness. The echo of the footsteps increased.

B'taav's eyes, so sensitive to the darkness, spotted the vague outline of the figure running toward them. It was a short man with a slight build.

He was carrying a fusion gun.

B'taav hastily picked Nathaniel up and rushed back around the corner.

As he did, the runners pace increased yet again. The approaching man spotted them.

Once around the corner, B'taav set Nathaniel down and turned. The running man was only steps away. The Independent leaned back and prepared to jump him the moment he rounded the corner. The man, however, stopped. He stood just beyond the corner, no more than a couple of feet from B'taav and Nathaniel.

B'taav didn't dare look past that corner junction and, likewise, knew the man on the other side was hesitant to do the same.

"B'taav? Nathaniel?" The voice came from around the corner.

"Maddox? What are you doing here?"

"Searching for Nathaniel. You have him."

"Yes."

"Don't you dare hurt him."

"Why would—"

"I saw the knife, B'taav. Don't you *dare* hurt him."

"I have no intention of doing so."

"Good. Slide your weapon my way and come out with your hands up."

"I can't do that."

"Why not?"

B'taav did not answer. Instead, he eased back a step while making sure Nathaniel remained behind him.

"What's this about?" Maddox asked. "Who gave you the knife?"

"Inquisitor Cer."

"Why the hell would she do that?"

"We found Rasp in his cot, dead."

"Rasp's dead?"

"Yeah."

"How?"

"Someone stabbed him."

There was a long pause.

"Let me get this straight: You and Inquisitor Cer find Rasp. He's dead, the victim of a stabbing. So the Inquisitor, in her infinite wisdom, decides to give you a *knife*?"

"Inquisitor Cer and I have been together the entire day. Neither of us could have killed him."

"Why should I believe you?"

"Thanks to the camera in the *Xendos'* engine room, you don't have to believe anything I say. Just look at your security footage. It will confirm everything. Did you put cameras anywhere else within the station?"

"No," Maddox admitted. "We only have the one. Looks like we should have brought more."

"Before we got to Rasp's room, someone exited through the side door. The corridor split, so Inquisitor Cer and I did the same. She gave me the knife, just in case I ran into his killer."

"You have any idea who did it?"

"None. Up until now, the only people I've seen are you and Nathaniel. If I had to choose a suspect between you two..."

"I have no reason to kill Rasp."

"As you put it so bluntly, Maddox, why should I believe you?"

"Listen, Independent, for all I know Rasp is alive and well and you took that knife from Inquisitor Cer's corpse. So now what? Do we spend the rest of the day here?"

B'taav noted movement coming from the far end of the corridor. Inquisitor Cer's yellow hair bobbed in the distance. She was on her way.

"Sit tight for a few more seconds, Maddox," B'taav said. "The cavalry is coming."

32

The first thing to come out from around the corner was Maddox's gun, held up gently by its barrel and pinched between two fingers. Maddox lowered the gun to the floor and released it. As he did, B'taav noted a dark stain on Maddox's shirt sleeve.

When the gun was down, Maddox stepped out from his hiding place. His hands were in the air.

"Satisfied?"

Maddox glared at the Independent. B'taav expected him to be relieved to see the boy was fine, but his expression remained stubbornly neutral.

"B'taav was right to take precautions," Cer said. She now held the only weapon, having taken B'taav's knife and demanded Maddox disarm himself as well. "I assume he told you about Rasp?"

"Yeah," Maddox said. "He was stabbed?"

"While he slept."

"May I retrieve my weapon now?"

Instead of answering, Inquisitor Cer picked it up.

"Allow me to hold it, for the time being."

She put Maddox's and her guns into holsters on her belt.

"Fine," Maddox muttered. "Let's see the body."

B'taav, Nathaniel, Maddox, and Cer walked back to the door leading into Rasp's room. The three Mercs were standing just inside the room. Each of the men carried a Bandera Fusion rifle.

The Merc with the harshest features stepped forward as B'taav and his group approached. He aimed his fusion rifle at them. In his burly hands, the fearsome weapon looked like a toy.

"Who goes there?" he asked.

"It's me," Maddox said. "I'm with Inquisitor Cer and Nathaniel."

"Don't forget me," B'taav said. "We wouldn't want them to think I'm not part of this group, too."

"Yeah. It would be too bad if they thought you were a meddling outsider and shot first and asked questions later."

Inquisitor Cer pushed past Maddox and stepped up to the Merc.

"Is the area secured, Balthazar?" she asked.

"Yes ma'am," the Merc identified as Balthazar said. His eyes drifted from Cer to B'taav. His mouth twisted into a grimace.

"Is everyone accounted for?"

"They are now. Everyone else is in there."

Balthazar pointed to Rasp's room.

"Good." Cer faced the other two Mercs and said: "Melchor, Kaspar, you two scout the corridors. Though the odds are very low, there is the possibility we might have an intruder."

"Yes ma'am," the two remaining Mercs said. They walked past B'taav and Maddox and disappeared into the darkness.

Inquisitor Cer motioned to B'taav, Maddox, and Nathaniel. Maddox put his arm around Nathaniel's shoulder and pushed him forward. B'taav followed along but at the entrance to Rasp's room Balthazar pressed the barrel of his gun against the Independent's chest.

Inquisitor Cer noticed Balthazar's actions and was about to say something. She didn't have to.

"Let the Independent in."

The voice was female, older. It was the gray haired lady. She spoke as she reached out to embrace Nathaniel.

Balthazar sneered at the Independent but nonetheless stepped aside.

B'taav entered Rasp's room. The remaining members of the escape sled, with the exception of the three Mercs, were inside. The gray haired lady escorted Nathaniel away from Rasp's corpse and to the far side of the room. They came to a stop before Stephen Gray, the morose man in white, and the man B'taav identified as a Phaecian Cardinal.

After a few seconds of talking with her boy, the gray haired lady approached Inquisitor Cer.

"You two found Rasp?"

"We did."

"Did you see who did this?"

"No ma'am."

"Any ideas?"

"No ma'am."

"Well, I certainly have some."

The gray haired stared deep into the black pools of B'taav's eyes.

"You've already had one run in with Rasp, Independent. Did you have another?"

"No."

"He's innocent of this," Cer said.

"Are you certain, Inquisitor? Rasp's murder was a cowardly act. Such actions are within the realm of an Independent's work."

"Whether typical of Independents or not, my lady, B'taav and I were together at all times up until the discovery of Rasp's corpse. This I would swear, even to my Cardinal."

The gray haired lady nodded, but was disappointed blame for this barbarous act could not be so easily determined.

"We'll get to the bottom of this, Francis," the man in white said.

B'taav stared at the gray haired lady and her boy.

"Francis?" he said. He recognized her at last. "Francis Lane?"

"You know me?" she said. "Yes, I suppose you do at that."

B'taav didn't have anything to add.

"If you weren't responsible for Rasp's murder, Independent, then one of us was," she said.

"Was anything touched?" Inquisitor Cer asked.

"No," the man in white said.

Cer took a long look at the room and its inhabitants.

"When was the last time each of you saw Rasp?"

"Earlier today, just after breakfast," the man in white volunteered. "He wasn't too happy, understandably, about what B'taav did to him yesterday. Maddox looked after him, making sure he didn't do anything rash. The rest of the group, everyone but B'taav and you, Inquisitor Cer, were there, eating."

"How about after breakfast? Anyone saw him then?"

"I did," Maddox said. "I kept watch on him through the morning, just as Mr. Frasier said."

B'taav eyed the man in white. Though he didn't recognize the man, the name was familiar.

"He was quite angry," Maddox continued. "It took a great deal of effort to keep him from visiting the *Xendos*. We –I– wasted far too much time babysitting him. Around lunch I got in touch with Ms. Lane and we decided to lace his meal with sedatives."

"You gave him spiked food?" Frasier said.

"Yes sir," Maddox said. "He was out in twenty minutes. I dragged him back to this room and laid him on the bed. Then I went back to the ship and—"

"Did you see him again?

"No sir."

"Did anyone else see him after he was dragged here?"

There was no answer.

"One of you did," B'taav finally said.

"If you have a suspect, feel free to enlighten us as to who it is, Independent," Frasier said.

Maddox fold his arms across his chest. Was he hiding the stain on his right sleeve? It was hard to tell.

"I have none," B'taav said. He shook his head. "We're wasting time. Time we don't have. We could spend hours going over each other's itinerary, checking to see if we have the motive, and opportunity, to kill Rasp. But our priority remains getting off this rock and as far away from Lieutenant Daniels as possible."

"Then you should get back to work," Maddox said.

"Not until you tell me what this is about."

"Are you crazy?" Maddox spat.

"At this point, you have to tell me. It is no longer debatable."

"You *are* crazy."

"Every second that passes where we don't identify Rasp's killer is another second where our lives, each and every one of our lives, is in danger. Rasp's murder was clearly a crime of opportunity. He was alone in this room, asleep, and far enough away from everyone else that he could be picked off without much effort and without anyone seeing. One of you is thinning the herd. One of you is here for their own purposes. And it won't be the last time he, or she, strikes."

The eyes of the passengers floated from face to face, as if trying to read their partners', their associates', their friends' minds.

"Unless I know exactly what we're doing out here, I can't trust any of you."

"You're asking us to explain ourselves?" Maddox mocked the Independent. "No. You've received all the information you're getting. From here on out, you'll follow orders."

"What if these orders come from the mouth of Rasp's murderer?" B'taav said. "Do you really want me to do whatever any of you ask, blindly, when that might be the case?"

The room grew silent. Francis Lane rubbed her chin and sighed.

"You can't seriously be thinking..." Maddox began, and then paused. "You're not going to do what he asks, are you?"

"The Independent's right. Why should he trust any of us?" she said. "What if the murderer orders him to do something that jeopardizes our mission? How would he know if the order is legitimate if he doesn't know what we're doing?"

"This is insanity!"

"I know where you stand, Maddox," B'taav said. "Why don't you let the others decide for themselves?"

Again the group eyed each other. Despite their weariness, despite their fear, they realized there was truth in B'taav's words.

"It's time we talked," Francis Lane said.

33

The group entered what was once the main conference room of the *Xendos* and sat before the room's single long table.

Francis Lane motioned for B'taav to sit before her, and he did so. Ned Frasier, Stephen Gray, and the Phaecian Cardinal sat on the other side of the table and faced the Independent. Melchor, Kaspar, and Balthazar assumed positions outside the room while Maddox and Nathaniel sat beside the door and out of the way. Like the Mercs, Inquisitor Cer chose to remain standing. She held the space between the door and the conference table.

When everyone was in place, Stephen Gray began the meeting.

"I would formally introduce myself," he told the Independent. "But you already know who I am."

"Yes I do, Mr. Gray. Your reputation as one of Epsillon's finest business men is equal only to your being an uncompromising patriot." B'taav paused and motioned to both Francis Lane and the Phaecian Cardinal. "So what are you doing with these two?"

"How well do you know them?" Gray inquired.

"Francis Lane is an aide to the regency of what is left of the old Epsillon Empire and her monarchy," B'taav said. "Today's Epsillon Empire neither recognizes her political party or their control over several lesser systems at our far borders. Given how small the systems are, neither have they made a big issue about their claims." B'taav's eyes turned from Stephen Gray and toward Francis Lane. "It was your monarchy that got us into the Erebus War."

"We are no longer a true monarchy," Francis Lane said. "We refer to ourselves as the Old Epsillon Empire. The new Empire may not give us much thought, but we exist nonetheless."

"So we have a high level representative from the new Epsillon Empire and a representative of the Old Empire," B'taav said. His gaze settled on the Phaecian Cardinal. "Joining them is you. Considering the shared history of these three distinguished members, it's not too surprising there's a murderer among us. Cardinal, you're an awful long way from home."

"You may address me by my name, Independent. Saro Triste."

"As you wish, Cardinal Triste."

"Given your knowledge of the others, perhaps I should be insulted that you didn't recognize me as well," the Cardinal continued. His voice was deep and commanding. He was used to intimidating his subjects.

"Don't take my lack of knowledge as an insult," B'taav said and smiled. "The galaxy is quite large. I have yet to memorize the names of everyone of importance within it."

The man in white, the only member sitting at the table not to formally identify himself, said: "I'm Ned Frasier. I'm a local at the *Titus* space station. It was my job to look at the material that came in from the scavengers."

"All material?"

"*Certain* material."

"Are you sure you want to do this, Ned?" Maddox said. "Once you speak, we can no longer go back. Think about what you're doing."

"We have," Francis Lane said.

The bartender's opinion no longer mattered.

"Then get on with it," Maddox growled.

They took their time to talk and B'taav wondered who would be the first to reveal their secrets. Stephen Gray chose himself.

"Given our diversity, you probably suspect us of some kind of treason against our respective political systems," Stephen Gray said. "That is the furthest thing from the truth. We came together because of a unique threat. A threat that could well result in the resumption of the Erebus War."

"I'm listening."

"As you know, the Erebus War ended in the destruction of almost every single one of the Old Epsillon and Phaecian Empire's most fearsome warships," he continued. "What you and almost everyone else do not know is that this was by *design*."

"Design?" B'taav repeated. "You mean this was planned?"

"Yes."

"By the Gods, why?"

"Our leaders were not fools," Saro Triste said. "Even if they were foolish enough to allow events to spiral out of control and push both Empires to the brink of war."

"Perhaps it was the cold reality of what they were about to get into that made at least a few of them realize the situation was critical," Stephen Gray said.

"Early estimates predicted when this war spilled out of Erebus and into either Empire, the fatalities would number in the billions," Saro Triste said. "Our leaders were facing not only massive deaths, but perhaps the end of humanity itself."

"You see, B'taav, by coincidence or not, both sides had developed an ultimate weapon," Francis Lane said. "We called ours Project *Charybdis*. They called theirs the *Tears of the Stars*. When detonated, these weapons released a tremendous energy wave. A wave capable of annihilating an entire solar system."

B'taav drew a sharp breath. He couldn't help but look out the room's single window and at the asteroid field beyond. The remains of Erebus.

"Yes, Independent, an entire solar system."

For several seconds, the room was quiet.

"Then what?" B'taav asked.

"This information was closely guarded. A group of twenty high ranking military, political, industrial, and clergy figures, ten from each empire, initiated top secret dialogue. They were aware their counterparts had their hands on this weapon. This realization proved sobering. They came to the conclusion that this war had to be stopped before it fully began."

"But too many events were already in motion. Ships from either side initiated hostile actions within Erebus. There were too many casualties and field Commanders were eager to advance. More and more ships were deployed in system. Even the citizens of the Empires demanded blood."

"The group of twenty grew increasingly desperate to find any kind of peaceful solution. But their fear was that peace treaties would be, at best, short lived. Even worse, they would afford each side time to create even more of these ultimate weapons."

"So someone in these negotiations offered a solution," Francis Lane said. "An ultimate solution. One that would eliminate the threat of any future wars for millennia. Time enough for the old hatreds to die down. Time enough for us to live together in peace."

"They agreed to explode these bombs in Erebus?" B'taav said. "Yes."

"H-how many people were sacrificed?"

"Far less than would have had this war spilled over."

B'taav shook his head. He eyed Inquisitor Cer. She stared back at him.

"And the military agreed to do this? They agreed to sacrifice all these lives along with the backbone of their fleets?"

"They did no such thing," Francis Lane replied. "The treaty

was known only to the group of twenty and a handful of very loyal, senior members of the two starships in question."

"The ones carrying the weapons."

"Yes. The *Charybdis* bomb was on board the Epsillon Empire juggernaut *Argus*. The *Tears of the Stars* was on the Phaecian Empire ship *Luxor*. Not only did they carry the weapons, these ships held the only copies of the complete schematics of these weapons along with the personnel who developed the devices. The group of twenty made sure no other copies of blueprints existed anywhere else. They set a time and date for the end and consulted with the Captains of each ship."

"The men and women in control of these vessels knew and understood their sacrifice. They, more than anyone else, were aware of the danger of introducing these weapons into a prolonged war. They agreed to do what was asked of them, even though it meant sacrificing their own lives."

"The *Argus* and the *Luxor* were to enter Erebus simultaneously and, at a given moment, set off their respective bombs. In the resulting maelstrom, the military might of both Phaecia and Epsillon would be destroyed, along with those ultimate weapons."

"They were mad," B'taav said.

"Perhaps, but their plan worked," Francis Lane said. "Neither Empire had the weapons or the desire to fight anymore. On that very day, the war ended."

"Investigations into the explosion at Erebus followed, of course," Triste added. "And because of the projects' secrecy, no one figured out exactly what happened. The group of twenty knew conspiracy theories would flower, but they could live with that, as long as their goal was realized."

B'taav mouth felt very dry.

"What happened to this group of twenty?"

"They suffered. How could they not? A year after their plan's implementation, thirteen of them were dead. Eight by their own hand. The others died in what was nebulously ruled as 'accidents.' Of the remaining seven, three left politics and disappeared forever from public life. The other four were victims of crime. Peculiar crimes. As nebulous as the accidents."

"Why are you here? Why is Lieutenant Daniels after you?"

"Despite their plan's success, the group of twenty realized something had gone wrong," Francis Lane said.

"They feared their deception would be revealed?"

"They never expected the secret to last forever. Indeed, they made provisions to reveal their handiwork. Their testimonials were recorded for posterity and are to be revealed at the five hundred anniversary of the end of the War. By then, hopefully, their distant relatives will not suffer for their forefathers' sins."

"What went wrong?"

"You're familiar with a scavenger by the name of Kelly Lang?" Ned Frasier asked.

"Yes."

"He was a nobody," Frasier continued. "One of many thousands of scavengers searching for any scrap from the war that a Homeworld collector might pay good money for."

"What did he find?"

"A nearly intact scientific probe from the *Argus*," Francis Lane said.

"A probe from the ship carrying the *Charybdis* bomb into Erebus?"

"Yes."

"How is that possible? Wouldn't the ship have disintegrated—"

B'taav did not finish his thought. He stared at the faces before him.

"Her bomb wasn't detonated?"

"No."

"You mean all this destruction...it was the result of the *Tears of the Stars* alone?"

"Yes," Frasier said. "Somehow, the *Luxor's* device exploded prematurely. The *Argus*, on the other side of the solar system, survived the explosion. If she's still in one piece, the *Charybdis* bomb is still on board."

"How could the ship survive an explosion of such magnitude?"

"Phaecian intelligence as well as the *Monnel* Displacer records indicated the *Argus* arrived through the inner Erebus Displacer just as the explosion's impact was felt on that side of the system," Saro Triste said. "When activated, all Displacers create a fold in the fabric of space, a negative space wormhole. It is what allows vessels passage from one point to another, many light years away. While active, this negative space wormhole is extra-dimensional and, in theory, unaffected by events occurring outside its fold. We suspect the *Argus* was still in this negative space for a fraction of a second *after* the explosion's energy passed."

"You think the ship was completely intact?"

"Obviously not," Frasier said. "Had she emerged into Erebus space unscathed, the crew would have blasted her out of the rubble of what remained of Erebus. No, she sustained enough damage from the blast to make her immobile or near immobile. Her life support systems obviously survived long enough to allow the crew time to release the ship's probes, including the one we found."

"You were looking for such objects? You knew the *Argus* was out there?"

"The group of twenty poured over all information collected from the explosion. As impressive as the destruction was, the data was incontrovertible. The explosion had the characteristics of only one solar bomb. Had both been detonated as planned, this area would *still* be a toxic cesspool. *Titus* and the Erebus Displacer would have been dust. Our ancestors knew the *Luxor* was gone. They couldn't be sure about the *Argus*."

"A year after the events at Erebus, the surviving members of the group of twenty set aside a stipend and created a secret organization," Francis Lane said. "To this day, the organization has no formal name and only one goal: To guard Erebus from both borders and see to it that if the *Argus* was somehow found, her cargo would never fall into the hands of either individuals or Empires."

"Several generations of sentries were stationed at *Titus* and the two other space stations in the vicinity of Erebus," Ned Frasier said. "Their job –eventually my job– was to sift through the scavengers' material and look for any signs of the ship."

"Why sit back and wait? Why not send in exploratory craft?"

"The chaos and fallout from the single solar bomb made trips deep into Erebus too dangerous," Ned Frasier said. "When things finally settled down some fifty years later, the group of twenty was out of power and our funds were limited. Besides, the area to cover was maddeningly broad and despite our fears, there was no clear evidence the *Argus* still existed. We chose to conserve what monies we had and let the information come to us, rather than go out to it."

"The probe Kelly Lang found proved beyond the shadow of a doubt that the *Argus* survived the explosion," Frasier continued. "We found markings on the probe indicating it was one of four hundred released afterwards."

"Why use probes?" B'taav asked. "Why didn't the crew use the escape ships?"

"Before venturing into Erebus, the *Argus'* Captain quietly sent all non-essential personnel on various trips, from shore leave to scientific conferences or intelligence gathering. The crewmen didn't even know they were being evacuated. When the *Argus* headed to Erebus, it was manned by a skeleton crew and there were no remaining personnel or escape crafts left on board. The scientific probes were the only means the crew had to get their message of survival out."

"Immediately after purchasing the probe, Mr. Frasier contacted us," Stephen Gray said. "We are what're left of the sentries."

"Before we arrived on *Titus*, Kelly Lang was dead," Saro Triste said. "Whether the explosion that took him and his ship was accidental, we couldn't know, but we suspected the worst. Especially when Lieutenant Daniels showed up."

"You think he was responsible for Lang's death?"

"While he arrived afterwards, it is possible Lieutenant Daniels had agents in the area and they killed the scavenger," Stephen Gray said. "Regardless, his interest in Kelly Lang's death confirmed our suspicions: There were others who knew what really happened in Erebus and, as you know, General Jurgens is behind Lieutenant Daniels. What is important is the fact that we're in a race with Jurgens and Daniels and their military might to find the *Argus*. I have little doubt they hope to recover the ship for their own purposes. Even if the super juggernaut is severely damaged, she remains the most powerful weapon in the universe. Should Daniels or Jurgens get their hands on her, all they have to do is keep the Erebus Displacer locked down. They'll have all the time they need to fix the ship. Afterwards...who knows."

Francis Lane laid her hand on B'taav's.

"Now you understand the urgency of our mission," she said. "Every one of their actions suggests they want the bomb for themselves. If they get it, what's to stop them from becoming absolute rulers of both Empires?"

"What about Rasp's murder?"

"Isn't it obvious?" Francis Lane said. "Someone among us works for them."

"Or for themselves," B'taav said. "The *Argus* offers enough temptation for anyone."

Francis Lane released B'taav's hand. The air within the conference room turned even colder.

"What if we find the ship first?"

"We get on board and finish the mission our distant ancestors tasked us with."

"You aim to destroy her?"

"Yes."

"Even assuming the *Argus* is still in one piece, the machinery within must surely be inoperative after all this time."

"This asteroid base proves you wrong," Stephen Gray said. "And, unlike the *Xendos*, the *Argus* was built to withstand the prolonged ravages of both space and war."

"If the ship was intact, her power supply would eventually run out," Francis Lane said. "Provided the asteroids surrounding her didn't crack her titalum hull, it's a good bet her core computer system is whole."

"When we reach the ship, we need only power up that computer," Frasier said. "Afterwards, we initiate the *Argus'* self-destruct mechanism and fly off into the sunset."

"Assuming we do all that, isn't there a danger that the self-destruct mechanism might also set off the *Charybdis* device?"

"While we know little about the *Charybdis* device, Independent, but it is highly doubtful the *Argus'* self-destruct mechanism would activate that device," Ned Frasier said. "The ship had at least ten quantum fusion engines."

B'taav whistled. Five such engines spread out at various points on a planet were enough to feed her energy needs.

"That kind of power, it stands to reason, could set off a solar system killer. It could also power the ship and allow the remaining crew to escape their burial in Erebus. Since that didn't happen, we know the ship's engines were silenced. Therefore, the self-destruct mechanism would only serve to break everything on board apart."

"Including the *Charybdis* bomb," Saro Triste concluded.

"What if the Captain of the *Argus* ordered the probes sent out and, when they didn't get a response, set off the self-destruct himself?"

"Captain Torin was no longer in control of his vessel by the time the probes were released," Francis Lane said.

"How do you know?"

"Because he, more than anyone else on board, knew the importance of this mission. He would never authorize the release of the probes."

"You think he was incapacitated?"

"There is no doubt."

"No one else on board could initiate the self-destruct?"

"Three people knew the proper codes," Francis Lane said. "Captain Torin, First Officer Ryan Mills, and the Epsillon liaison."

"We know the liaison was one of the people evacuated just before the *Argus* left to Erebus," Stephen Gray said. "That left Captain Torin and First Officer Ryan Mills. Mills was loyal to his captain.   He too wouldn't have allowed the probes to be released."

"Assuming all this is true, and even further assuming we get to the ship before Daniels does and manage to re-start the central computer. How do we initiate the self-destruct? Where do we get the security codes?"

"We've had them in the family for many years, B'taav," Francis Lane said.

"In the family?"

Francis Lane motioned to the boy. Reluctantly, Maddox rose from his chair and brought Nathaniel to her side. In the boy's hands was his ever-present red ball.

"Captain Nathaniel Torin, of the super juggernaut *Argus,* was a very distant relative of mine," Francis Lane said. "His wife, Angela Torin, was the Epsillon liaison on board that ship. She was meant to go into Erebus. Her position *required* her to do so. But Captain Torin couldn't bring himself to have her there. He...forced her to leave the ship."

Francis Lane took the ball from Nathaniel's hands. She twisted its upper half until it came off.

"Before she left the *Argus*, Captain Torin gave her one final gift." Francis Lane removed the top of the ball, revealing a small crystal cube concealed within.

B'taav's eyes opened wide with surprise.

"Project Geist?"

"Yes, B'taav," Francis Lane said. "A Project Geist cube. Stored within is the full mind scan of Captain Nathaniel Torin. He took the scan only hours before he ordered the *Argus* into Erebus."

"By the Gods, I never thought I'd see one of those. But...but they were banned. Every one of the Geist machines, and all the technology, was destroyed. Do you have one of those machines?"

"No, we do not," Francis Lane said. "Nor do we have the capacity to rebuild them. Even if we did, we dare not risk downloading the information on this cube with a machine built from scratch. The data storage on these cubes is delicate. Using an imperfect machine risks corrupting all its data."

"To get this information, we must find the machine Captain Torin used," Stephen Gray said. "The one that is still on board the *Argus*."

B'taav shook his head.

"More complications and delay," he muttered. "More time for Lieutenant Daniels to catch up with us. Why did Captain Torin make this memory cube?"

"We can only offer an educated guess," Francis Lane said. "I suspect Captain Torin knew the truth behind the end of the Erebus War would eventually surface. He wanted Angela to give the cube to the Empire for posterity. That way, all questions about his actions could be answered."

"That cube might have the plans of the *Charybdis* bomb on it."

"I doubt it," Francis Lane said. "Captain Torin knew very well what the *Charybdis* bomb was capable of, but he was ultimately a military man. I suspect he was unaware of the science behind the device and could no more replicate it than you or I."

"How did you come across the cube?"

"After the war, Angela Torin settled down on the planet Onia," Francis Lane said. "She was pregnant with Captain Torin's only child. That made the child a member of our royal family. The boy, now grown man, didn't learn of his heritage until Angela died some forty years later. On her deathbed, she told him who he was and gave him this cube. A pair of visitors came to see him that night. They told him about his father, and about the *Argus* and the *Charybdis* device. They were members of our organization."

"Angela's son joined the group," Ned Frasier continued. "He was one of the first stationed at *Titus* over one hundred and fifty years ago. He bought many relics over his lifetime, but nothing like what we found. When he died, the cube changed hands, going to his daughter, then his daughter's son."

"Until it was handed down to me," Francis Lane said. Her eyes watered, her lips quivered. "For his sake and the sake of all those in both Empires, I want to complete Captain Torin's last mission."

B'taav stared across the table and at the people before him. He then turned and looked at Inquisitor Cer, Maddox, and little Nathaniel.

"Every one of you knew this?"

"No," Inquisitor Cer said. Even as the words left her mouth, a look of apprehension filled her face. She eyed Saro Triste and said, "My apologies, liege. It was not my place to talk without your say so."

"Don't worry, child," Saro Triste said. "The Inquisitors, unlike you Independents, do as told without question. In the presence of their Cardinal, they are to speak only when permitted."

Saro Triste waved his arm.

"You've performed admirably, Inquisitor," Triste said. "You can understand why we kept this information from you. Until now."

"Nice to know someone else is in the same boat as I am," B'taav said.

Inquisitor Cer's eyes locked on the Independent. B'taav offered the Inquisitor a slight nod before turning his attention back to the people before him.

"You've told me what I need to know," B'taav said. "I'll get the *Xendos* running and keep you away from Lieutenant Daniels. You won't have to worry about me anymore. The same can't be said about whoever killed Rasp."

34

When the meeting was over, B'taav, Inquisitor Cer, and Maddox headed for the maintenance room and picked up the items they originally left the *Xendos* to collect.

On their way back to the ship they spotted the three Mercs wrapping up Rasp's body. They would leave the body in this room, for there was no reason to take it anywhere. At some point in the future maybe someone could retrieve the corpse and give it a proper burial. Until then, he would remain in the cot he used to sleep for the very last time.

As the three returned to the *Xendos'* engine room, B'taav thought about the events and conversation he had with the group as well as Rasp's murder. The silent man was indeed a very easy target. But why was he killed? As best as B'taav could tell, he was a relatively minor member in this group. If this was the first step in attempting to gain sole control of the *Argus*, as B'taav suspected, then the main suspects, and targets, had to be Stephen Gray, Saro Triste, and Francis Lane.

The trio entered the *Xendos'* engine room and laid the parts down. Inquisitor Cer and B'taav resumed their work while Maddox helped wherever he could.

The first hour passed in relative silence. Maddox helped move equipment around but, after a while, found little else to do. He hung back and watched what B'taav and Cer did. At times he stifled a yawn.

Despite his intense work, B'taav watched the bartender. He noted the stain on Maddox's sleeve and was certain it was Rasp's blood. The Independent kept that knowledge to himself. His attention gradually shifted back to Inquisitor Cer and their work. A smile crept onto his oil stained face.

"After the Tamarin Campaign, I didn't think I'd have to work this hard on a ship's engines ever again," he said.

Inquisitor Cer wiped sweat from her forehead.

"*If* you were there in the first place," she said.

"You don't believe the personnel files?"

Inquisitor Cer examined a patchwork of tubes and said, "For you, no. At least half the material on your personnel files is misinformation. I've written enough of it to know what it looks like."

B'taav slid a pair of clamps around one of the main coolant

tubes' joints and tightened the piece into place.

"I was there," B'taav said. When he was satisfied the clamp would hold, his attention returned to Cer. "There's little to be gained in admitting this fact."

"What side did you take?"

"I was with the mercenaries."

"Against the settlers?"

"They were the only other side."

"The world they fought for was rightfully theirs."

"That's not the way the Epsillon council saw it. Before the campaign, there were years of court battles. In the end, the Yakusho Corporation was granted rights to that land. The settlers took advantage of the court time to settle in, even though they knew the council might rule against them. They gambled Yakusho would relent."

"Because of their numbers?"

"Exactly."

"They also didn't think any corporation would be capable of such... slaughter."

"I'm not proud of what we did."

"Why not? Your mission was a complete success. You got rid of over seven hundred thousand mostly unarmed civilians."

"Mostly," B'taav repeated. "They were given time to make the proper choice. Two months before our operations began, they were offered a fleet of shuttles willing to take them wherever they wanted to go. Yakusho Corporation even offered them an alternative world to settle in, one they could rightfully claim—"

"A barren wasteland far away from any space lanes and supply routes," Cer interrupted. "Had they taken Yakusho's offer, they would have perished there as they did in Tamarin. If not from disease, then from starvation. Yakusho's choice was no choice at all."

"You're wasting time," Maddox growled.

B'taav and Inquisitor Cer worked silently for several more minutes before B'taav once again spoke.

"The Tamarin Campaign happened a long time ago. Why do you care so much about it?"

"I had relatives among the settlers," Cer said. "Be glad I am an Inquisitor of the Phaecian Guard and obey my superiors. If I didn't, I would have killed you when I had my chance back at *Titus*. Nothing would give me more pleasure than to rid the universe of every single mercenary involved in the Tamarin bloodbath."

Inquisitor Cer grabbed the toolbox.

"After we're done with this mission, I'll get my chance with one of them, at least," she said. She headed to the rear of the engine room and slammed the toolbox to the floor.

"You've made yourself an enemy," Maddox said and chuckled. "Well, *another* enemy."

B'taav wearily eyed Maddox.

"Easy, partner," Maddox said. "Best get back to work. There'll be plenty of time to settle scores afterwards."

"I suppose," B'taav replied. "In the meantime, you should clean that stain on your right sleeve. You wouldn't want anyone to get the wrong ideas."

Maddox looked down and spotted the crimson stain on his sleeve. His eyes opened wide with surprise.

35

Even though they barely talked from that point on, Inquisitor Cer and B'taav pushed themselves to their limits for the next two days. As impossible as it seemed at the start, all repairs were eventually completed and the exhausted duo headed for the ship's cockpit. B'taav sat behind the navigator's chair while Cer positioned herself behind the engineering station. Maddox stood by the door and out of the way.

B'taav ran his hands over the controls and hit various switches. After a few seconds several lights and monitors came to life.

"Computer is on."

"Primary engines online," Inquisitor Cer said. "Initiating slow burn."

A low rumbling filled the ship. Other lights turned on as the ship came to life after a two hundred year sleep.

"You did it," Maddox said. "You got her working!"

"We're not there yet," Cer replied. She pressed another series of buttons. "Going to fifty percent."

B'taav nodded. "Fixes are holding. Vents are clear. There is no sign of leakage and fluid levels are proper."

"Moving to sixty percent."

More rumbling filled the cabin.

"Patchwork is still holding. Fluid levels remain good."

"Going to seventy five percent."

The rumbling that filled the engine grew ragged. Despite this, B'taav grinned.

"Everything is holding," he yelled above the roar. "Go for one hundred percent."

Inquisitor Cer pressed another button and the rumbling became overwhelming. Maddox clapped his hands against his ears and winced in pain. B'taav cocked his head to his side and gritted his teeth.

"It's still holding," B'taav yelled. "OK, shut it down."

Inquisitor Cer hit several buttons and the rumbling dropped to a tolerable level.

"Back down to twenty percent," Inquisitor Cer said. She faced Maddox. "We'll keep the engine going for two more hours. If there's any problem, we'll find it. In the meantime, we need to fix the sound dampers. The ship will tear herself apart, or at the very least leave us all deaf, if we fly around like that."

"Agreed," Maddox said.

"They don't make them like they used to," B'taav said. "If everything holds, we'll be ready to go in another three hours."

Oscar Theodor rushed down the immaculate upper deck of the *Dakota* along with the rest of the fighter pilots. They were called back to the *Dakota* by Lieutenant Lester Daniels and ordered to be in the ready room by 0805. That left Theodor less than five minutes after landing to remove his pressure suit and get there.

The Communication OP's order was delivered without explanation, despite the fact that his fighter squad was still in the process of sweeping the asteroid field for signs of the survivors of the *Pilgrimage*. Theodor was angry they fell for the decoy ship trick twice. Whoever the pilots within that cargo craft were, they were clever. They had nearly decommissioned the *Dakota* and had managed, at least until now, to evade one of the Epsilon Empire's finest flight squads. The boys in the other squads back home would never let them live that one down.

Theodor hurried his pace. He passed several companions and found he was the first to reach the main elevators. He pressed his access code into the elevator paneling and found the personnel of his squad surrounding him.

"What do you suppose this is about?" Sandra Mortimer inquired.

Theodor shrugged.

"I have no idea."

"It can't be good," Jill Harris, one of the rookies on the squad, said. "Lieutenant Daniels can't be happy. We're going to get disciplined."

Theodor shook his head. Why was it that every rookie coming into the squad proved such a delightful mix of raw nerves combined with a boundless pessimism?

Was I like that?

"There's no use wasting energy on what might be," Theodor said. "How about everyone take a moment to compose themselves?"

"Sir, if I may?" Jill asked.

"Yes?"

"Don't you find it unusual for Lieutenant Daniels to call us in when we were just beginning our search? It's like he doesn't think we can find them."

It's unusual, all right, Theodore thought. But there was more to this. The higher ups always showed some lack of understanding about their underlings. However, this level of incompetence he never thought possible. For most of this pursuit, the *Tango* squad was told to keep back and not advance too far ahead of the crippled *Dakota*. His squad was treated like a dog on a tight leash. If the craft they were pursuing should escape, the Tango squad members, and not their superiors, would be the ones blamed.

"I don't know, nor question, my superior officer's orders," Theodor responded while those thoughts rumbled through his head. "I do know that whatever his plans may be, we will serve at his discretion and without question. Everyone here understands this, right?"

The members of the flight squad nodded. Within moments, the elevator doors opened.

The sound damper coils of the *Xendos*, it turned out, had disintegrated over time but proved surprisingly easy to fix.

After doing that job, B'taav and Cer ran a second major inspection of every component within the engines to make sure all the patchwork held and no leaks, tears, or burns were evident.

When they again ran the engines at full power, the sound and vibrations within the ship proved no more than a low murmur.

The *Xendos* was ready to fly.

The Independent and the Inquisitor left the ship's cockpit and met up with the other passengers. They were huddled around the escape sled and in the process of packing up their meager belongings.

"We're lifting off in a half hour," Cer said.

"A half-hour it is," Francis Lane said.

Maddox tagged along with Cer and B'taav as they headed back to the base's storage room.

"To get the *Argus'* central computer and Geist machine working, we're going to need every power cell we can find, just in case," B'taav said.

"There could be some compatibility issues," Inquisitor Cer said. "This place carried material for Phaecian, not Epsillon, spacecraft."

"We'll have to improvise," B'taav said. "We can get it to work."

"Good," Maddox muttered. "How about we grab what we need and get the hell out of here?"

Oscar Theodor was the first of the squad to enter the conference room. He was in for a surprise.

Seated around the table were members of the Blue Rogues, an elite anti-terrorist unit whose presence on board the *Dakota* was a whispered rumor since the ship's arrival at *Titus*.

The Blue Rogues were dressed in dark leather suits. Half the twenty members were male and they all carried gold insignias indicating they were squad leaders. The Blue Rogues' jobs usually involved insertion into hostile territory, identification of targets, hostage rescues, and, more often than not, threat elimination. Others, less charitably, referred to the later as assassinations.

Theodor swallowed. The *Dakota* was a very large craft, yet assuming each of the twenty squad leaders had a twenty person squad hidden away inside the ship...how had they avoided being detected this long?

But the biggest surprise proved to be the man sitting next to Lieutenant Lester Daniels. His suit was crisp in olive green, and the breast of his coat was filled with medals.

General Jurgens? Theodore thought. The situation must be even more serious than anyone thought.

"Fighter Squad *Tango 13* reporting," Oscar Theodor said. He addressed both Lieutenant Daniels and General Jurgens.

"At ease," Lieutenant Daniels said. "As you're undoubtedly aware, the gentleman to my right is General Anton Jurgens. You may also be aware that the men and women seated around this table are members of the Blue Rogues."

The Blue Rogue squad leaders acknowledged the pilot's presence with terse nods.

General Jurgens pointed to the large monitor immediately behind him. On it was a computer graphic that displayed the *Dakota* and her immediate surroundings.

"We don't have much time, so I'll be brief," General Jurgens said. "Since our abrupt departure from *Titus*, we've focused on pursuing a single craft. The craft had a considerable jump on us and has used guile to keep out of our reach."

Among other things, Theodor thought.

"We also fear they are listening in on our communications."

Several mouths hung open in shock at this revelation.

"If true," General Jurgens continued. "These people are not only fugitives, but they're also traitors to the Epsillon Empire."

General Jurgens let that revelation sink in for a few seconds before continuing.

"Since they may be using our equipment against us, we will change our procedures. Following your departure, we will use our sensor equipment very sparingly. We will also fly in formation, utilizing a phalanx of ships spread out in a broad area to canvas and, eventually, sweep our elusive prey into our grasp. All communications between individual fighter crafts are hereby shut down. You will only, and I repeat, *only* use communication between crafts in the event of an emergency. You will not talk to each other or to command. You will not update each other on your status."

Theodor raised his hand.

"Sir?"

"Yes?"

"What if we find them? Shouldn't we—"

"Let me repeat," General Jurgens said, his voice brimming with anger. "There will be absolutely no communication unless I personally rescind the command."

The pilots knew better than to argue with the General. Confusion and concern regarding these orders was evident in each and every one of their faces.

"From this moment on, our method of communication will rely on a relatively old, and primitive, technology. Breadcrumbs."

It took all his might for Theodor not to scream. *Breadcrumbs? As if we haven't been crippled enough in our search!*

The screen on the far wall activated, showing a diagram of a small, rectangular device.

"For those unfamiliar with them, a Breadcrumb is a battery powered mini-transmitter. It releases a continuous location blip and whatever information you choose to record on it. The device has enough power to last three months and its transmissions are limited to roughly fifty kilometers. When you have found the hostile craft and initiated pursuit, you will begin dropping these transmitters. One after the other every fifty kilometers. The fighter crafts behind you will have a very clear path to follow, and because the transmission signal extends in such a small area, there's no way the craft you are pursuing will realize we're coming, unless they double back. We don't anticipate this."

Bewildered looks filled the pilots' faces. Oscar Theodor raised his hand once again.

"Yes, Officer Theodor?"

"Given the device's narrow range, how many of them will we carry on each ship?"

"One thousand five hundred of the Breadcrumbs fit into a single missile tube. At this moment, all the missile tubes in your fighter crafts are being filled with these devices."

The bewildered looks turned downright hostile. Oscar Theodor noted the sour mood spreading like a thick fog. He worried his underlings might say something untoward.

"Begging your pardon, sir," Theodor continued. Though he tried his best to maintain a respectful tone, it was difficult to hide the bitterness from his voice. "Do you mean to send us after these hostiles unarmed?"

General Jurgens took several seconds before answering.

"Your ships' offensive weaponry will be limited to laser cannons," he acknowledged. "But you will have backup. Each of your fighter crafts will be assigned a squad of Blue Rogue officers. It is our hope the Blue Rogues unique skills will not, in the end, be needed. But if they are, you can rest assured you'll be in good hands. I know it'll be a tight fit, but I'm sure you'll make them comfortable."

General Jurgens pressed a button on the table and the diagram of the Breadcrumb was replaced by several blips.

"These blips indicate the various points your squads are to be positioned in the next hour. Where we go from there, as well as the particulars of your mission, will be revealed by the Blue Rogue commander in each of your ships. In lieu of any direct orders from me, you will follow the Blue Rogue commander's orders to the letter. *Any* deviation will be met with punishment. Is that understood?"

"Yes sir," the squad group replied in unison.

"Good," General Jurgens said. "Now let's get to it."

It took the full half-hour for Cer and B'taav to transfer the material from the storage room to the *Xendos*. When they were done, they met up with Dave Maddox in the cockpit of the ship and, for one last time, checked their instrumentation. Maddox sat in the engineer's seat.

"Is everything ready?" he asked.

"Ship's engines and computer systems are online and

functioning," B'taav said. "We cleaned out all usable spare parts and they're tucked into the ship's cargo bay. We're just waiting for our route."

"We'll get that soon enough," Maddox said.

The bartender was true to his word. Only seconds later, the cockpit door opened and Ned Frasier stepped in. As always, he was dressed in immaculate white and, like the other passengers, appeared exhausted. He reached into his jacket and pulled out a shiny metal disk and handed it to Inquisitor Cer.

"On the disk is all the information we could draw from the probe Kelly Lang found. If this information isn't accurate, all our efforts will prove a colossal waste of time."

Inquisitor Cer slid the disk into the navigational system and uploaded it into the computer. The general location of the *Argus* was listed as seven months full speed flight from their current location.

"We barely have enough supplies to get there, and certainly not enough to get back," B'taav said. "Is this a one way trip?"

"You forget, everything within the Erebus system is in motion," Frasier said. "The location you are reading is our estimate of the original position of the *Argus* following the explosion." The exhaustion on his face gave way to melancholia. "A...companion of mine and I made a detailed study of the asteroid migration. We examined the position the probe *thought* it was at, based on its final telemetry readings before its computers lost power, versus where Lang picked her up. Those readings allowed us to project an estimate of where the *Argus* is currently located, give or take a couple thousand kilometers."

Frasier reached between B'taav and Cer and pressed a series of buttons on the Nav Computer. A red sphere appeared in the schematic.

"That is our destination."

"It's an awfully big area," the Independent said.

"Yes," Frasier acknowledged. "But its outer edges lay no more than a week's travel from here, versus seven months. We will undoubtedly spend some time searching for the ship once we get there. But if things work out, it shouldn't take us very long. Who knows, we might even get lucky and find her right away."

Frasier rubbed his eyes. He returned to the door leading out of the cockpit and eyed his wristwatch.

"I'll help with the navigation but for the next few days, when Daniels' boys are closest to us, I'll leave the flying to you two.

When we've gained enough distance, we'll plot our search pattern. If you have any questions, please don't hesitate to ask."

"Of course," B'taav said. "My compliments on your estimates. You –and your companion– did a good job."

Frasier attempted a smile, but could only manage a slight nod.

"Let's get moving," Frasier muttered. His voice cracked with emotion. He stepped out of the cockpit.

B'taav and Inquisitor Cer looked at each other. Despite their glacial stares, there was a hint of anticipation.

B'taav flicked the intercom switch and said, "Ladies and gentlemen, we will be lifting off in five minutes. Make sure your seats are locked in an upright position and your seatbelts are on. All belongings should be stored in the upper compartment. We're in for a *very* bumpy ride."

Oscar Theodor swore as he steered his fighter off the *Dakota's* flight deck and into space. The lower compartment, where his crewmates waited for their shifts, was now crammed with twenty Blue Rogue troopers. Worse, in the very brief time they were together, prepping for lift off, it was clear neither group would get along.

Well that's too bad, Theodor thought. *We're all one big happy family even if we've been ordered to be glorified escorts to—* Theodor frowned. *—to wherever the hell we're supposed to be going.*

Theodor recalled the fearsome weapons the Blue Rogues carried. He didn't envy anyone who had to go up against *that*.

Theodor banked the craft to the right, away from the *Dakota,* and entered the asteroid field. The other fighter crafts of his squad spread out and hit their afterburners. In a few minutes they'd be locked into their positions and, in another few hours, they'd be sitting around in that asteroid field looking for the slightest movement.

And when they spotted it—

Theodor shook his head. He again recalled the Blue Rogues' fearsome weapons.

I guess we'll find that out when it happens.

He gunned the fighter craft's engine and steered to his assigned position.

Inquisitor Cer pressed a series of buttons and the gravity controls within the base shut down. Another flick of her wrist and the internal lights, the life support systems, and all remaining ancillary systems within the base shut down.

B'taav gently pushed the joystick before him and set off a small thrust under the *Xendos*. The ancient ship rose from her two hundred-year cradle.

"Decompression complete."

"Opening the outer doors."

Inquisitor Cer pressed a small green button in the center of the computer controls and looked up at the view screen.

The large outer door of the asteroid peeled away, revealing the darkness of space. In the near-distance floated several dozen other asteroids. A couple of them moved along as if they were orange clouds in a black sky.

It took a minute for the base door to fully open. When it was locked in place, B'taav pressed a button on the central panel.

"Get ready," he said. "Because here we go."

36

The first hour after departing the Phaecian asteroid base proved the tensest aboard the *Xendos*.

B'taav, Inquisitor Cer, and Dave Maddox stared out their windows while keeping a close watch of the ship's delicate internal instruments. B'taav and Cer were confident of their repairs but knew the ship's age and condition guaranteed things would not always run smoothly.

With the passage of time, B'taav's worries eased and his focus turned more to the asteroid field.

"We're doing well so far," he said. "Better than we had any right to expect."

"Agreed," Inquisitor Cer replied. "I haven't seen any sign of Daniels' fighter crafts."

"Is it possible they gave up?" Maddox said.

"I wouldn't count on...Look!"

Inquisitor Cer pointed out the window and to B'taav's left.

B'taav followed her gaze. Far, far away in the distance was what appeared to be a metallic object. Its surface reflected faint starlight.

"That answers your question," B'taav said. He pressed down on the controls and maneuvered the ship between a cluster of asteroids. When the ship was hidden from sight, B'taav eased on the accelerator.

"Did they see us?" Maddox asked.

"No idea," B'taav said. He accelerated the ship, until she shot around the asteroids and skipped to another group of rocks farther in the distance. "If they did, they'll be coming in." He faced Inquisitor Cer. "We should make a run for it. But I don't know if the engine will take that strain."

"One of us should watch it, just in case."

B'taav nodded.

"We'll switch off in a few hours," she said.

"Let's hope we're still able to."

Oscar Theodor noticed the flicker of movement out of the corner of his eye. He couldn't be sure if it was another spacecraft or a fast moving asteroid. By the time the magnification lenses were over his eyes, whatever he saw was gone.

Theodor turned his fighter craft around and increased the

throttle. Once his ship was headed in the proper direction, he pressed the intercom button.

"This is Theodor," he said. "I might have something."

"Might?" came the reply. The voice belonged to Richard Loo, the leader of the Blue Rogue 4 squad. He, along with his twenty soldiers, filled the lower deck of Theodor's fighter craft. Loo looked remarkably young, but there was little doubt he was fully in charge of his squad. His gaze was like steel and whenever he spoke his people listened.

"I saw movement, but only for a second. I'm going in for a closer look."

"Inform me the moment you can verify the contact."

"Yes sir."

Theodor reached for the communicator and was about to call in his finding to the other pilots and the *Dakota* before he stopped. He retracted his hand and shook his head.

This is so stupid, he thought.

What exactly were Lieutenant Daniels and General Jurgens up to?

B'taav stared at the monitor to his left.

It filtered through three different outer camera displays: The area directly above, the area directly below, and the view from the rear of the *Xendos*. The images were fuzzy, but B'taav wasn't complaining. It was a miracle they worked at all. Asteroids floated by at varying speeds. Some rotated while others were dead still.

Nearly five hours passed since he spotted one of Daniels' fighter crafts and ducked the ship among the rocks and out of the way. Since that time, Inquisitor Cer returned to the cockpit and B'taav made preparations to guard the engine. In between, the Independent saw no sign of any other ships or any evidence that the previous ship was following them.

This seemingly good news, nonetheless, made B'taav uncomfortable.

The *Xendos* was still well within Daniels' reach. If they were lucky, they might outrun the bulk of his fighter crafts in three to four days. Then they'd have another seven days' travel before reaching the outer edge of—

The Independent's thoughts were shattered by the high pitched whine of a fusion blast.

"What the hell?" Maddox sputtered. He jumped from his

chair in unison with Inquisitor Cer and B'taav. The bartender approached the door leading out of the cockpit but abruptly turned to face B'taav. He pulled his fusion gun out of its holster.

"Stay where you are," he said. "Keep the ship going."

Maddox pressed a button beside the cockpit entrance and the metal door hissed open. The acrid smell of charred flesh filled the cockpit.

"By the Gods," Maddox exclaimed and swallowed. He stepped just outside the cockpit door and leaned against the wall. He did not move any further.

B'taav pressed a series of controls and the ship slowed to a stop besides a large asteroid. Both B'taav and Inquisitor Cer headed to the door. Splotches of blood were plastered along the corridor wall and Maddox tried hard not to throw up.

"What is it?" Inquisitor Cer whispered.

Maddox pointed to the ground.

Lying on the floor were the gory remains of one of the three Mercs. The man's upper body just above his chest was charred black. His head was half gone, disintegrated by the fusion blast. Angry red embers throbbed along the lining of his clothes while smoke rose from the gash that at one point was his lower neck and upper shoulders.

There was enough of his face left to tell it was Kaspar.

Inquisitor Cer stepped past Maddox. Farther down the corridor she saw movement. She grabbed her fusion gun and aimed it into those shadows.

"Someone's there," she whispered.

B'taav and Cer stepped over the Merc's corpse and moved forward. Inquisitor Cer took the lead. Even though B'taav's eyes were better suited for the darkness, it was Cer who first recognized the figure hiding back there in the shadows.

When she did, she gasped.

37

Oscar Theodor couldn't help but yell in delight. Far, far away in the distance he finally spotted his elusive target.

"There you are," he muttered. He amplified the magnifier lens to their maximum. "*Posei*, but that ship is old!"

Theodor pressed the intercom button.

"I have visual of the target," he said. He heard his voice echo through the lower levels of his ship. "It's a Phaecian Cargo ship, classification unknown. She was weaving around some—"

"Hang on, I'm coming up," Richard Loo replied.

In seconds, the door leading to the cockpit silently slid open and Officer Richard Loo squeezed into the narrow space behind Theodor. He stared out the front window.

"Where is she?"

Theodor pressed a series of controls and portions of the forward window magnified. The Phaecian Cargo craft was displayed in the center of the view screen. She sat immobile next to a particularly large asteroid.

"Are you sure it's our ship and not some other scavenger?"

Theodor clicked the magnification controls until the digital image was clear.

"Based on their flight pattern before they stopped—"

"You're getting very close."

"Uh...isn't that what you want—"

"How long before we intercept?"

"Seconds."

"No," Richard Loo said. "Reverse course. Back us up and away."

"What?"

"That's an order."

Oscar Theodor pulled on the ship's control stick. His ship slowed to a crawl and stopped. Theodor nudged her behind an asteroid and out of sight of the Phaecian Cargo craft.

Richard Loo squeezed beside the pilot. The Blue Rogue squad leader examined the magnification image still on the view screen.

"Good work," he said after a while. "What were you saying about the ship not being a scavenger?"

"I can't be completely certain, of course," Theodor began. "We checked up on all ships in the area of *Titus* and they were accounted for. There were many different models, but none were of ancient Phaecian design."

"Are you close enough to get an ID of the ship?"

Theodor fiddled with the ship's image software. After a few seconds of doing so, he shook his head.

"No sir. We're too far away."

"What is the distance between us?"

"Two hundred fifty two kilometers."

Richard Loo nodded. His stare grew distant as he examined the view screen.

"Sir, we have them," Oscar said. "Shouldn't we call in the others? We'll have that ship and its crew captured before dinner."

Richard Loo did not reply.

"Sir?" Oscar insisted. "Shouldn't we—"

"Keep your distance," Richard Loo said. "We'll wait for them to move again, and then follow. If any of the other *Tangos* show up you are *not* to establish contact with them unless they make a move against that vessel."

"And...and if they do?"

"Intercept them."

"Intercept my own squad?"

"Yeah," Loo replied. "Do not use deadly force, but make *damn* sure they realize they're to stand down and follow our lead. The Phaecian craft is to be left alone. When they move, give me a call."

Theodor swallowed hard.

"Sir?"

"You have your orders."

Having said that, Officer Loo retreated from the cramped cockpit.

38

"I see him," B'taav said. He laid a hand on Inquisitor Cer's shoulder. "Let me."

B'taav stepped in front of her.

"No one's going to hurt you," B'taav said. He moved forward, until Inquisitor Cer and he were in the middle of the long corridor. Behind them were Maddox and Kaspar's corpse. An equal distance before them and in the shadows at the end of the corridor was the shooter.

"We know you're frightened," B'taav continued. "I am too."

The figure in the shadows remained still. Despite the violence committed just seconds before, his body was remarkably relaxed.

"I'm coming closer."

B'taav kept his voice low and mild and divorced of any emotions.

"We won't hurt you."

B'taav took another step, then another. The acrid smell of charred flesh filled his nostrils and made his stomach turn.

The figure in the shadows moved. B'taav spread his hands outward.

"I'm not going to do anything," he said. "I just want to talk."

The figure grew still. B'taav again moved forward. From somewhere behind, he heard the sounds of the rest of the *Xendos'* passengers rushing in from the opposite side of the corridor. The figure in the shadows once again stirred.

Inquisitor Cer spun around. Saro Triste, Balthazar, and Melchor ran to Maddox's side. Inquisitor Cer thrust her hand out and hissed, "Quiet!"

Balthazar and Melchor obeyed the command. Balthazar grabbed Triste by his collar while Melchor held his position. All was as quiet as before, and Inquisitor Cer gave Balthazar gave a nod.

The Inquisitor turned. B'taav was less than fifteen feet from the figure in the shadows.

"Easy," the Independent said. "I'm going to move nice and easy and nothing's going to happen. Do you understand?"

B'taav did not expect any reply.

"I'm taking another step," B'taav said. "Nice and easy. It's been a rough couple of days and I know you must be really tired.

We all are. All this excitement and movement wears you down.
So from here on out we're going to slow everything. I'm going to
take another step now."

B'taav lifted his leg. The figure remained still for a fraction of
a second as B'taav's foot left the ground.

And then the figure's fusion gun came up.

For the Independent, time slowed to a crawl. He lurched
forward even as the ear splitting blast roared throughout the
corridor. A wave of searing heat passed just over his head, a
fraction of a second before his body hit the cold metal floor. He
hoped none of the passengers behind him were in the path of this
deadly blast.

B'taav rolled away just as another blast slammed into the
ground, splintering and melting sections of the walkway.

Steam from a broken pipe hissed into the air and B'taav was
on his feet and running. Before his attacker could get off a third
shot, B'taav had his hands around him. He twisted the gun out of
his would-be killer's hands and threw it down the corridor. The
figure he held went limp, but B'taav did not relax his grip.

Through the mist of steam emanating from the broken pipe,
the Independent saw Maddox sprawled on the ground. The first
fusion blast clipped his left leg. He lay on the floor convulsing in
agony. Inquisitor Cer was already at his side. She ripped at the
fabric of his pants, revealing there was nothing left of the man's
leg below the knee.

Saro Triste, Stephen Gray, Ned Frasier, and the remaining
Mercs approached Cer and Maddox.

"This man needs medical attention!" Frasier yelled. "Does
anyone—?"

"Rasp..." Maddox gasped between clamped teeth.
"He...knew."

"But he's...gone."

Francis Lane pushed past the group. She ignored Maddox
and ran to B'taav. Tears filled her eyes when she stared at the
boy the Independent held so tightly in his grip.

"Nathaniel," she cried. "What have you done?"

39

Oscar Theodor hummed a few bars of an old love song and tapped his fingers against the cool plastic paneling of his fighter craft. To his right was a snow globe with the words "Douglas Gardens" written along its bottom. Within the globe was a holo-picture of a mountain range, one of the prime vacation spots for young military men with free time on their hands.

How he wished he was there rather than here.

The Phaecian cargo ship hadn't moved in what seemed like hours. He eyed his clock and sighed.

No, not hours. Exactly one hour and twenty-three minutes.

Oscar shook his head. In that time, he thought up various attack patterns he could use against the Phaecian ship. Each guaranteed their prey would be crippled and captured.

Captured.

Wasn't that their original purpose?

"Guess not," Theodore muttered.

He stopped tapping the panel and sighed. Outside, past the front paneling, lay the asteroid field and the other Tango crafts. They were heading in this general direction. Beyond them all was the Phaecian cargo craft. She hadn't moved an inch.

Once again Oscar sighed.

Why hadn't they?

B'taav and Inquisitor Cer finished patching up the ruptured coolant tube in the corridor. Because of the nature of the damage, they had to turn the *Xendos'* engines off, a dangerous proposition considering where they were.

Modern craft had cut off valves throughout their lines and didn't require a full engine shut off for repairs of this type. Of course, the *Xendos* wasn't a modern craft. After the patch was in place, Inquisitor Cer and B'taav headed back to the engine room. Inquisitor Cer noted the coolant line pressure sensor readings.

"We lost one hundred and twelve cubic kilos of coolant," she said. "Bad, but not catastrophic."

"Let's get the engines warmed up," B'taav said. "We've been here too long as it is."

Inquisitor Cer headed to the central computer panel and flipped a series of switches. The angry hum of an almost cold engine starting filled the room.

"This will take a few minutes. Let's get cleaned up."

When he finished wiping off the oil and sweat from his body, B'taav changed into fresh clothes and exited his room. The corridor outside was quiet. He walked to Inquisitor Cer's room and knocked on her door. For several seconds he waited for a reply, but none came. She was probably already back on the bridge.

Exhaustion was getting to him, and B'taav lingered by the door longer than he otherwise would have. He shook his head and moved off, pausing for a moment beside Maddox's room. Familiar voices came from within. B'taav knocked and opened the door.

Inside were Ned Frasier and Dave Maddox. Maddox lay on his bed. A pair of black straps was wrapped across his chest and kept him pinned to the bed. The blanket that covered him was fresh and clean, except for a stain in the empty space where his left leg would have been. Ned Frasier tried to comfort the bartender.

Maddox grimaced when he saw the Independent enter the room.

"How are you doing?" B'taav asked.

Maddox gritted his teeth and said, "F...fu...fucking great."

"The boy killed Rasp, didn't he?" B'taav said.

Maddox nodded.

"I was in the outside corridor, looking around for su.. supplies," Maddox said. "I saw...I saw some movement...in Rasp's room and figured he was up and about. Before I got there I...I saw someone run out...out the jammed door. I couldn't be sure, but I thought...I thought it was Nathaniel. I looked through the crack in the door...where he exited...I saw Rasp in his bed...the knife...the knife in his chest."

Another spasm shook Maddox.

"I went...went crazy...forced myself through the crack. I'm...I'm smaller than just about everyone else here, but I still don't know how I...did it...Rasp died...died in my arms. He didn't say anything. I ran back to that jammed door...forced my way out...I couldn't...believe what the boy did. I had to find him...to see for sure. I still can't...I still can't believe—"

Sweat oozed from Maddox's forehead and into his hair and the pillow below. Frasier reached for a first aid kit on the table next to the bathroom door. He opened it, produced a syringe, and used it to inject a colorless liquid into Maddox's arm.

"Easy," Frasier said. "Go to sleep."

Maddox shook for several more seconds before closing his eyes. His body went limp.

B'taav eyed the sparse contents within the first aid kit.

"Is this all we have?"

"We've got a little more in storage. Not much more. I'll have to check around."

"Provided no one else suffers any serious injuries, there's enough medicine here to keep Maddox going for a while. Three weeks anyway. But if that wound isn't properly treated..."

"What do you want us to do? Turn back? Give ourselves up?"

"He may die."

"Do you think I don't know that?" Frasier spat. "We've worked together for over twenty five years. He's like a...a brother to me. We have to complete our mission, B'taav. If anyone gets their hands on the *Charybdis* bomb..." Frasier shook his head. "I can't allow it."

"Where is the boy?"

"With Francis."

"Did you know the boy was a killer?"

"No," Frasier said. He let out a soft, hopeless laugh. "But back on *Titus*, we suspected there was a traitor among us. Little did we know..."

"When did you suspect?"

"After Kelly Lang's ship exploded. Our business with him was done. There was no reason to kill him, yet someone in our group did just that. Then Daniels and his ships arrived. It wasn't too long after that I found Janet dead."

"Who?"

"Janet Donaldson. She was the best damn mechanic *Titus* ever had. She was never a full member of our group, even though she was my...my wife."

Frasier rubbed his eyes.

"Janet did what I told her and never asked questions. She's the one that got the information from the *Argus* probe's computer. She did all the calculations and came up with a theory of where that damned ship was. She thought I wanted to find the *Argus* because it would be worth a fortune to me...to us. The last –the only– survivor of the Erebus explosion was within our grasp and she thought I wanted to find her, to salvage her, to sell her.

She never knew that was the last thing on my mind."

"I found her dead in the machine shop the day before we departed. She was in her cot and...she must have been napping. There was no sign of a struggle. Like Rasp, her killer entered the room and...and...stabbed her."

"Why would the boy do this?"

"How should I know? When Francis Lane arrived, she showed up with him. I couldn't for the life of me understand why she brought him along. She said he needed her care and couldn't be left with others...I insisted she take him back, but by then it was too late."

A wave of emotions passed through Frasier. When they were gone, the man in white stared hard into B'taav's black eyes.

"Promise me one thing, Independent," he said. "Promise me you'll get us to the *Argus* so that I can blow that fucker to pieces."

40

B'taav and Frasier exited Maddox's room. Further down the corridor were Saro Triste, Francis Lane, and Stephen Gray. They talked in hushed voices and quieted down even more when B'taav and Frasier approached.

Francis Lane broke from the group. She wanted to say something, perhaps an apology, but Frasier waved her off.

The man in white walked past the group and to his room.

"He's a good boy," Francis Lane said to no one in particular. "I know he is—"

"Don't blame yourself," Stephen Gray said. "How could anyone foresee this?"

"She did," B'taav said. "How long have you known?"

Francis Lane's body shook.

"He...he's never been violent before. Not ever. At home he's quiet. He can't do anything for himself. He's never hurt anyone."

"You should have left him behind," Saro Triste said.

"It's a little late for accusations and second guessing," Stephen Gray shot back. "Can't you see she's under enough stress?"

"Please, Stephen. Saro is right. I *shouldn't* have brought him along. Nathaniel can't handle all these stresses. He's acted out in the worst way possible." Francis Lane fought back a sob. "I shouldn't have brought him."

"Is he under guard now?" B'taav asked.

"Of course," Stephen Gray said.

"Good," B'taav said. "You better get back to your quarters. We'll be moving again very shortly."

Oscar Theodor shot up in his chair and slammed his fist against the intercom button.

"They're moving," he yelled. He flicked the switch off and added: "Finally!"

Theodor worked the controls. The engines of his fighter craft quickly warmed up.

The chase was on once again.

B'taav pulled at the ship's yoke. The *Xendos* rose over the edge of the asteroid and descended down its back before the Independent leveled her off.

"She's responding well," B'taav said.

"Like nothing happened," Inquisitor Cer muttered. She sat beside B'taav and checked the computer's system readings. The door to the cockpit was open and just outside of it stood Melchor, one of the two remaining Mercs. They had long since removed the body of Kaspar from the corridor. All that was left of him were blood stains and the smell of burnt flesh. Each proved a grim reminder, if any was needed, of the events of a couple of hours before.

"Doesn't this ship have air filters?"

"The smell bothers you?" Inquisitor Cer asked. "I figured Tamarin Campaign veterans would be used to the smell of dead."

B'taav ignored her taunt.

"Get to bed," he said after a while. "I'm good for at least three more hours."

Inquisitor Cer rose.

"By later today we'll be past the scavenger's grid," B'taav said.

"We may have to use our sensors. But Daniels..."

"If we're still free tomorrow, we can safely assume we've outrun Daniels and his ships."

"Is that wishful thinking or logical analysis?" Inquisitor Cer asked.

"A little of both," B'taav replied. "We'll find out tomorrow, won't we?"

Inquisitor Cer nodded and walked to Melchor's side. She paused for a moment and motioned the Merc into the room.

"I'm getting some rest," she told him. "If the Independent does anything funny, shoot him."

"Yes ma'am."

"Inquisitor?" B'taav said.

"Yes?"

"Does Mr. Melchor know what constitutes a 'funny' move while piloting a two hundred year old craft through an asteroid field?"

Inquisitor Cer offered B'taav a serpentine grin.

"You'll have to be extra careful. It would be a shame if you got shot for nothing."

The three hours passed slowly.

B'taav made sure to keep Melchor aware of every turn and twist the ship took on its way. All the while, he kept his eyes on any unusual movements among the rocks. He spotted none.

B'taav wondered if they had indeed lost Daniels' search party. It was, after all, a very large asteroid field and Daniels could not be sure of where they were or where they were going. Their fighter crafts might well have overshot the *Xendos'* location by hundreds of kilometers, perhaps leaving them in the clear many hours before.

We'll see, the Independent thought.

Oscar Theodor hit the intercom button and said, "Ready to disengage primary flight controls."

There was a crackle over the intercom. A female voice replied:

"Secondary flight controls are active. Whenever you're ready..."

Theodor pressed another button and the panel before him went black. His copilot was now flying the ship from the secondary cockpit below. Theodor pressed a third button and his seat lowered into the body of his ship. He unbuckled his seat belt and unscrewed several life support hoses. By the time the seat had fully lowered into the mid-level deck, he was free of all restraints.

Theodor rose and stretched. The middle compartment was just a little larger than a tearoom. A dozen Blue Rogue soldiers sat on the metal floor. Half of them were asleep while the other half killed time by either playing cards, reading, or examining their weapons.

Theodor turned to his right. A clear glass panel directly below him revealed Karina Wilson manning the secondary flight station and piloting the craft. Behind her was Ramon Mann, the fighter craft's reserve pilot. It was no secret Ramon was sweet on Karina, though the feelings weren't mutual. Theodor tapped on the floor and both Karina and Ramon looked up.

"If you want to take Karina's shift, do so," Theodor told Ramon. "Otherwise, she doesn't need distractions."

"Yes sir," Ramon muttered. To Karina he said: "Would you like to...?"

Karina was already up and out of the chair.

"Knock yourself out."

Ramon strapped himself into place as Karina walked to the ship's mid-section. She stopped before Theodor.

"Want something to eat?"

"Yeah, that would be great."

"Good," Karina said. "You know where the food's at. I'm getting some sleep."

Karina gave Theodor a mischievous smile and walked past the Blue Rogue Officers. A couple of them eyed the ship's co-pilot and one blew her a kiss. She ignored them and continued to the end of the corridor. She stopped before a set of doors. One lead to the crew quarters, the other to the food dispensers. Karina entered the door leading to the crew quarters. Before it closed, she pointed to the other door.

"In case you forgot, it's over here," she told Theodor.

Theodor walked to the food dispenser room door. He eyed the crew quarter door and, for a second or two, considered going there. It had been a long time—

No, Theodor thought. *If there was ever a wrong time to be thinking about that...*

Theodor sighed and entered the food dispenser room. He found Richard Loo sitting before the only table. He held a small computer pad in his hands and was reading something off its monitor.

"Oh," Theodor said. "I didn't mean to interrupt—"

Richard Loo pressed a button and the computer turned off.

"You weren't interrupting."

The Blue Rogue leader rubbed his bloodshot eyes and slid the computer into one of his body suit's many front pockets. "Your shift is finished?"

"Yeah. I'll be back to work in another ten hours or so."

"Who's piloting the craft now?"

"Ramon."

Richard Loo thought about that for a second.

"I thought it was Karina's turn?"

"They swapped," Theodor said.

"I see."

"He'll be fine. He's fresh."

"I'm sure he is."

Theodor chewed on his lip.

"I wouldn't let him pilot the ship if he wasn't ready. I can vouch for all members of my crew."

Richard Loo nodded but said nothing.

Theodor reached for the food dispenser. He put a cup under the faucet and filled it with thick brown Nutra-liquid. He sighed.

"Officer Loo, why do I get the feeling you don't approve of

our way of doing things?"

"As long as we get results, I don't much care," Officer Loo replied.

"We'll do whatever you ask. Even if it doesn't make much sense."

Richard Loo's eyes meet Theodor's sullen stare.

"We're alone here, soldier. Speak your peace. You've held it in long enough."

"Are we supposed to capture the people we are pursuing or not?"

Richard Loo leaned back in his chair.

"Go on," Loo said.

"We could have had them a long time ago, maybe even a little after *Titus*, with minimal effort."

"Yes."

"So why hide? Why let them move along? And why are we following them around like a horny schoolboy after a cheerleader? It makes no sense."

"When did your initial orders regarding this pursuit come through?" Loo asked.

"Back at *Titus*."

"How close were you to our prey at that point?"

"Not..." the words caught in Theodor's throat and his eyes lit up. "Not very."

"Precisely."

"Wait a minute," Theodor said. "We weren't expected to capture them at that time? Why?"

"You tell me."

"The only reason to go all out back then would be to...to make them *think* we wanted to capture them."

"The best way to do that was to have you pilots think the same. We held you back as best as we could, but without being too obvious."

"We were ordered to stick close to the *Dakota* after she sustained her damage. Is she..?"

"She's damaged all right, but it proved a good excuse to hold you back nonetheless."

"And calling us in for that meeting and forcing us to use the Breadcrumbs at the expense of our best offensive weaponry, it was all part of your plan?"

Richard Loo nodded.

"If you don't want them captured, what do you want?"

"Come on, Theodore. That should be obvious."

"Where...where are they leading us?"

"That information will come. In time."

Theodor took a sip of the nutria-drink and winced.

"Gods," he muttered. He put the cup down and gave his taste buds a few seconds to recover. "There's nothing out here but rocks and twisted metal, nothing worth bringing in a battleship and its full complement of fighters. Or is there?"

Richard Loo folded his arms.

"As I said, the information will come. In time."

41

B'taav awoke to the sound of a persistent buzz over the intercom. His limbs were stiff from lying in the cramped quarters assigned to him. The buzzing continued for what seemed like an eternity.

B'taav sat up. He took a quick glimpse at the door leading out of his room and found it closed.

Locked, too, he thought.

The Independent stepped into the bathroom. He ran water in the faucet and sprayed it on his face. When he was done, he looked in the mirror and sighed.

It had been a little over a week and a half since Nathaniel killed Kaspar and nearly did the same to both Maddox and he. Since then, tensions grew aboard the *Xendos*. In part it was due to the child and his actions, in part it was the monotony of flying around the asteroid fields all this time. Regardless, the anticipation everyone felt about searching for the *Argus* was tempered by the reality of the enormous area they had to explore and the fact that they were flying blind without full use of their sensor equipment. Even though they hadn't seen any sign of Daniels' fighters, they still dared not fully use that particular piece of equipment, for fear of revealing their location.

The ship's passengers, for the most part, kept to themselves in their quarters, as if hiding from either B'taav or Inquisitor Cer or the remaining Mercs. Perhaps they understood it was best not to interfere.

During B'taav's pilot shifts, either Balthazar or Melchor escorted the Independent. As sadistic and loudmouthed as Melchor was, he was the less threatening of the remaining Mercs. Melchor was the type that let out his emotions, often very loudly. But once those energies were spent, he settled down and became almost friendly.

Balthazar, on the other hand, neither talked nor threatened his charge. Like Rasp, whenever he was around B'taav, he was completely silent. His cold blue eyes, however, never strayed far from his subject and his fingers gripped the trigger on his gun or rifle much tighter than Melchor ever did.

There was little doubt he would act decisively if provoked.

Ned Frasier often came by the cockpit to check on the progress of the *Xendos* and point out where either B'taav or

Inquisitor Cer should take her during their shifts. He, more than any of the other passengers, kept track of the search for the *Argus*. Yet every time he examined the location estimates, estimates he made with his late wife, he fought off a creeping sadness.

At the end of his shift, B'taav made it a habit of looking in on Maddox. The man's condition fluctuated wildly from day to day. Several days before, he developed a high fever and the odds of his surviving grew bleak. Somehow, he fought the fever off and two days after spiking it was gone. During the past couple of days his temperature was near normal. It was starting to look like he might survive the coming week, and B'taav grew cautiously optimistic he would beat the odds and survive until their return to *Titus*.

Should they ever return to *Titus*.

Ned Frasier proved to be the only other person who regularly visited Maddox. He too tried to be optimistic about his friend's chances, but didn't share B'taav's glimmers of hope.

The Independent splashed some more water on his face. The steady buzz from the intercom continued to pester him, so the Independent stepped out of the bathroom and to the intercom's speaker. He pressed a button next to the speaker and said, "Is this thing working?"

B'taav released the button and found the annoying buzz was gone. Over time, several non-essential systems on the *Xendos* had spontaneously come to life, like electronic ghosts rising from the grave. Perhaps the intercom was the latest of the lot.

The Independent dressed in a black suit and walked to the door leading out of his room. He knocked on it.

"I'm ready to start my shift," he said. He took a step back and waited for one of the two Mercs to let him out. After a few seconds, he knocked again. No answer.

"Great," he muttered.

B'taav walked to the intercom and pressed the switch. He was about to say something but held back. A frown appeared on his forehead and he hurriedly returned to the door. He listened for any sounds coming from the outside. There were none.

B'taav returned to his bed and lifted the mattress. Hidden beneath it was a pair of pliers, a screwdriver, and a computer pad. He hid them away several days before, when Melchor seemed particularly distracted. The tools could be used at any point, should the need arise, but B'taav spent much of his free time working on the computer pad. Only a couple of days before he had successfully entered his own lock picking program within it.

You never know when these things come in handy.

B'taav approached his door and once again ran his hands along the paneling to its side. He used the screwdriver to cut through a piece of the plastic paneling and exposed a line of wires. He pulled the wires out and, after examining them, found the one he wanted. He used the pliers to cut two cables and shut the lights of his room off. B'taav then pressed the exposed metal from the wires into the computer pad's input slot. The lock picking program churned out a code and his door slid opened.

B'taav waited for one of the Mercs to come storming into the room, but no one did. Cautiously, the Independent looked out into the corridor while pocketing his tools.

There was no one outside.

B'taav exited his room. The other doors lining the corridor were closed and, upon closer examination, B'taav heard no sounds coming from them. An eerie silence filled the entire area. For a moment B'taav wondered if the rest of the passengers had somehow abandoned the Independent and the *Xendos*.

B'taav made it to the end of the corridor and stopped before the door to Francis Lane's room. He pressed his ear against it and listened for several moments. As with the other doors, he heard nothing. B'taav worked the door's keypad controls with the computer pad until it slid open.

B'taav remained in the corridor.

"Ms. Lane?" he said. He received no answer.

The Independent cautiously stepped into the room and, after seeing no one was within, noted an enormous window on the opposite wall. Beyond it a series of dark asteroids tumbled away. Just below the window was a communication device and monitor.

"They gave you the luxury suite," B'taav muttered.

The Independent ignored the communication equipment and focused on the room's other contents. Two small cots were lined up just under the window, their sheets ruffled. In the center of one of the beds was Nathaniel's red ball. B'taav picked it up and unscrewed the top. The Project Geist memory cube was no longer inside.

B'taav laid the ball back on the bed and walked to the closet. Inside were two suitcases. B'taav opened the smaller one, but before he could examine its contents he heard a muffled sound coming from the hallway.

B'taav hurriedly rose and ran back into the hallway. B'taav opened the door to the room next to Francis Lane's. It was Stephen Gray's room, but there was no sign of him within. The room next door was Saro Triste's. B'taav found no one inside that room, either.

B'taav fought off a growing unease. Each of his silent footsteps roared in his ears.

After he passed Saro Triste's room he stopped. The regular humming of the *Xendos'* engines, a sound he had grown accustomed to, grew muted.

The ship was slowing down.

Had the engines malfunctioned? No. Even if that was the case, it didn't explain where everyone was.

Could Daniels' fighter craft have found and surrounded the *Xendos*? B'taav shook his head. He didn't see any Epsillon craft outside Francis Lane's window, and unless something radically changed, capture was impossible.

B'taav walked to the last door in the corridor, the one leading into Maddox's room. As he did with the others, he pressed his ear against it and listened. B'taav heard soft, muffled sounds coming from within and detected the acrid smell of vomit.

B'taav accessed the control panel in the wall with his computer pad. Maddox's door slid open.

The *Titus* bartender lay on his bed. His eyes were shut and his face had an unhealthy yellow pallor. Ned Frasier sat before Maddox. His face was ghost white and lifeless, even whiter than the usually immaculate clothing he wore. Vomit dripped from the edge of his mouth. On the floor before him was a puddle of the stuff. In his hands was an empty glass of some clear liquid.

Even from a few feet away, B'taav knew the man was dead. Poisoned.

A sharp sound came from the Independent's left. Melchor stepped out of the bathroom. His hands were wet.

"B'taav?" the Merc said. A vicious smile appeared on his face, revealing crooked teeth framed by thin lips. "Fancy meeting you here." The smile broadened. "This is going to be fun."

42

The smile on Melchor's face disappeared. He reached for the fusion gun in his belt.

B'taav didn't wait for him to draw. He ran into the room, jumping past Frasier's body and crashed headlong into Melchor. The Merc had over thirty kilograms of muscle over B'taav, and should have swatted the charging Independent aside. But when Melchor saw the Independent move, he took a step back and slipped on Frasier's vomit. The gun in Melchor's hand came up too high, and a single fusion blast hit the ceiling, burning a large hole into it.

B'taav slammed into Melchor and plowed the Merc into the bathroom. He fell hard on the bathroom floor and lost the grip on his fusion gun. It clanged against the metal sink and fell away.

Melchor ignored the lost weapon and reached for the Independent's head while B'taav delivered a series of blows to the man's stomach. B'taav pounded him as hard as he could, but the Merc's light armor absorbed the brunt of the blows.

"If that's the best you can do..." Melchor taunted.

The Merc's left hand grasped the back of B'taav's head while his right hand savagely pummeled B'taav in the face.

"...then this is going to be *real* fun."

B'taav was groggy from the brutal punches. For a second he feared he would black out. But his instinct for self-preservation was strong and B'taav surprised Melchor by springing back and rolling away. Melchor's hands, for the moment, grasped at air.

Melchor let out a roar. He had no intention of losing his prey. The Merc pulled himself into a crouch. The anger in his face abruptly turned to euphoria.

To his delight, the dumb bastard Independent was right there, just a couple of feet away. He could have run. He might even have escaped.

For a little while at least, Melchor thought.

Instead, B'taav chose to stay where he was. A sadistic smile formed on Melchor's face. He chose to stay right where—

The smile abruptly vanished when the Merc realized B'taav held his fusion gun.

It was the last thing he ever saw.

"Wake up," the weak yet urgent voice said. It called B'taav out from under a blanket of darkness and into the light.

The Independent's eyes fluttered open. He was in Maddox's room. Lying beside him was Melchor's corpse. Smoke emanated from the Merc's neck. His entire head was vaporized.

For a moment, B'taav felt like he might again pass out. The pain along his jaw and face was intense. It took him a while to replay the events of the past few minutes. When he did, he looked down, at his hands. He still held Melchor's fusion gun. The Independent tucked it away.

"You came to *Titus* looking for Accelerant," the voice that took him out of the darkness said. "You found it. These Mercs can't live without it."

"Melchor was..?"

"You're lucky you got him before he got you."

The voice was Maddox's. He remained in his bed. With great difficultly he propped himself up.

"Yeah. Lucky," B'taav acknowledged. "For the second time. Won't be so lucky a third. What happened?"

"The Merc killed Frasier," Maddox said. "The two came down from the cockpit. They...they were here to see how I was doing. I was half asleep. They talked for a bit and I...I couldn't get it all. Melchor goes to the bathroom and brings out two cups of water. He gave Frasier one and wanted me to drink the other. I set mine aside. I wasn't all that thirsty."

B'taav noted the full glass of water on the table beside Maddox. He picked it up, stepped over Melchor's corpse, and drained the liquid into the sink.

"Frasier drinks up. For a while, he keeps talking," Maddox continued. "Only much slower...then he...then he seized up. Melchor –that bastard– laughs. Frasier knew he was poisoned. He tried to spit out what he could. It was too late. Melchor stepped closer to me. He was about to force the water down my throat. That was when...that was when Frasier threw up on him."

Maddox clenched his teeth as a deep shiver passed through his body.

"Melchor...he kicked Frasier. Then he sees his pants are stained. He says...he tells me he'll be right back. He goes to the bathroom to clean up. While he's doing that, he tells me they'll be plenty of time to take care of me, then *you*."

"I heard the intercom buzz in my room. Was that you?"

"Yeah," Maddox said. "I did it while the Merc was in the bathroom."

Maddox winced. The effort of talking to the Independent was sapping him of what little strength he had.

"I never liked you, B'taav, not from the first time we met," he said. "The others bought your stories but I never did. Your presence was too convenient. Especially when Daniels showed up and we...we couldn't get any other pilots or mechanics. It wasn't so long ago I worked in military intelligence. One of the things they taught me was the best way to infiltrate an enemy camp is to make your services crucial to whatever *their* mission is. You make them take you in. That's what you did...isn't it?"

B'taav's sunken eyes sparkled.

"I talked to every pilot I could, under the pretext of looking for someone willing to smuggle me out of *Titus*," B'taav said. "I made sure they were aware of just how dangerous going up against Daniels was. I made sure they were so scared they wouldn't take me or *anyone* out. I figured the pool of pilots was shallow enough that you'd eventually need me."

"Clever."

"Not really," B'taav said. "No offense, but if you saw through this ..."

"The others might have, too."

"Yeah."

"Look, I don't know what your game is and frankly don't care. But if you're right, we're the odd men out on this operation and we're obviously no longer needed."

"What's changed?"

"You don't know?"

"No."

"Then why don't you take a look out my window."

With effort B'taav rose to his feet. The room spun around him and he shook his head to lessen the pain and vertigo. He stepped past Maddox's bed and leaned against the window's frame. Like Francis Lane's room, Maddox's had a large window looking out into space. His window, however, was on the port side of the *Xendos*.

B'taav gazed at the darkness. At first, all he saw were the asteroids. Small and large, thin and fat, dark and light. But, out in the distance, he noted an angular, lean shape. It was long, enormous, in spite of the obvious distance from them.

"By the Gods," B'taav muttered.

The *Argus* lay between the chunks of asteroid like some rotting, half-buried corpse. Her hull was charred and filthy black.

Parts of her plating were warped from heat and wear. Others were ripped or twisted like used candy wrappers.

Yet there she was, damaged but in one piece.

For several long, breathless seconds B'taav gazed at her and held back the shivers rising along the back of his spine. There was the lost super juggernaut. There was the fate of two empires.

There was death itself.

43

B'taav stepped back, away from the window.

A stream of thoughts shifted into overdrive. One in particular hit him hard. The Independent thought of the Merrick Industries pleasure craft *DeCarlo* and the horrifying fate of its passengers. He wasn't there when she was found, but Merrick gave him the holographic walkthrough when they first met. In all its gory detail, it showed the Independent what happened to the passengers locked inside that vessel. Their deaths were like the blackest of nightmares.

With a shudder, B'taav realized those who remained alive on board the *Argus* immediately after the Erebus explosion suffered that same fate.

"You were right," B'taav whispered. "She's still in one piece."

"We can't leave her like that."

B'taav motioned to Frasier and the Merc.

"What happened?"

"It's so easy to swear you will destroy the ultimate weapon, but when it is before you, in the palm of your very own hands...Power corrupts, Independent. Especially when this power can make you the ruler of the known universe."

"Were all of them working against you?"

"I don't know," Maddox admitted. "When the group arrived at *Titus*, their manners were...different. Rasp, Frasier, and I worried something might be wrong. Ultimately, we thought they were simply excited knowing our mission was coming to its end. We weren't overly cautious, and that was a mistake."

Maddox gritted his teeth as a fresh wave of pain passed through his body.

"I don't know why you worked your way into our group," Maddox continued. "I don't know what it was you were hoping to gain. But right now you're in the same position as I am, so don't start thinking you can make some kind of deal with them. They have as much use for you as they have for me."

"So we join up? Tell me, Maddox, if they hadn't betrayed you and we found the *Argus*, would you have had *me* killed?"

"Yes." The admission came without emotion. "I swore on my life I would keep people from knowing about the *Argus*. I wasn't about to let a stranger, an infiltrator, be the exception to that rule."

"And now you're the person who saved, rather than took, my life."

"I would gladly have taken Melchor's poison if it meant the secret of the *Argus* was sealed in my grave as well," Maddox said. "But I will not let them take that knowledge back. You can't go to them, so you work with me. If we're smart, we might get out of this."

"Alive?"

"That might be asking too much. Whatever happens from this moment on, we must destroy the *Argus*."

Despite the defiance in his voice, Maddox's eyes held a mix of fear, hopelessness, and desperation. Would the Independent help him, or was his whole life's purpose at its end? The fear in his eyes was present in the tone of his voice.

"There has to be some part of you that knows the *Charybdis* bomb cannot find its way into the hands of these people."

B'taav nodded.

"I know," he said. "What's your plan?"

Maddox let out a relieved sigh but composed himself quickly.

"Exactly the same as before. We get the Geist memory cube from Nathaniel's ball, get it to the Geist machine on the *Argus*, and use its information to set off the ship's self-destruct mechanism. Afterwards, we sit back and watch the fireworks."

"I found Nathaniel's ball in Francis Lane's room. The cube wasn't there."

"Shit," Maddox muttered. "They have it with them."

"Where are they?"

"Probably in the cockpit, gazing at their treasure."

"What about Nathaniel? Why was he brought here?"

"You got me. Francis Lane knew there was a good chance this would be a one way trip, and still she brought him. The funny thing is, I didn't even know she had a kid."

"Is it possible...is it possible Nathaniel *isn't* her son?"

"Even if that's the case, does it really matter?"

"Maybe."

"How?"

"The kid killed Rasp and Kaspar and most likely killed Janet Donaldson."

"You think Francis Lane brought him aboard as an... assassin?" Maddox said. "You think he was programmed to kill us? I've heard of some degenerate things done in the cause of King and Country, but this one ranks among the worst..."

"What about the Mercs? Aren't they employed by Francis Lane?"

"Yes."

"Then there's more to this," B'taav said. "Nathaniel killed one of the Mercs. One of *her* people. If the child is a programmed killer, why would he do that?"

"Maybe there's no logic to his actions after all."

"On the contrary," B'taav said. "His actions have been *very* logical."

"What do you mean?"

"All this time, he's been trying to stop us, all of us, from getting to the *Argus*," B'taav said. "Nathaniel's first victim was probably Janet Donaldson. She was working on downloading the information from Kelly Lang's probe and using it to pinpoint the location of the *Argus*. Killing her slowed you down, didn't it?"

"Yeah," Maddox admitted. "We had to do the final calculations on our own. It cost us valuable time."

"And allowed Daniels to solidify his presence at *Titus*."

"I suppose..."

"Then we had that coolant leak on the *Pilgrimage*. It was deep in the engine room, in a a tight spot that took me great effort to reach. Not as much effort for a kid."

"He was there," Maddox said.

"Yeah. I didn't see him, and I passed out while fixing the air purification system. Good thing I managed to fix it before the fumes got to me. When I woke up, the boy was standing over me. If I hadn't awoken..."

Maddox suppressed a shudder.

"The next time Nathaniel acts up, it's in the cockpit of the *Pilgrimage*, when we've got Daniels' fighter craft are all around us," B'taav continued. "The boy is under constant supervision, except he somehow escapes Francis Lane and ultimately sets off our sensors and gives away our position to Daniels' boys."

"It wasn't an accident."

"Francis Lane and I talk about how we can't use the sensors, that doing so would give our position away, and some light goes off in the boy's head. He does exactly the last thing we needed."

"We set up an even tighter security on the boy after that," Maddox said.

"So he behaves for a few days and everything is fine. Then, when we get to the Phaecian asteroid base, he takes advantage of another opportunity and, as he did with Janet Donaldson, he takes out Rasp."

"But Rasp wasn't a key member of this mission."

"But he was another body in the way, and the only one of us with extensive medical experience. If someone gets injured, like you, we can't treat them properly."

Maddox's face grew pale.

"Our only alternatives are to turn back or do what little we can and risk our team member's death. Either way, we're hobbled."

"I'll be damned."

"And all the while the boy's creating tension and suspicion and distracting us from our goal."

"Regardless of what happens, he succeeds."

"A little later, the boy acts up once again. He gets his best chance to end the search for the *Argus* once and for all. While being walked around the ship and escorted by Kaspar, Nathaniel gets close to the *Xendos'* cockpit. The boy makes his move: He grabs Kaspar's gun and takes the Merc out. I'm thinking his next step was to take out everyone inside the cockpit."

"Why didn't he?"

"Who knows. Maybe he was distracted. Maybe he lost his nerve. Maybe he realized it would be impossible to kill us all before we got to him. Whatever the reason, he decided one less crewmember, for the time being, was enough. He ran."

"That brings us back to one of our original questions: Why would Francis Lane bring this kid along?"

B'taav didn't reply, for he had no answer. He again looked out the window. The *Xendos* was running parallel to the *Argus* and closing in. The ancient Phaecian ship was dwarfed by the enormous super-structure.

"B'taav?"

"Yes?"

"I lied."

"About what?"

"I *do* want to know why you infiltrated our group."

B'taav offered the bartender a smile.

"In good time," he said. "For now, let's focus on keeping ourselves alive."

44

Oscar Theodor couldn't believe his eyes.

"Take a look out front," he muttered into the intercom.

Excited voices filtered from the deck below. Far in the distance, the enormous black mass that made up the unknown super-juggernaut floated among the asteroids. The ship Theodore was pursuing became as insignificant as a grain of sand up against her.

"What is that?" Theodor asked.

The intercom crackled with static before Richard Loo replied.

"Come to a full stop," he said. As the *Xendos* approached the craft, he pressed the timer button on his wristwatch. "We wait here for the others to arrive. It shouldn't take long."

45

Maddox's door slid open. B'taav carefully leaned out and checked the corridor.

There was no one was around.

The Independent stepped out of the room. He dragged Melchor's headless body to the door leading into a storage room at the end of the corridor. He placed the Merc's corpse within the room and behind a stack of boxes. The boxes didn't completely hide the corpse, but B'taav couldn't waste time looking for a better hiding place.

The Independent hurriedly returned to Maddox's room and, with a grunt, lifted the bartender from his bed.

"Easy," Maddox said. The slightest movement caused the bartender enormous pain, and lifting him off the bed was excruciating.

"Sorry," B'taav said.

"You sound like you...actually mean it," Maddox muttered. "What about...what about Frasier's body?"

"They expected him to be dead," B'taav said. "When the others come and find his body but not yours, hopefully they'll think Melchor is out and about, getting rid of you."

"That'll confuse them for...what? A minute?"

"We'll take what we can get."

"Sure," Maddox said. He looked at Frasier's body one more time. "At least he's with Janet."

Inquisitor Cer guided the *Xendos* closer and closer to the fifth starboard side landing bay of the *Argus*, just as Francis Lane instructed her to. The landing bay door was closed. It's once smooth surface was scared by innumerable asteroid impacts. Despite being warped and caved in, it held.

"There," Francis Lane said. She pointed to the edges of the landing bay door. "That's where we begin."

Inquisitor Cer nodded but. To her the cockpit of the *Xendos* was uncomfortably crowded. Saro Triste, Stephen Gray, Francis Lane, and Nathaniel were all crammed within. Balthazar stood just outside the room. After discovering the *Argus*, Melchor was sent down to fetch Ned Frasier and B'taav. He should have been back by now, but Cer noticed none of the others were particularly worried by his prolonged absence.

A beep emanating from the control panel drew the Inquisitor's attention. The ship's sole laser cannon was charged up.

"Take it out," Francis Lane said.

Inquisitor Cer aimed the cannon at the landing bay door's uppermost hinge and pressed a button. A searing laser charge leapt from the cannon and streaked directly toward the hinge. It hit it dead on and metal exploded in a blast of brilliant orange.

"Again," Stephen Gray said.

Another laser blast slammed into the hinge. Its energy proved just enough. The upper landing bay door slid off its moorings and drifted up and away. There was an opening more than large enough for the *Xendos* to pass through.

The occupants of the cockpit grew deathly quiet. They stared at the dark entry and wondered, for the briefest of moments, just what they would find inside.

"Permission to proceed," Inquisitor Cer asked.

"By all means," Saro Triste said. "Take her in."

Before increasing the ship's thrust, Inquisitor Cer offered a silent prayer for those whose tomb they were about to disturb.

B'taav laid Maddox down on the filthy floor of the small room.

"You couldn't find a nicer place than this?"

"All the luxury cabins were taken," B'taav said. He placed a black knapsack beside the bartender. "There's enough food and water in there for a couple of days."

"Like we'll last *that* long."

"I've also gathered your antibiotics and what's left of the anesthetics."

Maddox gave the knapsack, and its sparse contents, an indifferent gaze.

"All the comforts of home."

"In spite of the engine noise, you'll hear them when they come in," B'taav continued. He knew these sounds would also make Maddox's stay very uncomfortable, but there were very few who knew of this maintenance room and of the coolant lines that passed through it. B'taav removed Melchor's fusion gun from his pant pocket and pointed out those lines to Maddox.

"If they rush you, don't bother taking them out, for there will be too many," he said. "Aim for the coolant drains. One shot and the *Xendos* is permanently crippled."

"Isn't the coolant toxic?"

"If you need to fire that gun, it's a fair bet coolant toxicity won't really matter."

Maddox took Melchor's fusion gun.

"What if I take the shot now and end this whole thing?"

"Your goal...*our* goal, is to rid the universe of the *Argus*. Crippling the *Xendos* will get rid of this bunch, but the *Argus* isn't going away. You can bet Lieutenant Daniels, if not someone else, will eventually find her."

"What's your plan?"

"I don't really have one. But I intend to make our friends' job that much harder."

"Come on B'taav, I'm finished," Maddox said. He offered the handgun back to the Independent. "You're going to need this more than I will."

Instead of taking it, B'taav said:

"Be careful with that. And don't go firing it off the moment that door opens. If we're lucky, the next person coming in will be me."

"You're a crazy son of a bitch," Maddox said. "Good luck."

"You too."

B'taav gave Maddox one last look before exiting the room.

46

Inquisitor Cer eased the *Xendos* closer to the rutted landing bay opening. Once the ship was lined up, she steered it straight in, all the while checking and double checking to make sure no debris or jagged metal around the hole scraped or got caught in the *Xendos'* body.

As they entered the bay, a stygian darkness descended upon the cockpit. Inquisitor Cer flicked a switch and the ship's exterior floodlights came on. They illuminated much of the area directly in front of their vessel and offered its occupants the first look at the *Argus'* cavernous interior landing hangar.

What lay before them was a monstrous pit filled with the discarded toys of a giant. Cables, boxes, small and heavy tractors, as well as massive hydraulic machines spread out in the darkness. A ten-ton crane floated a few feet off the ground, its weight in zero gravity no more than that of a feather. Thick metal cables hung between the floor and wall like colossal spider webs.

"Careful," Saro Triste said, keenly aware that these webs, like those of a spider, could easily snare the *Xendos*.

Tools, some as small as a screwdriver floated before the ship's front window. A hammer gently bounced off the ship's side and spun away into the darkness.

Inquisitor Cer eased the ship fully into the landing bay and avoided the larger debris. After several tense minutes, the *Xendos* bypassed the major barricades and neared its destination: the doors leading into the *Argus'* main body.

Inquisitor Cer gently touched the ship down amidst loose metal sheets and boxes. She left the ship's floodlights on and faced the occupants of the bridge.

"We're here."

B'taav silently moved down the corridor and to the stairs. He climbed them quickly and examined the crew compartment corridor. It was unchanged from moments before and there was no sight of anyone.

B'taav returned to Maddox's room. Frasier's corpse remained sitting in its chair. The Independent stole a glance at Maddox's window and was transfixed by the sight of the interior of the *Argus* before hastily pressing the timer button on his wristwatch. For longer than he should have, he watched the *Xendos* make its way inside the massive ship's landing bay.

B'taav forced himself to return to the outside corridor. He made a beeline to Francis Lane's room, pausing for a moment before the door to listen for any sound coming from within.

Satisfied no one was there; he again used the computer pad's lock picking software to open the door and stepped inside. He walked to the room's closet and removed the two suitcases he found in his previous visit. B'taav focused on the small case first. He opened the case and sorted through its contents. There was nothing within but clothing.

B'taav set the smaller case aside and turned his attention to the larger one. It was jet black and made of an exotic, and very expensive, nomilium plastic. When B'taav picked it up he found it to be very heavy.

B'taav suspected the case might have a security device within and inspected it carefully. He found security locks on each of the four buckles. They were a type the Independent was familiar with and took little time to disarm. Once done, he opened the suitcase.

Inside was more clothing but buried at the back was a small black box and two bags. B'taav opened one of the bags and found wires of different colors carefully tied together. B'taav laid that bag down and picked up the other. He found Francis Lane's toiletries inside. She had a brush, cleaners, and three plastic containers filled with blue, white, and red pills. B'taav identified the white pills as analgesics and the red pills as decongestants. The blue pills, however, had no labels or marking.

Something about them seemed familiar.

B'taav turned his attention to the black box. When he picked it up, he was surprised by the small box's considerable weight.

"Interesting."

B'taav lifted the box from the bottom of the suitcase and laid it on the floor. There were no markings and its surface was smooth. He ran his hands along its edges and felt an indentation near one of its sides and pressed it in.

A slit opened on the top of the box. Three holes and a square indentation were also revealed. B'taav reached for the blue pills. Recognition dawned on his face.

The Independent scowled and muttered a vile oath under his breath. For several seconds he seriously considered hurling the box against the wall and smashing it to pieces.

No. That won't solve anything.

The Independent calmed down. He pocketed the blue pills and once again felt for the indentation along the edge of the box. He pressed it and the slit at the center of the box closed. B'taav returned the box to its place in the suitcase before closing it up and re-activating the security locks.

B'taav placed the suitcase back in the closet. He knew time was short and couldn't afford to remain in Francis Lane's room much longer. In his hurry to leave, he failed to notice a thin slit along the base of the closet wall.

Inquisitor Cer shut down the *Xendos'* engines and rose. Stephen Gray, Francis Lane, and Saro Triste remained in their places, gazing out the window. All of them were in awe.

"Even now, even though we're here...I never thought—" Stephen Gray said. A smile cut across his face. "She's intact. By the Gods, she's actually intact!"

Francis Lane shared his smile. Her grip on Nathaniel's shoulders tightened. "We built them to last back then. The Old Empire knew what it was doing. Let's not waste any more time. Let's move."

The group hurriedly exited the cockpit. They walked down the stairs and to the crew deck. They sped along the corridor with the intention of continuing to the decompression chamber that lay in the next level below.

"How many power cells did we bring?" Saro Triste asked Inquisitor Cer.

"Fourteen large power cells and fifty small ones."

"Will they be enough?"

Francis Lane thought about that.

"The *Argus'* doors have two energy systems, the main system and a backup. If the connection to the main system fails, a backup cell feeds energy to the door, allowing those with knowledge of its code to open it."

"Do we have the codes?" Inquisitor Cer asked.

"My research into the *Argus* revealed one of their primary, non-secretive access codes," Francis Lane said. "Thirty three, forty-four, and sixty-six. They picked that code for all the minimum security doors."

"Easy enough to remember. What if we need to pass through doors with secondary security codes?"

"For now, let's worry about getting the main doors opened,"

Francis Lane said. "There should be enough energy cells to get us through them. And there should be enough of the big cells to get the central computers online. If we're lucky, we'll get the artificial gravity mechanisms working and maybe even get the life support systems operational."

"Life support? How long will we be—?"

"Never mind that, Inquisitor," Saro Triste interrupted. "We need to work quickly. It's only then that we can proceed to the next —"

His words were cut off by the sound of an alarm. A red light flashed through the corridor.

"Someone's activated the ship's airlock!" Stephen Gray yelled.

Inquisitor Cer broke off from the group and ran down the hall. She passed several rooms before abruptly stopping.

"What in...?"

The group caught up with her. Inquisitor Cer stood before the door leading into Maddox's room. Sitting in a chair in the room was the body of Ned Frasier. Inquisitor Cer approached the man in white and checked for a pulse.

"He's dead."

"And Maddox is gone," Saro Triste said. "He couldn't have moved on his own."

"We're also missing B'taav and Melchor."

"We can sort this out after we see who used the airlock."

Inquisitor Cer turned to Saro Triste for guidance. The Phaecian Cardinal nodded.

"Let's get to the airlock," he said.

Inquisitor Cer was the first one out the door. She took a sharp right and disappeared down the corridor, followed by Saro Triste and Stephen Gray.

The last people to leave Maddox's room were Francis Lane, Nathaniel, and Balthazar. Francis Lane took one more look at Frasier's corpse and Maddox's empty bed. She also noted the dry vomit on the floor.

"Where *is* Melchor?" Francis Lane asked the Merc.

Balthazar shrugged.

"Find him. We'll need him. *Very* soon."

"Yes ma'am," the Merc said.

Francis Lane and Nathaniel headed after the rest of the group while Balthazar walked in the opposite direction.

47

Inquisitor Cer was the first to arrive in the decompression room's antechamber. Whoever had used the airlock chamber was gone, as the room beyond was empty. As the others made their way into the antechamber, she was already working on the airlock's computer system.

Inquisitor Cer pressed several other buttons and the three monitors over the computer system came alive. They showed the area immediately outside the *Xendos*. Inquisitor Cer moved the outer camera until she caught sight of someone in an environmental suit on the *Argus'* flight deck. He was too short to be Melchor and obviously couldn't be the injured Maddox.

"It's B'taav," Stephen Gray said.

The man in the space suit carried a large black case in his right hand and a computer pad in the other.

"He's got the power cells," Saro Triste said. "What is he doing?"

B'taav walked to the door leading from the flight deck into the body of the *Argus*. It was already half open. With some effort, he slid it open the rest of the way. Without pausing, he disappeared into the darkness within.

"Son of a bitch," Stephen Gray spat. "B'taav killed Frasier and now he's inside the *Argus*. He means to get the *Charybdis* device for himself!"

"How far will he get without the proper codes?" Saro Triste asked.

"Not very," Francis Lane said.

"Reprogramming that computer pad to be a lock picking device isn't that difficult, if you know how," Inquisitor Cer said. "The Independent wouldn't take this action without some kind of plan."

"You believe he thought this through?" Stephen Gray said. "What, in your considered opinion, could his plan possibly be?"

"All I can offer are guesses," Inquisitor Cer said. "Once we found the *Argus*, the Independent likely feared his usefulness to us was at its end."

"You think he's trying to make himself useful again?" Saro Triste said. "By getting his hands on the bomb?"

"What else of value is there in this place?"

Stephen Gray shook his head.

"He has to be stopped."

"Indeed," Saro Triste said. He laid both hands on Inquisitor Cer's shoulders. "For a long time you've wanted to get your hands on the Independent, have you not Inquisitor?"

"Cardinal?"

"You are among friends," Saro Triste said. "We know you share little love with the Independent, especially because of his involvement in the Tamarin Campaign."

Inquisitor Cer took a step back.

"You overheard my conversations with the Independent?"

"It was for your benefit, child. We had to make sure no harm came to you." Saro Triste offered the Inquisitor a sympathetic smile. "It pains me that you spent so much time with that loathsome war criminal."

A savage darkness settled on Inquisitor Cer's face.

"You wish me to stop the Independent?" she asked.

There was a long pause as Saro Triste considered her question. When Saro Triste spoke next, his voice was deadly serious.

"You will stop him," Saro Triste said. "I do so order."

"Your lordship," Inquisitor Cer said and bowed.

Inquisitor Cer approached the lockers on the other side of the room and pulled out one of the eleven remaining environmental suits. She examined it, making sure that the Independent hadn't performed any sabotage on it. Once satisfied the suit was intact, she put it on.

"Remember, any communications between us must be limited," Inquisitor Cer said before screwing her helmet on. "B'taav will hear anything we say."

Stephen Gray swore.

"Frasier should have invested in better quality suits. Suits capable of sending encrypted messages."

"No use worrying about that now," Francis Lane said.

Inquisitor Cer nodded. She placed the helmet over her head and stepped to the airlock door.

"Good hunting," Saro Triste said.

Inquisitor Cer hooked her fusion gun to a holster on the suit's side. She keyed in the airlock entry code and the chamber beyond filled with air and was pressurized. When the environment mirrored that of the inside of the *Xendos*, the bulky security door slid open. Inquisitor Cer stepped into the airlock chamber. The door sealed after her, and the chamber's atmosphere was drawn and replaced with cold vacuum.

The moment the outer doors of the *Xendos* opened Inquisitor Cer felt little of the bitter cold filling the *Argus'* landing bay. With only minor hesitation, she took her first steps outside the *Xendos* and onto the landing bay of the super juggernaut. Though her mind was focused on her mission, it was hard not to stare at the wonders surrounding her.

The landing bay was massive. She looked up and past the dangling cables and long burnt out lights and saw a stygian darkness. It was impossible to guess how high the ceiling rose. To her right and left, the floor extended for what seemed like miles before it too disappeared into darkness.

Despite the Inquisitor's years of service and courage in the face of danger, it was difficult not to feel overwhelmed. She took a moment and allowed a chill to pass. Once gone, her jaw clenched. Whatever fears she felt were consigned to the back of her mind.

It was time to move forward.

The bay floor was covered in a thick layer of red dust and B'taav's footprints were clearly visible. Provided the dust made its way inside the super juggernaut, his path would be an easy one to follow.

Inquisitor Cer focused her attention on the door B'taav entered moments before.

Time to get to work, she thought as she followed his footprints and entered the *Argus* itself.

B'taav knew whatever time he had was short. He switched his communicator on and stepped deeper into the wide corridor leading away from the landing bay. B'taav worked his way to another heavy door, a security hatch, and knew it hadn't been opened since—

The thought made B'taav pause. He could imagine the fading screams of the *Argus* crew. The very last sounds as, one by one, the crew died. Without hope, they died in terror.

B'taav leaned against the wall. Thoughts of the bloody carnage from the *DeCarlo* assaulted his mind.

"Enough," the Independent yelled. His voice quickly dropped to a hushed whisper. "Enough."

He steadied his footing and shook the black thoughts from his mind as best he could before placing his black case on the floor. He opened it. Within were a collection of tools and batteries. B'taav grabbed a screwdriver and got to work on the large panel beside the heavy door. In normal conditions, forcing the panel open would take only a few seconds. Working in the cumbersome environmental suit proved far more difficult. Frustration added seconds to the task, but eventually B'taav removed the panel and revealed the ancient computer that operated the door.

B'taav unscrewed several plastic caps from beside the computer and pulled out two wires attached to a drained mini-cell battery. He removed the ancient battery and hurled it down the corridor, where it floated away until it was swallowed by darkness. B'taav then reached into his black case and grabbed a fresh new mini-cell battery. He fastened the wires to openings on the surface of the cell and pushed it into place.

Either this works or—

The Independent jumped when the computer came alive. Like the *Xendos* and the Phaecian asteroid base, the vacuum of space preserved this rugged instrument.

Hopefully, it preserved much more.

B'taav hurriedly closed his case and gripped it in his left hand. He pressed his computer pad against the numerical keypad in the middle of the massive door. A series of red lights flashed on the pad. One after another the lights settled until they displayed a sequence of numbers. 334466.

That was easy enough, B'taav thought. He entered the code and felt vibrations. The massive gears turn inside the walls and the door him slid open. B'taav recovered his computer pad and stepped into the darkness that lay beyond.

The drained mini-battery cell floated by Inquisitor Cer and headed straight toward the *Argus'* landing bay. Inquisitor Cer watched it bounce harmlessly against some debris before stopping.

Her target was very close.

48

Francis Lane scowled as Stephen Gray turned off the communicator.

"You look worried, Francis," Saro Triste said. "Don't be. Inquisitor Cer will find, and kill the Independent."

"Are you certain?" Francis Lane said.

"She will do as she's commanded," Saro Triste replied. "My orders are absolute and unquestionable." He stared past Francis Lane and Nathaniel. "Unlike those you issue to your Mercs."

A flicker of anger, a remnant of past arguments, appeared in Francis Lane's eyes.

"We agreed to these actions," she said. "Melchor had the honor of killing Frasier and Maddox. If there is blame, it will be shared."

"Yes," Triste replied. "But *I* suggested sending both Melchor and Balthazar together do the job, not Melchor alone."

"Frasier would become suspicious if both Mercs showed up to just escort him topside."

"My dear Francis, we are on the *Argus*. At this point, why bother with subtleties? By the way, where is Balthazar?"

"Searching for Melchor," Francis Lane said. "He's probably getting rid of Maddox's body."

"The bodies could wait," Stephen Gray said. "The Mercs could have helped your Inquisitor get rid of B'taav."

"You fear the Independent that much?"

"I don't fear the Independent, but it's a mistake to underestimate him," Stephen Gray said.

"She can take care of him on her own."

"Yeah, but why risk it? Besides, there were other alternatives, ways we could have handled this differently."

"You think B'taav could have worked for us?"

"Why not?" Stephen Gray said. "People like B'taav do their job for money. Besides, he is our second... "

The color in Stephen Gray's face evaporated.

"What?" Saro Triste asked.

"The Independent...He's our second pilot. Inquisitor Cer is our first."

"By the Gods," Francis Lane muttered. "They're *both* out there. How could we be so stupid!"

"Inquisitor Cer needs to return," Stephen Gray said. "Screw

the B'taav. Let him wander all he wants. Let's get Inquisitor Cer back!"

"She will take care of him!" Saro Triste said.

"Look, Cardinal, accidents happen. B'taav might—"

"B'taav is nothing compared to an Inquisitor of the Phaecian Empire. She will do her job, she will kill the Independent, and we'll have one less problem to deal with."

"You need to get her back," Stephen Gray demanded.

Saro Triste folded his arms. He made no move toward the communicator.

"What's the matter? Won't she follow your commands?"

"Issuing a death sentence is something we do not take lightly," Saro Triste said. "Once this command, is made, it stands. Until the job is done."

"Oh, for—"

"I would ask you not mock our beliefs."

"Look," Stephen Gray insisted. "We all may know, on a rudimentary level, how to fly this craft. But there's no way we could get through that asteroid field and back to *Titus*. Hell, I doubt we could even make it out of the *Argus'* landing bay. And even if we did, what if we had a mechanical failure on our way back to *Titus*? What would we do then?"

Saro Triste was unmoved.

"The matter is closed. Inquisitor Cer will complete her job."

"You noble types are so fucking stubborn," Stephen Gray said. "Let's hope that doesn't send us to the grave."

Francis Lane stepped between Stephen Gray and Saro Triste.

"All right," she said. "You've made your points. If Inquisitor Cer eliminates B'taav and makes her way back, we're fine. If things work out the other way, and B'taav somehow gets the better of her—"

"Such a thing will not happen," Saro Triste said.

"If such an unthinkable thing *should* happen, we're still fine," Francis Lane concluded. "In the end, B'taav has to come back here for he has no other choice. If he's shows up, we deal with him from a position of strength. We can tell him Inquisitor Cer acted alone, that she was out for revenge because of his involvement in the Tamarin campaign. In the end, he'll listen to what we say. He won't believe it, but we have the only means out of here."

Both Saro Triste and Stephen Gray considered Francis Lane's words.

"We're almost at the end," Stephen Gray said after a few

seconds. "We've hit a couple of bumps on the way but you're right. In a few more hours, we'll be done."

"Exactly," Francis Lane said. "But from here on in, we don't let anything else slip."

"Agreed," Saro Triste said.

Stephen Gray eyed young Nathaniel. The boy stood near Francis Lane. His eyes were half-closed and he didn't appear to have heard or understood a word of their conversation.

"What do we do now?" Francis Lane asked.

Stephen Gray's gaze remained on Nathaniel.

"It's time we got our money's worth from this boy."

49

B'taav stepped past cargo boxes the size of small buildings while pushing away packing material and other unidentifiable floating debris.

The lights coming from his environmental suit helmet illuminated the corridor before him. He swept the flashlight stitched into the suit's right forearm from side to side. He moved along quickly, but paused now and again to get his bearings.

B'taav eventually stopped before an enormous decompression chamber, the largest he had ever seen. A small fleet of ships the size of the *Xendos* could certainly pass through it.

"Nothing about this place is small," B'taav muttered.

The Independent adjusted the illumination of his helmet and ran the beam across the chamber's far walls. The opposite wall was crushed in, likely the result of a collision between the ship and an asteroid. The wall held despite the blow, but stress fractures as large as the *Dakota* were left in the thick metal paneling. At a few points the stress was severe enough to cause jagged cracks. B'taav spotted asteroids floating in space just beyond.

B'taav soon reached the other end of the chamber and paused before another enormous door. This one was at least ten stories high.

Really stretches the definition of a "door".

B'taav shone his flashlight across the base of the metal structure, eventually finding the computer paneling that operated it. As with the much smaller entry to the landing bay, he pried the paneling off and removed the drained battery, replacing it with a fresh cell. He then waited, and hoped, for the computer system to boot up.

His wait proved long, and the Independent worried his luck had run out.

"Come on," B'taav said. If he was to have any chance at all, he needed to get past this chamber.

More minutes passed, and B'taav grew increasingly concerned. He looked around, trying to see if there was some other way past this point. He saw nothing close by. A minute passed. Two. Worry filled the Independent's face. Just when he was about to look for an alternate route, the computer panel came alive.

"Took your time," B'taav said. He punched in the "334466" code and hoped the code was reused on these levels. The door didn't budge.

We'll have to do this the hard way.

B'taav retrieved his computer pad from a side pocket on his environmental suit and placed it over the computer keys. The lock picking software was initiated and several red lights flickered on the device's body. After a few moments, a display read "Alpha Alpha 345 Theta 1".

The Independent keyed the code in and a series of intense vibrations shook the ground around him. The Independent feared the whole ship was falling apart. And then the doors slowly opened.

B'taav stepped inside and shone his light at the chamber beyond. It was as large as the one he just exited and packed from floor to ceiling with even more supply crates. The crates carried labels identifying the cargo as machine equipment, spare parts, tools, and various brands of coolant and engine oils.

Before moving deeper into this new chamber, B'taav looked back into the chamber he just exited. He noticed a flicker of light coming from the door leading into it from the landing bay. As he feared, someone from the ship was after him.

B'taav ordered the enormous door shut.

Inquisitor Cer stepped into the decompression chamber and felt the floor vibrate. At the far end of the room she spotted movement and realized the far wall was actually an enormous sliding door. It was moving down, back to the floor.

Cer took full advantage of the weightless conditions and leaped forward. Despite her best efforts, she could not reach the door before it closed. With one final, heavy vibration, the door sealed and locked into place.

Inquisitor Cer examined the computer paneling beside the door. B'taav didn't have time to shut it down or, had he wanted to, destroy it.

Wouldn't be a good idea anyway, Inquisitor Cer thought. *This is your only way back out.*

Inquisitor Cer keyed in the main numerical code Francis Lane gave her and, like the Independent before her, waited to see if it would work.

Balthazar opened the door leading into the small maintenance closet. Francis Lane, Stephen Gray, and Saro Triste crowded into the closet and stood over the remains of Melchor.

Francis Lane noted the bruises on his hands.

"He put up a struggle," she said. "Frasier died in his chair, unaware he was poisoned. Maddox was incapable of fighting back."

"Then who?" Saro began. His eyes grew dark. "B'taav. How the hell?"

"Maybe we'll get a chance to ask him. He somehow found out what Melchor was up to. Maybe he entered Maddox's room while Melchor was in the process of disposing of Maddox's—"

Francis Lane gasped.

"Maddox isn't dead," she said. "That's why B'taav hid Melchor's body. He was buying time. He wanted us to *think* Melchor was getting rid of Maddox."

"Have Maddox and the Independent formed an alliance?" Stephen Gray said.

"If so, B'taav might not be looking for the *Charybdis* bomb after all," Francis Lane said. "He means to destroy the *Argus*."

"How?" Saro Triste asked.

"If he has converted a computer pad into a lock picking device, is it possible he's made it sophisticated enough to decode the *Argus'* self-destruct mechanism?"

"Picking the lock on common usage doors and accessing one of the most sensitive pieces of information on a military vessel are two very different things," Francis Lane said.

"Then B'taav took a great gamble and lost," Saro Triste said.

"Did he?" Stephen Gray said. "It is even more imperative than ever your Inquisitor take the Independent out. In the meantime, we have to find Maddox."

"What possible harm could that cripple do to us?" Francis Lane countered.

"Plenty. If I were B'taav, I'd place Maddox in a sensitive part of the *Xendos* and give him the means to disable this ship. Maddox would die a very happy man if he could seal us in this tomb."

"Then we need to find him," Saro Triste said.

"No," Francis Lane countered. "If B'taav did as you say, searching for Maddox would ensure we lose this ship."

"What should we do? Nothing?!"

"Time is on our side, not Maddox's," Francis Lane said.

"Assume our work takes several days. Perhaps even a week or two. To us, that's not so bad. We've got plenty of supplies and we're healthy. The same cannot be said of Maddox."

"You're hoping Maddox's injuries eventually kill him?" Saro Triste mocked. "Or do you hope to starve him out? What if he realizes we're waiting and decides to go ahead and sabotage the *Xendos* anyway?"

"He hasn't done anything yet, which means *for now* he believes B'taav will succeed in what he's doing," Francis Lane said. "So *for now* we keep everything as it is. B'taav undoubtedly left Maddox with some food and water and whatever medicines he could find. He'll last, but each minute that passes he'll grow weaker and his supplies dwindle. We just make sure Maddox doesn't know how B'taav –or we– are progressing. Waiting for good news may prove Maddox's downfall."

Inquisitor Cer's fingers ran across the computer panel beside the massive decompression door and typed in the 334466 code. When nothing happened, she re-entered the code. The computer took the information, considered it, and again rejected it.

Inquisitor Cer considered her options and realized there were none. She needed to get the code for this door or her pursuit of B'taav was over. She clicked her communicator on and attempted to reach the *Xendos* for instructions.

All she got was static.

The *Argus'* walls were thick and the communication equipment within her suit, already limited to a single channel that her target could hear, was also not powerful enough to breach such obstacles. Nevertheless, she tried again. And again. After her fourth attempt, she leaned back, frustrated. She would have to return, at least far enough to get her signal—

"—quisitor Cer... read me?"

The voice over her speaker was low and static-filled, but understandable. The message was repeated, even stronger than before.

"Inquisitor Cer, do you read me?"

The voice was that of Stephen Gray.

"Loud and clear," Inquisitor Cer said.

"Good. We sent out Balthazar when we heard your first transmission. He set up an amplification beacon. It will allow us to communicate across greater distances. Have you found

B'taav?"

"No," Cer said. "I'm at an airlock, number 354. The code Francis Lane gave me doesn't work. I need more access codes."

On board the *Xendos*, Stephen Gray manned the communications in the decompression antechamber. For the past few minutes he fiddled with the ship's computer, adding new code while eying both the view screen and Saro Triste. The Cardinal stood a few feet behind him. His attention was on the *Argus'* landing bay, visible through a window in the chamber. Whenever the Cardinal looked his way, as he did following Inquisitor Cer's last transmission, Stephen Gray paused in his work on the computer.

"I read you, Inquisitor," Stephen Gray said.

He motioned to Saro Triste and pointed to the computer monitor. On it was Balthazar, returning from the *Argus'* landing bay and entering the *Xendos'* airlock. He no longer carried the shoe box sized amplification beacon he was tasked to set up in the internal corridor Inquisitor Cer and B'taav first disappeared into.

"Let me get you Ms. Lane," Gray said.

Inquisitor Cer waited a few seconds before Francis Lane spoke.

"Inquisitor, whatever information I give will be overheard."

"There is no alternative."

"Please confirm: You are at airlock 354?"

"Yes."

There was another pause.

"The code is Alpha 345 Theta 1."

Inquisitor Cer was surprised by the speed with which Francis Lane found the code. She entered it into the airlock's computer panel and the massive door moved.

"It's opening," Inquisitor Cer said. "How did you know?"

Within her room in the *Xendos*, Francis Lane stood near Nathaniel. A thick layer of sweat covered the boy's forehead and his face was flushed, as if burning alive. The boy's eyes were closed tight and a small line of foamy drool ran down his chin.

"Never mind," Francis Lane said. "Finish your mission. Be safe."

Francis Lane shut her communicator off. She pulled up the

boy's right arm, revealing a small yellow disk attached just below his right shoulder. The disk was larger than most Epsillon coins, but only barely. A series of yellow lights flickered on its surface. Francis Lane pressed the center of the disk and the lights dimmed.

The boy let out a loud sob as the intense pain he suffered until that moment was gone.

Francis Lane peeled the deactivated disk from the boy's arm. Three small rings of seared flesh were the only evidence it had been there.

"It would be so much easier if you told me what I needed to know when I asked. I hate having to resort to such primitive tactics."

She dropped the yellow disk into her shirt pocket and chuckled.

"You know how much I hate hurting people," she added.

Tears fell from the boy's eyes, but his sobs abated. He gave Francis Lane an insolent stare.

"If looks could kill," she said.

Nathaniel opened his mouth and tried to speak, but no words came.

"You're quite the fighter. I'll give you that."

She walked to her closet and pulled out her large black suitcase. She disabled the security mechanism and opened it. When she looked inside and at the contents, her face filled with surprise.

"What the hell?"

Francis Lane knew someone had searched the suitcase. She threw aside her clothing before reaching the heavy black box and wires. She gently pulled these items out and examined the box to make sure it was in one piece. Afterwards, she returned to the suitcase and removed her bag of toiletries. She found her blue pills were gone.

"Damn."

Francis Lane pushed the suitcase aside and returned to the closet. She removed her smaller case and set it aside. She could barely contain her fury.

"Fuck," she whispered. She fell to her knees and leaned down low inside the closet. She ran her hands along the corner wall until she felt a thin slit. She then pushed at the wall and a small piece of plastic paneling fell away, revealing a small compartment. She reached into the compartment and pulled out a black box. The anger in her face faded.

"You didn't find this one, did you," she muttered. She opened the black box, revealing the casing for a computer. She allowed herself a relieved smile and gazed once again at Nathaniel. The boy's face returned to its blank, lifeless expression. Unseeing eyes stared at the walls before him.

"The pills were important, but there are alternatives," Francis Lane said. "You thought you could slow me down, didn't you? You're a clever bastard. I wish I could see your face when—"

Francis Lane let out an angry chuckle. She shut the computer casing and returned to Nathaniel's side. She pulled his shirt sleeve down, covering the singed flesh on his upper arm. She lifted him to his feet and pushed him out the door and into the corridor.

B'taav passed a series of storage rooms. Within each were crates stacked up to the ceiling. The Independent could only guess at the buried treasures lying within each box, but even if they contained all the gold in the universe they were little help to him now.

For what seemed like hours he moved, passing one after another room. At times he slowed whenever he spotted an open crate, just enough to take a peek inside. Deep in the corner of one cargo box were what looked like SR 1 missiles. He hadn't seen such ordinance since his early days of training in military OPS. In another container he found food packets and hygiene supplies. In another, what appeared to be pressed clothes.

Now and again B'taav looked back to see if his pursuer was near. Thanks to her communication with the *Xendos*, he knew the flickering lights he saw before were from Inquisitor Cer. And if the communications were to be believed, he also knew that Balthazar wasn't with her. In time, he would likely be on his way, too.

Two against one is so much worse when you're the one in that particular equation.

The Independent reached a staircase leading up into the darkness. He could only guess the length of the climb.

"Away we go," the Independent muttered.

It took a while to reach the top. Once there, B'taav found another decompression door. This one had a very large glass panel in its center. B'taav looked through the glass and spotted a second, heavier decompression door beyond the first. On the floor within the decompression room were several small supply crates. One of the crates had ruptured, and its contents, engine lubricants still in their individual containers, floated within the room.

B'taav went to work on the decompression door's computer, doing the by now regular routine of replacing its battery. He tried the two codes he knew before resorting to his computer pad's electronic lock pick. He was pleased to find the second code worked.

His good cheer abruptly vanished when the door slid open and a burst of gas knocked the Independent back into the railing of the stairs. The force was enough to almost take him over the edge. Several of the containers in that room sailed past him, one slamming with incredible force into his environmental suit's face mask. For several terrifying seconds, B'taav thought a mark left behind indicated the face shield was cracked.

Thankfully, the burst of air was short lived and gone as quickly as it came. B'taav regained his footing and examined the mark on the suit's face mask. It turned out to be a line of plastic resin that spilled out of the container. He rubbed it off as best he could.

The Independent stepped away from the railing and entered the small decompression chamber. The lingering atmosphere was gone, dissipated into the vacuum.

B'taav closed the outer door and sealed it. He approached the door on the opposite side of this room and removed the paneling from the security system. Once again he replaced a spent battery and, when the security control was activated, he accessed the computer system. This time he requested a reading on what atmosphere, if any, lay beyond the decompression door.

When the reading came, B'taav had to scan it twice to make sure what he was seeing was correct. The area beyond this door had an atmosphere consisting of sixty three percent oxygen, thirty five percent nitrogen, and negligible amounts of argon.

There was breathable air in the chamber beyond!

50

Francis Lane gave Stephen Gray and Saro Triste all the details she could. Once done, the men's eyes were on Nathaniel.

"B'taav took the boy's medication?" Saro Triste asked. "Are there any other medicines on board we can use as substitutes?"

"I did a quick search, but so too did B'taav before he left. He not only took anything Maddox could use, but also any medication I could use on Nathaniel. Without it, it won't be long before the boy is outside my control."

"We can force information through...other means," Stephen Gray said.

"We certainly can try," Francis Lane corrected him. "But it increases our risk of damaging him. Not his body, I could care less about that. We have to worry about damaging his mind."

"How long do we have before the current dose wears off?"

"Hours."

Saro Triste shook his head.

"We were wrong when we said time was on our side. We have a very tight deadline after all." The Cardinal sighed. "Summon Balthazar. We need to get into the *Argus*."

B'taav allowed the atmosphere from the outer room to fill the sealed decompression chamber. When a green light came on over the decompression door, indicating the atmosphere and pressure was the same inside as it was outside the chamber, B'taav opened the far door. Despite the all clear readings, he took great care in doing so.

The Independent then stepped into the darkness. Unlike the cargo and landing bays, he found considerable signs of rust and decay in this area. He stepped cautiously, aware that because of the oxygen rich atmosphere, any spark could set off a raging fire. B'taav wondered how such rich air came to exist on this doomed craft.

The fact that it would remain in place all these years, was less of a mystery. Despite the considerable wear on the outside of the *Argus*, the inner compartments were largely untouched. The seals on most doors B'taav ran into remained tight and it was reasonable to assume the thousands of others within the ship were in similar shape. If not, the atmosphere would have dissipated a long time ago.

B'taav continued marching through the rusted corridor. He soon reached a series of internal windows that looked in on a very large chamber. B'taav wiped the grime from the window and aimed his flashlight within. He spotted what at first appeared to be melting iron rods. It took B'taav a few seconds to realize they were the remains of plants.

A hydroponics level, B'taav thought.

The Independent now understood why the air was so rich. The plants were used along with the ship's purification systems to filter the atmosphere. Before the *Argus* finally lost all power and the plants froze, they, along with the ship's ventilation system, had no doubt continued their work.

The plants must have been quite a sight, when they were alive.

B'taav continued his long trek. The Hydroponics area alone was easily twice as long as the *Dakota*. It was a wonder that a military craft devoted that much space to something non-tactical. Then again, a ship this size never existed before or, for that matter, since.

Soon, B'taav reached the end of the Hydroponics glass paneling. The corridor turned sharply to the right and B'taav followed along. The windows that overlooked the levels below were replaced with a series of doors. He paused to look into the first one and found a crew compartment.

A set of three bunk beds lined the walls within. Against the opposite wall was a shattered video screen. On one of the beds was a framed photograph. B'taav picked it up and gazed at the image of a pretty blond woman. She was not much more than twenty years old at the time of the photograph and offered a warm smile to the cameraman. On the lower right corner of the picture was writing. Parts of it were blurred with the rot that permeated the area, but the Independent managed to read the note nonetheless.

I worry so much for you.
Please come back safely.
I'll always love you,
Deborah

B'taav put the picture back on the bed. He eyed the other beds and noted several more photographs taped to the walls, a collage of pictures of different places and different people. People who no longer lived and places that no longer existed.

B'taav stepped out of the room and approached the next. He froze at that room's door.

Sitting on a chair in front of a video screen was a withered corpse. Long brown hair hung down her head. In her left hand was an antique Emerson handgun. The bullet hole that brought a speedy end to her life was all too evident on the right side of her head.

This was only the first body he encountered, B'taav realized. Surely there were many, many more elsewhere.

In the corpse's right hand was a clothbound book. B'taav pulled it from the corpse's fingers and opened it up. He read a few passages of the woman's journal before closing and returning it to its place.

"Rest in peace, Rebecca," the Independent said. He walked out the room and abruptly came to a stop.

A figure in an environmental suit stood in the corridor, blocking his way.

Inquisitor Cer.

In her hand was her fusion gun.

The communicator buzzed in the bridge of the *Xendos*. Saro Triste, manning the system at the moment, motioned to Francis Lane and Stephen Gray. They quickly came to his side while Nathaniel stood banished to a corner. Balthazar was the only one missing in the group. He was tasked to guard the decompression chamber, in case B'taav somehow made it back.

"This is Inquisitor Cer," came a static filled message.

"I read you," Saro Triste replied. "You have news?"

"Yes, Cardinal," Inquisitor Cer continued. "I found B'taav."

"We read you. Please continue."

"The Independent is dead."

51

Francis Lane let out a relieved laugh. Stephen Gray and Saro Triste couldn't contain their smiles and nodded in satisfaction. Only Nathaniel showed no emotion toward the news. After a while Saro Triste shushed his companions and reactivated the communicator.

"That is good news, Inquisitor," Saro Triste said. Try as he might, it was hard to keep the elation from his voice.

"I've recovered the stolen battery cells," Inquisitor Cer continued. If she detected the Cardinal's tone, she made no mention of the fact. "There is atmosphere on this level. I'm transmitting my findings and position now."

The trio looked over the Inquisitor's readings. A map showed her path from the *Xendos* to her current location, while below it was the atmospheric readings.

"Oxygen?" Saro Triste asked. "How is this possible?"

"Who knows?" Stephen Gray said. "If we have the time, perhaps we can investigate. After she restores energy to the central computer."

Francis Lane pressed a switch and spoke into the microphone.

"How does the computer look?" Francis Lane asked.

"There was heavy rust in some of the corridors outside, but it was limited to that area."

"Can you reactivate the central computer?"

"I think so. Yes."

"Good," Francis Lane said. She stepped away from the microphone and Saro Triste took her place.

"We'll suit up and meet you there," he said before shutting off the communications. He then faced his companions. "As I said, the Independent was no match for an Inquisitor."

"I'm glad you were right," Francis Lane said.

"Before we celebrate, remember that Maddox is still somewhere, hiding out," Stephen Gray cautioned.

"He doesn't know B'taav is dead," Saro Triste said. "Let's make sure he continues waiting for the Independent's return, until it's too late."

Stephen Gray and Saro Triste headed for the bridge's exit. Francis Lane approached the sullen Nathaniel and tried to get his attention.

"Coming, Francis?" Stephen Gray asked.

Francis Lane shook Nathaniel.

"With Maddox around, we shouldn't leave the bridge unguarded," Francis Lane said. "I'll call Balthazar, tell him to come up."

"Good idea," Saro Triste said. "We'll see you downstairs in the decompression chamber."

Once Stephen Gray and Saro Triste were gone, Francis Lane rushed back to the communicator. She activated the intercom panel and directed her message to the decompression chamber.

"Balthazar," she said.

"I'm here, Ma'am," the Merc replied.

"You heard the message from Inquisitor Cer?"

"Yes."

"Then you know B'taav is dead."

"Yes Ma'am. That is good news."

"Stephen Gray and Saro Triste are heading down to suit up. I am a few steps behind them."

In the decompression chamber, Balthazar cocked his head. Francis Lane's words were innocuous, but they also announced the fact that their conversation was private.

"Understood," Balthazar said. "What do you wish me to do?"

"You will suit up and take the lead. I will ensure this lead is considerable." Francis Lane pressed a series of buttons and sent information down to the decompression chamber's computers. "The file I just sent has Inquisitor Cer's position. You will go to her. You will eliminate her."

"Should I make it look like an accident?"

"No need to waste any time," Francis Lane said. She bit her upper lip and eyed the atmospheric readings. A cold smile formed on her face. "Burn her. A single blast of your fusion gun."

"Understood," the Merc replied. "You will create anxiety with the others."

"I could care less about them. When they arrive at the *Argus'* central computers, take them out, too."

"But who will pilot us out of here, Francis?" Balthazar said and laughed.

"We'll speak later," Francis concluded. Her attention returned to Nathaniel.

52

When Stephen Gray and Saro Triste arrived at the *Xendos'* decompression antechamber, Balthazar wasn't there.

"Where the hell did that Merc go?" Saro Triste asked. "We didn't pass him on the way down."

Stephen Gray saw there were three missing environmental suits, but said nothing. The intercom let out a loud beep.

"We've got a message from the bridge," Stephen Gray said. He activated the communication system and Francis Lane appeared on the monitor. Behind her was Nathaniel. He was drenched in sweat.

"You're still in the bridge?" Saro Triste said.

"Yes," Francis Lane said.

"Where is Balthazar?"

"I sent him to the supply room, to look for medicines. Any medicines. The boy..."

"What's wrong?"

"He's emerging from the tranquilizers much faster than I thought he would."

"Can he suit up?" Stephen Gray asked.

"I don't think so."

"By the Gods," Saro Triste groaned. "We need to go!"

"Easy, Saro," Stephen Gray said. "If we lose the ship's codes, we're finished."

"Stephen is right," Francis Lane said. "Hopefully, Balthazar will find something I can use. Until then, I'll stay here, guarding the bridge."

Saro Triste shook his head.

"When will he be ready?"

"Maybe...maybe it's best I take Nathaniel back to his room," she said. "If he rests a little while, perhaps an—"

She never finished her thought. Nathaniel let out a howl and slammed his hands against his head. The boy collapsed to the ground, unconscious.

Balthazar walked past the landing bay doors and into the body of *Argus*. He wasted no time sightseeing for at this point the Merc only cared about his mission.

He pressed down on the Accelerant dispenser under his environmental suit and felt the warm, familiar burst of energy.

His muscles tightened and power surged through his body.

No, Balthazar couldn't waste time looking at all the wonders around him.

All he cared about was killing Inquisitor Cer.

Saro Triste and Stephen Gray stood several feet behind Francis Lane and Nathaniel. The boy was in bed. His body was covered in sweat. A look of terror filled his face.

"He's getting worse," Stephen Gray said. "Is this withdrawal or is something else going on?"

"I don't know," Francis Lane responded.

Saro Triste bit his tongue. He wanted nothing more than to suit up and force the boy to the *Argus'* central computers. There, the codes that only the child knew would unlock the computer's databanks. Once unlocked, they would know where in this massive ship the *Charybdis* device was hidden.

"You said the drugs would last a few hours," Stephen Gray said.

"I was obviously wrong," Francis Lane retorted.

She rubbed the boys' shoulders and, as she did, the terror in his face faded. After a few minutes, he closed his eyes. His breathing became deep and regular. Soon, he was sleeping.

Balthazar stepped back as a burst of air rushed past him. Inquisitor Cer was right, there was atmosphere within the *Argus*.

He stepped inside the decompression chamber door and closed the outer door. He allowed the machinery to do its work. Once the atmospheric pressure was stable, he opened the inner door and moved forward.

"Good," Francis Lane said. "Maybe when he wakes, he'll be better."

"We're wasting too much time," Saro Triste said. "We should suit him up, take him down, and hope for the best."

"That would be unwise," Francis Lane said. "If he has one of these attacks while we're out there..."

"Then force him to reveal the access codes now!"

"If I was able to do so, do you think I would have gone to all the trouble of bringing the boy along? Our best hope of getting those access codes is by sitting him down in front of the *Argus'* computer operating systems."

"And how do you propose to do that when we can't even get

him out of this fucking room?" Saro Triste yelled.

"If we can't bring the boy to the *Argus'* operating system, it might be enough to bring the operating system to him."

"But the computers within the *Argus'* are locked down, hardwired," Stephen Gray said. "The last thing the crew wants is an outside force hacking into their software."

"We don't need to link up to the actual computer," Francis Lane said. "We could set up a camera before the central computer's monitor. The camera signals can be relayed back here so the boy can see them. The quality won't be optimal..."

"But it'll be enough for the boy to remember the codes!" Saro Triste exclaimed.

"It just might," Francis Lane said. "Suit up and I'll guide you to the central computer room. Once we get the system activated, and provided Nathaniel tells us what we need to know, we'll unlock the security systems around the *Charybdis* bomb. When we secure the device, I'll tell you how to set the self-destruct mechanisms."

Francis Lane rubbed Nathaniel's forehead.

"You'll need to take tools to release the bomb from its moorings. You'll have to work as fast as you can, in case Nathaniel doesn't last."

"What if the bomb is located somewhere in the center of the ship?" Saro Triste asked. "How do we cut it out?"

"In one of his more...lucid...moments, the boy told me the device was located near an enormous exit hatch. It makes sense. How else would it be deployed? Provided there isn't any debris in the way, all we have to do is enter the activation code, unlock the device from her berth, and float her outside the *Argus*. Then we fly the *Xendos* to her, strap the bomb down, and we're on our way."

"Let's not waste any more time," Saro Triste said. "When Balthazar is finished searching for tranquilizers, send him after us. We'll likely need his help."

"I'm sure you will," Francis Lane said.

Both Saro Triste and Stephen Gray exited Francis Lane's room.

After the duo was gone and the door closed, Francis Lane straightened her skirt and let out a harsh laugh. Time enough had passed. Balthazar was surely close to Inquisitor Cer by now.

Very close.

Francis Lane pulled up Nathaniel's right sleeve and removed

the yellow disk she planted on his upper arm. She eyed the disk's readings and said, "Oh my. I set the level a bit too high. It must have hurt quite a bit."

The boy stirred but remained asleep.

"Good thing I shut it off after you fainted."

She pocketed the disk and once again laughed.

Saro Triste reached the end of the corridor and hurried down the stairs leading to the ship's decompression chamber. He caught up to Stephen Gray and grabbed him by the shoulder.

"Hold on a second," Saro Triste told the Epsillon industrialist.

"Every second counts."

"It most certainly does." Saro Triste lowered his voice to a whisper. "But for now, I'm sure you recognize our unique opportunity."

"What do you mean?"

"It's down to you, me, and Francis Lane, and all that Francis Lane and that brat kid have done is slow us down. She's even got us doing all the dirty work. I don't know about you, but I'm finding it harder and harder to justify sharing that bomb with her. She's a fossil, Stephen, a member of political party that hasn't had the sense to realize it's extinct."

Stephen Gray's eyes narrowed.

"Francis Lane has Balthazar."

"And I've got Inquisitor Cer."

"You want to send her up against him?"

"It worked with B'taav."

"It's not my place to tell you how to deal with your subordinates, Cardinal, but ordering her to take on Balthazar might make her suspicious."

"Why?"

"Inquisitors are tough bastards, one and all, but they're also noble to a fault. Having Inquisitor Cer kill B'taav was easy enough. He was never a part of our organization and she had good reason, both personal and professional, to do what you ordered. Getting rid of Balthazar, on the other hand, might tip her off."

"To what?"

"To the fact that you're here like we all are, to get our hands on the bomb. Destroying the *Argus* was always incidental."

"She'll do as I say."

"She might wonder, accurately, if your loyalties are still with the Religious Council."

"I have devoted my life to it."

"So you have," Stephen Gray said. "But you've decided they need new blood at the top. Yours."

Saro Triste opened his mouth to protest, but Stephen Gray waved him off.

"Come now, Saro. You've got your sandbox and I've got mine. I'd rather deal with you as the sole ruler of the Phaecian Empire than any of the Overlords or other Cardinals."

"You will get your wish."

"I hope so," Stephen Gray said. "However, Inquisitor Cer may not see things like you do. When you convinced her to come to the Epsillon Empire, you told her your purposes were noble. Back in the asteroid, when we were forced to explain to B'taav and the Inquisitor what we were doing here, we furthered that lie by saying our goal was to destroy the *Charybdis* device. Changing those plans, especially when there's the very real possibility doing so will make you the most powerful man in the Phaecian Empire, may not agree with her more patriotic sentiments."

Saro Triste said nothing.

"And that's the dilemma, isn't it?" Stephen Gray continued. "In time I'm sure you could convince her to kill Balthazar. But time, as you said before, is in short supply. Besides, even if we could come up with a good reason to order your Inquisitor to kill Balthazar, the only way to send that order is through her communicator. Balthazar or Francis Lane might hear, and things would get very messy."

Saro Triste swore.

"There are other possibilities," Stephen Gray said. "Given the fact that your Inquisitor will likely become as big a problem to us as the Merc is now, our best course of action is to eliminate them both."

"How?"

"We send them on a mission. Tell them to pick something, anything, up from the far end of the ship. It gives us the time we need to find and retrieve the bomb, return to the *Xendos*, and kill off Francis Lane and the boy."

"We kill...?"

"I know you're not used to getting your hands dirty, but special circumstances require great effort. After the woman and the brat are dead, we fly off."

"Leaving Inquisitor Cer and Balthazar behind."

"Absolutely. They'll be in the middle of their fool's errand while the *Argus'* self-destruct mechanism counts down to zero."

"Who will pilot the *Xendos*?"

Stephen Gray chuckled.

"Come on," he said.

"What?"

"Before jumping into any potentially dangerous situations, I make it a habit of knowing my companions. Saro, you've been overly modest in describing your piloting skills."

Saro Triste smiled.

"As have you," the Cardinal replied.

"I'm impressed. You've taken the time to research me as well."

Stephen Gray patted Saro Triste on the shoulder. "We dump Francis and the boy's bodies on the landing bay. When the *Argus* self-destructs, there will be no evidence of our having been here."

"None at all."

"So we're in agreement?"

Stephen Gray held out his hand and Saro Triste shook it.

The two laughed and headed down the stairs and to the decompression chamber. Neither of them noticed an obviously forgotten maintenance room door close by.

Within that room, Maddox lay on the floor. His face was pale, his lips were parched, and his eyes sunken in their sockets. Yet he still held a steady grip on the handle of his fusion gun.

The one time *Titus* bartender eyed the weapon and thought of B'taav. The Independent was dead, killed by Inquisitor Cer, and Maddox was the only person remaining who could fight these traitors.

They would all be off the ship. All except for Francis Lane and the boy.

Maddox eyed the crack in the maintenance room's door. Beyond it lay the stairs leading up into the ship. It would take all his energy to make that climb, especially on one leg.

But Maddox had to do it.

It would be one of his very last actions. He would climb those stairs and make his way to the crew quarters. Once there, he would finish this.

He would kill Francis Lane.

53

Balthazar stared through the glass panels and at the withered remains of the Hydroponics level. His gaze lingered only moments before moving on. Inquisitor Cer wasn't far.

When the Merc reached the corridor's end, he took a hard right into the crew quarters.

He passed several doors before spotting a faint light in the distance. He quickly shut his suit's lights off and hurried his pace. The Merc kept close to the walls, to minimize the possibility of being spotted. As he moved, he realized the floor below him was buckled. At some point, maybe even recently, a large asteroid slammed into the *Argus* and burst through the decks below. Here and there Balthazar spotted cracks in the floor, some of them large and very deep. The Gods alone knew how far the drop was.

The Merc wondered how the *Argus* retained her atmosphere after such a breach. Perhaps, he thought, there was an emergency redundancy system that took care of this. But the Merc didn't give it much more thought. There were other things to do.

As he approached the light source, the Merc slowed, inching his way to a door. Beyond it, he knew, was Inquisitor Cer. Balthazar cradled his fusion gun and pressed his back against the wall beside the door. He took a peek.

The room beyond was cavernous. Inquisitor Cer stood at its rear and beside the light source, an enormous computer monitor. She was working on the *Argus'* central computer. Beside her was the case of energy cells B'taav stole from the *Xendos*.

Inquisitor Cer leaned down to connect one of the larger cells to the system. She then tapped on the keyboard to her side and read the display on the monitor. She was quite busy.

Good.

Balthazar looked away from her. Between the door and her position was a large gash in the floor. The darkness below confirmed the destruction of the lower decks. It was a miracle the central computer was still in one piece. To get to the Inquisitor, Balthazar would have to cross the area very carefully.

Lying close by and to his left was a crumpled environmental suit. At first Balthazar thought it belonged to one of the crew of the *Argus*, but a closer look revealed it to be from the *Xendos.* There was a body within it.

B'taav's.

Dark drops of liquid spread on the front of his suit and floated around the body.

The Merc nodded in satisfaction.

The liquid was B'taav's blood.

54

Saro Triste and Stephen Gray struggled to put their environmental suits on. They desperately wanted to be off and get their hands on their treasure. Stephen Gray swore at his clumsiness while noting Saro Triste suffered the same difficulties. He let out a frustrated laugh.

"When I was young, I could get these things on in seconds," Stephen Gray said. "I've become too comfortable working behind a desk."

"As long as you're doing Gods' work, the location doesn't matter," Saro Triste said.

"Your faith is still strong, Saro?"

"Very much so, even if I've become... disillusioned...with the way we spread the good word. In the old days, dissent wasn't tolerated. Cleansing heathens was our one...our only...priority. We've become weak. We talk of tolerance and allow alternative views and praise cultural differences." These last words came out with a tone of contempt. "After I get my hands on the bomb, I will control the message. We will go back to the way things were. The way things should be. Purity of thought and action. What I do here will restore the Phaecian faith as well as the Empire."

"Or else?" Stephen Gray said. "Tell me, Cardinal, how do you stand being here, with me?"

Saro Triste's smile revealed very sharp teeth.

"I don't," he said. "What about you, Mr. Gray? What are your goals?"

"They're remarkably similar to yours, Saro. Cultural and religious differences in Epsillon are irrelevant. Our religion is profit, our church is capitalism. Those who control territory, precious metals, or any desirable product are the ones in charge. When I get my hands on the *Charybdis* bomb, I'll control them all. I'll issue proclamations and again devote ourselves to research and technology. There will be plenty of jobs. There will be plenty of profit."

"Or else?"

Both Stephen Gray and Saro Triste laughed. Stephen Gray tightened the straps about his waist and reached for his helmet.

"What about our Empires' relationship? You wouldn't turn the weapon our way, would you?"

"No," Saro Triste replied. "I will honor our agreement. The

Charybdis device, once in our hands, will be delivered to an equal number of our agents at an agreed upon neutral site. It will be dissected and replicated one time. We'll each receive a copy of the bomb's blueprints and one of us will get the original device while the other takes the replicate."

"We'll flip a coin on that."

"Agreed. Afterwards, whatever expansion we engage in as rulers of our empires will be limited to the Erebus border. The fact is, Mr. Gray, we gave up on your culture years ago, and we have hundreds of more years to go before our internal fractures are...healed. We will not bother you. At least not until then."

"By which time we'll be long gone, eh?"

"By then, we'll likely have even more powerful weapons and countermeasures. What will come in the future is, at least to me, irrelevant. My focus is on the work I need to do to get my Empire back to where it was."

Stephen Gray slipped his helmet on and adjusted the seals. He tested the air re-circulator and did the same with Saro Triste's suit. Afterwards, Stephen Gray pressed a series of buttons on the panel in Saro Triste's environmental suit's chest plate before eyeing the Cardinal.

"Everything OK?" the Cardinal asked.

"Yeah," Stephen Gray replied. He activated his communication system and said: "This is Stephen Gray. Do you copy, Francis?"

Gray's headset filled with a burst of very loud static. He winced and lowered the volume.

"I hear you loud and clear," she said.

"We're all dressed up and ready to go," Stephen Gray said. "Balthazar hasn't arrived yet."

"He's on his way to my room," Francis Lane said. "He's found some medication. I don't think it'll make much of a difference, but it's worth a try."

"Should we wait for him?" Saro Triste asked.

"Where's your sense of adventure, Cardinal?" Stephen Gray said. "Tell the big guy to join us when he's ready."

Stephen Gray switched the lights on top of his helmet and gave Triste a thumbs up sign.

In seconds, they were off.

Balthazar watched as Inquisitor Cer continued her work with the large energy cell. She hadn't spotted him, hidden as he was in the shadows at the opposite end of the large computer room. Balthazar was eager to take her out, but knew it was better to wait for her to get the *Argus'* central computer fully operational. It meant less work for him to do afterwards.

Now and again Balthazar stole a glance at B'taav's body. A curious feeling of regret rose within him.

Too bad I wasn't able to take out the Independent, he thought. *Then again, I get to kill his killer.*

It was something to look forward to after so many dull days of travel. The only question remaining was how he'd kill her. Francis Lane ordered him to not waste time, to shoot her with the fusion gun on sight. But that would be too quick, too impersonal, and there were so many other ways to get that particular job done.

He could announce his arrival, walk up to her, and for a little while actually help her out. The moment she turned her back on him, he could pull her oxygen line or stab her in the back. Then again, he could sneak up on her, and shatter her visor. Or...

Balthazar smiled. *So* many options.

Inquisitor Cer pressed a series of keys and more lights came on around the computer. The system was rebooting.

Balthazar marveled at the Inquisitor's ingenuity. Too bad she'd never see the end result of all that work.

Balthazar spent a few more seconds considering the ways to get rid of her. Finally, he decided there was no reason for further delay. He reached for his fusion gun and aimed it at Inquisitor Cer's back.

Francis Lane opened the closet door and leaned down to remove the paneling at its base. She flung the loose plastic aside and grabbed her hidden computer. She placed it on her room's only table and powered it up.

The *Xendos'* central computer link appeared first, but that was expected. Francis Lane read the ship's status report and was satisfied all was well. She made sure through this computer link that this ship's outer doors, the ones that lead into the decompression chamber, were sealed now that Saro Triste and Stephen Gray were out.

Francis Lane sat back and wondered how long it would take before she had the second, and most important, link up.

Her wait proved very short. When the signal came, it was sharp and very clear.

Francis Lane double checked the information streaming on the computer's thin monitor. She could barely contain herself. The logo of the old, the *only*, Epsillon Empire appeared. Below it, the words: "*Argus Main Computer System.   Please Enter Access Code.*"

Francis Lane clapped her hands and approached Nathaniel. The boy sat upright in his bed. A series of wires were taped to his forehead. They ran down the length of his body and connected to the heavy black box B'taav found in Francis Lane's suitcase. Sitting in the indentation at the center of the box was the clear crystal Project Geist cube.

"Inquisitor Cer got the *Argus* central computer working," Francis Lane told the boy. "It's time to finish this."

55

Balthazar lowered his gun. He was ready to take the shot, but the Accelerant flowing through his veins made him want to jump out of his skin. Something dark and deep kept him from pulling the trigger. He didn't want the excitement to end so soon. He wanted to see his victim's face. He wanted to see the bitch *beg*.

Balthazar reached to the controls on his space suit's sleeve and adjusted the settings on his communicator. He linked up to the amplification beacon and shut it down. Whatever conversation he had from here on would be between Inquisitor Cer and himself and no one else.

Balthazar then picked up a worker's rag lying among the other debris within the room and squeezed it into a ball. Tiny flakes of ice broke off it and floated away. Balthazar hurled the rag over the enormous crevasse and at Inquisitor Cer. It hit the computer monitor, startling the Inquisitor. She immediately turned.

"Balthazar?" she said. She saw the fusion gun in the Merc's hand. "What?"

"You're no longer needed," Balthazar said.

"Don't be a fool!" Inquisitor Cer yelled. "You fire that gun and we're *both* dead."

Balthazar smiled. She was already begging. This was going to be much more fun than he thought. Yeah, this was—

Realization dawned on Balthazar.

"The oxygen!" he muttered.

"You fire that gun and the oxygen rich atmosphere around us erupts. We'll *all* burn up."

The Merc was stunned that he no longer had the upper hand over his victim. He eyed the crevasse separating them and cursed the fact that the impact from that object hadn't dissipated the atmosphere on this level. Balthazar again stared at Inquisitor Cer. Although they both knew he wouldn't use it, the Merc kept his gun pointed at her.

"Looks like I'll have to do this the hard way," the Merc said. With his free hand he reached down and grabbed at a knife in its holster.

"Who ordered you to do this?" Inquisitor Cer asked.

"What difference does it make?"

"Did they tell you to use the fusion gun or was that your idea?"

"Lady, what the hell difference—"

Balthazar frowned. He recalled Francis Lane's orders.

We can't waste time. Burn her. A single blast of your fusion gun.

The Merc took a step back. His mind was swimming.

"She...she wanted me dead, too?" the Merc muttered. "We'll see about—"

Balthazar paused.

"Wait a minute!" he said. The Inquisitor carried a fusion gun as well. "If you can't fire a fusion gun here, how did you kill B'taav—?"

The words barely escaped his mouth when the glass of his helmet turned dark and the knife and fusion gun were ripped from him. Balthazar swung his hands around wildly, trying to connect with his attacker. He managed to swipe some of the dark liquid off his helmet and saw lights and shadows dancing around him.

The air circulating into his environmental suit abruptly shut off.

"You fucking bastards!" the Merc yelled.

With all his remaining strength he ran forward. He didn't know which direction he was going, only that he had to get away. He slammed into something very hard and the world spun around. His feet no longer touched ground, and the light from the room, what little he could see through the smudged helmet, receded, as if he were falling.

But there was no gravity here. The Merc couldn't fall. Yet the light receded. An ice cold fear gripped Balthazar. He couldn't fall, but his lurch forward had created momentum. He was hurling forward, down and down...

Into the crevasse.

The Merc twisted and turned. The light from above was almost gone. How far would he go before stopping? Would he *ever* stop?

The Merc pressed the control buttons on the forearm of his suit. A small shot of air hit him in his face. He couldn't get the full burst. He would slowly, slowly asphyxiate.

The horror of his situation sank in. The Merc yelled once before slipping into unconsciousness.

56

Saro Triste and Stephen Gray followed the stairs to the upper level of the *Argus* landing bay. They found a large door.

"We're at the top," Saro Triste said. He noted the door's computer system was alive with flashing lights. "Inquisitor Cer got the main computer powered up. We've got juice on this door."

"Good," replied Francis Lane. "The code to this door is theta 1666 AR 12. Hurry up. I don't know how much longer I can keep the boy talking."

Saro Triste entered the codes into the door's computer paneling and ancient gears in the walls slowly slid her open. What lay beyond was a long corridor that stretched for what seemed like many kilometers.

Stephen Gray and Saro Triste entered this corridor. They noted the many adjacent doorways, leading off to an innumerable amount of side corridors. Without a clear idea of where they were supposed to go, they could spend a lifetime exploring these passages. According to Francis Lane, this was the more direct route to the central computers.

"We're past the door," Saro Triste said.

"You should be seeing quite a few doors and corridors."

"It's like a maze," Stephen Gray said.

"It *is* a maze," Francis Lane replied. "So from here on out you listen to my instructions very carefully. You do what I say and you don't deviate. The last thing we need is for you guys to get lost."

B'taav wiped the black liquid from the front of his suit while approaching the crevasse. Balthazar dived into the hole so quickly that there was no chance for the Independent to grab him. B'taav could not see the Merc below.

B'taav wiped off more of the engine oil he picked up in the last decompression chamber and smeared on his environmental suit's chest plate. He watched it bubble up and float away. In the dim lights within the room and upon casual inspection, it looked exactly like what Balthazar thought it was: blood. Had the Merc bothered to look closely, he would realize the material was still in liquid form. At the frigid temperatures present within the *Argus*, blood would have crystallized. The engine oil, on the other hand, was specifically designed to remain in liquid form at these extremes.

Had Balthazar known this, he would have realized he was entering a trap. Once he stepped past B'taav, the Independent slapped a handful of the engine oil against the Merc's facemask and removed his weapons. Unarmed and blind, it was an easy task to shut down the Merc's oxygen supply. What the Independent hadn't counted on was Balthazar's subsequent actions.

Inquisitor Cer stepped around the crevasse and approached B'taav.

"What do you think?" Inquisitor Cer said. Because of the atmosphere in this section, she was able to talk directly to the Independent and without the use of the communicator.

"I don't know," B'taav replied. "I don't see him at all."

"We should go down there, get him."

"He was about to kill you."

"And for that he will pay. Tell me, B'taav, did you need to lure him *that* close to me? He could have fired before I turned."

"I was going to jump him, but then he started working on his suit's controls," B'taav said. "I think he switched off the communication amplification beacon. Only reason he'd do that is because he wanted to talk to you without anyone on the *Xendos* hearing."

"He wanted to see me squirm?"

"For as long as possible."

"Is that a unique skill of yours? Reading the mind of a psychopath?"

"Takes one to know one?" B'taav said and smiled. "Mind reader or not, we've gotten away from the *Xendos* group. As a bonus, we've disabled the last of their muscle. And I don't think they had any suspicions about you and me. The game isn't over, but I'd say our work so far has been remarkably successful."

"We should turn the beacon back on," Inquisitor Cer said. "We wouldn't want the others to think something is wrong."

"All the more reason to get Balthazar," B'taav said. "I'm sure he's the only one who has the proper—"

The Independent didn't finish his thought. An orange light flickered on the central computer monitor. Both he and Inquisitor Cer hurriedly returned to it. Inquisitor Cer pressed a series of keys. Her mouth opened wide in disbelief.

"What is it?"

"Someone's accessed the *Argus'* central computer. They're searching through the files."

"How can that be? Aren't all computer systems on military vessels hardwired?"

"It would appear the *Argus'* computer system has a backdoor," Inquisitor Cer said. "I can only imagine the complex access codes required to get through."

Inquisitor Cer pressed some more buttons before shaking her head.

"They're not using any of the active computers on this level."

A frightening thought occurred to B'taav.

"Whoever did the link intends to download the *Charybdis* bomb schematics," B'taav said. "Damn. My mind reading skills could use some sharpening. They were waiting for us to get power to the main computers so they could make their connection from the safety of the *Xendos*. You don't need the actual bomb when you have the plans."

"It's a good bet whoever's doing this linkup got everyone they didn't need off the *Xendos* and into the *Argus* to search for the bomb. Once they have the schematics for the *Charybdis* device, they're gone."

"Looks like you're something of a mind reader as well," B'taav said. "Anyone not on board the *Xendos* at the time of liftoff gets to sit around and experience this ship's self-destruct mechanism first hand."

"If they can fly the ship, maybe they've done so already. Maybe they're searching for the bomb's schematics while the *Xendos* is parked outside the *Argus*."

"No. This ship's hull is too dense. Look at what it did to the communicator signals. Attempting a computer link from outside the ship is probably impossible."

"What do we do?"

"We need to disconnect the central computer's power cell. It's the only way to stop them."

"Agreed. But wouldn't that tip them of? Wouldn't they suspect we know what they're doing?"

"They might think it was something else. A short circuit."

"Would you believe that?"

"Not for a second."

"In which case they'll fly the *Xendos* out of the *Argus* and wait from a safe distance for our environmental suits to eventually fail. All they have to do is wait a couple of days. Afterwards, they fly back, reconnect the electrical systems, and finish their work."

"So we leave things as they are and hope we finish our job before they finish theirs."

"We need to get back on board the *Xendos* quickly and without their knowledge."

B'taav eyed the crevasse.

"We won't have time to go after Balthazar."

"I don't like leaving loose ends."

"Neither do I."

"We could split up. One goes to the *Xendos*, the other after Balthazar."

"We could, but the *Xendos* is our primary objective. For all we know, the Merc is already dead."

Inquisitor Cer took a breath and nodded.

"Let's move."

57

Francis Lane adjusted the power level of the yellow disk, increasing the sharp stabs of pain shooting into young Nathaniel. The boy's face was as pale as bone. He shook as a fresh charge of electricity shot through his tiny body. The wires connected to his forehead were gone. The heavy black box and crystal cube lay to his side.

"You're only prolonging this," Francis Lane said. "You can end it. All you have to do is talk."

The child's frightened eyes focused on his tormentor. The boy opened his mouth a fraction of an inch. His swollen tongue rolled forward.

Francis Lane leaned in close, until her left ear was near the boy's mouth.

"Come on," she said. "Talk to me."

Instead, the boy spit in her face.

Francis Lane drew back and wiped the saliva away before slapping him hard. Nathaniel fell over. His eyes, so dead all these days of travel, were very much alive. They stared up at Francis Lane and silently defied her.

"You bastard," she said.

Francis Lane grabbed Nathaniel by his hair and pulled him back up to a sitting position. She reached for the yellow disk once more. Her finger floated just over it, ready to apply another jolt.

"Tell me the code," she said. "Tell me the code or we'll explore every single level of pain in this disc."

"You... don't...scare me," the boy muttered. But the defiance in his eyes wavered. His guardian let out a cruel laugh.

"We'll see about that," she said.

Francis Lane pressed down on the disk and the boy once again shuddered.

Saro Triste was pale with fear.

Stephen Gray and he wandered the tight corridors of level 12 of the *Argus* for more than a half-hour and only now did he truly understand just how lost he was. The Phaecian Cardinal, for perhaps the hundredth time, checked his radio communicator settings. Green lights indicated the system was on and functioned. He desperately punched a series of buttons and tried to communicate with Francis Lane.

There was no reply.

"That bitch," he muttered. "Why doesn't she answer?"

"She can't," Stephen Gray said. "The radio amplification beacon was shut off a while ago."

"What? How do you know this?"

"I tend to keep track of important things like that," Stephen Gray replied. He pointed to the display screen on the sleeve of his environmental suit. A single red light blinked on it. "She can't hear us, and we can't hear her. However, it doesn't change much. She meant to lead us in circles until we were completely lost."

"How do you know this?"

Stephen Gray didn't reply and instead offered the Cardinal a beaming smile. For the first time since losing contact with Francis Lane and the *Xendos*, the Epsilon industrialist took the lead in their trek. He stepped past one of the many doors on either side of the corridor they were in. Saro Triste followed close behind. They entered yet another dark and clutter filled corridor. After twenty meters, they found a door.

Nothing around Saro Triste was familiar. Nothing at all.

"I can't go on like this," the Cardinal said. "The walls feel like they're closing in."

"That's probably what the crew of this ship felt, right before they died."

"Please—"

"Why Saro, are you begging? I didn't think a man of your high status would ever do such a thing. It seems...undignified."

"Mock me all you want, but please, *please* get us back to the *Xendos*."

"I wish it were that easy."

Saro Triste took deep breaths and felt a heavy tremble work its way through his body. From the moment they first stepped onto the *Argus'* landing bay, Stephen Gray became silent. Saro Triste tried to engage the man in conversation and was frustrated when he didn't join in.

Now, Stephen Gray appeared eager to talk, and Saro Triste feared what he had to say.

"When I was a little boy, I used to capture bugs in our family garden," Stephen Gray said. "I'd put them in glass containers and set the containers on a shelf in my room. After a day or two of flying around, desperately hoping to find some way out, the bugs' energy was spent. They'd stop flying and begin dying. Slowly.

They'd walk around, one day on the inner lid of the container, the next on the side. Finally, I'd find them on the bottom. This ship...it's like those glass jars I used to have, and we're the bugs."

"Please...get us back."

"That's how Francis Lane planned our deaths."

The Epsillon Industrialist opened the door before them and stared in the room beyond. It was one of the ship's many kitchen areas. A long metal table lay in the center of the room and several chairs were stacked in the corner. Against the wall were food dispensers and cooking utilities. A half-open door lay to Stephen Gray's left. On the opposite side of the room were three meat locker doors.

Stephen Gray walked to the half-opened door and shone his light in all directions before turning back into the kitchen. He found Saro Triste before one of the meat locker doors, staring at the contents within. Unseen by the Cardinal, Stephen Gray worked the remote controls on his environmental suit sleeve.

He checked to see if the communication amplification beacon was still offline. No sense in others hearing this conversation. Satisfied it remained off, he readied another program. When he was done, he noticed Saro Triste was on his knees before the meat locker.

"By the Gods," the Cardinal whispered.

Inside the locker were the frozen remains of at least two dozen people. Every one of the bodies were cut open. Some were missing viscera while others were missing entire limbs. Stacked neatly next to the bodies were body parts, the remains of what could be another twenty or more corpses. There were arms and legs and, wrapped in a bloody rag, what looked like a woman's head. The crude tools used in this butchering lay on the floor.

"Cannibalism," Saro Triste gasped. "When their food ran out, they resorted to cannibalism. This was their refrigerator."

"They had to eat."

Saro Triste was incredulous at the man's cavalier tone.

"These were your people!"

"They lived longer than anyone else stationed in Erebus at the time of the explosion."

"You call this living? The Gods will punish you for your words. Unless I do first."

The pent up fury within the Cardinal was about to explode. Saro Triste reached for his gun, but as he grabbed for it he stopped. Stephen Gray's fusion gun was already out and aimed at Saro Triste's stomach. Saro Triste raised his hands while Stephen Gray took the Cardinal's weapon.

"You surprise me," Stephen Gray said. He tucked the spare gun into his belt. "I was told you were one of the more intelligent members of the Phaecian guard. I can't believe you didn't notice Francis Lane was leading us in circles."

"You...you knew?"

"I knew what she was up to even before we left the *Xendos*."

"How?"

"I look around, Saro. I notice things. Like the fact that three environmental suits were gone before we dressed up."

Saro Triste frowned.

"Who?"

"Come on, Saro. Do I have to spell out everything? Francis Lane's Merc, Balthazar, took the third suit. When she said he was looking around the ship for medication for Nathaniel, he was actually suiting up and heading out. He left the ship before us, no doubt sent by Francis Lane to take out your Inquisitor."

"You knew she was betraying us, yet you let her lead us out here? Why?"

"Because in this game, sometimes it pays to let your opponent show his –or her– hand before making your move."

"What...?"

"Neither of us are trustworthy, Saro. I knew you talked to Francis Lane back at *Titus* and planned to get rid of me once you got hold of the bomb, just like you and I planned to get rid of her on the *Xendos*. You've tried to be smart, playing to the party you hoped would come out ahead. Unlike you, I always knew everyone was in this for themselves."

"I swear by the Gods—"

"Don't insult me or your Gods. Even if they exist, they abandoned you years ago...the moment you abandoned them."

Saro Triste's face grew red with rage.

"You're so very clever."

"No, just thorough," Stephen Gray retorted. "As I said, I like checking everyone out. When I did, I found some interesting discrepancies."

"Discrepancies? Like what?"

"Two things," Stephen Gray replied. "The first, and most important, is that Inquisitor Cer probably knew about the *Argus* for quite some time, and that she was working against you."

Saro Triste laughed. When he realized Stephen Gray was serious, the laughter abruptly stopped.

"That can't be," the Cardinal insisted. "She's been at my side for five years. My orders to her are absolute. She knew nothing."

"During our lengthy trip to the *Titus* station, one of my agents intercepted a coded message sent from your so very devoted Inquisitor. I figured it was intended for the Phaecian Command, an update of what you were up to. Imagine my surprise when I found it was addressed to the Epsillon Military."

"You lie!"

"Saro, at this point, why would I bother?"

"It...it can't be."

"From that moment on, I had your Inquisitor watched. She didn't make any more attempts to contact anyone, so I focused on deciphering her original message. Unfortunately, it has proven a little too tough for my encryption software. Nonetheless, I can make a good guess what she wrote. It would certainly explain how Lieutenant Daniels and General Jurgens were onto us so quickly after we arrived in *Titus*."

"She is no traitor!"

"Oh, I agree," Gray acknowledged. "Unlike you, unlike all of us, I think she *is* one hell of a patriot. The only reason I can think of that she would reveal details of our mission to the Epsillon Military was because she was trying to stop us. As I said before, she already knew about the *Argus* and she realized we were not here to destroy her and maintain the peace between the Empires. You see, Saro, she gave away our mission to Lieutenant Daniels and his boys because she hoped they would prevent us from getting our hands on the *Charybdis* device."

Saro Triste swallowed hard.

"We sent her after B'taav. Do you suppose...?"

"*Now* you're starting to think," Stephen Gray said and laughed. "Of course she didn't kill him."

"W...why?"

"Come on, Saro. The answer's so clear."

"I don't..."

"Think about our Independent friend and the circumstances of his arrival a little more."

Saro was mute.

"Don't you think it peculiar that B'taav showed up just when we needed a pilot? Don't you think it peculiar this Independent just *had* to get away from Daniels, as we did, and we were his only means out?"

"He's an infiltrator?"

"Absolutely. I really thought you or Francis would have figured that out by now. Well, maybe Francis did. She's smart. Smarter than you. In the end, the only question left is whether Balthazar took care of them both. If Francis Lane knew the Independent was still alive, she would have warned him. If she didn't, then I wouldn't place the odds on his survival as being particularly high."

"You think Inquisitor Cer and B'taav will be waiting for Balthazar?"

"Why not?"

Saro Triste swore.

"You said you found out two things. What was the other?"

"This one is far less important, perhaps even meaningless to you," Gray said. "I found out B'taav was recently under the employ of a man named Jonah Merrick."

"Who is he?"

"I said it wouldn't mean all that much to you," Gray said. "But to satisfy your curiosity, he and I are...rivals in the business world."

"You think Merrick sent him after you?"

"It's likely. Which means our Independent friend might well be playing either or both sides against each other. I simply can't imagine Daniels and Merrick seeking the same ends in this little adventure, although, truth be told, stranger things have happened."

Stephen Gray looked at the time display on his wrist. "Well, it's been long enough, I suppose. I regret our partnership didn't prove fruitful, but that's the way things go."

Stephen Gray smiled a humorless smile and pressed two buttons on his environmental suit's control pad. They activated the program the Industrialist prepped on Saro Triste's suit back in the decompression chamber of the *Xendos*, when he pretended to check if the Cardinal's suit was on properly.

"What did you do?" Saro Triste yelled.

"You'll find out."

The warm air in the Cardinal's suit ejected violently. Like a deflating balloon, the Cardinal spun around in place. The glass on the face mask crystallized, but not before the blood in his veins froze and erupted.

58

B'taav and Inquisitor Cer reached the communication amplification beacon. While the device was still shut off, they were so close to the *Xendos* that they couldn't risk using their communicators for fear those inside the ship would overhear them.

B'taav, however, had a solution.

First he used his computer pad to discover the security codes Balthazar installed on the beacon. After cracking the code, he went to work the control panel and, in a few seconds, nodded in satisfaction.

"We can talk now," he said.

B'taav had reversed the beacon's controls. Instead of amplifying signals, it now inhibited them. Any communication signals in its immediate proximity were dampened and would not reach beyond a few feet from the source. Certainly not far enough to reach the *Xendos*. To communicate, however, Inquisitor Cer and B'taav had to stay very close together.

"Nice work."

The two walked a few feet from the amplification beacon and stopped at a series of windows that looked out at the *Argus* landing bay. The two kept to the shadows and were relieved to find the *Xendos* still in its place.

"They haven't gotten the plans yet," B'taav said. He adjusted the magnification in his helmet and pointed to the ship's still open decompression doors.

"They've also left the ship's exit doors open."

Inquisitor Cer noted the barren area she landed the *Xendos* in.

"But how do we get there undetected?" she asked. "They'll close the decompression doors as soon as they see us approach. We won't be able to bridge that distance in time."

The two eyed the rest of the landing bay, hoping to find alternative ways to get to the *Xendos*. After a few seconds, Inquisitor Cer patted the Independent on his shoulder and pointed past the ship and to the blasted landing bay doors she flew the ship through upon entering the *Argus*.

"Old saying: 'If the enemy expects a frontal attack, then assault his rear'."

"That almost sounds perverted."

"Inquisitors have nothing but the purest of thoughts, even if there is little purity in war. They won't expect us to approach the *Xendos* from outside the *Argus*. It'll take a while to circle around. Let's hope they don't finish their download before we get there."

The two headed back.

Maddox's eyes filled with bursts of light and deep veils of darkness. He blinked several times and shook his head.

How long have I been out?

He was lying on a corridor floor somewhere in the third level of the *Xendos*. Despite intense pain and exhaustion, he forced himself to a sitting position and examined his wound. The blood around it was fresh. However, it was coagulating.

At least that's something.

Maddox let out a chuckle. Tears streamed down his face. He wouldn't last much longer. He was dying. Dying and alone.

But armed.

The fusion gun was still in his hand. For a long moment he thought seriously about ending his suffering. The pain was too much to bear and his mission was a failure. Francis Lane or Saro Triste or Stephen Gray would get their hands on the *Charybdis* device and the Empires would return to their wars and death and—

Remember the children of Davanus 4.

"By the Gods," he muttered. Old memories flooded back.

Davanus 4.

The Phaecian Empire overran that system in the early days just before the start of the Erebus War. Their forces were hardly enough to conquer the planet, and the exhausted soldiers' only desire was to return to their Phaecian homes. They raided the colonist's supplies but otherwise treated the people of the planet well. They also showed uncharacteristic compassion by sending a message to the Epsillon Empire explaining the status of those colonists and their limited supplies of food and water. By the time the Epsillon forces were to arrive, the Phaecian soldiers would be long gone.

The message should have been enough to save the citizens of Davanus 4.

But red tape and bureaucratic screw ups, along with suspicions of a possible Phaecian trap, delayed the arrival of the Epsillon forces for six months. In the interval, the planet's bitter winter arrived. Over two million men, women, and children –the entire population of that planet– died of starvation and exposure.

Maddox suppressed a shiver.

He recalled the holo-images of Epsillon soldiers heaving the bodies of frozen children into a mass grave. Their bodies were like grotesque dolls with fully extended and rigid limbs. Their hair was spread out in all directions. The children that were still clothed had only broken rags to fight off the fifteen degrees below zero temperatures.

The Epsillon soldiers completed their jobs in a hurry. The bodies were buried in the mass graves and the official records were hidden for nearly two centuries. A single journal entry in a forgotten ship's log brought the tragic story to light. What followed were denunciations and high level meetings. Something had to be done for the forgotten lost of Davanus 4.

A decision was made and the Empire sent seventy six ships to the planet to finally, *finally*, recover the lost dead. Bodies were pulled from their mass graves, identified, and shipped to relatives. Those that had no relatives were given a proper burial.

A very young Dave Maddox was part of one of the recovery crews. During his two year tour, he came face to face with so many of the planet's victims. He swore, then and there, that if it were up to him, the suffering from war would never again stain either Empires.

Never, ever again.

The bartender gripped the barrel of his fusion gun. *Never, ever again.*

He planted his free hand on the slick corridor floor and pushed forward. Despite the pain, despite the exhaustion, he pushed forward.

Consciousness came slowly to Balthazar.

He gasped for air while keeping his movements to a minimum. The Accelerant high was spent, and his body was wracked with pain, exhaustion, and, most loathsome of all, weakness.

How he hated that weakness.

Balthazar moved his hand and felt firm ground below it. Had he reached the bottom of the chasm? He couldn't be sure. Everything around him was so very dark...

His mind went over the ambush orchestrated by Inquisitor Cer and B'taav. He could barely contain his fury.

His greatest anger, however, was reserved for within. For it was he who failed this mission; it was he who was taken for a fool. And not just by the Inquisitor and the Independent, but also by his employer. Francis Lane had arranged his death by his very own hand.

Balthazar took several short breaths. When he felt he could, he lifted his right arm and wiped some of the engine oil from his environmental suit's faceplate. He spotted a faint light far above him. It was the central computer room. Jagged lines extended from the light and down, making up the torn walls lining the crevasse he fell through.

They didn't come down to finish me off yet? he thought. Was he that harmless to them?

Balthazar let his arm drop to his side and fought off a fresh wave of drowsiness.

You two were clever, the Merc thought. *You cut my oxygen supply to the point where it's kept me alive but little else. If I sit up, if I try to stand, I'll black out. I'm a prisoner of this suit.*

Balthazar took several more short breaths. He again lifted his right hand, this time to feel his suit's belt and the remote controls lying on it. He reached for the communicator button but, when he pressed it, heard nothing through his headphones.

It's gone. Probably destroyed in the fight. Or the fall.

The Merc's hand slid back down. The main oxygen controls were at his side, but he feared working them. He wasn't familiar enough with the controls, and if he should accidentally cut his life support or the oxygen...

Balthazar fought off a fresh wave of rage and forced himself to relax. What else could he do? Surely B'taav and Inquisitor Cer were finishing whatever they were doing up there and would soon be on their way down.

They were still up there, right?

But...but what if they weren't? What if they left him here to die?

The Merc shivered.

Why should they show any mercy to me?

Why should they show any mercy at all?

The Merc stared at the light, trying to see any flicker or shadow. Any sign that someone was still up there. The light held steady, and Balthazar's fears were realized.

A line of sweat rolled down his face, then another. Minutes passed, and the Merc was certain he was abandoned. A despair greater than any he had felt before gripped him. It wasn't sweat rolling down his face. It was tears.

And then he saw it. The light flickered. Only for an instant, but it did.

Balthazar blinked the tears away. He wanted to yell, to tell whoever was up there where he was, even though he knew they wouldn't hear him.

He spotted a shadowy form. Someone up there looked down into the crevasse. At him. Did they see?

Yes! Yes they did!

Balthazar was beside himself with joy. It didn't last.

Was the shadowy figure coming down to finish him off?

The figure descended, moving slowly along the edges of the wall and using the environmental suit's thrusters to glide down. The figure landed feet away from the Merc.

"Please," Balthazar pleaded. "Please don't leave me down here."

The shadowy figure approached.

"Please," Balthazar repeated.

The figure was next to him, leaning over his body. Balthazar wanted desperately to reach up, to grab this person. Perhaps he could, with what little energy remained, take out one of the two before they killed him.

No, you don't even have the strength to do that.

More time passed.

The shadowy figure examined the controls on the front of the Merc's suit before focusing on those at the side. A button was pressed, and Balthazar felt a rush of fresh oxygen.

"Balthazar," came a muffled voice. "Your communicator was destroyed."

"Mister Gray?" Balthazar said.

The Epsilon Industrialist leaned close to him so the Merc could see his face and their voices could more easily travel in the oxygen rich air.

"I gave you a little bit more air," Gray said. "In the next minute, I either give you a steady flow or shut it down completely. Understand?"

The Merc didn't know what to make of Stephen Gray's threat. He nodded.

"Let's be clear," Gray continued. "I know you worked for Francis Lane. I know you and your mistress intended to kill us all. So killing you won't bother me one little bit."

Stephen Gray offered the Merc a cold grin.

"I know once Veil Mercs take on a job, they complete that job. Unless, of course, their employer betrays them. Francis Lane betrayed you, didn't she?"

"Yes," Balthazar managed. "She told...told me to use the fusion gun on Inquisitor Cer. If I had done so..."

"You would have killed yourself as well. Very clever. She knew B'taav was still alive. Had you fired the shot as you were told, all three of you would be dead now, which is precisely what she wanted. Do you still carry any allegiance to her?"

"None."

"Good. She is on one side and Cer and B'taav are on the other."

"What about—"

"Saro Triste? He's dead. You and I are the odd men out."

"How...how did you find me?"

"When they called me at my room that the *Argus* was in sight, I ran down to the *Xendos'* decompression chamber. I placed my own micro tracers on each and every space suit we had, just in case. Even those currently worn by B'taav and Inquisitor Cer."

Stephen Gray paused to let the words sink in. He produced a hand held tracker monitor.

"If you join me, this is yours. It'll tell you where Inquisitor Cer and B'taav are."

"What...what is your offer, Mister Gray?"

"Work for me or perish."

"It's you...and me...then."

"Do you swear to aid me?"

"I do."

"You will be paid for your work," Stephen Gray assured the Merc. "In fact, whatever Francis Lane offered you, I will double. That is *my* guarantee."

A fresh wave of oxygen entered Balthazar's suit. It didn't take long for the Merc to feel his strength return. He lifted his right hand and pressed down hard on his Accelerant patch and, for a second, felt lightheaded. He drifted on the edge of unconsciousness, but that ended as a wave of warm energy rolled through his body.

Balthazar sat up. He was energized. He was alive. Stephen Gray gave the Merc the hand held tracker monitor. He pointed to two dots far from its center.

"That's where B'taav and Cer are," Stephen Gray said. "We must get them before they leave us stranded."

"Yes, sir."

Balthazar wiped the remaining oil from his faceplate. Once done, he gritted his teeth and said:

"I'll tear their hearts out with my bare hands."

59

B'taav and Cer entered the *Argus'* enormous decompression chamber and aimed their lights at the back of that room, exposing the crumpled far wall and jagged holes that opened to outer space.

B'taav and Cer approached the gash with the intention of quickly exiting, walking along the exterior of the ship, and re-entering the super juggernaut through the demolished landing bay doors.

Their haste almost proved fatal.

A metal crate crashed against the floor before them and just inches from B'taav. Its top slid open and, in the zero gravity, skidded along the floor at a dangerous speed. The contents of the box, including heavy machine parts, spread out. B'taav and Cer fell back and away from the still moving debris.

They simultaneously spotted a figure approaching fast. From the oil stains on the environmental suit, they knew it was Balthazar. The Merc's speed in the environmental suit was almost superhuman.

"He's on Accelerant!"

Cer drew her fusion gun. Now that they were away from the oxygen rich chambers, she was free to fire the weapon. She aimed and fired several times, but the Merc anticipated her attack and hid behind a stack of crates and out of sight.

"Who freed him?" Cer asked. "And how did he find us so quickly?"

B'taav stood beside Inquisitor Cer. He eyed the back of her environmental suit, at the crack between the oxygen and life support equipment. He spotted a small object wedged in that crack.

"I don't know the answer to the first question," B'taav said as he pulled the small object out. "But here's the answer to your second one."

Inquisitor Cer eyed the tracking device and swore.

"You probably have one on your suit, too."

"No doubt," B'taav replied. "We don't have time for this."

"Agreed. Turn around."

B'taav did. Inquisitor Cer examined the back of the Independent's environmental suit.

"You see it?" B'taav asked.

"No," Inquisitor Cer replied. "Maybe whoever put the device on my suit didn't put one on yours."

"Then again, maybe it's inside," B'taav said. "Either way, we're wasting time. Let's move."

The two pushed forward. Soon they were at the base of one of the jagged tears in the *Argus'* outer hull. Inquisitor Cer carefully stepped through it and on the ship's outer surface. It was like slipping out of a tunnel and onto a long abandoned city that stretched out for many, many miles. Structures as tall as the largest buildings in the Empire rose from the ship's surface. Some of them were shattered or wilted, like burnt flowers.

Inquisitor Cer adjusted the magnetism on her boots and clamped down. She noted the enormity of the asteroid field surrounding the super juggernaut. The blackened cityscape before her, bizarrely, stood in the middle of a frozen rock slide.

B'taav stepped through the hole seconds after Inquisitor Cer. He carried Balthazar's gun and aimed it at the opening.

Inquisitor Cer pointed past B'taav's right shoulder.

"That way," she said and began moving.

B'taav, however, remained in place.

"What is it?" Inquisitor Cer asked.

"Balthazar, and whoever else knows of these tracker signals, sees where I am and where I'm going," the Independent said. "They can't see you anymore."

"What are you suggesting?"

"We split up. I lead Balthazar, and whoever else might be tracking us, away, while you go to the *Xendos*."

"What if there is another tracking device on me? What if you don't have a device on you?"

"The odds my environmental suit has a tracking device on it is far greater than either of your scenarios. You know that."

"Yes," Inquisitor Cer acknowledged. "But you're facing a killer on a full Accelerant rush. You saw how he moved. To him, we're in slow motion. You spoke of odds. What are the odds of you surviving Balthazar?"

B'taav didn't answer, but they both knew she was right. Even with a fusion gun, an Accelerant engorged Veil Merc would be almost impossible to stop. But there was no alternative. They had to get to the *Xendos*, or all would be lost.

"When you get back to the ship, be quick," B'taav said. "The only one on board you can trust is Maddox, and I'm afraid he may not be of much help. Don't linger, take control of the craft, by whatever force necessary, and then come for me. I'll hold off Balthazar as long as I can."

"I *will* come back for you," Inquisitor Cer said.

"I'm counting on it," B'taav replied. He handed her his computer pad. "And I expect nothing less from the finest Inquisitors of the Phaecian Empire."

Inquisitor Cer stared deep into the shadowy pools of B'taav's eyes and B'taav stared back. For a brief second, there was a connection.

Inquisitor Cer turned away from the Independent and began the trek to the *Argus'* landing bay entry.

Balthazar lingered behind several crates and watched as Inquisitor Cer and B'taav exited the *Argus* through a hole in the outer wall. He let out a laugh.

The two could run to the very ends of the super juggernaut and back but they weren't getting away from him. He eyed the two small blips on the tracker monitor.

Not only wouldn't they get away, they *couldn't* get away.

The Merc approached the ripped wall and paused. Behind him, inside the decompression chamber, lay utter darkness. The Merc could not see Stephen Gray back there, even though the man followed him until this point. For a moment, the Merc wondered where he was.

"What difference does it make," he growled. To his ears, his voice overflowed with bloodlust. All that mattered was killing Inquisitor Cer and B'taav. He searched for and quickly found several other holes leading out of the super juggernaut.

"You can't cover them all," the Merc muttered.

Though there was no way B'taav or Inquisitor Cer could hear him coming, a fusion blast screamed through the hole the duo just exited. The blast blackened a crate a few feet behind the Merc. The shot was a blind one, yet came dangerously close.

"Lucky shot," the Merc said. He bit his upper lip so hard he drew blood. "Now it gets exciting."

Balthazar spotted a long metal tube along the edge of the wall and picked it up. He approached one of the tears in the ship's outer wall and pulled himself through.

Stephen Gray watched from the safety of the far side of the decompression room as Balthazar exited the *Argus*. A graphic display on the corner of his faceplate showed the position of the

Merc and the two he pursued. Stephen Gray smiled.

His way was clear to get back to the *Xendos*, and he would make it there well before B'taav or Inquisitor Cer. Provided, of course, they should somehow overpower Balthazar.

But Stephen Gray didn't understand why they retreated to the decompression room after being in sight of the *Xendos*. He walked the corridor outside the room and approached the communication amplification beacon. A few steps away from there he paused by the windows overlooking the landing bay and the vessel. He now understood why the Independent and the Inquisitor back-tracked.

"Oh, Inquisitor. You parked her a little *too* out in the open," Gray muttered and laughed. "Anyone could see you coming and close the Decompression doors before you got there."

He eyed the beacon and noted its controls were set to dampen rather than amplify any signals.

"Clever," he said. Balthazar told him, back in the crevasse, what the codes were for activating the beacon, but either B'taav or Cer had already cracked the code and didn't bother setting up another. The equipment had served its use, so Stephen Gray shut it off.

The Epsilon industrialist began the walk to the *Xendos*. Unlike the Independent and the Inquisitor, he didn't fear anyone seeing him approach. In fact, he fully expected Francis Lane to try to shut him out. She wouldn't. Stephen Gray had seen to that before he left.

For as Balthazar was originally setting up the amplification beacon, Stephen Gray hastily changed the computer codes used to close the decompression chamber doors as well as activate the *Xendos'* flight controls. Because Saro Triste was near him all that time, Stephen Gray was forced to keep the encryption codes simple. But even simple codes would take a few minutes to crack, and that was all the time anyone needed to enter the ship from here.

He imagined Francis Lane's despair as she furiously tried to shut him out and fly away.

He laughed.

He could only imagine Francis Lane's face when he finally confronted her...and squeezed the life out of that scheming bitch.

B'taav saw Balthazar exit through one of the holes above him.

He fired a shot but the Merc ducked away. B'taav jumped past a series of twisted and melted antennae and landed in a small service pit. The Independent ran its length before climbing out. Once again he looked for Balthazar, but there was no sign of him.

B'taav ran away as quickly as he could, taking a moment after each series of steps to look back. Now and again he thought he saw some movement, but could not be certain if it was the Merc or his imagination.

The asteroid dust on the outer surface of the *Argus* was very thick and B'taav's steps kicked it up. His footprints and the cloud of dust made him an easy target.

And that's ignoring the trackers, B'taav thought. He still held Inquisitor Cer's tracker unit in his left hand. He could have thrown it away, but he wanted to lead Balthazar as far from the Inquisitor as possible.

A shadow flickered behind him, and B'taav whirled around. His eyes opened wide in horror as a metal tube slammed against his right arm. The impact shattered the bone and sent the Independent flying backwards. He lost his grip on Cer's tracker unit and it too went flying.

Fortunately, B'taav still held his fusion gun, but at the moment, and despite the intense pain, he was more worried about the condition of his suit. If the metal tube ripped a hole in it, he would be dead in seconds.

B'taav quickly assessed the damage while in mid-flight. He was relieved to find there was no tear in the suit's fabric.

B'taav slammed against a twisted post. Waves of pain splashed throughout his body. Several meters away and approaching fast was Balthazar. The Merc no longer bothered hiding.

B'taav raised his fusion gun and fired, but again the Merc was quicker. He dropped low and scurried away.

Though B'taav could fire well with his left hand, his accuracy, especially in these zero gravity conditions, simply wasn't as good. And given his injury, if the Merc got close enough to engage in hand to hand combat, there was no way the Independent could offer even the ghost of a fight.

B'taav stumbled away from the twisted post. As he did, he once again spotted the Merc approaching.

Balthazar had no intention of letting B'taav get away.

60

Inquisitor Cer jumped the melted remains of a defensive cannon unit and looked back. B'taav was a small figure moving farther away from her with Balthazar following close behind. The Inquisitor aimed her fusion gun at the Merc, not caring that she might draw his attention. If she could take him out...

Just as she was about to pull the trigger, the Merc slipped out of sight behind a rectangular post.

Inquisitor Cer tried to re-acquire her target, but the Merc was gone. So too, she realized, was B'taav.

For several seconds she remained where she was, hoping to catch sight of either man. The clock in her head told her she couldn't afford to waste any more time. Reluctantly, she turned away. As much as it pained her to abandon her ally in the middle of a fight, the mission was too important. If she didn't make it to the *Xendos* in time, they were *both* dead.

Maddox fought off a fresh wave of nausea and resumed his slow crawl. His mind was a jumble of images from the past and the present and nothing made much sense anymore. Nothing but one thought:

You need to kill *Francis Lane.*

The words gave him strength. Strength enough to crawl another few feet.

"I need to kill Francis Lane," he muttered. Each move was a small victory. Each move got him closer to that woman.

When he heard a voice coming from down the corridor, Maddox stopped. He feared he was suffering a hallucination. The voice persisted. He listened to it, tried to identify it. It was Francis Lane. With a start, Maddox realized he was only feet away from her room.

I'm almost there.

A fresh surge of energy that almost eclipsed the pain and exhaustion filled him. He crawled forward.

He was almost there, and he inched along.

He was almost there...his work would be done. He'd be able to rest...to sleep...to...to...

Maddox could no longer move. His body had given all it could and would not move another inch.

Come on! He thought, but his limbs felt like they were

encased in cement. *I should be upset. I should be angry.*
I should...

Exhaustion gripped him. He closed his eyes and was gone.

Stephen Gray reached the door leading into the *Argus'*
landing bay and entered the code. The door slid open.

Before approaching the *Xendos*, he crouched down and eyed
the far side of the landing bay. He adjusted the magnification on
his suit's faceplate until the distant entry became crystal clear.
All details of the area came into focus, including wrecked
equipment and antique machines. Of greatest importance was
the missing landing bay doors, the route Inquisitor Cer and
B'taav intended to use to get to the *Xendos*.

They were nowhere in sight.

Stephen Gray expected this. The display on the side of his
visor offered the latest readings of their positions, and it
indicated they were running the opposite direction with
Balthazar close behind. Still, Stephen Gray gave the landing bay
doors a look. He was a cautious man and wanted to be sure
before moving.

When he was, he ran toward the *Xendos*.

"I'm trying hard not to get angry, but you're making it very
difficult."

Nathaniel withstood another burst of energy from the yellow
disk. Afterwards, the young boy offered his guardian the same
contemptuous stare.

Francis Lane shook with rage.

"You're going to talk," she said. "I've got plenty of time and if
the disk doesn't do the job, there are other means. Primitive
ones."

The boy said nothing.

Francis Lane sighed. She reached for the pain disk and,
instead of raising its settings, actually lowered the intensity.
There was little to be gained in melting the boy's brain. At least
at this point.

Nathaniel went limp. He fell sideways onto the bed and let
out a whimper.

"Rest up while you can."

Francis Lane eyed the small computer she brought along on
this journey. It remained linked to the *Argus'* central computer
operating system. A cursor flashed in a blank box. To gain access

to the super juggernaut's data banks, she needed the proper access code.

The one the boy refused to give.

Francis Lane walked to her closet and pulled out a container from her small suitcase. She laid down its contents on the bed. Among the various toiletries was a small knife. Francis Lane examined its blade before running it over the palm of Nathaniel's left hand. She pressed down hard, drawing blood.

Nathaniel shrieked and tried to pull his hand away, but Francis Lane held tight.

"That was just to get your attention," she said. "You have ten fingers, child. For now."

She grabbed the boy's pinky finger, twisting it away from the others while thrusting the blade at its base.

"Last chance, Nathaniel," she said.

The boy still did not reply.

"Have it your way."

Francis Lane gripped the boy and pressed the blade down hard. A horrific snap was followed by a scream.

Francis Lane released the boy's arm and drew several breaths.

"Nine more," she said.

Tears flowed down the boy's face. He dared not look at his tormentor, but neither did he speak. More seconds passed, and Francis Lane's patience was quickly exhausted.

"You asked for it," she said.

Francis Lane again grabbed the boy's arm. He tried to pull away, but didn't have the strength to free himself from her grip. Francis Lane pulled at the pinky finger on his other hand and placed the blade against it.

"Talk, Nathaniel," she said. "Don't make me do this again."

The boy let out a whimper. Still he did not talk.

Francis Lane's jaw tightened.

"Fuck you!" she spat. The grip on the knife's handle tightened. "You can stop this, Nathaniel. Remember that!"

She drew a deep breath and was about to press down—

A loud buzz roared from the outer corridor and was amplified through the ship's speaker system. It was a proximity alert. Someone was approaching the *Xendos*.

Francis Lane released the boy and ran to the window. She saw someone in an environmental suit run past the debris in the *Argus'* landing bay. The person was moving directly toward the ship.

"Who the hell?" Francis Lane muttered. What did this person hope to gain? The ship's decompression doors were closed. She had closed them herself—

Suspicion filled Francis Lane's mind. She pressed her face against the window and looked to the far right. She saw a light coming from the rear of the ship. From the decompression chamber.

The outer doors were still open.

"Son of a bitch!"

Francis Lane ran to her computer and clicked on a series of keys. The *Argus'* operating system was replaced with that of the *Xendos*. She clicked on another series of commands.

Decompression doors closed and locked, the monitor read.

"You fixed the controls, didn't you?" she muttered. "You made me think they were closed when they were still open."

She ordered the computer to shut the doors, but received an error message. The computer believed the doors were already closed, so any command to close them was therefore in error.

Francis Lane swore and switched to the navigation controls. Like Stephen Gray and Saro Triste, she too had hidden her piloting skills from the rest of the group. Now, if she could lift off and take the ship outside the *Argus*, it wouldn't matter if the decompression doors remained open or not. All she had to do was...

"*Fuck!*" she yelled.

The navigation controls were frozen. Francis Lane's face grew pale. The person on the landing bay was getting closer...and closer.

There was only one thing she could do: Get to the decompression chamber and use the manual over-ride to shut the outer door. But would she make it in time? She had no other choice but to try.

She slid past Nathaniel and approached the door leading out of her room.

"I'll get back to you," she said as she stepped into the corridor.

She only made it a couple of steps before coming to an abrupt stop.

Lying on the floor less than ten meters from her was Maddox. His fusion gun was cradled in both hands and aimed at her.

"Don't move," he said.

61

Inquisitor Cer reached the outer landing bay entrance of the *Argus*. The hole was massive.

She didn't linger, quickly climbing the melted metal remains of the hinge and entering the super juggernaut. She was at least a kilometer from the *Xendos*. The smaller ship's engines faced the landing bay and there would be no way for anyone on board to see her approach.

Inquisitor Cer ran, kicking up a mist of asteroid dust. She did not pause, she did not slow. Even a second delay could mean the failure of her mission.

Her breath grew ragged and sweat dripped down her face. In normal gravity and unencumbered, bridging this distance wouldn't have been taxing at all. But in these conditions, she had to muster every ounce of her energy to keep her legs moving.

When she was a little less than halfway to the *Xendos*, she spotted someone approaching the spacecraft from the front of that ship. He was only a few feet away from the craft's decompression doors and moving quickly to enter. The person wore the same environmental suit as B'taav and Balthazar, but was shorter. Inquisitor Cer activated her communication system and, although she couldn't be sure if the signal would reach that far given the dampener, nonetheless asked: "Who is that?"

The person beside the entry to the *Xendos* paused. He saw Inquisitor Cer.

"You found the tracker units on your suit?" a voice said over the Inquisitor's speakers. "Very clever, Inquisitor. B'taav carries both trackers with him and leads Balthazar away while you storm the castle. Well done. Too late, but well done nonetheless."

"Stephen Gray?"

"Yes dear," he replied. "Give my regards to your Cardinal. I'm sure you'll see him again, in the afterlife."

Inquisitor Cer hurried her pace as panic filled her mind.

Stephen Gray frowned.

Even though he stood next to the *Xendos'* decompression doors and there was no way the Inquisitor would reach him before he closed them on her, he couldn't help but admire her continuing fight.

"I doubt you'll miss Saro," Stephen Gray continued. "Both you and your Empire deserved better. When your final minutes run out, be content in the knowledge that his kind will no longer soil this universe."

Inquisitor Cer ran with all her might.

"Besides, we'll be far better off with people like me in charge. I suspect you'd beg to differ."

Stephen Gray laughed as he stepped into the decompression chamber. He took one last look at Inquisitor Cer.

"I've turned the communication amplification, or rather the dampening device, off," Stephen Gray said. "Since you're close enough to hear, I'm certain you're listening as well, B'taav. When Balthazar is finished with you, Independent, I'll make sure he has enough time to take care of Cer as well."

"What did you do with Saro Triste?" Inquisitor Cer asked.

"The same I'm going to do to Francis Lane. You probably hear this as well, don't you, Ms. Lane? I'm coming for you next."

Stephen Gray gave Inquisitor Cer one final wave before stepping into the *Xendos*. He held his fusion gun and aimed it at the decompression antechamber door, in case Francis Lane was on the other side. She wasn't.

Stephen Gray keyed his code into the computer controls and the heavy outer door slid closed. There was no way Inquisitor Cer could force her way inside the craft now, at least with fusion blasts alone. There were other means, from using the *Argus'* computers to override the *Xendos'* systems to finding and using explosives left behind in one of the *Argus'* cargo holds to blast the door open, but Stephen Gray wasn't about to give Cer time to try these alternatives. He meant to fly the ship out as soon as possible.

Air filled the decompression chamber and the lights inside changed from dark red to bright green. Stephen Gray quickly removed his space suit. When he opened the decompression chamber's inner door, he expected to find Francis Lane there. Again he was disappointed.

"Where are you, Francis?" Stephen Gray called out. "It's been an awfully long day. How about we make this easy on both of us?"

There was no reply.

"Fine. We do this the hard way."

Stephen Gray climbed the metal stairs leading to the decompression antechamber. From there, he stepped into the lower corridors of the ship and began his trek to the crew level.

Inquisitor Cer reached the decompression doors well after they were sealed. She pulled out B'taav's computer pad and hoped there was some way it might help her open the decompression doors. But there were no outer door panels. She ran her hands along the ship's smooth metal surface and searched in vain for any hidden compartment or keypad that could allow her entry. But she knew, from her previous work on the craft, there were no other usable entry points.

Cer took a step back and eyed the ship. She worried for those trapped inside with Stephen Gray and then thought of B'taav.

She clicked on her communicator.

"B'taav? Can you read me? Stephen Gray got into the *Xendos* before me. He's locked me out."

Inquisitor Cer waited for a reply but none came. Had Balthazar killed the Independent? If so, he was surely on his way here, to finish the job. She would have to be ready...

A sad smile appeared on Inquisitor Cer's face. She couldn't think of a bigger waste of time and energy than fighting off Balthazar while Stephen Gray gained control of the *Xendos*. Once he did, he would leave both Inquisitor Cer and Balthazar behind, fighting over a worthless, burned out relic while her self-destruct mechanism was armed and ticking down.

Inquisitor Cer's smile faded.

Everything had fallen to pieces.

62

B'taav tripped against a line of exposed wires and momentum sent him to the ground. His broken right arm twisted under his body and a corrosive pain paralyzed him. Without realizing it, he dropped his fusion gun. When the pain receded and he opened his eyes, B'taav saw the gun slip into a narrow crevasse.

The Independent crawled forward and shone his wrist flashlight into the hole. It was deep. His light faded before reaching the bottom.

The fusion gun was gone.

B'taav spun around. Balthazar was just out of sight, but somewhere close.

"We did a hell of a job," he muttered. While it was static filled, he heard most of the exchange between Stephen Gray and Inquisitor Cer. It was the reason he wasn't paying as much attention as he should have to the debris on the ground before him. Another message came through.

"—av? Can you—Gray got into the—before me. He's locked me out."

B'taav switched on his communicator. He was about to reply when the burly Merc grabbed him. Balthazar locked his hands on B'taav's wrists, rendering him helpless.

B'taav looked directly into Balthazar's faceplate and saw the Merc's Accelerant distorted face. Fiery bloodshot eyes stared back at the Independent. It felt like he was once again staring at Gail Griffen.

"By the Gods," B'taav said.

The Merc had purposely overdosed. Perhaps he knew Stephen Gray would ultimately abandon him along with Inquisitor Cer and Francis Lane. He had neither a master nor a patron, and if he was to die, he would do so while taking his most hated enemies with him.

Saliva dripped off the side of Balthazar's mouth. He screamed at the Independent, but because his communicator was smashed, B'taav could not hear any of his words.

He didn't need to.

Stephen Gray climbed the stairs from the decompression chamber. He waved his fusion gun at each and every shadow along the way.

The Epsillon Industrialist noted a blood stain on these stairs. It led up, toward the crew compartment. Towards his destination.

No one could lose that much blood and live. At least not for very long.

Just as well, he thought.

The bloody trail continued beyond the crew quarters closed door. Stephen Gray pressed his head against the door, to listen for any sounds coming from within.

He took his time.

Francis Lane was frozen in place. From the way he cradled the gun, she knew Maddox was barely consciousness. He had not noticed the small red knife in her right hand, the one she used to snip off one of Nathaniel's fingers. With little effort, it could easily slit Maddox's throat and drain what little blood was left in him. Francis Lane drew that hand away and behind her.

"I'm pleased you're alive, Maddox," Francis Lane said.

The gun in Maddox's hand shook, as if it weighed several tons. She looked past the gun, at Maddox's bloody stump. Even now, blood seeped from the grotesque wound.

Maybe I won't need the knife after all.

"You need help, Maddox. If you don't get it, you'll die."

"Die?" Maddox mumbled. He sounded confused, disoriented.

"Let me help you," Francis Lane continued. She kept the tone of her voice gentle and dared take a single step closer to him. "I'll save you."

"Me?"

"Yes."

She took another step and her confidence grew. She took several more steps. Easy. Slow. Soon, Maddox's gun was just inches away from her. She could almost touch it.

Francis Lane tightened her grip on the knife. One jab was all she needed, right in his eye.

Maddox struggled to keep his head up.

"You..." he began.

"Easy, Maddox. Just take it easy."

Maddox lowered his head. His eyes closed. The fusion gun went down, settling onto the floor.

Francis Lane smiled. The *Titus* bartender's breath was deep. He was unconscious.

"For a moment there, you actually scared me," Francis Lane whispered. She kept her right hand and the knife within it hidden behind her back, just in case. Maddox didn't move. Not at all.

With her left hand, she reached down to grab Maddox's gun.

"Sleep well, Maddox."

Her fingers were only inches away. They were practically touching the gun's barrel...

"*Freeze!*"

Francis Lane stiffened. At the end of the corridor, at the doors leading to the stairs, stood Stephen Gray. His fusion gun was aimed at her.

Francis Lane took a step back. She kept her right hand, and the knife in it, hidden.

"Did you get the plans?" Stephen Gray asked.

"What?"

Stephen Gray fired a shot. The blast slammed against the corridor wall and sent a cascade of white hot embers onto the floor. Several of them struck and burned Francis Lane's face. She held her ground while the Industrialist approached.

"Don't screw with me," Gray said. "Before joining this crew, I checked up on the building and supply manifests of the *Argus*, just as I'm sure you did."

"You know?"

"Of course I know. Now, did you get the fucking plans?"

"No. I'm...I'm having problems with the codes."

"The boy still isn't talking? I figured a cold blooded bitch like you would have him singing operas by now."

"He'll talk."

"In time, I'm sure he will."

Stephen Gray stopped a couple of feet from Francis Lane. He raised the gun's barrel until it was aimed at her head.

"You had your chance. It's my turn."

"He won't say anything to you," Francis Lane said. She grasped her knife tight. *Come closer, Stephen. Just a little bit.* "I'm the only one capable of making him talk."

"Yeah. You've more than proven your effectiveness in that regard."

"Fuck you."

Stephen Gray laughed. He eyed Maddox and shook his head in mock sympathy.

"Imagine all the pain he's suffered. You think you could take it?"

"More than any of you."

"Maybe, just for the hell of it, we'll see if that's the case." Stephen Gray pressed the gun's barrel against Francis Lane's left cheek. "I'm in no hurry."

"Are you trying to scare me, Stephen? What is it with you capitalists? Winning the game isn't good enough. You need your opponent to grovel before you as well? You'll make an excellent dictator. Up until the day someone puts a bullet through your skull."

Stephen Gray slammed the gun against Francis Lane's cheek. She fell against the corridor wall. Her lower lip quivered and when her teary eyes opened, they stared into Stephen Gray's cold blue eyes.

The Epsillon Industrialist saw her pain and fear and let out a bitter laugh.

"That's better," he said. "I wouldn't want you to miss a second of this."

The Epsillon Industrialist kept his gun on Francis Lane and reached down to grab Maddox's weapon. His hand touched the corridor floor and sought out the weapon, but it was just out of reach. For a moment, only a moment, Stephen Gray looked away from Francis Lane, to see where it was.

It was all the time she needed.

With a bloody yell, the gray haired lady drew her knife and slammed it into Stephen Gray's right cheek. The blade tore through the Industrialist's flesh and smashed against something very hard. The blade snapped inside Stephen Gray's mouth and blood gushed out of the wound.

Stephen Gray stumbled back.

"You want pain?" Francis Lane yelled. "I'll show you pain!"

Stephen Gray tried to lift his gun, but the attack against him was so sudden and the pain so extreme he was paralyzed. Francis Lane was on top of him. Her fingers clawed at his eyes.

Stephen Gray feebly lifted the gun. Its barrel was pointed at Francis Lane's stomach.

"Fuck you," he muttered. The words sounded like they were coming from under water. Blood and torn flesh dripped from the Epsillon Industrialist's mouth and wound and down his neck. He pushed the barrel of the fusion gun harder, until Francis Lane let out a yelp. She no longer struggled, and instead took one deep, last breath.

A fusion blast reverberated like thunder through the corridor. For several seconds, Francis Lane was frozen in place. She couldn't think, she couldn't feel. And then she took one more breath and realized, with a start, that she felt no pain. For several more seconds she didn't move. How could this be? Her hands balled into fists, and very, very gingerly she moved her legs. She was still standing. She didn't feel any pain.

Francis Lane opened her eyes.

She stood only inches away from Stephen Gray. In his eyes was the fear she felt. He tried to say something, but the blood in his mouth choked off any sounds.

The Epsillon Industrialist slid to the floor. There was a large black hole in his right side, a fatal fusion blast delivered at very short range. On the left side of his body was a gaping hole. That side of his body was almost completely vaporized. Burned organs spilled from his wound and onto the floor. The wall next to him was charred black.

"Maddox," Francis Lane whispered.

The bartender held the still smoking gun. He aimed it at Francis Lane and tried desperately to take one more shot. He couldn't. The gun slid to the floor. Maddox's eyes once again closed.

Francis Lane leaned against the corridor wall. Tears ran down the side of her face.

"Thank the Gods," she said before savagely wiping them away. She stood over Stephen Gray's corpse and spat on it.

"My lucky day," she said and approached Maddox. She kicked the gun from his hand before leaning down close to him.

"Wake up you son of a bitch," she said. She held Maddox by his collar and pulled his face close to hers. "I want to personally thank you for saving my life."

Francis Lane slapped Maddox until his eyes opened.

"You hear what I said?" she yelled. "You saved my life you stupid bastard. You saved my life and ended yours. How does that make you feel? *How does that make you feel?!*"

Maddox stared into the face of rage and madness. There was nothing he could do.

"You're going to wish you never heard of the *Argus*," she continued. "You're going to wish—"

Francis Lane's words abruptly ended. Maddox looked at Francis Lane but thought he was staring at a hideous nightmare. In what to him appeared like slow motion in an action vid,

Francis Lane's head expanded like a grotesque balloon. It expanded until her flesh could stretch no more. Skin ripped and her head exploded in a mist of blood and flesh.

Maddox closed his eyes as the remains of Francis Lane's face sprayed him. The woman's grip on his collar loosened and he fell heavily back down to the floor.

When he stopped shaking, the *Titus* bartender opened his eyes.

Francis Lane's headless body lay crumpled on the floor. Blood spurted from her torn neck and drained onto the corridor floor. Like her still pumping heart, her body twitched. Slowly now. What little life remained in the husk faded. Maddox looked past Francis Lane's corpse and at the door leading to her room.

Little Nathaniel stood there, holding Maddox's fusion gun. Somehow, he got a hold of it after Francis kicked it from his hands. The boy appeared both shocked and relieved, and for a moment Maddox wondered if he was next.

They watched each other for what Maddox felt was a very long time.

Finally, Nathaniel dropped the weapon and slid down until he sat on the corridor floor.

"You saved my life," Maddox said.

He crawled past Francis Lane's body and to boy's side. He took back his gun and tucked it into his belt holster. When he looked the boy over, he realized the child was missing a pinky finger. Blood still dripped from the wound.

"She...she didn't."

Maddox gently grabbed Nathaniel's hand. Along with the missing digit, he noticed the fresh scars and burns on the boy's upper arm, as well as the yellow torture disk.

"What did she do to you?" Maddox said. Despite the visual evidence, he couldn't believe Francis Lane's cruelty.

Maddox removed the disk from the boy's arm and violently threw it away. The little boy started to cry and Maddox held him tight.

When the boy was done, his eyes were sharp and alive. This Nathaniel wasn't the same lifeless boy Maddox knew from *Titus* until now.

"Who are you?" Maddox asked. He didn't expect any answer, which made the boy's answer all the more amazing.

"My name is Nathaniel Torin," the boy said. "I am the Captain of the Epsillon Royal Fleet starship the *Argus*."

63

Maddox was stunned.

"You...you speak?"

"Despite Francis Lane's best efforts, yes. She kept me drugged through most of this trip. I tried stopping her from finding the *Argus* as best I could, but I...I wasn't always sure if what happened around me was real or not. I fought them as best I could. I'm sorry about your leg."

Maddox held his tongue. He was sorry too, sorry for the deaths of Janet Donaldson and Rasp. Was the boy aware of those actions, too?

"What do you mean you're Captain Nathaniel Torin?"

"I may not inhabit the body of the man who commanded this ship into Erebus two hundred years ago, but I *am* Nathaniel Torin, nonetheless."

"Explain yourself. Slowly."

"I don't know who this body belonged to," the boy said while pointing at his chest. "Most likely an orphan Francis Lane and her group picked up, someone nobody would miss. She used Captain Torin's mental recording—"

"The Project Geist cube?"

"Yes, the Project Geist cube," Nathaniel repeated. The ball he played with during the trip lay on Francis Lane's night table. Nathaniel left Maddox's side and retrieved it. The Geist Cube was inside. He held it in his hands for several seconds before dropping it to the ground and crushing it under his foot. "She used it to make me."

"She transferred Nathaniel Torin's memories to a child's body? How is that possible? I thought the only reliable way to access the information on a Geist cube was through the machine that created the cube. The one on board the *Argus*."

"Accessing the information via computer is, as you say, difficult without using the original Geist machine that made the recording," the boy said. "But the moment the cube was first discovered there were those in your group who were desperate to find a way to access that information. The fact that they had this in their hands may well be the reason they were originally corrupted. For years they conducted experiments, almost all failures, in their increasingly desperate attempts to access Nathaniel Torin's thoughts. They realized that while computer to computer links were extremely unreliable, there was a way of imprinting pieces of Geist information on living organisms. By the time Francis Lane became a member of this group, they knew their best hopes in accessing the cube's information lay in transferring it to a human host. An infant. Preferably a newborn."

A chill ran through Maddox's body.

"They didn't discover this on the first try?"

"No."

"How...how many experiments were conducted?"

"I don't know. But given the many decades they worked on it..."

"What happened to the...to the subjects of the experiments that failed?"

"The children's minds were wiped or... worse. The Gods alone know what they did with the bodies. Each failure, however, produced some small results. They continued their work." Nathaniel's voice trailed off. "I was the last, and only, success in transferring Captain Nathaniel Torin's complete thoughts into another human being. From infancy until this age, I was a blank. My developing brain worked on the memory imprint until it finally took. At that moment, I awoke. I was Captain Nathaniel Torin in everything but body. That was five months ago."

"How...how did you feel?"

"Confused. I recalled Captain Torin's childhood and his training and his personal and professional ups and downs. I love...loved his wife and was incredibly proud of my command."

Nathaniel lowered his head.

"When I came to, the first face I saw was that of Francis Lane. She said she was my distant granddaughter, and that the Erebus War ended two hundred years before. The information was extremely difficult, to say the least, to take. She feigned sympathy and allowed me time to assimilate to this new era, at least within her palace and while under her supervision. She explained what I was and how I came to be, but left out all the brutal experiments and failures that preceded this one success. She tried hard, too hard, to act nice. I knew she was holding back, that there was too much desperation behind her questions and an unusual thirst for knowledge that I swore would never fall into anyone's hands. So I feigned difficulties with my memories and didn't tell her everything I knew. This worked for a while, but like I did with her, she saw through me. Eventually there was a confrontation, and all her pretenses of being a sympathetic relative from the far future were gone. Francis Lane turned on me, and that's when she started using drugs and torture. But she couldn't take things too far. She knew the memory imprint was delicate and there was danger I could be damaged. Had she the time, I would eventually have given her every bit of information she wanted. By the greatest stroke of luck, word came down from you and your group that the first solid evidence of the *Argus'* survival, and along with it a strong theory as to where she may lie, was found. Francis Lane and I were off to *Titus*."

"Two hundred years have passed, Nathaniel. Why put yourself through all this? Why not simply tell Francis what she wanted to know?"

"I sacrificed my ship, its remaining crew, and myself for one cause: Peace. Why would I risk that sacrifice by giving anyone, even a distant, distant relative, the means to resume this terrible war?"

"You still want to destroy the *Argus*?"

"I made that decision centuries ago."

"Then let's finish what you started."

Nathaniel helped Maddox to Francis Lane's bed. The rugged bartender winced in pain when he sat down. He eyed the small computer Francis Lane used to access the *Argus'* main computers.

"She was using this computer to download the plans of the *Charybdis* device."

"Everyone...everyone was in this for themselves. All but one."

"One?"

"Yeah, B'taav. You...you remember him?"

"Vaguely. The blond haired man with the dark eyes? The one who took the gun from my hand when you were—"

"Yeah. We...we picked him up on *Titus*. He saved my life, but...but it doesn't matter anymore. They're all dead. All—"

The communicator suddenly came to life, and the two heard Inquisitor Cer's voice.

"B'taav, do you hear me?"

Inquisitor Cer listened for any response. After a few seconds, she thought she heard some words amidst the static.

"—tor Cer?"

Inquisitor Cer increased the volume to maximum. Painfully loud pops and hisses filled her ears.

"I hear you, B'taav. I'm at the *Xendos*. Stephen Gray is inside. He locked the decompression doors and I cannot enter the craft. Do you read?"

There was more static.

"B'taav, do you hear me?"

Nathaniel was at the room's window, looking outside.

"Someone's out there."

Maddox leaned forward until he too could see out the window. A person stood on the landing deck beside the *Xendos*.

"Could it be Inquisitor Cer?" Nathaniel asked.

"It's possible," Maddox said. For a second he saw a face through the glass at the front of the person's environmental suit helmet. "It...it looks like her. Raise the volume. Let's hear what she—"

"—go help you?" Inquisitor Cer voice echoed throughout the room. "B'taav, do you need help? Should I go help you?"

She received no reply.

B'taav was near death and he knew it.

As the Independent did to the Merc, Balthazar cut his oxygen supply until he could barely breathe. The Merc then threw B'taav around as if he were a useless rag. He slammed B'taav's body against the uneven hull surface or any jutting pieces of metal with incredible force, only to pick him up and start the process all over again.

B'taav felt his ribs fracture. His mouth filled with blood.

The Independent was near death and he knew it.

But he wasn't dead yet.

Inquisitor Cer's voice came to him as if from a different reality. The Independent focused hard on her voice, but even as he did, Balthazar grabbed him by the waist and spun him around. When he was done, he thrust his bloated face at the Independent.

Despite his rage, the Merc wanted B'taav's death to be slow and painful.

Balthazar shouted at B'taav and laughed and shouted some more. When the Merc's rant was over, he again flung him.

B'taav's limp figure flew many meters before touching ground and sliding into a wall. The Independent came to rest facing Balthazar, now a small figure in the distance. The Merc was laughing and drinking in every bit of the sadistic pleasure gained from beating another man to death.

B'taav turned away, to look at the trail his body made through the asteroid dust. The dust was brushed away, revealing glass paneling below.

"Tinsel glass," B'taav muttered. The Independent reached forward and wiped more dust away. The tinsel glass was at least three meters thick. By shining his light on it, the Independent could just make out a series of frozen stalks and withered leaves.

The hydroponics level, B'taav realized. He was on top of it.

Despite his pain, the Independent forced himself to his feet.

"Inquisitor Cer," B'taav said. "You've...you've got to order the central computer to...to jettison the hydroponics paneling."

Inquisitor Cer could barely hear, much less understand, B'taav's words.

"You want me to get to the central computer and do what?"

"—etison the hydroponi— paneling."

Inquisitor Cer considered B'taav's request. It was a very long walk back to the *Argus'* central computer. Would B'taav still be alive when she got there? Were there any other alternatives?

As if to answer her question, B'taav's said, "It's—only way."

Maddox listened in on the conversation and shook his head.

"That sounded like B'taav," he said. "But...but they said he was dead."

"I'll go," Inquisitor Cer said over the speaker. "Hang on, B'taav. I'll get there!"

"I don't understand," Maddox said. "They sent Inquisitor Cer out to kill B'taav. Why...why are they talking to each other?"

"They're working together," Nathaniel said.

"How is that possible?"

The boy shrugged.

"Why don't you ask her?"

Inquisitor Cer took two leaps toward the exit of the *Argus'* landing bay when her communicator came alive.

"This is Maddox on the *Xendos*, calling Inquisitor Cer and B'taav. Do you...do you read me?"

Inquisitor Cer abruptly stopped.

"Maddox? What is your status in there?" she asked.

"I'm...I'm in control," Maddox said. "Stephen Gray and Francis

Lane are dead."

"And Saro Triste?"

"Unknown. But I don't think he's here anymore. What about B'taav?"

"We disarmed Balthazar but Stephen Gray found him and sent him after us. B'taav and I split up. He took on the Merc so that I could get to the *Xendos*."

"For what purpose?" came a child's voice.

"Who's that?" Cer asked. "Nathaniel!?"

"Never...never mind that. What is your purpose?"

"The same as B'taav's. We intend to destroy the *Argus*."

Sweat dripped down Maddox's face.

"How...how do I know you're telling the truth?"

"There isn't the time, or a way, for me to convince you. So if you can do it, set off the *Argus'* self-destruct mechanism and try your best to get the *Xendos* out of here. Because if you can't, I will."

Inquisitor Cer resumed her run. She managed three more steps.

"Wait!" Maddox said.

Inquisitor Cer stopped. Behind her, the decompression doors of the *Xendos* slid open.

64

B'taav felt Balthazar's vice like grip on his side. The Merc's hands sent sharp waves of pain throughout the Independent's body.

For a second B'taav blacked out.

The tranquility within the darkness was a welcome release, but a fresh wave of pain tore through it like a supernova. B'taav again stared into the crazed eyes of Balthazar.

By now his perverse joy was dulled. He was like a cat grown tired of its half-dead mouse. B'taav could no longer run and he could no longer fight. There was little fun in continuing this game.

The Merc's eyes drifted to the exterior of the *Argus*. For a moment he seemed confused, as if realizing for the first time that Inquisitor Cer was not around. B'taav took advantage of his distraction and, with his little remaining strength, kicked the Merc in the stomach and twisted out of his grip.

B'taav fell backwards, eventually hitting the ground while Balthazar went airborne. His hands flayed at his side and the hints of boredom in his face were replaced with rage. He yelled and flung his arms around wildly. He was unable to control his flight.

B'taav got to his feet and stumbled away. He took only a few steps before Balthazar landed. The Merc readjusted the magnetism on his boots and slowly walked after B'taav.

There was no need to rush, for B'taav's pace was slow. The Independent could not get away from Balthazar. Indeed, his energy quickly dissolved and B'taav crumbled to his knees.

Balthazar was at his side. He picked B'taav up and pulled him close. The sadistic fire was back in the Merc's eyes. He turned B'taav around and fiddled with his life support controls. The heat in the Independent's suit was replaced with an unbearable cold.

The Merc gave B'taav one last smile before hurling him away.

B'taav's body fell into a pile of thin metal cables. Like a fly in a spider's web, B'taav was tangled up and could not move. In the distance he saw Balthazar pick something from the ground. It was a long metal rod with a jagged spike at its end. The Merc eyed the fearsome weapon and nodded.

This would do.

Balthazar's dance with the Independent was over.

In desperation, B'taav looked around for something, anything that he could use to fight off the Merc. His eyes followed a cable that wound around his right arm and down into the asteroid dust. The floor under him, B'taav realized, was solid metal. He was no longer on the tinsel glass that made up the hydroponics roof. He continued his desperate search for a weapon of any kind, but instead of finding one he spotted what looked like the hand of a life sized statue half-buried under the cable and asteroid dust.

B'taav blinked. Though he was keenly aware of the approaching Merc, he couldn't help but wonder what a statue was doing outside the *Argus*.

The statue's hand was missing several fingers. Despite this, it was remarkably life-like. Remarkably...

With a start, B'taav realized he was not looking at a statue. The hand was human. B'taav followed it through the tangled cables. He made out the form of a man buried beneath the web. He had probably died of exposure, for he did not wear an environmental suit. Instead, he wore a Royal Epsillon fleet blue uniform.

B'taav slid to his right and pulled at the cables. The man's upper body was revealed and his features, even after all these years, remained untouched. The man had a lean face and black hair and his eyes were closed. His mouth was open, frozen in the middle of his last, painful death rattle.

B'taav couldn't know for sure who this man was, but his uniform and the gold insignia on his chest identified him as a Captain in the Royal Epsillon Fleet.

The only Captain aboard the *Argus* when she entered the Erebus Solar System was Nathaniel Torin.

65

Inside the *Xendos'* decompression chamber, Inquisitor Cer stepped out of her environmental suit and ran up the stairs and to Francis Lane's room, pausing only for a moment when confronted by the bloody corpses of Stephen Gray and Francis Lane.

She found Maddox sitting in Francis Lane's bed and Nathaniel working on a small, very sophisticated computer.

"What is this?" Cer asked. She was surprised to see the boy so nimbly operating such a piece of high tech.

"You no longer have anything to fear from me, Inquisitor," the boy assured her.

"He's more than he seems," Maddox added. His stump was re-wrapped and there was life in his tired features. "We can talk about that later, after we rescue B'taav."

Inquisitor Cer sat beside the boy.

"B'taav wanted the tinsel glass shielding over the hydroponics level ejected. Can this be done from here?"

"Why does he want to do this?"

"I have no idea. But with the atmosphere trapped in the level, ejection will create one hell of a blast. Can it be done?"

Nathaniel pressed a series of codes into Francis Lane's computer. In a matter of seconds his work was done.

"Tell me when."

"Stand by," Cer said. She pushed her communicator button. "B'taav? Do you still want me to eject the tinsel glass?"

B'taav tore his eyes from the lifeless form of Captain Nathaniel Torin and back to Balthazar. The Merc stood only a few feet away and was approaching fast.

"Yes," B'taav whispered. *"Now."*

After he spoke, the Independent's head settled back while his eyes remained on the Merc. The man drew closer, and closer, and nothing happened.

Nothing at all.

"Now," B'taav repeated.

Still the Merc approached. Closer...

Inquisitor Cer failed, B'taav realized. She had—

The Independent felt a rumble.

It was as if the corpse of the long dead ship was coming back to life. Asteroid dust kicked up several feet before B'taav. The dust enveloped Balthazar and spread out for what seemed like many kilometers into the distance.

Balthazar spun around, confused by the vibrations. He released the metal spike and it floated off. Metal fragments lying on the surface of the *Argus* jumped up and shot past him. The tinsel glass that made up the hydroponics shield was, for a second, fully exposed. Balthazar saw the field of withered vines and plants below him. Each and every one of them shook. Fiercely.

Air hissed out from cracks and blew past the Merc and into the vacuum of space.

B'taav could do little more than sit back and watch. He lay on a solid metal surface, and not the tinsel glass. Even so, the rumbling grew so strong he feared the *Argus* itself would shatter.

And then the tinsel glass exploded.

Millions and millions of jagged pieces shot directly upwards, like an erupting volcano.

In less than a fraction of a second, Balthazar's body was ripped to shreds by the shattered glass. His pulped remains along with the entire tinsel glass shield shot straight up, hurling many kilometers in seconds, before colliding against a giant asteroid floating above the *Argus*.

Just as suddenly as it began, the area around the Independent was calm. The ejection of tinsel glass and atmosphere was complete and all energies were spent.

B'taav, though he lay only feet away from the edge of the blast, had nonetheless escaped uninjured. In the zero gravity conditions, all shrapnel was hurled up, and away, from the Independent.

B'taav let out a breath. His body was growing rigid from the cold, but he survived. B'taav heard a beep within his suit. The timer on his wristwatch was signaling the ten minute notice. In the distance, he spotted movement.

The *Xendos* gracefully exited the super-juggernaut's landing bay, made a sharp turn, and floated his way.

"Just in time," the Independent muttered.

B'taav closed his eyes and, as he drifted into unconsciousness, managed a very relieved smile.

66

Oscar Theodor checked the fighter craft's internal systems for what had to be the thousandth time since parking his fighter within visual range of the *Argus*. He wondered how the other two members of his group, as well as all the members of the Blue Rogue squad, were doing down below.

Start and stop. Hurry up and do nothing.

It made no sense. The other Tango fighter crafts arrived shortly after the discovery of the super juggernaut. They knew where the ship they were pursuing landed. If the order was given, they could fly down in force and neutralize any potential hostiles. If there were any.

Of course there are. You've been ordered to keep your weapons hot, your communications silent, and await the arrival of the Dakota. Once it arrives, all hell will break loose.

Won't it?

Oscar Theodor, and the rest of the ships lying in wait, had a little less than two hours before finding out.

"Do as you're told and don't ask questions," Theodor muttered.

He wasn't the only one growing irritated with this wait. Even the usually stoic Richard Loo had a look of exasperation about him.

Theodor felt his eyes glazing yet again.

"How's it going up there?" Karina Wilson called from the compartment below.

"How do you think?"

"Tell us when it gets exciting."

"That should be any day now."

Theodor's gaze drifted from his ship's monitors and back to the juggernaut. The massive ship's stern was closest to his spacecraft and her bow was hidden behind a wall of asteroids. He could only guess at her exact dimensions. He could only guess why Lieutenant Daniels made it so important to find her, only to then order everyone remain far away.

Don't ask questions.

Easier said than done.

Theodor shrugged. He followed the super juggernaut's visible lines from bow to stern and admired the craftsmanship. Halfway through his latest gaze, he stopped.

Theodor spotted what appeared to be a puff of smoke rise from the middle of the ship.

"What?"

He leaned forward and adjusted the magnification on his goggles.

"I'll be damned."

A plume of dust and debris rose from the ship and violently collided against an enormous asteroid floating just above. The asteroid slowly spun up and away.

Theodor hit the intercom.

"We've got activity!"

Richard Loo was up the stairs and at Theodor's side in a microsecond.

"What did you see?"

"Exhaust. It came from the center of the ship."

Richard Loo put on his magnification goggles on and adjusted their settings.

"I see it. You think the hostiles somehow got the ship's directional thrusters working?"

"No. It looked more like a sudden decompression, like when a ship's walls crack and the atmosphere leaks out."

"The ship had atmosphere?"

"It would appear so."

"Was this done on purpose?"

"It had to be. You don't have atmosphere trapped for all these years in a space craft only to have it shoot out accidentally right here and right now. You know, we could take a closer look."

"We'll need permission to break formation."

"Yes sir."

"We'll have to break communication silence."

"It's your call, sir."

"Yes it is."

Richard Loo pulled the spare headphones from beside Theodor's chair and placed them over his head. He looked at his wristwatch. The timer had run down to ten minutes. Ten minutes before they were supposed to act. Ten minutes before the *Dakota* would fire her long range Lancer torpedoes at the super juggernaut. He was ordered to wait the full four hours, and they were damn close to being spent.

Orders are orders. Even if there are only ten minutes left.

Was the atmosphere purging cause enough to break the communication silence?

Reluctantly, Richard Loo activated the communicator. Theodor was surprised by the man's hesitancy.

The higher ups must have made radio silence an absolute imperative.

"This is Officer Richard Loo of the Blue Rogues. We have a—"

"Sir," Theodor interrupted. He pointed to a small ship exiting the juggernaut. Richard Loo again adjusted his magnification goggles.

"It's the ship we were following," Theodor said. "They're moving away from the juggernaut. They're picking up speed."

"This is Officer Loo," Richard Loo repeated. "The craft we were pursuing has left the juggernaut. What are your orders?"

Lieutenant Daniels and General Jurgens stood on the bridge of the *Dakota*. They, along with all the officers on the bridge gazed at the central view screen. Despite the asteroids and distance from their target, they could see the ancient craft. They also heard Richard Loo's message.

"All *Tango* crafts, you may now break communication and sensor silence," the General said. "Get a full scan on the derelict."

Oscar Theodor hit several buttons in the panel before him. Dormant monitors came alive with long-range sensor information. He locked in on the juggernaut and, after examining the data, drew a sharp breath.

"All levels of the juggernaut's internal compartments show energy spikes," Theodor said. "They're expanding. She's—"

Theodor faced Richard Loo.

"Sir, she's going to blow!"

Richard Loo grabbed his microphone.

"All *Tango* fighters," he yelled. "Surround the escaping craft and lead her to the *Dakota*. Let's get the hell out of here before the juggernaut takes us with her."

It was impossible for Inquisitor Cer not to notice the sudden, blinding sensor activity surrounding the *Xendos*. She counted thirty fighter crafts appear out of the emptiness of space and move on an intercept course toward them.

"This is Inquisitor Cer of the Phaecian Empire calling all unknown crafts," she said over her communicator. "I'm on board the cargo vessel *Xendos* and present no threat. Please be advised that the derelict juggernaut's self-destruct mechanisms are engaged. She will explode within five minutes. You must maintain a minimum three hundred kilometer distance from the derelict or risk grave damage or destruction to your craft. I repeat, you must maintain..."

67

For two hundred years the *Argus* laid hidden deep inside the Erebus asteroid field. She was the last remnant of a war that most in the Epsillon and Phaecian Empire would rather forget.

When the five minutes was up, she erupted.

Her blackened hull blew outward as her guts were ripped open by the charges hidden in every one of her levels. For a brief second the darkness that filled the asteroid field was bathed in a stark white light. For a brief second it appeared this lonely, forgotten place had gained a new sun.

And then everything went black again.

The remains of the *Argus*, small, twisted pieces of metal, drifted off in all directions. Asteroids remained the only testament to the destruction caused by the Erebus War.

68

When B'taav came to, he was lying in a bed within the *Xendos*.

The room was small and dreary and could fit only two small cots side by side. The other bed, B'taav found, was enclosed in a germ free stasis container, the type used for people who suffered grave injuries. Within the container, however, was someone long past suffering of any kind. Within the stasis container was the body of Captain Nathaniel Torin. The asteroid dust was removed from his face and body and he looked like he just passed away. The only things that suggested otherwise were the missing fingers on his right hand and a missing left leg.

Sitting before the body was little Nathaniel. His eyes were stained with tears. When B'taav rose from his bed, the boy barely noticed.

B'taav's right arm was in a splint and his midsection was wrapped. Despite the pain that lingered from his encounter with Balthazar, he felt remarkably good.

Why not, he thought. *You're alive.*

"How do you feel?" Nathaniel asked.

"Not bad," B'taav replied. He noticed the boy had a heavy wrap around his left hand. He was missing his pinky finger. "Yourself?"

"Could be worse."

"You really aren't him," B'taav said. "Despite what you may think."

"You knew? When?"

"Before I left the *Xendos* and entered the *Argus* I searched Francis Lane's room. I had to know who you were and why you were here. In one of her suitcases I found the download box and the medication she used to keep you under control. In my...travels, I heard about efforts to imprint memories. I put the Geist Cube together with the items in Francis Lane's possession and guessed she figured out a way to do this. On you."

B'taav sat on the edge of his bed.

"It sickened me when I realized what she was up to, but there was little I could do to stop her, at least at that moment. The best course of action was to make things harder for her. I took the medication she used to keep you sedated."

"Then I have you to thank for all the things she did to me

afterwards."

"Sorry," B'taav said. It was clear he meant it. "But if I allowed her to continue using the medication, she might have tricked you into giving her all the access codes."

"You're probably right," Nathaniel said. "The medication made me more pliant. Had she shown me the *Argus* operating system while I was under the meds, I might well have given her everything she wanted. In spite of all I went through, you saved me nonetheless. I had to return the favor."

"You issued the command to eject the hydroponic level tinsel glass?"

"I didn't know how close you were to it. I was afraid you would die along with Balthazar. It must have been quite a sight."

"It was like seeing the *Argus* let out one last breath."

"She was a magnificent ship, B'taav. I wish you could have seen her back then, before..." Nathaniel shook his head. "I miss my crew and I miss my ship. They deserved better."

"Did you...is she destroyed?"

"Yes." The boy pointed to his head. "And it won't be long before the memories Francis Lane implanted within this body will also be gone, as I'm sure you're aware."

B'taav was. Even the most successful memory imprints were like shooting stars. In a few years' time, perhaps less, there would be little of those memories left within the boy. With stunted mental growth, he'd be lucky if he eventually become a semi-functioning adult.

"I wish there was certainty Captain Nathaniel Torin would finally get his rest," the boy continued.

"Francis Lane wasn't carrying the real Geist Cube, was she?"

"You're a mind reader, B'taav."

"So I've been told."

"The group behind Francis Lane, they'll be back. If they discover what happened here, they may even come after all of you."

"What happened here will be kept secret."

"They still have the Geist Cube, and there remain memories within it that could make up for this loss, even if they don't know it."

"Did you tell the others?"

"No. Maddox is a small man in what was ultimately a very small organization. Inquisitor Cer, she's...she's Phaecian. Despite her noble actions, it is difficult for me to trust someone from the other side. We were at war with them, after all."

"You're willing to trust a lowly Independent?"

"You're hardly that," the boy said. He produced a small diskette and handed it to B'taav. "Since we left the *Argus*, I've been making this recording. Most of what I know about Francis Lane and her organization is there, along with other information Captain Nathaniel Torin kept to himself. If you have any hopes for the Empire's future, you'll treat this material well."

B'taav took the disk.

"If the people behind Francis Lane try anything, we'll deal with them."

"Take them lightly at your own peril."

There was a moment of awkward silence. The boy's gaze returned to the body of Captain Torin.

"Why was I...he...out there?"

"My only guess is that the surviving crew mutinied. They probably expelled him."

"No. They were loyal."

"I'm sure they were," B'taav said. "But these circumstances were beyond extraordinary."

"No," Nathaniel insisted. "I –he– must have been trying to save the ship. Maybe there was an accident, and...and he was somehow blown out...perhaps a faulty hatch gave way."

"Yeah. Maybe that's what happened."

B'taav looked out the room's tiny window. In the distance he spotted two fighter craft flying alongside the *Xendos*.

"We're being escorted to the *Dakota*," Nathaniel said. "What will they do with us?"

"Nothing. There's nothing more to be done. Where are the others?"

"Inquisitor Cer is piloting the ship," Nathaniel said. "Maddox's at her side."

"Oh? They didn't take him to get medical care?"

"They wanted him to come with them but refused. He told them to patch him up as best they could and let him take the *Xendos* back in. Either he's the strongest man in the universe, or the stupidest."

"Probably both," B'taav said.

The two shared a short laugh

"What did he tell them, about his injuries?"

"That the Mercs were responsible. It was an easy enough lie to tell."

"Yeah. I suppose. I better go talk to them."

Inquisitor Cer and Maddox were in the *Xendos'* cockpit just as the boy said.

"Remind me never to book any vacations with you," Maddox told the Independent when he entered the room.

Though the *Titus* bartender's features remained pale, the wound on his leg was freshly dressed with a sophisticated milky white compress. A low hum came from within the dressing. Machinery fed medicine as well as regenerative tissue into Maddox's wound. In time and with the proper procedures, it was possible for Maddox to eventually grow a reasonably analogous artificial limb, provided his body could take it. Perhaps in a matter of a year or two he might even be able to walk on it.

"The crew of the *Tango* fighter ships at our side insisted on boarding us after the *Argus* blew," Maddox said. "Since the *Xendos* remains the property of the Phaecian Empire, they had to ask Inquisitor Cer, our only Phaecian representative, permission to come aboard."

"No sense being rude to our gracious hosts," Inquisitor Cer said. "Their medics gave Maddox, Nathaniel, and you a good looking over."

"I'll have to thank them for their care," B'taav said. "What else did I miss?"

"There were more than a few Blue Rogues among the boarding party. They insisted our ship also get a proper looking over, in case of any mechanical issues."

"A formality, I'm sure," B'taav said.

"While looking over the engines they somehow...accidentally I'm sure, checked the computer banks. They were no doubt pleased to see we didn't have any illegal Royal Epsilon Fleet information stored within."

"What about Stephen Gray, Francis Lane, and Saro Triste?"

"Saro Triste was lost on the *Argus*. The Blue Rogues took away the bodies of the other two."

"What was the cause of death?"

"A tragic accident," Maddox said. "And that's the way it'll remain."

"What about you, B'taav? How are you feeling?" Inquisitor Cer asked.

"Not bad, all things considering."

"Look," Maddox interrupted. "There she is."

The crew of the *Xendos* stared at the view screen. The *Dakota* was visible in the far distance.

"Lieutenant Daniels caught up with us after all," Maddox said. "That is, if he was even chasing you to begin with. Care to share the whole story?"

B'taav slipped into the Navigator's chair and sighed. "I don't know. This information is classified."

Inquisitor Cer gave Maddox a cold stare. "It is illegal for Inquisitors to share Empire secrets."

"Yeah, but—"

"I'm sorry, Maddox."

Maddox looked like a lost puppy.

"The Independent and I need to discuss other matters now, and I must ask you to leave."

Maddox opened his mouth to protest.

"No exceptions."

The *Titus* bartender nodded. He was about to rise from his chair when Inquisitor Cer spoke again.

"Now that Maddox is gone, B'taav, perhaps we could share some information. On the condition, of course, that it remains between you and me."

A sly smile found its way onto Maddox's face. He put the metal crutches away.

"A few years ago, the Overlords began voicing... concerns...about some of Saro Triste's policies and activities," Inquisitor Cer said. "I was assigned to his staff as his personal Inquisitor. In reality I was there as a spy for the Overlords. It wasn't long before I discovered he was part of a Phaecian chapter of the organization Maddox and Frasier belonged to."

"There was a fear that Saro Triste's priorities were, at best, improper, and at worse compromised. Yet none of his actions, other than being part of this shadowy group, proved he had betrayed his post. The group of twelve Overlords met to discuss his future and decided to be patient. They ordered the other Cardinals to do so as well and had me commit to finding all the details about Maddox's group. When I did shortly afterwards, the Overlords were in a quandary. They agreed with the need to keep information on the Solar System killers a secret, and therefore had no problem with Saro Triste being a part of this organization. However, the fact that he kept his involvement so secretive made my superiors suspicious. They feared he was using Maddox's group for his own ends."

"At some point Saro Triste changed from a man seeking peace to a man looking to uncover, and possess, the secrets of the *Charybdis*. His goal was obvious: To use the weapon to spread our holy word by force throughout the galaxy. We kept an eye on him and let him go about his other business, content that it was unlikely the *Argus* would ever be found. And then it was. The very next day, Saro Triste and I were on our way to *Titus*."

"I had little time to warn the Overlords of Saro Triste's movements. When I did, they ordered me to get in touch with certain operatives inside Epsillon. It appeared people within your government had similar concerns about high ranking individuals on their side. I contacted General Jurgens, sending a single encrypted transmission to his operatives. I warned them of the search for the *Argus* and my fears the mission was perverted. Because of the intense scrutiny I faced from all members of this group, I did not identify myself. I told General Jurgens that if he managed to get someone to infiltrate us, they could identify me because I would claim not to know anything about this mission."

"I'll be damned," Maddox said.

"I see you've returned to the cockpit, Mr. Maddox," Inquisitor Cer said. "Finished stretching your legs?"

"That's cold," Maddox said and smiled. "Since when do Inquisitors have a sense of humor?"

"Your culture is very corrupting," Cer deadpanned. "Anyway, I knew B'taav was Jurgens' inside agent, but because he was being watched so closely, it was impossible for me to reveal myself directly to him. Instead, I allowed B'taav to find the appropriate time. After Rasp's murder, we all gathered together and B'taav insisted on knowing what we were up to."

"I asked if everyone knew about this mission to find the *Argus*," B'taav said. "Inquisitor Cer said she didn't. After apologizing for speaking without Saro Triste's permission, I told her not to worry..."

Maddox could no longer contain himself.

"...because you two were in the same boat," Maddox said. "You communicated with each other right in front of us all!"

"Inquisitor Cer's response was what I needed, and I in turn gave her my acknowledgement."

"What about all that business about the Tamarin Campaign?"

"Perhaps you don't recall, but when I first noted his supposed presence in that campaign, I said I recognized the information as false," Inquisitor Cer said. "It was my way of offering him a means of making the others think we were at each other's throats. This proved helpful once B'taav entered the *Argus*, and Saro Triste tried to use my supposed hatred of the Independent to get me to kill him."

"What about Lieutenant Daniels? Was that an act, too?"

"He and I don't see eye to eye," B'taav admitted. "In fact, he doesn't like me much at all, for the reasons I stated before. But he was following General Jurgens' orders. He was to make things hot on *Titus* and make sure I came across as a hunted man. That got you guys thinking, at the appropriate time, that I would be worth the risk of taking along on your mission."

"It worked," Maddox said. "With most of them, anyway."

"But why all this deceit? Daniels had an overwhelming force at *Titus*. Why not simply run us down, get all the information we have on the *Argus*, and go destroy her?"

"Last I heard, the highest ranking members of both governments knew the *Argus* was about to be found," B'taav said. "Phaecian and Epsillon leaders were in the process of mobilizing their fleets on both sides of Erebus. There was a very real fear things could escalate to war. After several rounds of diplomacy, a course of action was agreed to. The Phaecians knew Inquisitor Cer was dedicated to destroying the *Argus* and would not be corrupted. Our side needed their own agent in your midst, and by circumstance I was available and had a decent cover story to explain my being here."

"Pursuing Accelerant supplies?"

"When we finally took off from *Titus*, we were to be pursued. Hard, but not too hard. Once we found and boarded the *Argus*, we had four hours to set off her self-destruct mechanism. Had we not done so, the *Dakota* would have bombed her until she was in pieces, regardless of whether we were aboard or not."

The bridge grew quiet. The *Dakota* neared.

"What about Nathaniel?" Maddox asked.

"He's useless to anyone now," B'taav lied. "The *Argus* is gone and whatever security codes he has in his head are worthless. As Francis Lane herself said, he was the ship's captain. He could no more replicate the device than any of us could."

"Then the danger is over," Inquisitor Cer said. Although he couldn't be sure, B'taav detected a note of suspicion in her voice. Perhaps she too realized eliminating Saro Triste, Stephen Gray, and Francis Lane didn't mean their organization's end.

"The flotillas will stand down, and peace between our Empires continues," B'taav said and smiled.

"Exactly what I was thinking," Inquisitor said. "Perhaps I am something of a mind reader after all."

Inquisitor Cer offered the Independent her own smile. It was frosty. The Independent no longer had any doubt that she too worried about the future.

"We're agreed then," Maddox added. He was blissfully unaware of the unspoken messages between Independent and Inquisitor. "We'll make sure Nathaniel is treated as an innocent in this whole affair."

"Agreed."

The three stared out the front window and at the *Dakota*.

In only a few minutes they would arrive at the Epsillon battleship.

69

The *Xendos* flew into the main landing bay of the *Dakota* and touched down. After atmosphere was pumped into the area, the decompression doors of the *Xendos* and *Dakota* opened.

Inquisitor Cer, Nathaniel, Maddox, and B'taav exited the ship. A large group of officers stepped off a lift and approached them. At the head of the group were Lieutenant Daniels, General Jurgens, and, standing at General Jurgens' side, Jonah Merrick.

Another man dressed in flowing robes accompanied the group but kept his distance. B'taav recognized him as Overlord Octo, one of the twelve most powerful Phaecian Overlords.

"Permission to come aboard," Inquisitor Cer said. She offered a crisp military salute.

"Permission granted," General Jurgens said. He mirrored the Inquisitor's salute and said, "You must be exhausted. Please allow my men to escort you and Overlord Octo to your quarters. Should either of you need anything, food, medicine, whatever, please ask."

"We appreciate your hospitality," Overlord Octo replied for his subject. "Our ship may require service. I'm certain your officers can provide this without forgetting the *Xendos* is property of the Holy Phaecian Fleet."

"Absolutely," General Jurgens said. He motioned to several of the crewmembers standing behind him. "Provide whatever services Inquis...Overlord Octo requires. I want the ship in tip top shape."

The crewmembers saluted and spread out. One group, armed with computers and tools equipment walked up to the entry ramp of the *Xendos*.

"You won't find anything," B'taav told the General and the Overlord.

"This is reassuring to hear," Overlord Octo said. "However, there is no reason for mistrust, is there, Inquisitor?"

"No sir. General Jurgens' technicians may board the ship as they please."

General Jurgens nodded and the technicians headed into the craft. When they were gone, Inquisitor Cer motioned to the Overlord.

"Permission to speak, sir?"

"Granted."

Inquisitor Cer addressed General Jurgens and said:

"Your agent served admirably. I hope one day his work is recognized and properly rewarded."

"Perhaps it will be," General Jurgens acknowledged.

"As should yours, Inquisitor Cer," B'taav added for the benefit of the Overlord.

Inquisitor Cer offered General Jurgens another crisp salute before stepping away from the group. Both Overlord Octo and she, along with a couple of escorts, headed for the lift.

"You look better, Mr. Maddox," General Jurgens said when they were gone. "However, it would be wise to get you and Nathaniel to our medical center."

The last of the escorts appeared at Maddox and Nathaniel's side. Maddox tensed, but relaxed when B'taav laid his hand on the man's shoulder.

"They'll take good care of you," the Independent said. "I'll come down to visit shortly."

Maddox nodded. Both he and Nathaniel were taken to the lift, leaving B'taav, General Jurgens, Lieutenant Daniels, and Jonah Merrick alone on the deck.

"Who is the boy?" Merrick asked.

"His name is Nathaniel," B'taav replied. "He was adopted by Francis Lane. She couldn't bear to part with him, so she took him along on the trip."

"That's surprising," Merrick said. "Given the gravity of her mission, wouldn't she feel bringing along a child would be a burden?"

"I'd be the last person to ask about what was going on in Francis Lane's mind."

"He's missing a finger. How was he injured?"

"The liftoff from the *Argus* was...hurried. His injury was accidental."

It was an easy enough lie to tell.

"What of the *Charybdis* bomb? Did you get any of the schematics?"

"Not a one."

The Industrialist nodded.

"Just as well. It wouldn't be of much use, anyway."

"What do you mean?"

"It's been two hundred years since the Erebus War. In all that time neither Empire was able to make even one regular sized juggernaut, much less anything approaching the dimensions of the *Argus*. We have neither the materials, the manpower, nor, frankly, the interest in doing so. You do know why the ship was so damn large, right?"

B'taav shook his head.

"Because the *Argus* was the *Charybdis* bomb."

"What?"

"Did you think a device capable of destroying an entire solar system would fit into a suitcase?"

"So making the bomb is...?"

"A dream. At least at this point. Where would the makers get the money and material? And if they did, just how many years do you think it would take them to build it? A hundred years, if not more. Even assuming the project was somehow started, it wouldn't be long before word of its construction leaked. At that point, Epsillon and Phaecian agents would come swarming in. Depending on who arrived first, the project would either be seized or sabotaged."

"That's why Francis Lane was after the bomb's plans, rather than the device itself," B'taav said. "She had everyone thinking the device could be towed away with the *Xendos*. She had them chasing after something that was all around them. How did you know?"

"Francis Lane was a strong, intelligent woman," Merrick said. "I've had my eyes on her for quite some time. She kept most of the information about the *Argus* well hidden. Once she left her palace, my agents searched her files more thoroughly. We didn't discover the truth about the *Argus* until after you guys were in *Titus*. Good thing, too, as the Phaecians were more than ready to resume the war right where we left off. Once they realized schematics were all that could be retrieved from the *Argus*, cooler heads prevailed. We even convinced them to send Overlord Octo as an observer on the *Dakota*. He witnessed firsthand our good intentions of routing out the traitors and destroying that damned ship."

"If she knew the bomb might not be replicated in her lifetime, what did Francis Lane hope to gain?"

"Maybe she hoped to start the project and leave it for her offspring. Maybe she envisioned the Royal Epsillon Empire rising once again."

"Why did you guys keep up the facade that the *Charybdis* device was an imminent threat?"

"We couldn't simply assassinate a Phaecian Cardinal and one

of our highest ranking Industrialists. We had to let events work themselves out. Besides, the more people on the *Argus*, the greater the temptation. There was too much of a risk that someone might just sprint off with the ship's knowledge. No, it was better to keep the number of people on board at a minimum. In the end, Inquisitor Cer will tell Overlord Octo how we in good faith rid ourselves of that ship and kept the War's biggest secret a secret."

"There is more, though."

Merrick smiled. "Of course there's more. I've suspected for quite some time Stephen Gray's industries were in league with the pirates raiding my ships. If Gray's death at the hands of my personal agent doesn't send a message to those bastards to stop messing with my property, then nothing will."

B'taav nodded. Profit and loss, industrial one-upmanship. It was something so banal, yet easy to understand. The Independent suddenly felt very exhausted.

"Am I done here?"

Merrick's smile remained firm. "Yeah. You've earned a good vacation. Your room aboard our ship is..."

"Number 5334, fifth level crew quarters," General Jurgens said. It was the first time he spoke since the four were left alone. It was clear who the power in this group was and who were the underlings.

"Thank you."

"Why don't you come back to see me in a month or so and we'll plot out your next job?" Merrick said.

"Sure."

B'taav broke away from this small group and headed for the lifts. Lieutenant Daniels followed him.

"Next time," he said. "Maybe they'll let me catch you."

"If it's in the script," B'taav replied. Despite his exhaustion, he laughed. Lieutenant Daniels joined him.

Soon the elevator arrived, and the Independent was gone.

70

B'taav spent the next few days resting in his room aboard the *Dakota*.

From his window he saw the Erebus asteroids fly by at incredible speeds. At first there were many but their numbers slowly dwindled. It wouldn't be long before they arrived at the *Titus* space station. From there, everyone involved in the search for the *Argus* would return to their respective homes and jobs and lives.

Once, while taking a walk outside his room, B'taav spotted Maddox and Nathaniel on the ship's leisure decks. The two had obviously grown close. Nathaniel acted like a normal child, and Maddox wisely kept up that act. If anyone suspected the boy was something more than he appeared, they never showed it.

B'taav didn't see much of Inquisitor Cer during the return trip, nor did he expect to. She was an Inquisitor, and she had to remain at the side of Overlord Octo, both as her duty and, certainly, for debriefing. Despite this, he spotted her a couple of times walking the forward decks alone and watching the stars. They avoided talking to each other, because on a military craft, every wall had ears.

After two more weeks of flight, the *Dakota* was hours away from the *Titus* Space Station. B'taav watched the station grow larger from that same forward deck. It felt like several lifetimes passed since he was this close to civilization.

"I'll be leaving soon."

B'taav turned. Inquisitor Cer stood beside him.

"They finished with your ship?"

"Days ago," Cer said. "But they nonetheless had to re-check it a few more times. Just in case."

"You'll have to pardon our suspicious nature."

"If the roles were reversed, I would do the same to your ship. I might even be in charge of taking it apart."

"When are you leaving?"

"Soon."

"It's been a pleasure working with you," B'taav said.

For a few moments the two watched the approaching space station. She was a very old and battered piece of equipment, but she was a survivor. Until recently, the only known survivor of the Erebus explosion. That title was hers once more.

"I hope we see each other in the future," Inquisitor Cer said. "I also hope that the circumstances for such a meeting don't prove quite *this* interesting."

"Agreed," B'taav said. "Have a good flight back."

Inquisitor Cer gently laid her hand on B'taav's cheek. Her stony brown eyes lost their harshness in the *Dakota's* artificial lights.

"You too," Inquisitor Cer said. She retracted her hand, turned, and walked away. B'taav remained on the forward deck. An hour later, he spotted the *Xendos* fly out of the *Dakota* and begin her slow approach to the Erebus Displacer.

For a moment, the ancient ship was parked just outside the Displacer's hollow core. And then the Displacer gate came alive with energy. The *Xendos'* thrusters ignited and the tiny cargo ship entered that core.

There was a burst of light and the *Xendos*, and Inquisitor Cer, were gone.

EPILOGUE - ONIA

The Epsillon light cruiser *Goodwin* exited through the Onia Displacer at exactly 1600 hours local time. The ship corrected its course and began a standard approach into the desert planet over which the Displacer orbited.

At one time, Onia was a fertile garden of a planet. When the Phaecian and Epsillon Empires assigned the Erebus system as their neutral border, the proximity of the Onia system made it a logical choice for an Epsillon Military Intelligence base. The planet's lush flora was decimated as countless space ports, industry, and spy centers were created. Stripped of her vegetation, the planet heated up and eventually turned into a barren desert.

After the war, the Epsillon Empire abandoned the planet. All the military bases and industry were swallowed up by the shifting sands and forgotten by all but the few scavengers that remained planet side. Since then, she has housed no more than a few hundred thousand people.

"Captain Torin wanted her to go here," Nathaniel said as the ship kissed the planet's atmosphere. "That's what he was going to tell her. Afterwards..."

B'taav and Maddox eyed the planet's yellow surface. Nathaniel chewed on his lower lip but otherwise tried to keep his emotions in check.

The *Goodwin's* heat shield glowed a fiery red as she broke into the planet's atmosphere. After a few minutes of maneuvering, B'taav had the ship on a steady course toward the airbase in the city of Monier.

The light cruiser came in for a landing just past 1650 hours. Its passengers were off the ship and their cargo was loaded into a waiting vehicle at exactly 1714 hours.

The driver of the vehicle, an ex-military man personally recommended by Lieutenant Daniels, drove the desert buggy out of the city and deep into the shifting sands that made up the planet's surface. He kept quiet for most of the journey, though at times checked to make sure his passengers and their cargo were fine.

Nathaniel couldn't bear to look through the buggy's window. He had an especially hard time looking at the casket that lay in the pad behind him. His emotions grew even more pronounced when their vehicle approached the villa.

Once there, it was hard for Nathaniel to keep still. The place was withered with age, but the walls of the four main buildings still stood, even if each of their roofs collapsed in time.

B'taav asked the driver to stop in the middle of what was left of the villa's entry. He asked the driver to wait and, along with Maddox and Nathaniel, exited.

Maddox still had considerable trouble moving. While he had become proficient with the use of crutches, the soft sand proved tricky to maneuver. Nathaniel helped the *Titus* bartender step away from the buggy. Once done with that task, his eyes returned to the complex.

B'taav headed to the rear of the vehicle. He opened the trunk door and activated a compressed mechanized derrick. It hoisted the casket out of the buggy and onto the sand. The derrick remained locked to the casket and, after B'taav pressed a series of buttons on its control panel, the casket's antigravity function kicked in. The casket hovered a couple of feet off the sandy floor.

The derrick and casket followed B'taav as he walked back to Maddox's side. Nathaniel stood several feet away. Tears formed in the boy's eye as memories of his ancient home flooded his mind.

"I never thought I'd see this place again," he whispered. Though his voice was still that of a small child's, B'taav and Maddox thought of him as the adult he was. "I didn't think—"

Nathaniel stopped.

"Where is it?" he asked.

"It's behind the buildings and over a hill," Maddox replied.

"Show me."

They walked past the rotted villa and closer to a desert hill that lay beyond. They noticed a fragrant smell drift over the barren sands. It was coming from their destination.

"There it is," Maddox said.

Nathaniel ran up the hill and stopped. Maddox and B'taav, followed by the derrick and casket, soon reached the boy's side. Before them was an incredible sight.

In the desert world of Onia, there existed one place that still contained a large amount of vegetation. A wild bush grew for several hundred meters into the distance. Bright red flowers protruded among vibrant green leaves. The flower's scent overwhelmed the dusty nothingness that filled the Onia air.

Nathaniel walked to the edge of the bushes. He reached out to touch them, but stopped. The flowers were protected by thorns.

"Where is it?" he asked Maddox.

"Keep going along the edge of the bushes," Maddox said. "You'll find it there."

The boy thanked Maddox and headed off. B'taav and Maddox allowed him his space, but followed nonetheless.

"What is to become of him?" B'taav asked.

"The boy will need help. Good thing for him I've suddenly got a lot of free time on my hands."

"Sounds like you won't have that much free time after all."

"Let's just say now that the purpose in my life is fulfilled and the *Argus* is gone, I've found something else to do," Maddox replied.

"His memory imprint is already decaying."

"I know. He gets...lost...sometimes. He'll be in the middle of a conversation and just stop talking. He'll..." Maddox paused. "I'll be by his side. I'll make sure once the memories are gone, he grows up to be a fine, normal, and *healthy* man."

Up ahead, Nathaniel stopped. He bent down and stared at a small, rectangular stone marker. He brushed the sand aside, revealing an inscription. B'taav and Maddox approached. They all read the writing on the marker.

Angela Torin, dedicated wife and mother
She belongs to the heavens now.

Nathaniel's breath grew labored and more tears rolled down his cheeks.

"She was my life," the boy said. "When Admiral Cambridge ordered me to take the *Argus* into Erebus, I knew our time together was at its end. She was to be the last to leave the ship, so that I could give her my legacy, the Geist...the Geist Cube—"

He stopped talking. His voice was choked off by the emotions swelling within him.

"My very last memories from the *Argus* are of sitting in the Project Geist chair. It hadn't been used in a long time and it was...dusty. When all was ready I told my First Officer to turn the machine on. There was a bright light and...and I was thinking about my wife. I was going to see her immediately afterwards, to give her the cube and send her off. I was going to say goodbye. I...I must have done so, but my memories end right there."

Nathaniel sobbed for several more minutes.

"I don't know what I said to her. I don't have those memories. I wish to the Gods I knew what I told her when I saw her that last time."

B'taav instructed the derrick to lower the casket and dig a hole next to Angela Torin's grave. In a few minutes, the machine was done.

B'taav ordered the machine out of the pit and to the casket.

"They were good people," B'taav said. "I doubt any of us would have been able to make those sacrifices."

"To the sacrifices of true heroes," Maddox said.

"We commend your soul to the Gods," Nathaniel said.

B'taav pressed a button on the derrick. It gripped and lowered Captain Nathaniel Torin's casket into the freshly dug grave. When it reached bottom, young Nathaniel was composed. The derrick rose from the grave and buried the casket. Captain Nathaniel Torin would rest for eternity beside his beloved wife.

Nathaniel returned to the red flowers that surrounded them.

"She spent many hours in the Hydroponics level of the *Argus*," Nathaniel said. "I heard from others that gardening was her greatest joy. I was so jealous. You don't know how often I wished she would spend more time with me. I had it all wrong. I should have spent more time down there with her."

Nathaniel reached for one of the flowers and gently pulled it to his nose.

"It smells so...beautiful."

"When she got to Onia, she proved quite a gardener," Maddox said. "Everything you see around us she planted. When she died, they thought the plants would die, too. They were wrong."

"She created everything here?"

"Yes," Maddox said.

"The plants," Nathaniel said. "What are they?"

"Roses," B'taav replied. "They're roses."

As the words left his mouth, his gaze drifted. The first wave of starlight made its presence known through the dull orange sky.

THE END

Atomic Rocket

The Works of
E. R. Torre

Available
now

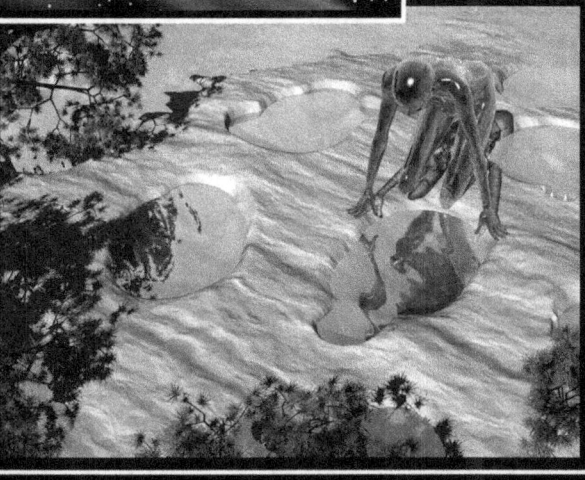

All images copyright 2010 E. R. Torre

From the grittiest corners of a dark metropolis...
...to the coldest reaches of outer space...
...and all those uneasy places in between...

SHADOWS at DAWN

E. R. Torre

Fourteen tales of Mystery, Suspense, and the Fantastic.

Visions of a dead actor haunt a lonely young man...
Fate leads him on a journey to the man's home town...

E. R. TORRE

HAZE

It started with Blood...

...see how it ends.

Return once more to the world of
The Dark Fringe.

COLD HEMISPHERES

E. R. Torre

An elderly Hitman's most dangerous job
Is the one he can't complete.

SUSPENSE...MYSTERY...ACTION...

E.R. TORRE

CORROSIVE KNIGHTS

MECHANIC

GHOST OF
THE ARGUS

CHAMELEON

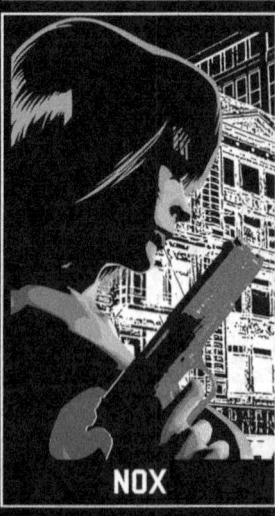

NOX

FOUNDRY OF
THE GODS

AN EPIC STORY
OVER TWENTY
THOUSAND YEARS
IN THE MAKNG...

E. R. TORRE
MECHANIC

Arizona, 1925: A Sheriff makes a discovery in the fiery desert that changes everything.
Bad Penny, the Present: On an idyllic island army base, a hidden menace is about to be unleashed...

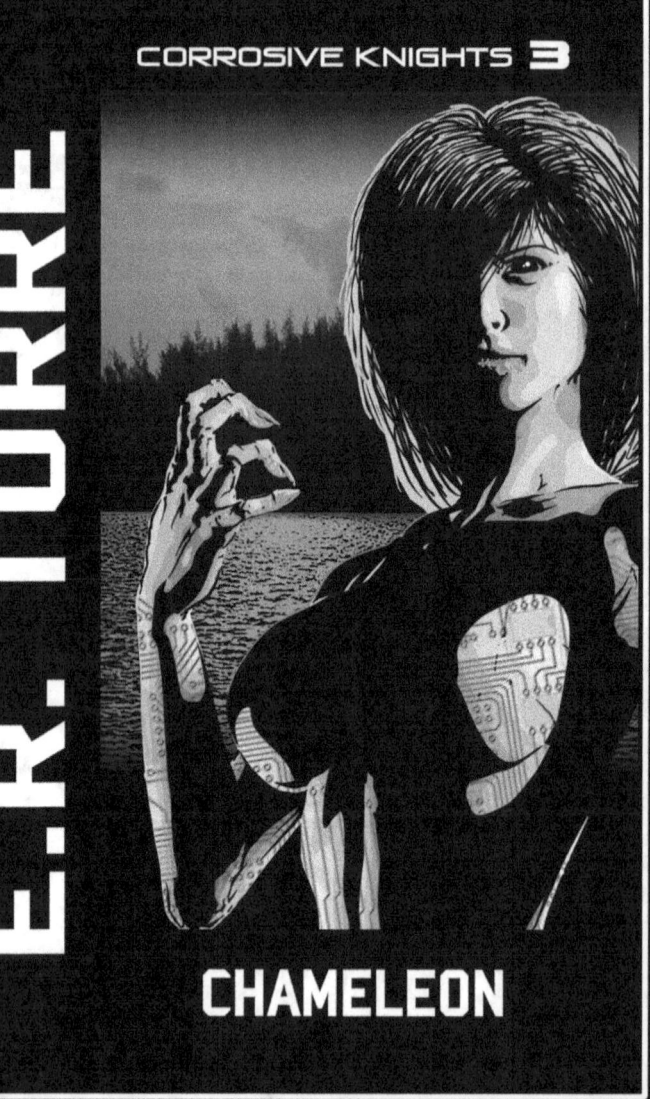

CORROSIVE KNIGHTS **3**

E.R. TORRE

CHAMELEON

For the seven passengers of a military transport helicopter, the next twelve hours could signal the end of mankind.

Nox the Mechanic is back and this time she faces
a threat that could destroy all of mankind...

CORROSIVE KNIGHTS 4

E.R. TORRE

NOX

Copyright © 2012 E.R. Torre

A threat she carries in her own blood...

Centuries ago, an unstoppable enemy
forced humanity to flee to the stars.

CORROSIVE KNIGHTS 5

E.R. TORRE

GHOST OF
THE ARGUS

Copyright © 2014 E. R. Torre

Today, humanity will take the fight to *them*.

A scavenger on a lost planet
carries a terrifying secret...

CORROSIVE KNIGHTS 6

E.R. TORRE

FOUNDRY OF
THE GODS

What lies beneath the desert sands
within the Foundry of the Gods?

ertorre·com

Atomic
Rocket

Science Fiction, Mystery, and Suspense

www.ingramcontent.com/pod-product-compliance
Lightning Source LLC
Chambersburg PA
CBHW071512260626
47170CB00002B/347